KISSING THE KAVALIER

ANNETTE NAURAINE

For more information contact annette@annettenauraine.com

Book design by Libby Waterford

Cover design by Aimee Martello of Code Cherry Designs

ISBN 9781736308011

Library of Congress Cataloging-in-Publication Data has been applied for.

This book is dedicated to my own beloved soldiers, Peter, Lincoln and Ulysses, without whom my life would be boring.

A brief note on the opera, *Arabella*.

Composer Richard Strauss, and his librettist, (the person who writes the lyrics) Hugo von Hofmansthal, collaborated on several critically acclaimed operas: *Elektra, Der Rosenkavalier, Ariadne auf Naxos, Die Frau ohne Schatten, Die ägytische Helena* and, lastly, *Arabella*.

When Strauss read the libretto for Arabella, he returned it to von Hofmansthal and requested he change the heroine from Arabella, to her more interesting, cross-dressing, younger sister, Zdenka. Tragically, before this change could be executed, von Hofmansthal died of a heart attack while dressing for the funeral of his son, who had committed suicide two days earlier —an operatic demise if there ever was one. Devastated, Strauss used von Hofmansthal's original libretto, which became *Arabella*.

This book is an outgrowth of my love of opera and *Arabella*, in particular. I have always been touched by Arabella's transformation from a beautiful girl willing to obey her parent's demands to marry someone rich to an intelligent young woman who genuinely falls in love with Mr. Right.

Perhaps *Kissing the Kavalier* is what Strauss and von Hofmansthal had envisioned.

Set in 1867, Vienna, in a world of royalty and tradition teetering on the brink after a devastating defeat in the Austro-Prussian war, *Kissing the Kavalier* is a sweetly funny and enchanting reimagining of a timeless romance that embraces independence, forgiveness, and hope.

I encourage you to listen to the operas of Richard Strauss. They are some of the greatest German operatic works of the Twentieth century. Strauss approaches tonality, the orchestra, story, and women in new and original ways. Some are musically challenging but worth a listen. The Metropolitan Opera streams many performances of Strauss operas where you can listen to, and see, some of the great singers of our time.

To stay informed about future book releases and to stay in touch, please sign up for my newsletter at www.annettenauraine.com.

You can also find me on Facebook at https://www.facebook.com/annettenauraineauthor or Instagram @ANauraine.

I would love to hear from you.

GLOSSARY TERMS

Allegemeines Krankenhaus – General Hospital
Bei Männer, welche Liebe fühlen – In men who feel love, a good heart is never lacking (the duet which Matteo loves).
Fiaker – A Fiaker is a form of hackney coach, a horse-drawn four-wheeled carriage for hire. In Vienna such cabs are called *Fiaker*
Friedenheim – Peaceful home
Gottes im Himmel – God in heaven
Grosse Gott – Great God
Gräfin – Countess
Gräfinnen – Countesses
Graf – Count
Grafen – Counts
Grossmutti – Grandmama
Hauptalleé – Main street
Kisber Felver – A rare sport horse breed developed at the former Kisber Stud Farm in Hungary.
Mecklenburger – Warm-blooded horse bred in Mecklenburg-Vorpommern used as a utility and cavalry horse prior to WWII
Mein Gott – My God!

Trakehner – Trakehner is a light, warm-blooded breed of horse, originally developed at the East Prussian state stud farm in the town of Trakehnen.

Schwimmen – a card game played with a 32-card Piquet pack. The was first mentioned in 1718 and is still popular in Austria and Germany.

PROLOGUE

L ieutenant Matteo von Ritter, of the Austrian Fifth Cavalry, lay in a dirt culvert, and surveyed the situation. They were hemmed in on all sides. Blood streamed from his head where a bullet had grazed his temple. He tasted the sulfurous gunpowder. Smoke choked him and burned his eyes. The ground vibrated with the hail of shelling. Shrapnel whistled overhead. Screams of men and horses mixed together in a symphony of death. Tree trunks, blasted apart by artillery fire, lay like matchsticks, their sap sizzling as they burned.

The dead and dying, both Prussian and Austrian, littered the forests and fields and low-slung rock formations around the villages. Fighting had commenced at sunrise. By four in the afternoon, Matteo knew that only a humiliating retreat to the other side of the Elbe could save the Austrian army. Neither side held their ground for long, beaten back by the inaction of timid generals and driven forward by the arrival of reinforcements.

A sheer rock wall blocked advance. To the right, dirt and rocks sprayed into the air, pounded by Austrian artillery. In the dense forest on the left, Prussians with their new breach-loading needle guns lay on the forest floor and picked off the Austrians when they stood to reload. Escape or advancement was impossible.

Against impossible odds, Matteo was determined to carry out the mission: find a way around the Prussian flank. Matteo and two infantrymen from his regiment, Kurt and Luther, lay belly-flat in the dirt. Matteo pointed to a cluster of boulders and scorched scrub around a depression in the field.

"Run!" Matteo shouted.

Kurt bent low and sprinted toward the boulders. Luther lumbered after him. Matteo launched himself out of the dirt.

Two Prussian cavalrymen, astride enormous black Mecklenburgers, galloped full tilt out of the forest. Swords flashed against the sky. Their eyes were wild with battle lust.

Luther drew his pistol, fired, missed. His target wheeled his horse and pinned Luther's torso against the rock wall. He held Luther there to watch him suffer.

The horse crushed bone to stone, forcing the breath from Luther's body. His face turned red, purple. The Prussian aimed his pistol at Luther's head. The horse shied. A shot resounded.

Luther collapsed, screaming and holding his face in his hands. Blood spurted through his fingers and ran down the front of his uniform.

Matteo fought the cold white horror flashing through his chest.

Lungs burning from the smoke, the taste of his own blood in his mouth, Matteo ran and leapt onto a smoldering tree trunk. He unsheathed his sword, the grip as familiar as a dinner knife. Muscles straining, he extended his arm, forearm rigid. With a roar, he swept his sword in a wide arc at Luther's attacker.

Sword sliced flesh, caught at bone, carried through. The soldier's head rolled off into the blackened undergrowth. The

Mecklenburger careened towards the forest, dragging the corpse from one leg hung up in the stirrup.

Matteo spun around. Where was Kurt?

The second Prussian knocked Kurt on his back. The soldier reared his horse. Hooves descended with a sickening crunch.

Kurt let out a blood-curdling shriek and bucked off the ground. He cradled his mangled hand and writhed on the ground. The Prussian raised his sword to spike Kurt. Matteo struck a blow to the Prussian's midsection, unseating the rider. The attacker pulled his pistol, but with one thrust of his sword, Matteo pinned him to the ground like a stag beetle.

Matteo put one arm around Kurt's waist, looped Kurt's arm over his shoulder, and hauled his screaming friend off the ground.

"We have to bring Luther. Get back to the horses," Matteo shouted above the din, dragged Kurt beside him.

Through the murk of smoke, Matteo spotted Luther leaning against the rock wall, his breath heaving.

"Horses," Luther sputtered, eyes wide. "Horses. Black monsters."

Muscles twitching with exhaustion, Matteo grabbed Luther by the shirt front and helped him to stand. "Luther," he shouted into the man's face and gave him a shake until Luther's eyes fixed on him. "Follow me."

Blood streamed from a jagged gash on Luther's forehead. He staggered, fell. "Don't leave me," he gasped. "The horses."

"Get up! Not a moment to lose," Matteo shouted. "Run! Now!"

Matteo half-dragged, half-carried Kurt as they dodged burning trees, swamps of blood, bodies piled upon one another. "Not much further," Matteo repeated over and over. Bullets whistled past. Mud sucked at his boots. Blood soaked his shirt.

"Should have turned back," muttered Kurt. "Impossible."

When Luther stumbled, Matteo bellowed, "We have all sworn the oath to love the name of honor more than fear death. Get up! I got us here. I'll get us back."

Luther staggered upright and lurched after Matteo.

Grimly, Matteo pressed ahead through the smoke and gunfire. When he couldn't go further, they found the place where they had been forced to tie their horses and advance on foot.

Matteo's horse, Reinhold, a steady, battle-hardened mount, was still alive, though squealing in fear. Kurt and Luther's horses lay snorting and pawing the ground, mortally wounded and suffering horribly. Matteo pushed Kurt and Luther up on Reinhold, then pulled out his pistol and put the two animals out of their misery.

A shell exploded nearby. Dirt shot skyward in a volcano of dirt and rocks.

Matteo hurtled to the ground. Something tore through the back of his jacket. Pain sheared across his shoulder blade, and wet oozed down his back. He gritted his teeth, got up, and took hold of Reinhold's bridle.

He led Reinhold through the carnage, blast holes, and dead soldiers until they reached the village of Predmaritz. A few remaining medics had taken refuge in an old granary and set up a field hospital. Prussians had taken most of the medics prisoner, leaving men who might have survived with medical treatment to die on the battlefield.

Matteo stumbled the last few steps into the granary and grabbed a young medic by the collar. "Help," he gasped. "Help. Them."

He collapsed.

Two days later, in a hospital on the other side of the Elbe river from where the Fifth Cavalry had been evacuated, Matteo remembered nothing of the Battle of Königgratz.

CHAPTER 1

VIENNA, AUSTRIA, 1867

G räfin Zdenka Waldner tugged at her gentleman's evening jacket. "Cousin Thomas's suits are becoming a bit snug. I can't button it."

"Your bosom is growing." Gräfin Arabella, Zdenka's beautiful older sister, giggled.

Zdenka moaned. "Just what a boy like me needs. I don't mind being your brother..." She squirmed and pulled at the tight wrappings. "But these bindings are bothersome."

"After the Coachman's Ball in a few weeks, you can give up being a boy and return to your rightful gender," Arabella said, trying, Zdenka knew, to nudge her toward respectability.

"I'm not eager to return to being a woman. I've rather come to enjoy the freedom I have as a gentleman. I can do as I please, walk about unescorted, ride when and where I please." Zdenka pressed her nose to the windowpane of the *fiaker* and watched as the houses and apartments, lit by gaslight, became elegant houses and then *palais*.

The Waldners had been in Vienna since January, through snow, rain, and sleet. The city was beautiful but noisy, with sooty air from coal fires, dwellings crowded together, and women like

Arabella hunting for husbands. It all made Zdenka want to steal a mount and gallop the distance back to their run-down, indebted estate in Hohenruppersdorf with its fields of wheat and pine forests, its pastures, the cows, sheep, and chickens. Back to where she was most herself and no one cared if she wore pants or petticoats.

"Don't become too fond of being my brother," Arabella said, using her big sister know-it-all voice that chafed Zdenka. "Galloping about in trousers on the farm is one thing, but next *Fasching,* you'll be looking for your own husband and you'll have to wear a dress."

Fasching, the Viennese social Season that commenced in November and ended on Shrove Tuesday, consisted of endless parties, balls, soirees, and general carousing—all meant to foster advantageous matches between the upper classes. The Coachman's Ball was the final ball before the gloomy descent of Lent when all of Catholic Austria refrained from life's pleasures— even drinking hot chocolate. The Season's best matches were often made at The Coachman's Ball.

"I like dresses fine, but they're impractical for birthing lambs, riding, pitching hay, and bringing in crops." Zdenka scratched behind her ear where a blob of pomade had lodged. Mama had shorn her hair so she could pass as a boy, but the pomade used to control her curls was the consistency of horse glue. "You, of all people, know how much I want to go home and rebuild the farm."

With Papa having gambled away most of their fortune, there wasn't money for two debuts. Zdenka didn't want a debut anyway. There wasn't even money for Mama to buy a new gown, and the ones she had were out of date and threadbare. Mama dreaded going out in a Society where she had once been young and beautiful but was now grey-haired and as worn-out as her dresses.

Arabella had only this one Season to make a good match, so Zdenka, dressed as a young man, was pressed into service as Arabella's chaperone for every tea, soiree, dance, theater, orchestra, and opera performance. Zdenka was willing to do anything, including stand on her head on the *Platz* in front of the Stephan's Dom, if it meant Arabella found a rich husband who could save the farm—Zdenka's farm—from the debt collectors.

Arabella seemed not to hear her. "Next year, you'll return as my distant cousin, and no one will be the wiser. You'll have a brilliant Season, and we'll find you a tolerant, indulgent husband."

Zdenka knew how to quiet her sister. "As far as I can tell, men only want a mindless vessel for their children."

"Zdenka, how vulgar," Arabella chided. "This is what comes from reading all those foreign newspapers and essays by those so-called emancipated women. It makes you appear unattractively intelligent. Really, you mustn't forget you are still a lady underneath those trousers."

"Intelligence isn't a bad characteristic in a lady. And I haven't forgotten I'm female, but marriage isn't necessary for running a farm." Or for much else, as far as Zdenka could see from her parent's marriage.

"You do need marriage," Arabella said, with an edge to her voice. "Mine. Don't forget my marriage will save your beloved farm from Papa's gambling."

Guilt washed through Zdenka. "I want you to marry someone you love, not just to save the farm. I appreciate your sacrifice for the family."

But Zdenka had made a promise to her *grossmutti* to keep the farm in the family, and she intended to keep that promise, even if it meant pushing Arabella toward the altar. Zdenka could still feel her grandmama's knob-knuckled hands gripping her own small, dirty hands. In a quavering voice, Grandmama had said,

'You are the last hope of our ancestors. Promise me you'll never let the land leave our family. You can be whoever you want here at Friedenheim. I know you love the farm as much as I do. My destiny was here and yours is too.'

A week later, Grandmama died in her sleep. Zdenka swore on her grave she would never let Friedenheim leave the Waldner family.

Arabella's feet tip-tapped a rhythm on the floor of the *fiaker*. "To think the Coachman's Ball has been held for two hundred years. That our parents attended the same ball."

"By the last night of *Fasching*, you have to make up your mind which of the Grafen you will marry."

"I know you think it's silly, my waiting for the right man," Arabella said with a wistful note in her voice. "But it's all I've ever wanted since I was a child."

Arabella could be such a giddy featherhead. Except for her obsession of finding the right man, ideas floated in and out of her mind like dandelion puffs.

"And what if he's not rich, like one of the Grafen?" Zdenka asked. Because if the right man wasn't rich, the once wealthy and noble Waldners would be homeless, as well as penniless. And Zdenka was determined to not let that happen.

"Then I'll make a practical and good match. I know what's expected of me, and I'll live up to my obligation," Arabella said, affecting the more elevated tone and accent pervasive of Viennese upper class.

She had changed into a husband-hunter again. Zdenka missed the carefree sister who laughed from her belly, skipped when she was happy, and let her hair trail down her back. This Arabella, in her heavy emerald brocade gown that fit her like a second skin, was almost unrecognizable.

The *fiaker* jostled over a hole in the cobblestones. Arabella's head bumped against the side of the carriage, mussing her hair.

"I'll have to make a trip to the ladies robing room to straighten myself out."

"Not a problem I have." Zdenka touched her curls and winced, missing her once-long braids. Sacrificing her waves of russet hair was the only thing she disliked about being a young man. She consoled herself with the certainty her hair would grow back.

Their carriage pulled up to the *palais* of one of Vienna's most infamous hostesses, Gräfin Thea Prokovsky. Arabella gave her fluttery Viennese laugh. "Let's not spoil the evening bemoaning a marriage of necessity. Let's enjoy ourselves, shall we, *brother?*"

Zdenka leapt out of the carriage, flipped the step down, and helped Arabella descend. As usual, heads turned to watch her. With Arabella on her elbow, the two started up the marble stairs. In front of them, an elderly man slipped and collapsed down on one knee with a groan of pain.

A strapping soldier quickly brushed past them, took the stairs two at a time, and helped the man to his feet. The soldier bent his head to speak to the old man. He brushed the knee of his trousers and steadied the man until he resumed climbing the stairs under his own power.

The soldier turned. For a moment, he peered—not at Arabella—but for once, at Zdenka. Lamplight fell across his face, turning his features to sharp angles and shadows. His narrow-eyed gaze seemed wary and challenging.

Something in Zdenka bubbled like hot butter on a griddle. The sensation was not altogether unpleasant, but it was unfamiliar and confusing.

Men were unnecessary.

Weren't they?

CHAPTER 2

Lieutenant Matteo von Ritter's eye twitched, and the scar at his temple throbbed. He leaned against the wall until the pain receded somewhat. Considering what other soldiers around Vienna had endured, his pain was of little consequence. A few headaches and diminished night vision were nothing. He squared his shoulders. No matter how great the pain, he would surmount it. That's what soldiers did. Push down the pain, ignore it, forget how it happened.

If only he could remember how he'd received his wounds, perhaps it might ease his conscience.

Taking a deep, steadying breath, he strode into the familiar, glittering drawing room of his aunt's *palais*. Soldiers milled about the room. Like him, they all had the questionable good fortune to return from the Battle of Königgratz. After arriving home from the battlefield, a party was the last place he wanted to be, but he couldn't let his aunt Thea down. A string quartet played the Blue Danube waltz, and the melody caressed his ear and slowed his heartbeat. The new gas chandelier cast a warm glow over the crowd, reflected off the gilt mirrors, and gleamed on the wine-red brocade drapes.

Wine red. Thank God, not blood red.

He searched the crowd for his aunt, the Gräfin Thea von Ritter Prokovsky, but there was only a sea of ladies waltzing in the arms of their dashing escorts. Light glimmered over the whirling satin skirts and made the backs of his eyes ache. The chattering of the crowd grated against his bones. Vibration in the floor reminded him of the way the earth shook under the bombardment of Prussian cannonballs.

He waved over the footman carrying a tray of champagne flutes. First order of business: make sure the fellow kept up a steady supply of the mind-numbing drink so he could get through the evening.

As was expected, his cousin Edward was on the other side of the room, wooing a gaggle of beauties. Edward was his slightly older, libertine cousin. He never met a woman he didn't try to seduce, although he preferred married ones so that permanent entanglements never became an issue. Edward, like other members of the Viennese aristocracy, had remained in Vienna, dancing, drinking, and flirting. They didn't know, or didn't want to know, how close the Prussians came to overrunning all the beautiful *palais'*, their spacious squares and pretty parks, crushing their way of life. They didn't know how close they came to losing everything. How close they came to death. How many good men had died so these people wouldn't have to forego evenings like this?

Since the war with the Prussians, nothing had changed in Vienna.

Only Matteo had changed.

Aunt Thea's throaty voice carried through the crowd. She was across the room, lambasting the French ambassador for the failure of the French to come to Austria's aid when Kaiser Wilhelm invaded Austrian territory. The poor ambassador was backed up against a statue with no avenue of escape.

Matteo crossed the room to Aunt Thea. Seeing him, she paused her tirade, gasped, and threw open her arms wide. Her generous embrace flooded him with the sense of safety he had known growing up in this home.

She held his face in her hands, tears in her eyes. "I was afraid you wouldn't come back."

She turned her cheek for his kiss and he gladly obliged.

"I only returned last night. I had to at least clean up before I made an appearance." He gestured to the room with his champagne flute. "Nice of you to invite so many of the returned soldiers."

"Someone must do something for them," she said, her tone acid with righteous indignation. "The Emperor seems to have forgotten them entirely. A party isn't much, but it's the least I can do."

A fearsomely intelligent, diminutive woman with a tongue like a horsewhip, Thea had raised Matteo when his parents were killed in a carriage crash. He adored her. She championed every injustice, ignored propriety, and spoke without reserve. Even though her hair was shot through with silver and wrinkles traced her forehead, her brilliance and fearlessness made her one of the handsomest women in the room.

At that moment, Matteo's eye chose to twitch. He blinked fast and hard to still the infernal thing.

Thea leaned closer to inspect his face. "Have you something in your eye?"

"Only a cinder of some sort." Rubbing his eye, he turned away to stop his aunt's questioning stare. Nothing another glass of champagne couldn't cure. He waved the footman over and exchanged his empty glass for a full one.

Fräulein Drossler, a husband-shopping debutante, swept past. Her brazen, appreciative glance down Matteo's frame culminated with a lingering gaze of invitation.

Matteo appreciated the dangerous dip of her neckline and her narrow-cinched waist. She was tall and comely, with upturned brown eyes and a lascivious pout, but Matteo couldn't seem to will his body to respond with desire. Something about her left him cold.

Thea raised an eyebrow and smiled knowingly as the young woman passed. "No one has offered for her hand."

He looked at his aunt reprovingly. "She, as most of these women, are only seeking men with a good pedigree or a fortune. I have neither."

A string quartet broke into an arrangement of a duet, *"Bei Männer, welche Liebe fühlen,"* from Mozart's opera, *The Magic Flute,* Matteo's favorite tune. The lilt of the strings floated out of the music room, wrapped around Matteo's heart, and eased the wire of tension running up the back of his neck. He recalled the words to the duet.

For men who feel love, a good heart too, is never lacking.

The high purpose of love proclaims there is nothing higher than wife and man.

The violins, viola, and cello, traded the melody back and forth like a feather on a breeze, filling the room with Mozart's unquenchable joy. It was such a hopeful, happy tune. For what seemed like the first time since he had returned, Matteo smiled to himself.

Thea smiled up at him. "I requested they play that for you."

"Thank you, but I suspect the Mozart wasn't the only reason you wanted me here this evening."

Thea threw her head back and laughed unabashedly. "Gräfin Arabella Waldner, the queen of the Season, is coming tonight. I want to introduce you."

"Ah ha," he laughed. "I knew it."

She gave him an innocent-seeming smile. "Can you blame me? I've given up on Edward ever settling down, and I thought a young woman might lighten your spirit in a way not even Mozart can."

The champagne was beginning to do its work. Matteo's shoulders relaxed. Faces softened. Eyes were less accusatory, voices less abrasive. A few more drinks and he might feel almost normal again.

"I suppose it won't hurt," Matteo said. "Is she as beautiful and intelligent as you? Educated? Well-read?"

"I'm glad you have such high standards." Thea sighed in mock dismay. "But you may have to settle for pretty."

"Why is she the queen of the Season?" He motioned for the footman with the champagne again and sensed Thea's silent condemnation as he tossed back the drink.

"She is gorgeous, sweet-natured, charming, and unattached."

"As are you," Matteo said.

"But not for my lack of trying," said Prince Dimitry Vladimir Gornostaev as he strode up.

The Prince was Thea's much-younger Russian lover, with whom she lived openly. Her defiance of all social conventions had earned her the reputation of being scandalous. Consequently, she had been exiled from many Society drawing rooms. The Prince was short, witty, and darkly handsome. His thick brown hair was combed back over his boxy head, and he wore a sharply trimmed beard. Best of all, he loved Thea.

The Prince shook Matteo's hand. "The woman she's trying to get you to notice has arrived. She is in the ladies' robing room and will make her appearance momentarily. The brother, her chaperone, is waiting in the foyer."

"Thank you, my darling," Thea said to the Prince. "She is perfect for Matteo."

The Prince gave Matteo a long-suffering look then said to Thea, "You are the most meddlesome, forthright woman in the world, and I love you." The Prince kissed her soundly on the mouth, causing several guests to stare.

Matteo was touched by these signs of affection. Theirs was the kind of love he wanted, not the stormy relationship of his long-dead parents.

"Lead the way, General," Matteo teased. He winged his arm at Thea and escorted her through the crowd.

In the foyer stood a strangely lovely young man.

"Graf Zdenko Waldner," Thea said. "How nice of you to come. I'd like to introduce my nephew, Lieutenant Matteo von Ritter, Fifth Regiment of the Imperial Cavalry."

There was a flash of recognition in the young man's eyes. They'd seen one another outside on the stairs.

Matteo was stunned by his angelic face. Matteo was definitely the sort who preferred women, but the young man was startlingly—well, there was no other way to put it—Graf Zdenko Waldner was *pretty*. Not just pretty, but almost alluring. Sensuous even. He had creamy skin and his cheekbones looked as though they had been smeared with peaches. Other men weren't pretty. They were handsome, rugged, leathery, or even lumpish, and they didn't have lush lower lips, like Zdenko. Men didn't have such thick brown lashes on their green eyes. Matteo had never seen dancing amber flecks in another man's eyes.

Matteo was embarrassed at his thoughts. Had that bullet to his temple done something to his male parts as well? Since returning from the war, it was the first thought he'd had that resembled something like lust.

But pretty Graf Waldner was a sartorial disaster. His ginger curls were plastered to his head with enough pomade to grease a pig. His overlarge coat had frayed sleeves and was missing buttons. Trousers sagged at his knees, and his floppy vest reminded Matteo of a scarecrow.

Or of the white Carrera marble statue of the Adonis in the

museum. Matteo was shocked when the word 'nudity' passed through his mind.

His reaction made no sense whatsoever.

Thea stared at him, her eyebrows raised, a look of alarm on her face.

Matteo blinked. Graf Waldner had his hand out, blushing like a schoolgirl. Matteo wasn't sure if he should bow or shake his hand. Thea slipped her hand into his elbow and pinched.

"I've come with my sister. She's fixing her hair," Graf Waldner was saying.

Matteo managed a smile, but not a single word came to mind.

Thea turned to Phillipe, the head butler, to discuss some logistical matters pertaining to the party leaving Matteo alone with Graf Waldner. The young man took a few steps into the drawing room. His eyes swept the room.

"So many soldiers," he murmured in his peculiar voice. "I've seen so many wounded men in Vienna since the war ended. I hope much is being done to take care of them." He turned his green eyes to Matteo. "Your aunt said you were in the cavalry."

Matteo nodded.

"I read in *Die Zeitung* that the cavalry was decimated at Königgratz. I'm sorry if you lost friends."

No one wanted to know. Didn't ask. But the first words out of this soft young man were words which Matteo had waited to hear since he'd returned.

Graf Waldner's attractive mouth opened and closed. "Pardon me if I've spoken out of turn."

"Not at all. It's kind of you to think of it," Matteo said. "No one knows what it was like, and even we soldiers want to forget."

But then, there were things he wanted, needed to remember, but could not.

♫

Zdenka's heart sped up. When she least expected it, the evening had become much more interesting. This was the same handsome soldier she had seen help the old man up from the steps outside.

Matteo von Ritter was strapping and clearly toughened by months on the battlefield. His jacket snugged over his powerful shoulders, but he had tightened his uniform belt several notches to gather the extra fabric. Chestnut hair tumbled across his forehead, accenting vigilant brown eyes. His hair barely covered a jagged scar at his temple. His trousers stretched over long legs, bulked with muscle earned, no doubt, by riding in the cavalry. He had hollows in his cheeks, an angular chin, and skin tawny from the sun. His dark eyes darting around the room, as if wary of attack, gave him a haunted aspect. For some reason, Zdenka was compelled to reach out and comfort him.

Inside, it was as if cold water sloshed against her ribs, turned to steam, and rushed out again. As she waited for Arabella to return, the cycle of cold and steam cycled faster and faster.

Finally, Arabella appeared from the robing room. Lieutenant von Ritter's eyes immediately, and predictably, latched on to her.

Their hostess, Thea something-or-other, made introductions, but Zdenka only heard the lilting melody of the string quartet.

"How kind of you to invite us, Viscountess." Arabella dipped a curtsy.

The Viscountess said, "I deplore formality. You must call me Thea. All my friends do and it's far better than the names my detractors call me." Her throaty laugh was unaffected and genuine.

The Lieutenant gazed down at his aunt with obvious affection.

What a kind smile he had.

"Please call me Arabella and my brother Zdenko," Arabella said.

So far, so good. Last week, Arabella had slipped and used the feminine version of her name and blushed right up to the tips of her ears.

Matteo bowed deeply. "And I would be honored if you would call me Matteo."

"Why don't you introduce Arabella and Zdenko to our other guests, Matteo," said Thea.

Matteo offered Arabella his arm and escorted her into the drawing room. Zdenka tripped along after them, following not only because she wanted to protect her sister's reputation, but because she wanted to be near Matteo.

He turned and stared at Zdenka with such intensity, she took a step back. His eyes reduced her mind to the consistency of cold porridge. What if he recognized she wasn't a boy? Did he notice something? Perhaps her bindings had come loose. Or her unmanageable hair had betrayed her secret. She dropped her glove on the parquet floor to avoid his scrutiny.

"The resemblance between you and your brother is remarkable," Matteo said.

Arabella said lightly, "I don't think you would mistake one of us for the other."

"Most certainly not," Matteo said.

Zdenka wished her smile sparkled like Arabella's, that she could be fluffy and flirty. How lovely if Matteo von Ritter smiled back at her the way he smiled at Arabella.

Where had those thoughts come from?

He was handsomer than any of Arabella's other suitors. Judging from this gilt-covered, satin-draped *palais,* he must be monied. He was unmarried. Handsome. Kind. He would make a fine husband for Arabella. If Zdenka wasn't so interested in him.

CHAPTER 3

When he'd first arrived, Matteo had been acutely aware of the chaffing chatter, the cloying ladies' perfume, the shoes scraping against the marble floor, and all he had wanted to do was flee. But Arabella provided a beautiful distraction. Her exquisitely fitted gown displayed her petite figure. Brother and sister shared the same high cheekbones, russet hair, slightly pointed chin, and startling green eyes flecked with gold and long dark lashes.

Zdenko was the tall, lithe, effeminate version of Arabella, but he carried himself with the stiff awkwardness of a man much younger, as if he wasn't used to his body. Earlier, on the street outside, Zdenko had returned Matteo's gaze with his own boldly masculine one, but his voice betrayed a girlish character, and he had yet to grow a single whisker.

Enchanting as Arabella was, it was Zdenko who *disturbed* Matteo, and this made Matteo want to get away from the young man.

Matteo asked, "Are you enjoying *Fasching*?"

"Oh, yes." Arabella stared off across the room at someone.

Zdenko said, "We've been on sleigh rides, to balls, teas,

soirees, parties, the theater, the opera and several masses at St. Stephan's. Such a huge cathedral!"

Matteo hoped the young man would find some attractive young lady to dance with and leave him alone with Arabella for a minute or two. "What did you find most memorable?" he asked Arabella.

Annoyingly, again, Zdenko piped up. "I liked Wagner's opera, *Tristan und Isolde*, the most. I love the way the orchestra builds and builds and builds to the earth-shattering climax."

At the words 'earth-shattering climax,' a deep flush crept up Arabella's neck. However annoying Zdenko's presence, he knew his music.

"Wagner's music is splendid, but his anti-Semitism is despicable," Matteo said.

Arabella's eyes were dreamy. "Mostly, I loved the story's romance. How Isolde loves Tristan so much, she leaves her entire world behind and, in the end, dies of love for him."

Zdenko's tone was derisive when he said, "Would have been more interesting if she'd realized she didn't need Tristan."

"But then there would be no love story," Arabella said. "And everyone loves a happy ending."

That Arabella was a romantic, fairy-tale-believing woman, for some reason, endeared her to Matteo. Despite his protestations about the ignorance of pretty women and his insistence on an intelligent, surprising woman, he found Arabella's grace and softness alluring. The velvet of her voice and the swells and curves of her body piqued something in him that wasn't exactly lust.

Perhaps it was because he'd been away from charm and beauty and sleeping in tents among smelly soldiers for so long, that Arabella's sweetness captivated him.

He glanced at Zdenko and a surge of something not exactly

pure, sped through him. His reaction so unnerved Matteo that he had an urge to escape the young man.

"It's quite noisy in here, would you like to go somewhere quiet to sit?" Matteo asked.

Arabella nodded.

He escorted her to a pair of unoccupied chairs in a solitary corner beside the bookcase. Zdenko followed close behind, clinging like a barnacle. Matteo was glad for a respite from the crowd and the pleasure of Arabella's company.

Several young ladies passed by and batted their eyes at young Zdenko, but he shyly avoided their glances.

"Wouldn't you like to dance with some of the ladies?" Matteo asked. "There are plenty to choose from. I could intro—"

"Oh, no, no." Zdenko gasped and blanched like a scared schoolboy. He grabbed a book from the shelf and buried his nose in it.

Just being around Arabella made Matteo feel lightness spark in his chest. "Do you like to read?" Matteo asked Arabella.

The gold flecks in her eyes twinkled. "I've been reading Jane Austen's books. I like the way she pokes fun at the aristocracy. Despite all their bumbling, mistakes, and understanding, everyone finds true love in the end."

Matteo waved an open palm around the room at the guests. "Ah, true love. I'm not sure that enters into many of the marriage contracts of present company."

"You sound skeptical. Do you disapprove of marriage?" Arabella said. "Surely there are some love matches to be made amongst the guests."

How could he not be skeptical? Being loved and loving in return required allowing oneself to be known. If anyone besides Kurt and Luther knew the truth about Matteo's disastrous performance on the battlefield, they would find him as unlovable as he thought himself. Love played no part in his future, as far as he could tell.

Fool. Don't be a boor.

He made an effort to lighten his tone, or at least sound less bitter. "I don't disapprove of marriage. It's perfect for many people. Do you believe in true love?"

"Of course. I thought everyone did." Arabella sounded slightly wounded. "The right man, or woman, will turn up if you wait and know what you're seeking."

Glancing up from his book, Zdenko interrupted again. He spoke pointedly to Arabella. "But sometimes, the person you think you want isn't really the right one for you. Sometimes, you really need someone else."

Arabella ignored her brother. "Have you never been in love?" Arabella asked Matteo.

The question caught him entirely off guard. "Not exactly."

"But you could be, couldn't you?" Zdenko asked.

Why didn't Zdenko go off and drink champagne elsewhere?

Matteo gazed at Arabella. "I'm not immune to the charms of the right woman."

Arabella's lush lips curved into a smile. To his dismay, she glanced away, and he sensed a wall drop between them. She was shutting him out, and he wasn't one to storm the battlements.

A drink was called for. Luckily, a footman carrying a tray of champagne glasses passed by. Matteo handed two glasses to his guests and took one for himself. Without thinking, he drained his in one go and set it on a table.

He was aware of Zdenko studying him.

"When did you return from the Front?"

Matteo's eye twitched. "Yesterday."

Somber, Zdenko replaced the book on the shelf slowly and with care. "How can the wounded soldiers recuperate in this sooty, crowded, noisy city? They need fresh air and quiet."

"I doubt that will help all of them," Matteo said.

Arabella's vague smile became frozen on her face. Matteo followed her gaze to see Graf Dominik lumbering through the guests. Sweat beaded Dominik's piggish face as he bowed to Arabella. "Arabella, how delightful to see you."

Matteo stood to greet the lout.

Instead of acknowledging Matteo, Dominik plopped his corpulence into the spot vacated by Matteo. "Thank you for the chair," he snuffled.

Perhaps the legs would give way. He was spectacularly ill-mannered for nobility.

"How lovely to see you again," Arabella said, greeting him with a breath-taking smile.

She hadn't smiled at him that way. How could she stand Dominik? Women were so changeable; it was confusing.

"Did you miss me? I certainly missed you." Dominik slathered a kiss on Arabella's hand.

He should have taken to the stage, except he had excessive perspiration, breath like rotten potatoes, and worse manners.

"Are you enjoying yourself?" Dominik didn't take his eyes off Arabella for a second.

"We were enjoying a pleasant conversation with the Lieutenant here," Zdenko answered.

Matteo took pleasure in Zdenko's slightly edgy reply. Dominik had always been an oaf, but a rich oaf whose fortune allowed him the attention of the ladies.

"Oh, yes," Dominik said. Not bothering to stand, he extended his hand to Matteo.

Such pure-bred loutishness gave the aristocracy a bad reputation.

"Congratulations, by the way, on making it back alive from the war." Dominik clucked his tongue like an old woman. "Abysmal failure, wasn't it?"

Matteo stiffened. "Particularly for the soldiers who died." He wanted to add *defending pompous fools like you* but, in deference to Arabella, he held his tongue.

In the music room the string quartet struck up the Strauss's "Farewell to St. Petersburg" waltz.

"Will you dance?" Dominik pleaded with Arabella, in the tone of a spoiled five-year-old.

"I believe the host gets to dance with her first," Matteo said, taking her hand and not bothering to disguise his disdain.

Batting her thick lashes at Dominik, Arabella called over her shoulder, "I'll dance with you next, *liebchen*."

Feeling slightly smug, Matteo bowed before Arabella. He placed his hand decorously in the small of her back and resisted the ungentlemanly temptation to pull her closer.

Zdenko slouched against the bookcase, his eyes watching their every move. Something about the brother... something...*bothered* him about the young man. And that internal disruption unnerved Matteo.

Waltzing around the room, the music buoyed Matteo, momentarily unburdened him in a way he hadn't experienced since returning from the war. He wondered at his attraction to her. She was graceful, dainty almost. She was also romantic, hopeful, and believed in love, which he didn't. At least not love for him. Not yet.

Still, he found himself inexplicably drawn to her.

Somehow, the weight of Arabella's diminutive hand on his shoulder seemed to reach down and touch his heart. A heart, since the war, he'd given up for dead.

CHAPTER 4

After their dance, Matteo relinquished Arabella to Graf Dominik who was waiting like a slavering animal where he'd left him. Next, she danced with Graf Lamoral, a foppish dandy with social ambitions to rival a woman's, and Graf Elemer, who was old enough to be her father and richer than the Emperor.

Matteo propped himself against a doorframe and watched Arabella. It seemed as if some inner light in her had dimmed. A trio of young ladies started toward Zdenko and he ducked behind a statue.

Matteo chuckled.

His cousin Edward sauntered up to him and clapped him on the back. Matteo gritted his teeth against the pain on his shoulder. His pain was nothing compared to the suffering of others.

"Good to see you, cuz," Edward said. "How's the nick on your noggin?"

"Fine, just fine," Matteo said, downing his champagne. "Good to see you, as well. I see you haven't slowed your pace of seduction since I left for the battle."

"I consider each lady a battle in her own right." Edward gave a half-smile, lifted a glass in salutation at a dark-eyed, generous-bosomed beauty crossing the room.

Matteo marveled how his cousin could communicate lust, thanks, and greetings, with just the raising of a glass and a twist of the corner of his mouth. These were skills Matteo had never acquired.

"Why so down in the mouth?" Edward asked.

Arabella whirled around the dance floor in the arms of Graf Elemer. As they passed, Matteo had the urge to trip the old goat.

Edward followed his gaze. "Ah! Now I understand. You've been smitten with the prize of the Season. Gräfin Arabella Waldner."

"Unlike you, I don't think of women as prizes," Matteo said.

"I simply like variety," Edward said, putting on his most innocent face. "So, despite all your protestations of pretty girls being uninteresting, you have fallen under Arabella's spell."

Edward's triumphant smugness made Matteo laugh. Even though they were so different, no one knew him as well as Edward. "All right. I concede, she's delightful, seems clever and well-read. She's graceful and charming. Oh, I nearly forgot ravishing."

Across the room, the three Grafen buzzed around her like hornets at a nest. "What about those three?" Matteo asked.

"Gossip is she has offers of marriage from each of them."

"Then I may as well relinquish the field now." Matteo straightened up and prepared to leave. "No need to pursue a woman who is already practically engaged."

"Just because she has suitors doesn't mean she wouldn't consider you." Edward's voice was suggestive of intrigue.

"I'm a lowly soldier of no title or fortune. How can I get her to notice me?" Matteo scoffed.

Edward snorted. "You soldiers. You think only of the direct approach."

"It is the most honest."

"Women are well defended because they *expect* the head-on attack." Edward lowered his voice. "You must use stealth, connivance, trickery, the oblique maneuver. You must *woo* them." He pointed to Zdenko hiding behind a statute. "The brother is your entrée to the boudoir of the Gräfin Arabella Waldner."

Matteo's head snapped back. "Her boudoir is not my target." Then, "Well...not immediately, anyway. I'd like to make her acquaintance first."

"Do you or do you not want a chance at courting Arabella?"

Matteo had to admit Edward was far more experienced with women than he. He'd had a few dalliances, but Edward made a hobby out of seduction and pursuit. However, Matteo didn't want a dalliance. He wanted an honest woman who could surprise him with her originality; a woman with a mind of her own. Someone like Aunt Thea. Arabella seemed like such a woman, but he couldn't be sure unless he got to know her better. "All right, what battle plan would you suggest, General *D'amour?*"

"Her chaperone, the brother, is where part one of my scheme comes in. He is the one you must impress. Make him your ally. Get to know him." Edward set his glass on a passing footman's tray.

"He's not my type."

Or was he?

"Think of him as the sentry to her, uh, virtue. All chaperones hold the key."

"You should know," Matteo conceded. His eye twitched. He rubbed it and it stilled.

Concern flooded Edward's face. "Are you all right?"

"Nothing another glass of champagne can't cure," Matteo said.

The footman with the champagne paused as Matteo reached for another glass. Edward gently plucked at his sleeve. Matteo scorched him with a glare and yanked his arm away. Edward hadn't been moved by patriotism to set foot on a battlefield so who was he to deny Matteo the calm found at the bottom of a champagne glass?

Unwaveringly, Edward met Matteo's gaze. There was only concern and brotherly love in Edward's eyes. Matteo resisted the champagne and let the footman pass. "What about the brother?"

Edward pointed at Zdenko. "Looks like he dressed in clothes out of a rubbish bin. Take him out and civilize him. Befriend him. He hides from girls practically begging him to ask them to dance. I doubt he even knows how. Show him how to be a distinguished gentleman. Invite him places, teach him how to hold a fork, take him riding and fencing, use Mama's box at the theater and the opera. Take him to the burlesque at *Rue Divorcee*."

"I most certainly will not!" Matteo said, appalled. "Those girls wear hardly any clothing at all."

"That's the whole point," Edward said.

"How am I to get him to do all this?" Matteo asked. "He'll be with his sister most of the time."

"Invite him during the day or early evening. From him, you discover where Arabella's engagements are, who she's calling on, and so on. Then you happen to appear there. If you have trouble gaining entry to a house, send me word and I'll finagle an invitation for you." Edward frowned and muttered, "Except not from Madame Druzay." He rubbed his chin. "Or Fraulein Brüder. And probably not Gräfin Kotlavarisch."

Matteo laughed. "You should have been a spy. It's all quite devious."

"Of course, it is. That's why I know it works. It took me two months of these sorts of machinations to endear myself to a certain Principessa Ricciardi of Lucca." A dreamy smile transformed Edward's face. "And it was worth the entire two month's work."

"As much as I want to court Arabella, I'm not going to stoop to lying and trickery. I despise that sort of thing. I won't be false in any way."

Edward smacked his forehead. "Ah, yes. I forgot. You're honest one hundred percent of the time. I'm not suggesting you bribe the lad. Simply make friends with him. You like doing good deeds, don't you? Get him a decent haircut—doesn't appear to need a shave—and a handsome set of clothes. The ladies will appreciate the improvements."

The whole business rankled Matteo. But Arabella seemed like the sort of woman with whom he could spend a lifetime and for this reason, for a moment, he considered Edward's scheme. "And once I've made friends with him?"

"Then comes part two. You write a letter, which you'll ask the brother to deliver to his sister. But not merely a letter. A love letter," cooed Edward, affecting a woman's swooning gaze. "Women love that sort of intrigue. And if you need any help composing the letter, I'm happy to assist. I've written several that brought successful outcomes."

Matteo brushed a bit of lint from his shoulder and Arabella's lavender scent rose from where her hand had lain. It still seemed an impossible chance, but she was worth it.

He was used to undertaking a challenge but recruiting, polishing, and convincing Zdenko--a rose of a different color-- had all the appeal of pouring sand into one's underwear.

CHAPTER 5

Zdenka tiptoed up the back steps of the Hotel Prinz to her family's apartments, relieved to have avoided the manager's pursuit. As soon as Arabella selected a husband, all their debts would be paid, and Zdenka could enter through the front door.

Once the servants' quarters, the Waldner's apartment was crammed up under the attic eaves. It was like living in a henhouse. Her room, which opened directly onto the hallway next to the main living quarters, was the size of a broom closet. Arabella's was scarcely larger. Zdenka gave the balky apartment door two hard shoves. In the sitting room, Mama and Arabella sat at a rickety round table with an odd-looking Romany woman. The three of them stared intently at cards laid out in neat rows atop a table.

Zdenka sighed. "Mama, really?" At least this time, fortune telling didn't involve pig entrails. What a colossal waste of their precious few coins. They didn't need a mystic to predict that their fortunes would improve when Papa stopped gambling.

In a reverent whisper, Mama said, "Shush, Zdenko, Madame Serena is concentrating."

Zdenka rolled her eyes and pushed the sagging door shut.
Arabella's gaze remained riveted to the cards.

The gypsy was of indeterminate age, with hair the color of
shoeblack. Her face was the color and texture of an old leather.
She reeked of cigars, wine, onions, and fakery.

Glancing about the room, Zdenka cringed at the condition
of their apartment. The furnishings consisted of mismatched
chairs, the wobbly table where the three women sat, a settee
propped up on books, and a cold fireplace. Zdenka and
Arabella's spartan rooms had thread-bare rugs, cracked
mirrors, and cots so narrow that Zdenka had fallen out twice.
The cramped space was no place to invite a guest, even a
gypsy.

Zdenka peeled off her hand-me-down overcoat and cap and
hung them on a hook by the door. Ordinarily, she would remove
her vest, but with a visitor present, she tugged it close to hide her
bosom. She crept up to stand behind Mama, laid her hand on
her shoulder, and peered down at the cards.

Mama gave her hand a nervous squeeze.

Madame Serena fixed Zdenka with an apprising glare. Zdenka's heartbeat spiked. She had the uneasy impression the old
woman could see right through her vest to the bindings
beneath. Blinking like a sleepy snake, Madame Serena turned
her attention back to the cards.

Mama plucked at a hairy wart on her chin. "What do you see
in Arabella's future?"

"I zee marriage," Madame Serena said in her raspy Romany
accent.

Zdenka choked back a laugh. "With three Grafen courting
her, that isn't hard to predict."

"Shhh," Mama hissed.

The crone laid down three more cards and muttered softly in
a foreign language. "But zer vill be trouble."

A chill crept along Zdenka's arms. Arabella and Zdenka exchanged glances.

Mama asked, "Will the wedding be this season?"

"Can you make it tomorrow?" Zdenka asked.

Arabella squinted at her.

"Sooooon," crooned Madame Serena.

"Who is he?" Mama asked.

"Zee carts zay only zat he iz not arrived. Zat he comes from far away."

"*Another* man? From far away?" Zdenka said. "He'd better hurry up. She has to decide by the end of *Fasching*."

"What else can you tell us?" Mama asked.

"A dark man. A broooooodink man." The gypsy spoke like a basso singing a long note. "Bik man. Mysterirrous...viz black eyes and dark hair."

Arabella glanced at Zdenka. "The *right* man," Arabella whispered.

"What if he mistakes someone else for you?" Zdenka said. When would Arabella give up this foolish fantasy and pick one of the three Grafen?

"Oh dear!" exclaimed Mama. "Lamoral has light brown hair, Elemer's is silver—."

"Dominik has no hair, but we could get him a wig," Zdenka said.

Madame Serena scowled at Zdenka and rasped, "Zere vill be trouble from a younger zeeister."

Zdenka's skin crawled. Her mouth went dry. Did the gypsy know she was a girl?

Arabella gestured to Zdenka. "I have only my brother, and he would do nothing to bring shame on our family."

Madame Serena rose from her chair, arms outstretched, so she looked like a black crow. "You dooo not belief me?" She flapped her hand at them all. "Pffft! Den zo be it." She stabbed her finger toward Mama, whose eyes were wide with fear. "But you vill pay de price."

The gypsy flung her shawl about her shoulders, hobbled to the door, and stomped out.

Zdenka turned to Arabella and her mother. "Who does the old bat think she is, threatening us with some bizarre disaster?"

But her stomach was cold as an icicle, then hot as a poker.

♫

The last of the parishioners departed St. Stephan's. Vespers was Matteo's favorite services. The choirboys' sweet, pure voices rose to the rafters and reminded him when the Fifth Calvary's tow-headed drummer boy sang. Such a dear, innocent boy.

The scar on Matteo's temple throbbed.

Father Benedict, plump as a dumpling with his tidy tonsure and spectacles perched on his pug nose, waddled down the aisle. Matteo rose from the last pew and greeted him.

"Good evening, Matteo. Were you here during the service?"

"Yes. Lovely singing as always."

Father Benedict's eyebrows rose. "And words about forgiveness? Did they speak to you?"

Matteo had heard them, but he didn't deserve forgiveness. Cowardice was unforgivable. "Not tonight, Father."

"Keep listening. I'm sure they will."

"Have you any word of Luther?" Matteo asked. "I've looked in every boarding house, hospital, and cure spa. Discharge records reveal no address."

Candlelight reflected off Father Benedict's spectacles. "Nothing. You're sure he's alive?"

He wasn't sure. Because he couldn't remember.

"I hope he is." Matteo held up a heavy sack for Father Benedict. "I've got more supplies for Kurt. Will you take them to him?"

Father Benedict accepted the sack and sighed. "Why don't you take it to him yourself? It was lucky you found him. He's grateful."

After several weeks of searching, Matteo had located Kurt in a flophouse, eking out a daily existence on the paltry government stipend for disabled soldiers. Matteo had contacted Father Benedict for help delivering goods to Kurt.

"You know where he lives," said Father Benedict. "You arranged and paid for the apartment. I'm sure he'd be happy to thank his mysterious benefactor for all you've done for him."

Matteo shook his head. He wanted to do as much as possible for Kurt before he realized Matteo was behind the money. Kurt, a former professional violinist, was a proud man. Somewhat arrogant, even. Matteo expected Kurt's fury might cause him to refuse assistance. Who could blame him? Matteo had cost Kurt his hand.

"Soon enough. How is his hand?"

Father Benedict gazed at the cold stone floor; his eyes filled with sadness. "He will never play the violin again, but he's copying music for Herr Brahms. He is grateful for the work, and he never complains. Such a cheerful fellow. Might cheer you up if you visited." Father Benedict scratched behind his ear, knocking his spectacles askew. "Why don't you let me tell him?"

They'd had the same conversation several times, and Matteo wasn't about to change his mind. Action, not religious platitudes about forgiveness, would restore his honor and make him feel worthy again.

"I'll be back next week." Matteo reached into his pocket, withdrew an envelope, and laid it in Father Benedict's hand. "For the church, Father. Thank you and good night." Matteo slipped out the heavy wooden doors of the cathedral. He turned and waved. Father Benedict made the sign of the cross, as though he despaired for Matteo's soul.

Father Benedict needn't have worried. After failing his comrades, Matteo had no soul.

♫

Soon after Madame Serena swept out of the apartment, taking her odor of garlic with her, Papa shuffled in as if walking through mud, his head down. He flopped down on the armchair and held his head in his hands.

Her father's gloom followed him into the apartment.

The droop of her mother's face said it all. She knew what they all knew. Papa had lost money in yet another card game.

"How much did you lose?" Mama asked.

"Fifty *gulders*," he whispered. "To a man they call the Argentinean. He's a crude, cruel beast. They say he once shot a man for an unpaid debt. I couldn't take the chance of giving him a promissory note."

Mama gripped the back of a chair with white knuckles. "That was our last money." She glanced at Arabella who was still sitting at the table. "Arabella, there's not much time."

Arabella's smile pinched.

Zdenka went to her sister and laid a hand on her shoulder. Arabella placed her hand over Zdenka's.

Mama's face looked like a red-hot steam kettle ready to blow. "Can't you stay away from the gaming tables?" she hissed at Papa. "How will we finish out the Season? I haven't had enough money to buy a decent dress in which to chaperone Arabella all Season, and now, I can't buy her a new dress for the Coachman's Ball. And how will we eat, for God's sake?"

"Don't worry, Mama," Arabella said. "I'll be fine in a dress I've already worn. I don't mind, and no one will notice."

Zdenka glanced down at her sock and wiggled her toes. The pale skin of her big toe poked through the worn wool. At least they didn't have to buy her a new suit.

"We have been allowed into Society because of Arabella's beauty, not because of our fortune or fame." Mama stomped about the room. "It's necessary for her to look her best, and now that's impossible."

"We still have a few weeks. I know luck will find me. I just have to find the right card game." He gazed at Arabella with his 'sad puppy' eyes. "Have you made a decision as to which of the Grafs you will marry? There are three. Won't one of them do?"

"I'm waiting for the right man," Arabella said, sounding convinced someone would materialize out of thin air.

It was such a foolish idea, but how could Mama and Papa deny her a few more days for the right man to appear? If the right man didn't appear, Arabella would sacrifice to save the rest of them.

Fear flashed in Mama's eyes like a bird right before the cat pounces. "Without a match, we will go from penniless to homeless. The farm is indebted. The manager hasn't been paid in months. We won't even be able to return there."

Zdenka was terrified of losing the farm, as well. Keeping her promise to her grandmother depended on Arabella, but her sister deserved happiness and love.

"The right man will be rich *and* handsome," Arabella said dreamily.

"Arabella, we have talked this over dozens of times. There is no such thing as the right man. Look at Papa and me. We have been married nearly twenty years, and we didn't see one another until two weeks before we married."

If Mama and Papa were an example, it wasn't in favor of marriage.

"And what if he isn't rich? Are you going to marry him anyway?" Papa asked, his color rising.

Arabella straightened. "I know my duty. I will marry someone who can save our family."

And the farm, Zdenka wanted to add, but she kept her mouth clamped shut.

"Then do it now, please," Papa pleaded.

Zdenka found herself unable to keep silent. "Papa, she has until the Coachman's Ball ..." She paused, not wanting to be disrespectful to her father, but it was his fault they were in this situation. "If you didn't gamble away all our money, Arabella wouldn't have to save us all from the gutter."

"When I make my decision, my girlhood will be over. I want it to last as long as possible, or until the right man comes," Arabella said.

Zdenka dressed as a boy so Arabella could have the best chance at a good match. If she had to do it all over again, she would. Arabella was dear to her. She didn't want her sister to simply yoke herself to one of the buffoonish Grafen who were pursuing her like hounds after a fox.

A rich love, hopefully.

Matteo von Ritter came to mind. He was dashing. Handsome. He and Arabella made a beautiful couple. Perhaps he was the right man.

"The Grafen have been patient and waited all Season. We need money now," Mama said as she paced the creaky floor.

Arabella's mouth drew into a narrow line, a sure sign she was not going to budge. She was even more stubborn than Zdenka. Would she have as much fortitude as Arabella if it was her responsibility to save the family? No, she realized. She would not. Love made a woman chattel, and she would not relinquish her independence for even a man so handsome as Matteo von Ritter.

"We must wait until the Coachman's Ball," said Zdenka.

Mama scowled at her. "Don't forget. Next Season will be your turn. We can't possibly let you marry someone from Hohenruppersdorf, after all. You are a Gräfin."

As if being a Gräfin mattered when you didn't have two potatoes for dinner.

"I don't want a turn," Zdenka said, planting her feet firmly. "I'm sorry if I sound disrespectful, Mama, Papa, but I'm going home to put the farm on good footing. Viennese men want to live in Vienna, but my life is the farm."

Mama glowered at Papa. "Have you asked everyone for a loan? Tresslauer? Bauerbock? Heim? Koch? Feuertag?"

Papa slouched deeper into the chair cushions. "Everyone. I already owe them money, and no one will help me. I'm still waiting to hear from Mandryka. He is my final hope."

Mama squinted at him. "Who?"

"Mandryka. My friend from when I was in the army. As rich as the Emperor and lives in Slavonia. He has lands, forest, tenant farmers, livestock. I sent him a letter along with Arabella's portrait. I asked him for a loan and to save my daughter and her beauty from poverty."

"Are you sure he's still alive?" Mama asked.

Papa blinked. "Oh. I hadn't considered that he might not be."

Papa had lost their last bit of money. Arabella would not give up her fantasy of the right man. Mama was beside herself with worry.

It was as if someone had stepped on a china cup that were Zdenka's insides. If she was independent, she would never have to suffer someone else's poor decisions. That would be real freedom. But would she really be free if her freedom was bought at the expense of Arabella's happiness?

CHAPTER 6

Matteo shifted from one foot to the other. He shoved his hands in and out of his pockets. "Why are we skulking around in front of a ladies' shoe store?"

"Haven't you ever heard of an ambush?" Edward poked his head around the corner then pulled it back.

"Yes, I have heard of an ambush." The scar on Matteo's shoulder grew hot as a brand. He strode back and forth on the pavement, irritation flicking at him. "Your foolish plan about the brother won't work."

"Ahhh, naïve youth. Watch an expert in action." Edward laughed. He poked his head around the corner again and jumped back. "Here she comes with her brother."

Matteo's heart jumped. "What? Why didn't you tell me it was Arabella we were ambush—uh, meeting?"

"I just did. Follow along, will you?" Smiling and laughing too loudly, Edward dragged him around the corner by his arm. Edward sauntered along, prattling on about the current style of men's hats in Paris.

Matteo kept pace with him, but sauntering wasn't exactly his manner of walking.

Sure enough, Gräfin Waldner and her brother were down the street. His heart was lighter for having seen her. The air smelled sweeter, and the clattering of the carriage wheels receded.

She wore a fox-trimmed cape, hat, and muff. The russet color matched her curls. The skirts of her dark green dress swung with the rhythm of her stride.

Her brother, Zdenko, wore day clothes as tatty as his evening suit. He was all long limbs, fair skin, and dreadful haircut, but he had a smile as delightful as his sister's.

"Ah, Gräfin and Graf Waldner," Edward bowed. "A pleasure to see you."

Zdenko drew himself up. "I know Lieutenant von Ritter," he nodded at Matteo. "But I'm sorry, sir, do we know you?"

"This is my cousin, Edward Prokovsky, my Aunt Thea's son," Matteo said. "I don't believe you met one another at her party. Let me introduce you properly."

Zdenko's grin was infinitely girlish. "Oh, well then, if he's related to you, he must be acceptable."

"I wouldn't go so far as all that," Matteo said and bowed to Arabella. "Gräfin."

She curtsied in return. The sun turned her skin to pale cream. Cream he wanted to brush his lips against.

Zdenko, except for the freckles strewn across his nose, had the same complexion.

"Lieutenant von Ritter," Arabella said, her consonants silken.

"We were heading over to Dehmel and Sohns for some chocolate," Edward said.

Matteo jerked his head at his cousin. It wasn't precisely a lie. Dehmel and Sons was the best coffee shop in all Vienna. And the most expensive.

"Would you like to join us? Since I didn't get a chance to make your acquaintance the other evening." He gestured to

Matteo. "My cousin and I would enjoy your company for a bit. That is, if you haven't anywhere to rush off to."

"Of course, we'll join you," Zdenko answered.

A tiny wrinkle appeared between Arabella's brows, but her smile never wavered. "Only a short while. We do have an engagement a bit later."

Zdenko glanced at his sister. "Oh, yes. I'd quite forgotten."

"Let me lead the way," Edward said, enthusiastically. He made a sweeping gesture down the street towards Dehmel and Sohns.

The sidewalk was wide enough for Matteo to walk alongside Arabella while Zdenko balanced on the edge of the curb.

"So, what brings you to this street today?" said Matteo.

"Fraülein Brüder invited us to call this morning," Zdenko answered.

Matteo recalled that, the previous evening, Edward had warned him against asking Fraülein Brüder for any favors. "Isn't she a friend of yours?" Matteo asked Edward.

Edward, who sauntered along in front, spun around, and walked backwards a few steps. "Yes, she is. A lovely one at that." To Arabella, he said, "I trust you enjoyed her company."

"Oh, yes." Arabella giggled. "So, *you're* the Edward she mentioned."

Edward's smile slipped. "In a positive light, I hope." He turned back around.

"She warned Arabella against you," Zdenko said.

"I'm hardly dangerous." Then, "Here we are."

They had arrived at Dehmel and Sohns. The doorman opened the door to the venerable institution. Warm, humid air, saturated with the aroma of coffee, chocolate, and buttery pastries greeted them. In a glass case, the famous Sacher Torte, a confection of dense chocolate cake, sat temptingly on pedestals. White tablecloths draped the tables. Dark walnut paneling and silver coffee pots that reflected light from crystal sconces imparted a cozy and elegant atmosphere.

The maître d' greeted Edward by name and led them to a table. Matteo slowed his pace and murmured to Edward, "What did you do for Fräulein Brüder in order to, uh, encounter Arabella on this particular street, at this exact time?"

"Something she appreciated very much," Edward responded with an inscrutable smile. "Now, invite Zdenko to go riding with you tomorrow. Arabella will be occupied tomorrow afternoon, so she won't need Zdenko as a chaperone."

"We could have used you in reconnaissance during the war," Matteo said.

"I was acting as Vienna's chief morale officer. My work was here."

Matteo held Arabella's chair for her. Her lavender scent wafted to his nostrils. Edward took the chair on her left, and Zdenko settled to her right. Matteo made sure to sit with his back to the wall and facing the door, so no one could sneak up behind him.

Somewhere, a pan clanged. His pulse kicked up. Matteo reached up to still his twitching eye. He noticed Zdenko staring at him before the young man looked away.

Soon after they'd ordered, the waiter brought their hot chocolate and coffees. Zdenko had ordered a hot chocolate with Dehmel's signature *schlag*, a dollop of rich whipped cream. Matteo sipped his coffee nervously, wishing someone would say something to give him an opening. He felt a kick in the shin and suppressed a wince. "What are you doing tomorrow, Graf Zdenko?"

"Not much. I wanted to read a bit of Pride and Prejudice by Jane Austen," he said, then reddened. "I like to know what ladies think about, so, occasionally, I read women's literature." He cleared his throat and straightened his jacket. "Other times,

I read articles on new methods of farming and livestock rearing."

"How interesting," Edward asked. "What kind of livestock?"

Matteo could tell it was killing him to restrain his irony about livestock. To Edward, livestock held as much interest as dirt.

"Horses. I'm interested in adding horse farming to our estate in Hohenruppersdorf."

"Do you have horses now?" Edward asked.

Zdenko glanced away. "At home, I used to have a fine stallion —Kessler—but my father, um, sold it. I miss riding him."

Matteo wouldn't have been able to live with himself if Reinhold had been killed in the war. He understood how Zdenko felt.

But he didn't *want* to understand how Zdenko felt.

"I like horses. They keep me from having to walk." Edward leaned back in his chair and crossed his legs.

Zdenko arched a brow. "I like them because I feel free when I ride. I can ride into the woods, up the mountain, to the pond, to town."

Matteo understood this impulse too. It was when he felt most calm, safe. He was uncomfortable with the number of things he had in common with Zdenko. He was a soldier. Had faced death, seen slaughter, and yet, this young man made him recall things—soft things, about himself, he'd tried to set aside.

"It just so happens that I'm going riding tomorrow," Matteo said. "Would you like to join me?"

Zdenko's face beamed in a way which made him look even more like his sister. "I'd love to. Where and what time?"

That was painless. The painful part would be avoiding looking into Zdenko's attractive eyes.

"Meet me at the Regimental barracks. I stable my horse, Reinhold, there. Where do you keep yours?"

Zdenko flushed up to the tops of his ears. If Matteo didn't know better, he would have sworn the boy was half girl.

"We don't have horses in Vienna," Zdenko said.

"Why don't you borrow one?" Edward said, sounding much too hale and hearty. He turned to Matteo. "Perhaps from a soldier friend of yours?"

"Of course." Matteo sipped his coffee and barely tasted it. He badly wanted to speak with Arabella, but she seemed preoccupied with glancing around the room and nodding at acquaintances. He wasn't sure she even knew he was there.

Zdenko sipped his hot chocolate. When he set his cup down, there was a great smear of whipped cream across his upper lip. Probably the only thing that would ever appear on that feminine lip. Matteo couldn't help laughing. He lifted his napkin to wipe the *schlag* but stopped himself in time. He looked at Zdenko and pointed to his own lip.

Zdenko reddened and dabbed, *dabbed*, at his upper lip. Teaching him the manners of a gentleman was going to take longer than Matteo would be alive.

"If you're ever going to attract the ladies, Zdenko, you are going to have to stop blushing so easily," Edward joked, which only made Zdenko hunch his shoulders up to his ears as if to hide.

It would be impossible to train that out of him.

"He's rather shy," Arabella said.

"Am not," Zdenko muttered with a frown.

There was an uncomfortable momentary lull until Edward picked up the conversation. "Where will you ride tomorrow?" he asked Matteo.

"Have you ridden in the Prater yet?" Matteo asked Zdenko,

Zdenko brightened. "No, and I've wanted to. We've walked and had carriage rides there, of course, but I've not been in the meadows or by the Konstantinteich pond."

Edward smiled and tapped a finger on the table. "Excellent choice."

It was settled; they would ride together. And that was the most unsettling result Matteo could have hoped for. He hated admitting Edward's machinations were working. It was Matteo's manner to be straightforward, but this convoluted strategy might end up as badly as his strategy on the battlefield had.

At least in this case, only his own ego would be bruised, and no one would be killed.

CHAPTER 7

Matteo and Zdenka rode along the southern Prater Road, which followed the Donau canal. At the horse racing track, they turned north. Through the trees they could see the swift, dark Donau, which demarcated the northern border of the Prater. Sun filtered through the black-green shade, throwing shivering spots of light on the path. Everything smelled green, damp, loamy. Leaves whispered in a brisk breeze. Bright green patches of moss dotted fallen logs. Crocuses pushed up where sun fell between the branches.

We're almost there," he called. "Konstantinteich Pond is up ahead."

He directed his horse, Reinhold, off the well-worn path. They ducked under low branches and, when she raised her head, the wind-rippled pond spread out before them. Ducks paddled near the edge of the sun-glittered water. The sight made her homesick for the forests surrounding Friedenheim. Vienna was lovely, but it couldn't compare with the lush pine forests of home.

She followed Matteo until he stopped at a shady nook. He dismounted, tied Reinhold to a fallen tree, and inhaled deeply.

"This is one of my favorite spots." He gazed across the pond. His eyes were no longer wary and the tension around his mouth was gone. Even his back seemed less rigid. She dismounted and tied her mount to a tree.

Zdenka struggled to keep up as she followed his long-legged stride to a sunny spot where he flung himself down on the grass. Trying to imitate his loose-limbed movements, she joined him on the grass, but her body felt awkward and disorderly.

He was quiet a long time, face tipped up, eyes closed as he soaked up the sun and hummed a tune.

"What's that melody? I don't recognize it." She shifted her weight to be close enough to feel the heat radiating off his body. Sharp licks of lightning ran up her spine.

He smiled. "A favorite tune of mine. It's from Mozart's *Die Zauberflöte*. Pamina and Papageno are sitting around singing about the virtues and joys of married life."

"*That's* your favorite tune?" A song about married life?"

"Don't ask me why," he said with a low laugh that vibrated in the base of her throat. "I don't know, I've just always liked it. It does lack the lust and murder which dominate opera."

"I thought perhaps Edward would come," she said. She was glad he hadn't, but Edward would have provided some distraction from Matteo's nerve-wracking closeness.

He snorted. "Off chasing some woman some place. An inveterate libertine, Edward."

She'd always managed to avoid having a 'male' conversation with a gentleman. But now, here in the forest, next to a very masculine man, a man who made her think more about being a young lady, she had to turn her mind upside down in order not to betray her gender, as well as seem gentlemanly.

This was getting impossible.

He seemed not to notice her silence. "Edward prefers married women. Can you imagine? Says he doesn't have to worry about marrying them, and, because they'll be the ones to worry about their husbands. I love my cousin but hate his deceptiveness. He could have been my father's son."

"Why?"

"My father never told the truth about anything." His voice took on a bitter edge. "I despise lying."

A lump, rather like a stone, landed in the pit of her stomach. Perspiration gathered in the crooks of her elbows.

"You know, once, Edward even dressed up as a priest for an assignation? I can't believe he hasn't got a bastard around somewhere."

"Um hm." The stone rose to her throat, and she swallowed hard. What would he think of her if he figured out her secret? She had to steer him clear of this sort of talk. Otherwise, she wouldn't be able to navigate the shoals and rocks of her own disguise.

"Edward told me the Gräfin of Belgrade was—"

"Oh, look. Up on that branch!" she exclaimed, pointing to a bird. "What sort of bird is that?"

"Uh, I believe it's a robin. They live here. In the woods," he said dryly. "Lots of them."

"Really? I mean, yes, of course they do."

He propped up on his elbow and rested his head in his hand. "Last night, I noticed several young ladies eyeing you, but you didn't ask any of them to dance. Might I ask why?"

She hadn't noticed. And why *would* she notice the glances of interested ladies? Struggling for an excuse, she stammered, "I ... I ... I'm not a good dancer. I wouldn't want to tread on the young ladies' feet."

"You don't weigh enough to cause any real damage." He poked her waist.

Ticklish, she grabbed his hand and *giggled*.

He squinted at her.

She quickly lowered her laugh to make it sound more masculine, but she ended up sounding as though she'd swallowed a frog.

"I enjoyed dancing with your sister. She's a fine dancer and a charming woman. Do you think she might allow me to call on her?"

One more suitor, particularly one who was kind, thoughtful, and charming, would only create further chaos. Arabella didn't need any more men appearing. What if Matteo was the 'right man'? His inquiry gave her a shudder of jealousy.

Zdenka pointed towards a bird pirouetting in a patch of blue sky. "Isn't that bird a red kite? I think it's got a catch in its beak."

His gaze followed where she pointed. "You seem terribly interested in birds." He grinned. "Particularly the ordinary ones."

"I ... I like birds. And animals." She pressed a blade of grass between her thumbs and blew a honking whistle.

His rumbling laugh resounded in the forest. "You can always attract geese who have the croup." He gave her slender leg a smack with the back of his hand.

There he was, being physical again.

"If I didn't know better, I'd say you were too shy to ask a lady to dance."

Her throat seized momentarily. "Yes ... I'm shy. Very shy."

Matteo levered off the ground and stood. His form cast a shadow over her like one of the towering trees. Arms outstretched, he struck a pose, one brawny leg in front of the other, as if ready to execute some complicated dance step.

He meant to be funny, but his inner thigh was truly exquisite. What would it feel like to run her hand down that thigh?

No! What if he's Arabella's right man and he could save Friedenheim?

"No one would dance with me if I looked like that." She laughed.

"I'm no dancing master," he gave a flourishing bow, "but I've heard the ladies think I am a passable dancer. I could certainly show you a few things."

He broke into a waltz and spun about the grass. Muscular as he was, when he moved about, he was as sleek and agile as a cat. His movements made her heart bump.

She plucked a blade of grass and twirled it in her fingers. She wanted to appear relaxed, when really, her heart thumped like a kettle drum. "Why should I learn to waltz? I prefer watching from the sidelines."

He raised one eyebrow. His voice was low and kind. "Unless I've made a mistake and girls aren't your flavor."

Heat rushed up her neck to her hairline. "No, no! I like girls. I—I like them very much. Only not to dance with." Her emotions battled inside her. She wanted to be in his arms but was afraid he would figure out she was a girl. But she *longed* for him to figure out she was a girl.

Zdenka felt like a pretzel.

No, no, no, she reminded herself. He'll be a good husband for Arabella.

He leaned against a beech tree. "You've seen people waltz dozens of times. You must know how to dance by now."

The truth was, often when she and Arabella returned from parties, they rolled up the ratty Persian rug in their hotel room and waltzed around the room, bumping into things, not stopping until they were laughing too hard to continue. She loved dancing but had only ever danced with her sister.

At his aunt's party, when he'd waltzed Arabella around the floor, Zdenka had stifled a yearning to be the one in his arms.

"Waltzing is the best way, and the only way, to hold a young lady in your arms. This is your first Season in Vienna. You can't go without dancing."

Dancing with a young lady terrified her. She would be devastated if she broke some poor girl's heart.

He nudged the toe of her boot. "Come on. You can't be *that* scared of dancing." He laughed and made a dramatic show of looking around. "There's not a single soul about."

"Thank you for the generous offer, but truly, I prefer being a wallflower." She bit her lower lip. "The male equivalent of a wallflower, that is."

"Here's one way to get you up." With a rascally glint in his eye, he reached down and plucked her cap off.

Her curls sprang loose, and her pulse surged. She launched to her feet. "Hey! That's my favorite hat." She jumped up, grabbing as he dangled it over her head, but he kept her at a distance with a hand on her shoulder. She felt the heat of his oversized palm through the thick fabric of her coat.

Then, he ruffled her hair.

She leapt back as if he'd set her hair on fire. Her heart pounded, and the hair on the back of her neck prickled.

He shook his head. "It looks as though whoever cuts your hair is blind. I can take you to my barber."

"I have great affection for my barber. I'm loyal." One last bound and she snatched her hat back and jammed it on her head.

"Are you using your barber as a girl-repellant?" Matteo laughed.

She couldn't think of anything to say, so she gave into laughter.

His wide smile and crinkly eyes turned him into a different man than the one who'd dismounted at the shady nook. When had he turned so light-hearted? At home, whenever she was despondent or lonely, she rode or walked in the forest because she firmly believed that Friedenheim had restorative powers. If he married Arabella, he might go there to live and always feel as happy and relaxed as he was now.

"For now, let's work on your waltzing. Dancing gives you the best chance of holding a warm, curvaceous body against your own. Everyone knows dancing is merely a poor imitation of sex."

"It is?" she squeaked.

"Now, you must be careful not to hold the lady too tightly or you'll cause a scandal."

"Can you show me how tight is too tight?" she asked. As soon as she said it, she realized her mistake. He would feel her curves, her bindings. She stiffened, trying to keep a hands distance between them.

"Like this." He grasped her waist and pulled her to him with such force, he knocked the air out of her.

Once, during a tremendous summer storm, she'd seen a tree hit by lightning. The oak had exploded. Orange and blue tongues of flame danced in the rain as it caught fire and blazed up against the dark sky. Sap sizzled and popped. Tree branches snapped.

This was how she felt as he held her, gazing down from what seemed such an enormous height.

Her thumb accidentally brushed the inside of his wrist, and a bewildered look came into his eyes. He dropped his hands, glanced away, and stepped back from their embrace.

Sweat coated her palms. Did he know she was a girl? Her whole body felt hungry for fire, for water, for lightning and thunder.

"There," he said, his voice strangely gruff. "That should get you through at least one dance."

CHAPTER 8

Matteo had been up most of the night. He had gone through pages and pages of paper, trying to compose a letter to Arabella. Soldiers were not given to romantic rants or flights of fanciful prose.

It was easier to kill a man than to lay bare his heart.

Now, as he walked the distance to Bösendorfer Hall, he repeatedly reached up to pat his breast pocket where the letter lay.

The previous day, Zdenko had mentioned that he and Arabella were to attend a piano concert to hear Herr Franz Liszt. Tonight, Matteo would meet them at the hall with a letter for Zdenko to give Arabella.

Friendship; that was all he was asking. When he regained his honor and made things right with Luther, Matteo would be worthy of courting her. Until then, he wasn't worthy of being a suitor.

Matteo looked forward to spending more time with Zdenko. The ride in the forest, the laughter, even the way Zdenko disconcerted him, made his chest lighter, made it easier to move about in his own skin. The time had been a refreshing change from soldiering. If he had to put a fine point on it, Zdenko took Matteo outside of his own head. Perhaps Zdenko could tell him more about Arabella. If she had as much humor and liveliness as her brother, she would indeed be a catch.

When he arrived at Bösendorfer Hall, Zdenko, Arabella, and Graf Lamoral were disembarking from the latter's gold-trimmed carriage. Zdenko and Matteo waved at one another.

Just then, Corporal Niedermeyer, a soldier from Matteo's regiment, passed by. Once a strapping man with sharp blue eyes and a rascally smile, Niedermeyer had been a fierce fighter. Now, the man walked with an exaggerated limp. Instead of his handsome uniform, the soldier wore a torn, dirty overcoat not nearly warm enough for the sharp weather.

Zdenko bounded over, prepared to chat, but Matteo wanted to speak to Niedermeyer first. He held up a polite hand to give Zdenko pause.

Matteo called out, "Niedermeyer."

The man turned.

Niedermeyer's face was badly burned turning his smile into a grimace.

Matteo froze.

"Hello, Lieutenant von Ritter. How are you?"

Matteo's eye twitched madly. Damn the infernal thing. "I am well. I lost track of you after we were discharged. Where are you living now? I assume you've been...discharged."

Niedermeyer's face twisted. "Without a *gulder*. I've been living in the Prater. I make do as I can."

"Have you seen any of the others from our regiment?" Matteo asked.

Niedermeyer shook his head. "Are you looking for anyone in particular?"

"Luther Klesper, the cannoneer, was a good friend. I've been looking for him."

"I haven't seen him."

"If you do, will you tell him I'm looking for him?"

Niedermeyer nodded.

"May I embrace you, for old time's sake?" Matteo asked.

Niedermeyer nodded. As they embraced, Matteo slipped money in his comrade's pocket.

Niedermeyer lifted his chin proudly. "Don't forget our regiment's motto. From Shakespeare's Julius Caesar, it was."

Matteo nodded gravely. "I live by it still. 'I love the name of honor more than I fear death.'"

"I'll tell Luther you're looking for him if I see him." Niedermeyer nodded and departed.

"Who was that?" Zdenko asked.

He had been watching and stood at Matteo's side.

"A former soldier from my regiment," said Matteo. "Wish I could help him."

"I saw you slip money in his pocket."

Zdenko wore his evening scheme with the frayed jacket cuffs and the disheveled shirt front. His red curls escaped the lacquer of pomade, making his head look like a russet shrub in need of pruning.

"He wouldn't have taken it had I offered." Matteo watched Niedermeyer limp around the corner and out of sight. "Soldiers are a proud bunch and often refuse help."

"Why?"

He took a deep breath. "We like to think we're invincible. Capable of managing whatever happens."

Zdenko's eyes searched his face. "Do you let people help you?"

A kind of darkness swept over Matteo. An irritation he hadn't expected. The scar at his temple stung. "Help with what? I'm quite fine."

Arabella walked toward them on the arm of Graf Lamoral.

Resplendent in gold silk and her red fox cape, the lamplight cast a glow over her that gave her the iridescence of a butterfly. She smiled graciously and asked in her refined voice, "Are you coming to hear Herr Liszt, as well?"

He had intended to, but after seeing Niedermeyer, what he really wanted was a drink. Then another. And perhaps another.

Matteo bowed. "I thought I might, but I've got a headache and think I'll walk home."

"Good evening, von Ritter," Lamoral said in such a way as to make clear his disdain for Matteo.

It wasn't going to be possible to give Zdenko the letter for Arabella with this fool around.

"Herr Liszt is going to play some transcriptions from Mozart's *Die Zauberflöte* tonight," Zdenko said.

Zdenko's smile gave him his own sort of glow, putting Matteo at ease. Matteo had spent so much time around gruff, battle-weary soldiers, the friendship of someone as lively as Zdenko was a welcome change. Matteo felt a certain affinity with the younger man he couldn't explain. Somehow, Zdenko calmed his wire-tight nerves. Even if Matteo's ultimate aim was the sister, he had enjoyed his time with Zdenko the previous day. Matteo was already thinking of other outings for the two of them.

Matteo said, "You'll find him sublime. I heard him play the transcriptions in Budapest last year. It includes my favorite theme, *Bei Männer, welche Liebe fühlen.*"

"The tune you hummed yesterday," Zdenko said.

"If you are finished," Lamoral said, sniffily, "I'd like to go in."

Matteo would like to have thrown the fop under a carriage. How could Arabella consider him as a husband? He was a shallow, preening social climber.

"Will you walk to the door with us?" Zdenko said. "Perhaps you'll change your mind about going to the concert."

As they walked, Matteo slipped the letter from his pocket. He didn't like the subterfuge of the entire scheme, so he wanted to be as straightforward as possible when it came to asking Zdenko to deliver his letter to Arabella.

Matteo pressed the paper into Zdenko's hand.

Zdenko's eyebrows scrunched. "What is this?"

"A letter for Arabella. Would you give it to her?"

Zdenko stopped in his tracks. His gaze followed Arabella's back as she ascended the stairs on Lamoral's arm. The two paused at the top of the stairs to chat with Fanny Bösendorfer, a young woman whose father was the Emperor's piano maker and owned the concert hall.

Zdenko turned to Matteo, and with a hurt look in his eyes, said, "I must guard my sister's reputation. I can't allow her to be compromised by a letter."

"It's unsealed so you can read it. If there is anything you find objectionable, return it to me."

"I think you would ..." Zdenko tugged his wrinkled evening jacket. "... make a fine husband for Arabella."

Matteo dipped his head. "I was afraid you might think I made friends with you only to access your sister, but it's not the case. Yesterday, when we went riding, I had the best time since I've been back from the war. I do consider you a friend and hope you think of me as yours. You're quite relaxing to be with. I can't approach her directly until I have some things...settled. I would like her to know I found her charming and gracious, sweet and genuine, and I would like to be her friend, should it please her."

Arabella and Lamoral moved to enter the concert hall.

"I must go." Zdenko slipped the letter into his pocket.

"All right. And thank you. Let me know how she receives it." Matteo didn't know if Zdenko would truly give the letter to Arabella. He might destroy it or give it to their parents. If one of Arabella's other suitors found the letter, Matteo might even be called out for a duel. Not that he was worried, but he didn't feel like killing another living soul. He'd had enough of running men through with his sword.

Matteo watched Zdenko's scrawny figure climb the stairs to the music hall, his coat flapping around him rather like a loose bedsheet. Matteo remembered about the tailors. He ran up the stairs after Zdenko and grabbed his arm as he was about to go inside. The slim, softness of Zdenko's arm was a surprise. "I nearly forgot. Edward wants us to meet him at his tailor's tomorrow. Mr. Boughton of Savile Row Tailors. Can you come?"

Zdenko stopped. The crowd flowed around them. "Why?"

Matteo smiled and flicked a bit of imaginary lint off Zdenko's jacket. "Edward thought you might like to look at a new suit."

For some strange reason, Zdenko's face became a mask of fear.

"I...I have to go. I'll meet you tomorrow, but really, I don't need a suit."

"It will improve your chances with the ladies," Matteo said.

Zdenko blinked, and his brow furrowed as if trying to discern Matteo's meaning. "Oh, yes. The ladies," he muttered and fled into the concert hall.

♫

Zdenka waited until the rest of the family had gone to bed before she dared read Matteo's letter. She lit the lamp on her bedside table and pulled the thin coverlet up to her chin. His handwriting was upright and exact, without flourishes or cross-outs. Here was a man who knew what he wanted to say.

Sehr Geeherte Countess Waldner,

I know I should not be writing to you, but after meeting you, I am compelled to do so. If you are reading this, my letter has passed your brother's approval. He is dedicated to protecting your reputation, as am I. I assure you, my intentions are wholly honorable, and I will do nothing to publicly compromise you.

At my aunt's soiree, I was struck by your grace, peaceful demeanor, intelligence and love of music.

Tell me about yourself. How do you spend your time when you are not in Vienna? What do you think of Goethe? Do you prefer the snows of winter or the breezes of spring? Do you speak French? (I do not. I hope that does not disappoint you.) What is your favorite place in the entire world? What do you want most in life?

Forgive me for asking so many questions, but I would like to get to know you better, to become your friend. I think a gentleman and a lady must first be friends before all else. Perhaps, in the future, I can hope for more. Until then, I hope you will answer my letter.

If you reward me your friendship, with even the slenderest of hopes for something more, I will repay you with my undying faithfulness.

As she read, Zdenka's skin went from hot to cold and back to hot again.

You are of noble birth, highly sought-after, beautiful and lovely beyond compare. I am a soldier who has put his life to the test for his Emperor, country and Vienna. Would that I could show you the same dedication.

I pray this letter doesn't take you too much by surprise.

With warmest regards,

Lieutenant Matteo von Ritter

When Zdenka finished reading the letter, she exhaled and stared at the water spot on the ceiling above her bed. She held the letter to her chest and considered whether or not to give it to Arabella.

What if Matteo was the right man Arabella had been waiting for? If he was the man the gypsy predicted would come, she would be doing Arabella a favor by giving her the letter. The gypsy said the man's eyes would be dark and brooding. Matteo's eyes were more than that. They were hungry, wounded, and there were glimmers of hope, too. But when he smiled, Zdenka had felt a furry feeling blossom in her chest. Was his chestnut hair the color the gypsy had in mind when she said he would have 'dark' hair?

Matteo was robust. Broad and solid, with a simmering fierceness about him. He was proud too because he tried to hide the scar on his temple. When he'd helped the old soldier up the stairs, he showed compassion and kindness. He was charming without being insincere, unlike the Grafs, who acted as if Arabella was an *accoutrement* to their persons. Matteo admired Arabella and treated her as if she was a person, not a mere woman.

And he was heart-stoppingly dashing.

An unfamiliar tickle fluttered in her lower abdomen. Thinking to still it, she flopped over on her tummy, but the sensation didn't abate.

If Matteo *was* the right man for Arabella, Zdenka must slam shut the door of her heart, lock away and silence whatever stirred there. She would sacrifice her heart for Arabella's happiness, if necessary.

She reread the letter to ensure nothing would compromise Arabella. Not a single line suggested impropriety. Of course, their parents couldn't find the letter or Matteo would have no chance at all with Arabella. Mama and Papa wanted not merely wealthy, but madly rich, like the three Grafs. And she wanted Friedenheim. Zdenka folded the letter, returned it to the envelope, and tucked it beneath her pillow.

Arabella was busy. How would Zdenka find time to plead Matteo's case? Tomorrow, she and Arabella were to take the tram to the Schloss Belvedere Museum. Zdenka's *Baedeker's Guide to Vienna* said the museum was quiet and filled with beautiful works of art. Tomorrow, undisturbed, she would share Matteo's letter with Arabella and let her decide if this bold soldier was 'the right man.'

But what if he wasn't the right man for Arabella? Growing up with someone as unreliable as Papa, Zdenka held that the safest thing for a woman was not to depend on a man. Society believed a woman had to give up herself, her dreams, her own will, if she was to love. A choice had to be made, and most women, including Arabella, didn't have a choice.

Zdenka, in pants and boots, did have a choice. The problem was, her heart wasn't listening. Her heart pulled her toward Matteo as inexorably as the sun to the horizon.

She clutched her bedclothes tight to her chest. Give up Friedenheim for Matteo?

Impossible. She could not give up her promise to her grossmutti to follow her fickle heart.

If Arabella didn't agree that Matteo was the right man, she would decide on one of the richer suitors.

And Zdenka would have to forget she ever saw him.

CHAPTER 9

The swaying tram rolled to a stop at the Oberes Schloss Belvedere and Arabella and Zdenka rose to disembark. As they made their way down the tram's aisle, Zdenka made sure to stay close behind her sister. Men were known to occasionally take liberties with women's backsides on public transport. When she overheard stories at parties where women blushed and refused to repeat what had been said or done to them, Zdenka had the confused impulse to apologize for her gender.

Did *all* men do such vile things? Surely not a man as gallant as Matteo von Ritter.

With her *Baedeker's* tucked under her arm and Matteo's letter in her pocket, Zdenka leapt off the steps to the pavement. How lovely not to have to worry about skirts or propriety.

Zdenka assisted her sister.

As they headed up the gravel path toward the magnificent castle, Arabella said, "Be careful. You won't always be able to act so freely."

Zdenka could have walked faster in her gentleman's boots, but Arabella's dainty slippers kept them at a slower pace.

Arabella paused to gaze at the castle. "It's incredibly grand."

Zdenka said, "If you lived in such a place, you would have to act proper all the time. Never running or skipping down the stairs."

Since coming to Vienna, Arabella had become as proper and reserved as a dowager. Zdenka missed the carefree sister who shared laughter and teasing. Marrying one of the Grafen would seal Arabella's fate as a stiff Society woman with a boring husband.

She would have to convince Arabella that Matteo could save her from that fate.

"If I live in such a place, I'll be able to save Mama and Papa from ruin." She tapped Zdenka's elbow. "And save your beloved Friedenheim."

"There is that." Inside her pocket, Zdenka's fingertips brushed Matteo's letter. "What if there were someone else besides Lamoral, Elemer, and Dominik?"

"Someone else? Such as who?"

Unable to contain herself any longer, Zdenka spun on her heel and walked backwards, in front of Arabella, talking animatedly. "Like Lieutenant Matteo von Ritter. What if he wanted to be friends with you? What if he was in love with you?"

Arabella stopped and frowned. "It's impossible. You know that. Fräulein Brüder let it slip that he's a penniless soldier."

"But his aunt's quite rich. Surely there's an allowance for him, and he will inherit one day." Zdenka turned back around and walked beside Arabella. "And, he's the sort of man, who, one day, might make a lot of money in trade.... or something."

"Allowances don't save farms."

"Matteo is handsome, nice, intelligent, and I think he cares for you."

"Matteo is it now? Not Lieutenant Matteo von Ritter?" Arabella scowled. "What are you about, Zdenka?"

Zdenka blushed and clapped her mouth shut.

Inside the Schloss Belvedere, they found themselves in the snowy marble vestibule of the splendid *Sala Terrena*. Four monumental nude male figures, twisted in agonizing positions, muscles straining, served as columns holding up an arched roof. The nudes, with their bulging sinews, took Zdenka's breath away.

"Exquisite," Arabella murmured. She pointed to the Grand Staircase leading up to the galleries. "Matteo von Ritter seems nice, but he must know I'm already being wooed by the Grafen."

"He knows, but is it possible that he is your 'right man'?"

Ignoring the question, Arabella paused before a painting by Carl Goebels the Younger. "See how he's shadowed the face so you can barely see it? Only the eyes show such pain."

The character in the painting appeared desperate and broken. The eyes bore the kind of pain Zdenka thought she'd glimpsed in Matteo's eyes. What had happened to him in the war that he carried such grief? Perhaps Arabella's love was precisely what could heal him. She was loving, patient, kind. She might be just the right wife for him, as he might be the right man for her.

Zdenka trailed behind Arabella. "Just hear him out. He has written you a letter. Will you read it?"

"A letter?" Arabella's skirts rustled as she rounded on Zdenka. "You let him write to me? What were you thinking?"

"You'll like him. Seems to be forward-thinking about women." Zdenka dashed around to Arabella's other side to cajole her. "He's considerate and kind. And I've read the letter. There's nothing in it that might compromise you. Won't you at least read it?"

"Don't cause trouble, Zdenka." Arabella shook her head.

"I'm not. I'm only trying to help you find the right man you've been waiting for."

Zdenka thought she must have looked crushed, because Arabella stared down at her hands and said, "All right. I will let you read it to me."

Zdenka grinned. She crossed the gallery to a bench in the middle of the room and patted the cushion for Arabella to join her. When Arabella had settled, Zdenka took the letter out of her pocket and read in a hushed voice. Out of the corner of her eye, Zdenka snuck glances at her sister's face, which remained placid the entire time. When she was finished, Zdenka flapped the letter at Arabella. "Here, see? Harmless. He only wants to be friends."

"For now. You know as well as I that later he wants to be more than friends."

"At least he wants to get to know you. The Grafen don't even care about you. They just want to marry you for your looks. They don't know how gentle and kind you are. Matteo is interested in you as a person."

"Even if I wanted it, Mama and Papa would not allow it. Aside from his lack of income, there is his aunt who is a social pariah. Mama made an exception to allow us to attend her party, but she would never countenance a union with the nephew of Thea Prokovsky, even if she is a Viscomtess." Arabella swiped her hand through the air in a gesture of finality. "I consider the matter closed."

Zdenka wadded up the letter and shoved it back in her pocket. She wasn't ready to give up. "I know you better than anyone, and I think he'd make you a fine husband. And as for Friedenheim, Matteo is an honorable man. A man of character and commitment. I know he'd find a way to save the land of our birth."

Arabella's voice came like icy daggers. "You, who wants your blessed Friedenheim, urge me to consider tying myself to a penniless man? Haven't you learned from our parents' marriage that it's much worse be unhappy and poor than to be unhappy and rich?"

As quickly as she had angered, Arabella thawed, and her eyes brimmed with tears. "I know you think I'm selling myself to the highest bidder. But even if I had feelings for Matteo, which, after meeting him, I don't, you know I'm still waiting for the right man to come before I make a choice."

Zdenka leaned her head on her sister's shoulder. "I'm sorry. I know. It's just that he seems nicer than all the Grafen I don't mean to pester you like Mama—"

"Then don't." Arabella shrugged off Zdenka's hug and stood, her back straight as a fence post.

Zdenka nodded and sighed. "I'll write back to him and tell him it's impossible." She rose from the bench. They strolled down a long hallway to the next gallery filled with ocean paintings. "Would you mind if I kept him as a friend? I'll learn more about being a man from him."

"He doesn't suspect?"

"No."

"It's dangerous. He might discover your secret, and the scandal would ruin your Season next year."

Didn't Arabella understand anything? Zdenka stared at a painting of a stormy sea. Whitecaps foamed. Jagged bolts of lightning stabbed through boiling black clouds. Boats lay tossed like toys on the roiling water. The piece captured what she felt inside, but she wasn't entirely sure why. "I don't intend to have a Season."

"What do you mean? Of course, you'll have a Season," scoffed Arabella. "You must have your coming out if you're to be married."

Zdenka faced Arabella and stacked her fists on her hips. "I don't want to be married. Friedenheim has been in Mama's family for generations, and I promised Grossmutti I would not allow it to leave the family." As she spoke the words aloud, her jaw tightened, and her heart gained pace. "I want to buy back the lands Papa sold off. Start a stud farm and raise horses. Replant the forests. Grow crops. Raise cattle and sheep. I don't want to follow the rules society imposes upon women. There, I can be who I want to be. I can wear pants and make something of myself, and I don't need a husband to do it. I can do it on my own."

Arabella's eyes widened. She spoke in a hushed, shocked voice. "What are you saying, Zdenka? I knew you loved Friedenheim, but you've never said anything so radical before. You're frightening me."

"I've seen what you're going through, Arabella. It's killing your spirit. Your sense of fun, your personality." Zdenka shook her head. "You've changed so much since we came to Vienna. It's like we're not even sisters anymore."

"Change was necessary." Arabella tipped Zdenka's chin up so she could look in her eyes. "And you will be required to make adjustments, as well. You cannot live on your own. You must have a husband to make a way in the world. As a woman, you can't even hold title to property. Life simply demands marriage."

"No," she said adamantly. "I won't make *adjustments*, as you call them. That's another word for giving up who you are, your freedom to choose how you want to live. I want to change things, if only on the estate. I can ride about in pants. I can make my own decisions. I can deal with matters of money. I don't have to depend on some man who gambles and drinks like Papa."

Arabella sighed, her face pale. "You have been too long in pants, sister."

"And when I return home to the estate, I don't intend to change out of them." Zdenka strode to the door. She'd long ago made up her mind, as Arabella had hers. Zdenka wasn't about to make any *adjustments*.

They returned to the tram stop. Zdenka stuck her hand in her pocket and squeezed the balled-up letter. Matteo was the finest man she had ever met. He loved music, books, his free-thinking aunt, his Emperor. He was compassionate, courageous, and thoughtful. He didn't deserve to be snubbed. Zdenka wanted to keep him as a friend. It would be rude not to respond. His brilliant smiles were so few. The apprehension in his gaze, the tautness about his mouth, his darting eyes. These were all evidence of some hell he'd lived through. A letter from Arabella would aid in healing whatever dark memories lurked in his soul.

Surely Arabella wouldn't mind if Zdenka wrote him back over her sister's signature. So Arabella's reputation remained entirely above reproach, Zdenka wouldn't tell her.

What could it hurt to exchange a letter or two?

CHAPTER 10

"Y ou've explained to Edward that I'm not looking for a new suit?" Zdenka asked Matteo as they walked along the Ringstrasse toward Edward's tailor, Boughton's.

"He suggested we meet to look at some of the latest fashions," Matteo said.

His breezy tone suggested he was up to something.

They came to arched double doors. Over the entrance hung a gold-lettered sign: *Mr. Boughton, English Tailor*. Inside, the shop smelled of money, leather, and imported bay rum cologne. Folded lengths of woolen fabric in an array of blues, blacks, and grays were layered on several tables. White linen shirts hung in rows, and silk cravats nestled against one another like colorful little birds.

"Doesn't Edward have enough suits?" Zdenka fingered an expensive length of cashmere wool, as soft as one of her new lambs. Papa never had a suit of this quality fabric.

"Yes," Matteo stroked a sky-blue cravat. "He's late as usual."

The tailor, a dapper man with side whiskers the size of a whisk broom, was busy fitting the shoulders of a jacket on a customer, who stood in front of a mirror, turning this way and that, admiring himself from every angle.

"*Guten tag*, I will be right with you," Herr Boughton said in greeting.

The door opened, and Edward blew in. He wore a dark blue suit, a maroon waistcoat, a silk paisley cravat, and a top hat. He even carried a silver-topped ebony walking stick like an Englishman. He could have stepped out of the Emperor's carriage.

Edward removed his leather gloves and put them in his pocket. "Sorry to be late, you two. Glad you could come on this expedition. Have you looked around yet?"

Before either of them could answer, the man trying on the suit turned.

It was Graf Lamoral, Arabella's suitor.

"Why Graf Waldner, what are you doing here?" Lamoral's lips pressed into a shape not quite a smile. He nodded curtly to Matteo. "Lieutenant."

Matteo's eyes darkened.

"Lamoral. I didn't see you there. How are you? Zdenko is to be fitted for a new evening suit." Edward clapped her on the shoulder and roughly rubbed her the way an older brother might do to a younger sibling, causing her to sway on her feet.

Edward's proclamation made her heart clench. There was no way she could afford a new set of evening clothes. Now, she'd be embarrassed to say as much in front of everyone. And how was she to keep her gender a secret while being fitted for a new suit?

"I don't need a new set of evening clothes. I like the one I have quite all right." She glanced at the door and estimated how many steps it would take to escape.

Edward strode across the shop with an attitude befitting a king. He surveyed Lamoral's suit, circled and inspected him up and down until Lamoral snorted impatiently.

Musing aloud, Edward murmured, "Yes, yes. Something precisely like this, I think."

Lamoral looked absolutely apoplectic.

The glint in Edward's eye indicated this was precisely the reaction he hoped to provoke.

Lamoral glared at Edward. "If you'll let Boughton finish, I'll be down from here in a moment."

Edward stepped back, crossed his arms, and tapped his lips with a finger. "I believe we'll take one exactly like that," he said to Boughton.

Boughton looked startled and glanced from Lamoral to Edward and back.

Lamoral smiled. His voice dripped with condescension. "This is a very expensive suit." He glanced at Zdenka. "I hardly think Graf Waldner would be comfortable in a suit such as this."

"Oh, I don't know," Zdenka said, getting into the spirit of things. "I rather like the fabric." She leaned over and peered at the coat. "Don't you think your potential-brother-in-law would look illustrious in an identical suit?"

She shot a look at Matteo, but his back was turned. The shaking of his shoulders betrayed his laughter.

Lamoral turned to the tailor. "I'll take the entire bolt of cloth."

The tailor's eyebrows shot up. "Yes, sir. But there's the matter of your outstanding—"

"And I'll order my bank to send payment for the entire amount I owe, plus the bolt," Lamoral snapped as he marched behind the curtain where men changed their clothes. In a moment, the jacket and pants came sailing out from behind the curtain, forcing Herr Boughton to catch them.

"*Schade!*" said Edward, affecting a pout. "I suppose we'll have to find something else for you, Zdenko."

Lamoral stomped out of the dressing room in pants and

shirtsleeves. As he strode between the tables, he jammed his arms into his coat sleeves. Boughton rushed to help him, but Lamoral brushed him off. He tipped his hat. "Good day, gentlemen. I'm sorry if I inconvenienced you regarding the fabric." He stared at Zdenka with a raptor's glare. "I had to have it. Just like I have to have Arabella."

A shot of cold chased up Zdenka's spine. The Grafen acted as if Arabella was a fox to be hunted and captured.

Guilt soured Zdenka's stomach. A fox whose marriage, perhaps to Lamoral, would save her beloved farm.

"Give her my fondest greetings, won't you, Graf Zdenko?"

Coldly, she replied, "Of course." She gave a little bow, but Lamoral was already out the door.

Matteo and Edward burst into laughter. The tailor spluttered and scuttled off to some back room to hide his mirth.

When Edward and Matteo had recovered themselves, Edward looked Zdenka up and down. "Now," he said, "let us get down to the real reason we've come here. To get you..." He tugged at Zdenka's frayed cuff. "...a fine evening scheme which will make you the envy of Lamoral, Dominik, and Elemer."

"But I thought we were merely playing a joke on Lamoral."

"Zdenko, look at your suit. It's practically falling off you," Matteo said. "You need a new one."

She lowered her voice. "You two know I can't afford a suit. Why did you bring me here?"

Matteo laid a hand on her shoulder. "Edward has offered to pay for it."

Edward grinned and held out his hands in a there-you-have-it gesture.

Surprised, Zdenka asked, "Why would you do that?"

"First, I can't stand Lamoral, Dominik, or Elemer." Edward perched on a stool and rested his hands atop his walking stick. "They're condescending, self-important asses. They should show you more respect. A good suit of clothes will go a long way toward that."

"I can't possibly accept such a gift." She inched backward, toward the door. "And besides, I like my evening suit. It fits me quite well."

Matteo tugged on her lapel. "How can you chaperone your beautiful sister around those three when you wear your tattered evening scheme?"

She moved nearer the door, but Matteo crossed in front of her escape route to examine a row of cravats.

Boughton emerged from the back room. In German with an English accent, he asked, "Herr Edward, how may I help you?"

Edward explained what they wanted.

Boughton said, "I see. Quite simple."

He took a measuring tape from around his neck and held it out toward Zdenka. She maneuvered hastily between tables, pretending to examine a stack of fabrics.

As soon as Boughton neared within arm's length, she darted to the next stack of fabrics and the next.

Matteo watched her every move, a bemused look on his face. "Hold still a minute so he can measure you. Don't be so worked up. It's only the gift of a suit."

Zdenka looked around the store until she found a half-finished suit on a hanger. She yanked the hanger off the rack. "What about that one?"

The tailor frowned and coughed into his fist. "That was for a gentleman who..." He cleared his throat and swiped his mustache. "Died before he could wear it."

Perfect.

"I'll try it on." Hanger in hand, Zdenka dodged into the dressing room. She cowered in the corner, clutching the suit to her chest. If only there were a back door.

"Once you've put it on, come out so we can see it," called Edward.

The curtain parted and Boughton stepped into the dressing room.

Zdenka recoiled. "No!"

The man jumped back. "Pardon me, sir, but don't you wish me to help you?"

"I have been dressing myself since I was five," Zdenka sputtered. She flapped the jacket at him as though he were a pesky fly, gave him a little shove out, and yanked the curtains shut.

Her heart raced. She bit her lip. If she put the pants on, Boughton would want to measure her inseam and nothing would give her away faster. She squeezed her eyes shut and tried to think how she could get out of here.

Boughton called from the other side of the curtain. "Sir, would you like to come out so I can make the alteration measurements?"

Her mouth was dry as dust. "The suit is perfect. Requires no alteration." She paced the floor of the tiny cubicle, trying to wait them out.

Finally, with impatience that sounded as if he might march right in there, Edward said, "Zdenko, come out of there and let us see it."

She gulped. There didn't seem to be any way around this.

"Wait, just a moment," she called. She sat on a bench and pulled off her boots.

There was that hole in her sock again. She pulled off her threadbare pants and pulled on the new ones. When she let go of the waist, they tumbled to the floor.

Zdenka shed her jacket with the holes in the pockets, slipped on the new one, and surveyed herself in the mirror. The suit was gorgeous, except it hung on her like a sack and would require a great deal of tailoring, which meant measuring by the tailor.

"Hurry up, we're getting old waiting out here." Matteo laughed.

She thrust her arm out through the opening in the dressing room curtains. "See? It's nice. Fits well."

"Come on now, we want to see it," Edward said. "Don't be shy."

"It's lovely. Really. Trust me."

"Sir," said the tailor. "May I measure the pants?"

"No!" she said. "They're perfect." Even holding the pants up, the hems puddled around her ankles.

The curtain jerked aside. Matteo's imposing bulk filled the opening. "Why are you so shy?" he asked. "Have you never had a suit fitted?"

Zdenka quailed in the corner. "N, n, n...no."

He held the curtain back and motioned her to come out of the dressing room. "Come on out of there and let Herr Boughton make you look like a rich young man."

She clutched the curtain and shuffled to the opening. If only she would drop dead.

Herr Boughton smiled indulgently. "Sometimes the young gentlemen are somewhat...timid. Perhaps my young assistant would make him more comfortable."

Only if the assistant was a girl. The front door was too far away to escape now, and she would never get far, holding up the waist with the pants sagging around her ankles and the jacket sleeves so long. A vein in her neck jumped with a rapid pulse.

She stripped off the jacket while struggling to hold up her pants. "Here, shorten the sleeves a bit, and it will be fine."

Matteo's laugh split his face in a grin. "It's not like Herr Boughton hasn't seen everything before."

She choked back a cough. *Want to bet?*

"Let me call my assistant." Boughton went to the door into which he had earlier disappeared. "Willem. Come here."

A slight young man came out of the back room. Judging by the smoothness of his cheeks and the unruliness of his straight, white-blond hair, Willem wasn't much more than a boy. He wore an apron with a tape measure looped around his neck. "Yes, sir, Herr Boughton?"

Matteo stumbled backwards, knocking a pile of fabric to the floor. His chest rose and fell rapidly, and his face drained of color. His gaze was riveted on the apprentice.

Everyone froze.

"Matteo?" Zdenka asked softly. "What's wrong?"

Edward stared at his cousin, his brows drawn. "Matteo, what's got into you?"

Matteo swallowed and seemed to gather himself. He whirled on Edward and snarled, "This was a stupid idea." His hand shot out, and he pointed to Zdenka. "That suit is fine." He glared at each of them in turn. "Why is everyone making such a fuss about it? Pay for the damned suit, and let's be done with it."

Edward's eyes widened. Boughton's fat cheeks blanched. The apprentice scurried away into the back room.

Matteo flung his arm out, accidentally knocking over a rack of cravats. He stared down at the silken pile, breathing raggedly. "He doesn't want the suit altered, well, damn it all, let him be!"

He turned and stalked out, slamming the door.

Zdenka caught her breath as the window in the door rattled. She glanced at Edward, who frowned and shook his head.

What had Matteo so upset? His lightning-fast temper, his wariness, the way his eye twitched, his headaches were symptoms of a deeper illness. The scar at his temple was a mere scratch compared to how gravely wounded the war had left his soul.

If they became closer friends, perhaps she would learn what

had caused his spasm of anger. But to do so, she would have to continue to deceive him, wounding him again. Perhaps she could help heal his soul, but at what cost? Breaking his heart and destroying his trust might be the greater loss.

♫

Matteo strode down the Ringstrasse until his stomach unclenched then slowed to a walk. He avoided looking at passersby, certain they could see his heartsick countenance. The apprentice was a reminder of his failure to keep his unit's drummer boy, Hans, alive. They must have been about the same age. The apprentice shared the same pale-as-an-angel hair and startling blue eyes as Hans. Matteo had promised Hans' mother he would keep the boy safe. Never had he expected the battle to be so barbaric. Matteo recalled Hans playing his drum, laughing around the campfire, trying to learn a game of cards. He had been a child.

Once Matteo's men had lined up to charge, he instructed Hans to stay behind the cannons. The boy was excited by the chance to do something for his Emperor, and Matteo had been unable to convince him to stay behind the lines. He should have been more forceful with Hans, told him it would be a bloody mess, but he, himself, couldn't have imagined the carnage.

Matteo paused and braced his hand against a stone wall, sickened by the image of Hans lying face up, blue eyes staring at the sky, his lips parted as if to say one last word. Matteo's breath burned in his throat. The scar at his temple throbbed.

Zdenko strode down the street toward him with a kind of feminine swing to his hips. Zdenko was older, but almost as naive as Hans. Men, bullies and predators, would make a target of him. Boxing, and later, fencing, gave Matteo the confidence and ability to defend himself.

Already, Matteo felt an affinity for his slight friend. If he could keep Zdenko safe, teach him how to defend himself from bigger, more physically imposing men, he would be doing something he'd failed to do for Hans: keep him safe.

Zdenko approached and put his hand on Matteo's shoulder. He carried a bag with the suit. "Are you all right?"

Was he? He had to be all right. Soldiers didn't simply fall apart when they saw someone who reminded them of a dead person. He wouldn't succumb to that madness. Instead, he said to Zdenko, "Meet me tomorrow at the Arsenal. I'm fencing, and I want to show you a few things."

CHAPTER 11

Zdenka had agreed to meet Matteo in the fencing hall in the vast, new *Kaiserlich und Königlich* Arsenal. The crossed broadswords over the heavy oak door made the hall easy to locate.

Zdenka pull the dagger which served as the door handle and entered a cavernous hall. Sun splashed across the wooden floor from the tall windows. Shields with crossed swords of various regiments hung on the walls, and flags fluttered on poles. The scents of beer, cigar smoke, sweat, and raw masculinity assaulted her nostrils. Soldiers reclined in a kind of viewing gallery above the fencing floor and men loitered in various states of undress or in their shirtsleeves.

Heat rushed to her face.

Men were so casual about their bodies. Why did women have to be so scrupulous, cosseting themselves in layers of bindings, lacings, and all manner of restrictive clothing? Wearing pants on the farm—and for her masquerade as Arabella's brother—had been a necessity. But now, those accommodations afforded her a close view of the most exquisite male flesh she'd ever laid eyes on. She felt a flutter in her lower abdomen which reminded her of her own femininity and its vulnerabilities. Vulnerabilities which she would not allow to limit her destiny.

On a kind of observation platform, men sat and chatted, as fencers in the middle of the floor tried to kill one another, their swords flashing through the air with a singing sound.

A thrill, sharp as quicksilver, ran through her as some of the men cheered and shouted out encouragement. "That's it, Franz."

"Thrust, now."

"Huzzah!"

"Don't let him back you against the wall!"

"Stiff arm! Quick step."

Thrusting and parrying, pushing one another back, the duelists grunted with exertion. Their silver swords had basket-shaped hilts and the tips had leather covers. Padded vests protected their chests and they wore elbow-length leather gloves. Wire masks hid their faces. All the protection was presumably so they wouldn't *actually* kill one another.

Not only was this place exciting, it was thrilling to be where no other lady would never venture. She searched the ring for Matteo and spotted him on the far side.

He was naked from the waist up, rubbing a towel over his chest, glistening with sweat. His torso was as sharply defined as the statues she'd seen at the museum. When he threw his head back and laughed with a friend, her heart galloped.

With her blood running hot and cold, she would never be able to hide her feelings from Matteo. This was a mistake. She didn't belong here. Wearing pants to the opera was one thing but trying to appear as a boy in a group of half-clad, muscled, fighting military men was something else altogether. Someone was bound to suspect the scrawny young man wasn't really a young man.

She prepared to sneak out when Matteo saw her and waved. "Hey! Zdenko. The view from here is better."

The view was already *quite* spectacular.

Zdenka nearly tripped over her feet as she made her way around the ring to Matteo. Her skin seemed to be popping like water thrown on a hot griddle. How would she hide the fire flushing across her cheeks?

"Hello, Zdenko." Matteo stuck out his hand. "Good to see you." He cocked a grin. "You look a bit queasy? Feeling all right?"

Bracing for his iron grip, she placed her hand in his. "Just fine." She nodded numbly as the knot in her stomach twisted tighter.

He turned his back for a moment, and she caught a glimpse of a long, ragged scar on his shoulder blade. She winced. It must have been a brutal wound, and yet, he'd never once mentioned it. How had he gotten it? Did it still hurt?

Matteo drank from a glass of water. A trickle ran down his chin, dribbled the length of his neck, and tracked through the dusting of dark hair on his chest.

Zdenka glanced at the floor, the viewing stands, the walls, the toes of her boots, anywhere but at his eyes or the ridges of his abdomen. What would it be like to stroke a single finger down the dip in the middle of his chest? What would it feel like to run her hands over the broad expanse of his bare shoulders? Hair tumbled around his head, making her want to reach out and tug her fingers through it.

He slipped his bulging arms into his shirt. "Did Arabella write back?"

The question was like a punch to the solar plexus. With all the sensations thrashing through her body and mind, she'd forgotten why the letter in her pocket.

"Yes. She can't see you, of course, but here's the letter." Slowly, Zdenko handed him the letter she'd dashed off so as not to lose her nerve.

"She's written back, so at least she doesn't think me too forward." He turned the letter over in his hands. Tension bracketing his mouth faded as he smiled, and his eyes lit up.

He stepped away to read the letter. She watched his expressions intently. He looked like a little boy on a Christmas morning.

She was overwhelmed with confusion.

Had she written to him for his sake, her own, or Arabella's? She hadn't wanted to disappoint him, so she'd written back. A man like Matteo von Ritter would make a fine husband for Arabella.

So why did her heart flip and spin when she saw him? Why did she lay awake thinking about the curve of his lower lip, the slope of his shoulders, the way his eye twitched when he seemed uncomfortable?

She couldn't be in love, could she?

♫

Matteo ran his finger under the flap of the envelope and held it to his nose, seeking Arabella's lavender scent.

Oddly, he smelled vanilla. Her handwriting was side-slanted and a bit sloppy, not looped and fluid, as he expected, yet he savored every word like a piece of Sacher Torte. In his mind, he heard her voice, her sweet inflections, as though the words flowed from her lush lips.

Dear Matteo,

Thank you for inviting Zdenko to the fencing hall today. He enjoyed your ride in the Prater. He loves to ride. I'm afraid he's quite bored with chaperoning me while I'm here in Vienna. As long as it doesn't interfere with our social obligations, he would enjoy doing more things with you.

You asked me to tell you about myself. I will answer your questions, but I'm really rather ordinary, and you will probably find me uninteresting. Zdenko is much more colorful than me.

My favorite season is early spring when the yellow and purple crocuses begin to push out of the ground. Then I know the snow will melt soon and flow down from the mountain, swelling the brook and the pond with ice cold water, that the pink and white apple blossoms are not far behind. You must tell me what season you like most.

My greatest joys are these: to listen to the birds in our woods at home, to work on the farm with the animals, to walk the fields where my ancestors walked. These endeavors make me feel part of something greater than myself, something eternal that will last after I pass on, as our ancestors passed their legacy on to my parents. It is my greatest wish to return to Friedenheim. That is where I feel most at home.

What in nature do you love best?

As for my favorite song, it is Die Taubenpost by Schubert. I love how he describes how the man sends his message to his beloved on wings like a bird. Zdenko will be our little bird, carrying our messages back and forth. He is entirely trustworthy. I hope you and he will be great friends. The more time you spend with him, the more I will get to know you from his recounting your words and actions.

The fact that I have suitors should not prevent two friends from exchanging letters. Write back and tell me about yourself. I am most eager to get to know you better.

Sincerely,
Arabella

Matteo returned the letter to his pants pocket. Arabella welcomed his friendship. It was but a tiny chink in the strictures of social convention, but it gave him hope.

He didn't yet feel worthy of Arabella. When he'd restored his honor, he would offer for her. He could not have the story of abandoning Luther and Kurt hanging over his head like the blade of a guillotine. If she—or anyone, for that matter—found out what had happened at Königgratz, he would be revealed as a coward.

For one brilliant-as-a-diamond second, the war, the past, seemed far away. He wished he could throw wide his arms and laugh out loud.

Was this what it felt like to be in love?

CHAPTER 12

Matteo found Zdenko sitting on a bench, staring slack-jawed and wide-eyed at the fencers.

"You've obviously never seen fencing?"

Zdenko was mesmerized. "No...it's amazing to watch."

"I've fenced since I was a boy."

"Did your father teach you?" Zdenko asked, not taking his eyes off the action.

He didn't know whether to tell Zdenko of his parents. Perhaps he had already heard the story through gossip. "No. When I came to live with Thea after my parents died, she arranged training for me in boxing and fencing to fend off the other boys who taunted me for being an orphan."

Zdenko turned to him, a question in his eyes. "Your parents died? I didn't know. How old were you?"

"Seven. They were killed in a carriage crash." Telling Zdenko felt like punching a hole through a brick wall and letting sunlight in.

Zdenko let out a gasp. His hand hovered over Matteo's knee as if to comfort him, then he withdrew it, as though thinking better of it. "How awful. Was it here in Vienna?"

"No, we lived in Klagenfurt at the time. My father--dishonorable cur--was a banker and a philanderer."

"Did one of those two things lead to the crash?" Zdenko asked quietly.

"The latter."

In the ring, two fencers circled one another then came together, their sword hilts locked. With a shout, one pushed away the other, and they continued to spar. The fencers repeated the action twice more as practice. It reminded him of the way his mother begged his father to remain faithful, how she fought and pushed him away when she found he had returned to one of his mistresses.

Rage boiled inside him. He wanted to pull the two men apart and tell them...what? To make up? He shook his head.

He was aware Zdenko watched him carefully, listening. Matteo found he wanted, for the first time in his life, to tell his childhood secret, a secret only Aunt Thea knew. He'd kept the truth hidden inside for so many years he'd gotten used to it like one of his scars. "I was in the carriage when it happened."

"Oh, no. And you were just a child," Zdenko said. Now, he did rest his hand on Matteo's knee. Matteo found the gesture comforting instead of uncomfortable, the way he expected he would if another man laid his hand on his leg.

He pushed the words past the tightness in his throat. "My mother had had enough. She packed me and her things into a carriage, and we were traveling to her parents' house. My father rode after us on his horse and forced the carriage to stop. He climbed in and told her more of the same lies, but she, finally, was having none of it. She ordered the carriage driver to start." His blood went cold, congealed, as it always did when he remembered the event. "Enraged that she refused to return to him, my father struck her and attempted to drag her from the carriage. She screamed. The door hit a tree, threw the carriage off balance, and tipped it into a ditch. She had wrapped me in thick blankets against the cold, so I wasn't more than bruised, but they were both killed. He died instantly. She died a few hours later at Thea's."

Zdenko's face was colorless. Tears glittered in his eyes. "You must have been devastated."

"I was, but my mother gave me the values by which I have lived my entire life. As she died, she told me to be honorable and honest in all things."

"Unlike your father," Zdenko said.

"That was implied, but she never tried to turn me against him. He did that himself." Matteo gazed at the younger man's green eyes. "Because of my father, I hate lies."

A strange, strangled sound came from Zdenko. He put his fist to his mouth and coughed.

The two fencers slashed viciously at one another, their duel having surpassed practice into malice. If the skirmish continued much longer, he or one of the other men would call a halt to the match. It was an unspoken rule in the fencing pavilion that no one be killed or injured here.

The men saved that for the battlefield.

"So that is how you came to be raised by your aunt."

"Thea, my mother's sister, was as good and generous to me as any mother could have been, and Edward and I are close as you and Arabella. There are no secrets between us."

Zdenko blinked and glanced away.

"I've made it my mission to restore the honor of the von Ritter name, which my father wasted." He rubbed his palms up and down his thighs. "As a son, I'm sure you understand the principal of retaining the family honor."

Zdenko gulped. "Yes. Of course."

The two fencers in the middle of the ring had worn themselves out and could no longer run at one another or push each other back. One fencer locked his leg around his opponent and pushed him to the floor. The man fell with a cry, and the victor raised his sword above his opponent's chest as if to stab straight down.

Zdenko jumped up, eyes wide. "No!"

Someone shouted. The fencer stepped back and dropped his sword. He yanked off his face guard. His hair and face were sweaty and red. Instead of helping his opponent off the ground with the expected courtesy, the man stalked away.

Matteo was acquainted with such rage. His father had been equally wrathful when it suited him. Matteo had sworn to never become the kind of man who lost his temper. So far, he'd succeeded.

Slowly, Zdenko sat again on the bench. "I thought he would kill him."

"He might have. The chest guard wouldn't have protected him from a thrust of that sort."

"Practice fencing seems as dangerous as dueling," Zdenko said, a tremor in his voice.

"When I learned to fence, I was taught that you always treat your sparring partner with respect. That man didn't. I don't know if they'll let him back in."

He slapped Zdenko's thigh and he winced. Matteo reminded himself to be gentler with his puny friend. "You're a skinny fellow and bigger men might try pushing you around. I invited you here to give you a lesson in fencing so you can protect yourself."

♫

Zdenka rose and inched away. "I don't like pugilistics. I'm a pacifist." She jammed her girlish hands under her armpits. "Perhaps another time."

Matteo said, "All right, no pugilistics today. But I'll give you a lesson in fencing."

"Fencing?" Zdenka squeaked. "I don't anticipate having to answer a challenge. Ever."

"Swordsmanship is not necessarily for dueling but for rounding out your experiences as a young gentleman. It's invigorating. Good exercise. Come, let's get you a vest and mask." Matteo marched off across the hall toward a rack where white vests, gloves, and wire masks hung on hooks.

Zdenka hesitated to follow, but Matteo returned to her, flung an arm over her shoulder, and half-dragged her along.

Matteo examined the vests. "Here," he said, holding one up. "Try this on."

From the front, he reached around her to fit the vest on her.

Her entire body felt as though she'd been dipped in hot water. His chest brushed against her bound breasts. She sucked in her chest and stomach, holding herself motionless until he moved around behind her to buckle the straps. He handed her a pair of leather gloves and a facemask.

"Your slight build makes you a mark," said Matteo. "Fencing will put some muscle on that frail body of yours."

She quickly slipped the mask over her face to hide the rush of pink to her cheeks.

Matteo led the way to a spot where there were no other fencers. "All right. First thing, you must learn the *en garde* stance."

He demonstrated and she imitated, bending her knees and poking them in opposite directions. It felt supremely dangerous to have her knees bent in two different directions with her unguarded crotch as a perfect target. For once, she felt unladylike.

"Are you sure this is right?" She heard the quavering in her voice.

"Quite perfect. Now raise your rapier," he said.

He coached her to the correct positions, but hard as she tried, her body felt like a collection of wayward sticks. Crossing behind her, he encircled her waist with his arms and fitted his body against her back. When his pelvis pressed against her backside, she bit her lip to smother a moan.

"A little bit taller. Like this." He pulled her body slightly more erect when she really wanted to sag back against him.

In the way one man looks over another, he visually apprised her from head to toe. Dissatisfied, he moved behind her again and repositioned her left arm.

The press of his chest against her back felt like fire.

Stepping back, and looking her over, he said, "Good. That's right. Now the fighting arm."

She nearly groaned in painful delight when he took her arm and raised her hand holding the rapier.

"Excellent. That's the position you start in."

Her skin was so hot she didn't think she could stand his touch one more time.

"Use your muscles to stay erect. Let's try it now."

She let her arms flop to her sides, her knees go limp. "I'm not sure I understand. Can you show me again?"

He gave a half smile of resignation. "Watch."

There was nothing she wanted to do more than watch him. He struck the *en garde* pose, his magnificent thighs parted so his crotch was exposed. He raised his rapier high and brought it down slowly. She crossed his rapier, and he drew his sword against hers. A metallic zing filled the air.

"Defend yourself," he said. Then, his sliced the air in swift strokes as he rapidly advanced towards her.

Her heart leapt to her throat. She retreated until she backed into the wall behind and he pinned her to that wall with the full weight of his body. His face was inches from hers, their breathes mingling, their eyes locked together like swords locked at the hilts.

Breathlessly, she said, "I surrender."

CHAPTER 13

Zdenka shifted from foot to foot outside the beerhall, *Das Keller,* where military men came to drink. This was where she'd agreed to meet Matteo so he could give her another letter for Arabella. She wore the new pants Matteo had bought her. Mama had taken the hems up several inches and nipped in the waist. The jacket would take more work, but at least Zdenka had escaped the tailor's shop undetected.

As soldiers came and went from the beerhall, she witnessed the results of their injuries: heads in bandages, arms in slings, missing legs and arms. The sight broke her heart and infuriated her. Such a tragedy for so many.

A man sailed out the door, not of his own accord, and landed face down in a puddle. The mud seemed to have a revivifying effect. He picked himself up and lurched off down the street.

Matteo wasn't the only one drowning himself in drink.

Smoke hung low in the sky. Smelly trash piled against buildings. Heavily laden wagons thudded down the street, splashing through puddles. Dogs rummaged through garbage. A rat darted under a barrel. How could a wounded soldier recover in a city so noisy and dirty?

Friedenheim, or someplace like it, would provide peace and quiet to bring these soldiers back to health. So many men needed care. After serving their country, they deserved better.

Men like Matteo.

When Matteo strode around the corner, his chestnut hair ruffling in the wind, her heart gave a whiz-spin. She hoped she wasn't smiling too much. If being in love was a plague, at least it was a pleasant sickness.

He looked ravishing in charcoal pants, blue wool coat, and a white shirt. "Have you been waiting long?"

"No," she lied, trying not to stare at his chest, which only the day before she'd seen bare and glistening with perspiration. "I just arrived."

He pulled open the heavy oak door, and they entered a cavernous room. The barrel-vaulted ceiling made her feel as though she was standing in half a beer barrel, turned on its side. Dozens of men, many of them soldiers, sat at long plank tables, drinking beer from heavy glass steins. Men played cards, arm wrestled, snored with their heads on the table. It was loud with laughter and the pounding of the steins on the tables. The sour stink of spilled beer hung thick in the air. Matteo chose a small table in the corner. He sat with his back braced against the wall, a foot resting on the bench. Zdenka sat across from him.

"I drink here often. The Bock lager is good."

A round-faced girl with forearms like a woodcutter greeted them. She carried three steins of dark lager in each fist. "Guten tag, Herr Lieutenant von Ritter."

So, he was a frequent customer.

"We'll take two, Mathilda," Matteo said.

Mathilda slammed down two steins of *dunklebier*, a dark beer with a foamy head.

Matteo raised his stein. "*Prost!*"

Zdenka clunked her stein against his. "*Prost!*" She sipped, and a bit of foam dribbled down her chin.

Matteo laughed and pointed. "Your first whiskers."

She managed a laugh and wiped it with the back of her hand the way she'd seen other men do.

"It won't be long now until your whiskers sprout. You just wait."

Not a reassuring thought.

"Where's Arabella? And who's guarding her virtue, if not you."

"She's playing *Schwimmen* with some other young ladies at the home of Fraülein Brüder."

Matteo withdrew a letter from his pocket and placed it in Zdenka's hand. The paper felt filled with promise, affection, and hope.

But not for her.

"Will you give her my letter? Her previous letter gave me hope our friendship might become more."

Zdenka didn't want to break his heart, or he would give up and she might never see him again. She would lose the chance to even look at the man before her. Worse yet, she might be forced to reveal herself to him and he might expose her to all Vienna, which would destroy all of Arabella's prospects of marriage, as well as her own. Neither did she want to lie to him and promise him Arabella loved him. That was too great a lie, even for her.

"I will," she said.

"After you read it, of course."

"Of course."

"You know my intentions are honorable," he said.

Yes, and that was a problem.

"Now that I know you, I wouldn't expect anything less."

He smiled and sipped his beer. His gaze swept the room.

"Are you waiting for someone to join us?" she asked, disappointed she wouldn't have him to herself.

"Oh no, just looking to see if my friend is here." He slapped the table with his palm.

He rubbed at the scar on his temple, and she wished she could kiss that scar, press her cheek to it. "Who's the friend for whom you're looking? Maybe I can help you find him."

His eye twitched. "A canonneer from my regiment."

"What exactly does a cannoneer do?"

"Loads the gunpowder and lights the fuses. Sort of a fire man."

"What's this man's name?"

"Luther Klesper. He was injured at Königgratz. I've searched everywhere for him." He frowned. "I've checked the military wing of the *Allegemeines Krankenhaus*. I've also asked after him at the Office of the Military, but they have no record of his address."

"You are putting great effort into finding him. May I ask why?" Her bindings suddenly seemed so tight she was having trouble breathing.

He hitched his shoulder. "He was wounded, and I'd like to help him if he needs it."

And who was helping Matteo? With the twitching of his eye; with his bursts of temper such as she'd seen the day before at the tailor's shop. If he would tell her what was wrong, she might be able to help him. He had already finished his beer. "You're drinking quite fast," she said. "Perhaps you should slow down."

He raised his eyebrows. "I am?"

"As usual. Are you drinking to forget something?" She watched his face for the minutest change and chose her words carefully. "Yesterday, at the tailor's, you knocked over a rack of cravats and stormed out of the shop. What upset you?"

Matteo glanced away, as if to deter her questions. "Upset?"

he snorted. "I wasn't upset." He clutched his stein so his knuckles turned white.

"Breathe deeply. It will settle your mind," she suggested.

He flexed his hands open and closed. "The apprentice reminded me of a dead boy, that's all. Just a bad memory."

His voice was a growl, which made her understand he was finished talking about the incident. She would ask him later.

"I've been...thinking about something." Matteo looked up and smiled. "Something besides Arabella."

It was meant to make her feel good, but it felt like a stab of ice in her heart. She forced a smile. "What are you thinking?"

He drew a deep breath and let it out slowly. "I joined the cavalry to make my name and fortune. For a man with neither, it's one way to distinguish myself, but if I stay in the cavalry, I must return to the deplorable act of killing other men. Men as innocent of crime as me. I'm thinking of leaving the cavalry altogether."

It was wonderful news. She would never again have to worry about his safety, that he might get hit by bullets or cannon fire or sliced in two by a saber. "The war is over now, and you served your country. What else are you good at?"

He closed his eyes and leaned his head back on the wall behind him. "I'm only good at killing, really."

His voice was so desolate, it struck a blow to her heart. It was such a hopeless assessment. She had to make him see a life of possibility, instead of death and war. "The night of your aunt's party, I saw you helping a man who'd fallen on the stairs." She leaned forward on the table and stared hard at him. "That's your destiny. Not killing men; helping them get better."

His eyes widened, and she could tell her words reached into his soul.

"I read in the newspaper about a veterans association in Reichenberg," she said. "They raise funds for impoverished veterans. To pay for medical care and, if necessary, a decent burial. I haven't heard of anything like that in Vienna. Perhaps you could set one up. That way, you could help even more men. Why settle for what is expected: being a soldier. Do what you love most. Help these brave men."

He gazed around at the soldiers. "Could I really help them?"

Zdenka said, "Of course you can. Look at how much energy you've put into finding your friend. Think of that multiplied and directed toward creating an association to help these men."

"If I set up a veteran's association here in Vienna, Luther might come for help." He mumbled, "This endeavor would repay them all."

"What do you mean, repay them?"

His eyes clouded as they had the day before at the tailor's. As if he saw the drummer boy, soldiers, friends, comrades in arms, all dead.

A star burst in her mind; the realization hit her. They were dead, wounded, maimed. And he was alive and felt guilty for some reason. He didn't even recognize his own injuries. The scar on his temple and his back. The way his eye twitched and the headaches. His temper. She wanted to gather him in her arms and comfort him, tell him it would be all right. To say, "there, there."

But it would never again be all right, and she was only now beginning to understand this. To understand him. She was quiet for a long time, watching him stare into his empty beer mug. Then, she said, "You couldn't save them all, but if you start an organization to help those yet living ..."

His eyes locked on hers, and she felt as if she might melt like a puddle of butter. "Yes," he said, softly, nodding. "I believe you're right, but it would require money, which is something I lack."

"Sell your commission to raise the funds to start with. Helping comrades is an honorable reason to leave the cavalry."

His face opened so that dark circles under his eyes disappeared and tight lines at the corners of his eyes turned to crinkles as he smiled. "I can't do this alone. To undertake a mission this great, a man needs a woman's help. I can't foresee everything these men need. If she chooses me, do you think Arabella would help me?"

Zdenka laid her hand on her chest where it felt as though he'd run her through with a sword. She wanted to be the one to help. The soldiers touched her. Their injuries made her angry.

But that was not his question, nor his invitation.

"I ... don't know if she would. Possibly."

"She has a big heart. A compassionate heart. I think I could convince her, if she accepts me." He pounded the table with his palm. "As a matter of fact, let's go right now and tell my Commandant that I am resigning my commission." He stood abruptly. He threw his arms around her and drew her into a hug.

Now she knew why women sometimes swooned. His hug was like being transported to heaven.

He slapped her on the back, and she stumbled forward a few steps.

"Thank you for the suggestion. I don't know why I didn't think of it myself. Come along." He motioned towards the door, and she led the way. He followed.

Somewhere behind them, glass shattered. She was hurled backwards. Her head banged against the wall. Stars spun before her eyes. The breath was knocked out of her.

Matteo crushed her to his chest, smashing her face into the crook of his shoulder. His breath was hot and ragged against her ear. He curved his shoulders to protect her. Through his coat, she felt the rise and fall of panicked breathing. The room went silent as people looked around to see what the commotion was about.

Right then, she knew his wound was so deep, it tore at him over and over in ways he could not predict or control.

And she had to help him. Somehow. Some way.

"Are you all right?" she whispered hoarsely into his chest. He smelled of rosemary and juniper. His soft chestnut hair brushed against her forehead.

Someone laughed. It wouldn't do, having all these rough military men see two men in an embrace. "Shhh, shhh," she whispered. "Take a deep breath."

He breathed deeply. The iron bands of his arms eased from around her. He stepped back, his face pale and drawn. Men stared. Then, as though they understood, they turned away and returned to their activities.

Matteo jerked back, red-faced, and glanced around. His withdrawal made her feel as though she'd been robbed of her heart. "You're all right. I'm here now," she whispered. "Don't worry. I'll get you home."

"*Heiligen Gott*, I'm a damned fool," he muttered with disgust.

"Lean on me so they think you've had too much to drink." She arranged his arm across her shoulder and wrapped hers around his waist. She gripped the hand of his draped arm around her shoulder and pretended to half-carry him. It was a glorious feeling, to have his arms around her, even in this sort of circumstance. Together, they feigned something of a drunken stagger and went out the door. When they'd reached a corner, they stepped into an alleyway.

"You must think me mad," he said.

"I think you believe you are mad, but I don't."

Without a word, Matteo turned and disappeared down the alley.

Walking home, Zdenka thought of all the injured soldiers:

men missing legs and arms, faces pockmarked by shrapnel, heads swathed in turbans of bandages, men who limped. Men who'd been at Königgratz. Matteo hid his wound inside, where he *thought* no one could see.

But she saw. She knew, and her heart ached for him.

They were alike, she and him. Neither could really tell anyone else who they were or what was truly in their hearts.

♫

That night, Zdenka lay in her bed thought about the fencing hall and the dark hair trailing down Matteo's sculpted chest, the distinct spot where it vanished into the waistband of his trousers. The way he pressed her into surrender against the wall. Warmth started in her breastbone and spread, with increasing heat, down her arms and to her fingertips. By the time the heat dropped into her lower abdomen, it was a raging bonfire of desire she was forced to satisfy.

Zdenka couldn't lie to herself anymore. She was in love with him. Every idea she'd had about not falling in love, about independence, paled against the urge to see his naked torso again. Her heart felt as though it had tumbled down a mountain in an avalanche. She couldn't concentrate and food had either no taste or too much flavor.

Zdenka held her sleeve up to her nose, inhaling Matteo's spicy scent redolent of rosemary and juniper. With his letter pressed to her chest, her skin tingling where he had touched her, she ran her knuckles over the spot on her cheek where his jacket had pressed into her, feeling again the press of the wool. He had crushed her in his arms, as she had so often dreamed he might. It had been heavenly, even with the bang to the back of her skull and having the wind knocked out of her. The scene must have been awful and humiliating for him. She vowed to protect him when they were together so he wouldn't have to experience such humiliation again.

She slid her finger under the flap of his envelope and opened it. Seeing his handwriting across the page made the hair on the forearms stand.

Dearest Arabella,

Zdenko dutifully delivered your last letter to me. He is a faithful friend, and I enjoy him a great deal.

I long to see you again. Your grace, serene character, and intelligence have captured my heart. If you and I could exchange a few words in private, one chaste kiss, I would be the happiest man alive. When I returned to Vienna after the war, I found little joy in daily living and even less hope for a happy future. But I have fallen deeply in love with you through your letter. You letter has revived my heart. Hope for a future filled with love and happiness has taken hold of me once more. Do I dare to dream of such a life with you, sweet girl of my letters?

Zdenka gasped and held her breath. He was in love with the girl who'd written him the letter. Her heart felt as if fireworks were exploding in her chest. Now if Arabella would hurry up and make a decision as to which of the Grafen she would marry, Zdenka could tell Matteo she was a woman.

That she loved him.

Oh, dear!

She turned back to the letter.

You wrote of your dream to return to your beloved Friedenheim. I've always lived with my aunt. As much as she has treated me as her son,

I've never really had a home of my own, so I understand your desire to return to the place you feel most yourself. A woman should also have the freedom to follow her heart. I would spend my life filling your days with joy should you grant me more than friendship.

I know I press my case hard, but there is so little time before you must choose a husband. I know your parents would rather you marry one of the rich Grafen, but the girl who has written to me is not a typical woman. She deserves her dreams, and I would be honored to be the man to help make those dreams come true.

Fondly,
Matteo

After today in the beerhall, Zdenka realized what misery Matteo must be suffering. She had to help him—keep him out of crowds, make thing quieter, watch his face for signed of discomfort and irritation. To stop him drinking so much and see if she could get him to talk about his experiences in the war. It wasn't certain to help him, but something deep and soul-destroying tore at him. Perhaps he would confide in her if she was a woman. But loyalty to her family and, most of all, to Arabella, required she deceive him.

She shuddered.

He hated lies and liars. If he discovered Zdenko was Zdenka, Matteo might hate her. But if she told him, he might come to understand that he had loved the girl in the letters all along.

CHAPTER 14

Zdenka's heart galloped, burned, thrashed, and flung itself against every distraction during the three days since she had seen Matteo. Her preoccupation with him made her doubt everything she had ever considered about love.

Tonight was the Coachman's Ball, and she had to find some way to tell him of her feelings before the ball, or her entire scheme of writing to him as Arabella, would fall apart.

Arabella and Zdenka strolled the *Freyung* market in the heart of Vienna. Every Tuesday, vendors laden with goods streamed into Vienna from the surrounding countryside. The smell of yeasty, fresh-baked pretzels tempted. Aromas of cinnamon and cloves rose from pots of warm, spiced *gluwein*. There were stalls with carved figures, a shoe repairman, scarves and caps, children's toys, candy, hair combs, used books, ribbons in dozens of colors, buttons and thread, writing paper and ink. The market was a profusion of small luxuries to daily necessities.

Occasionally, the two sisters stopped to look at and touch things they could only afford to admire, not buy.

Zdenka was anxious that Matteo might accidentally run into Arabella; but today, the crowd was so big, she doubted that even if he searched, he could find them. If Arabella caught wind of the scheme, Zdenka would be the one setting their futures afire.

They stopped to browse at a table of lace. Nearby, a hulking man with black eyes set deep in their sockets appeared. He had a blocky head, and his bronzed, weather-beaten face was hand-some in a craggy sort of way. He caught Zdenka's attention, not only because he was a head taller than everyone else, but because the cut of his coat, his long mane of hair sweeping his collar, and his tooled leather boots made it obvious he wasn't Viennese. He stared at Arabella, but Zdenka ignored him. Men always stared at Arabella.

Arabella stopped so fast Zdenka nearly bumped into her. "Mama wanted a bit of embroidery thread and new thimble because she lost hers. There was a sewing woman here last week, but I can't remember which stall."

Zdenka glanced over her shoulder at the man and pointed to a row of stalls. Would he follow them? "We can try over there." They wandered about looking for the sewing supplies stall, but when they came to the bookseller's stall, Arabella touched Zdenka's arm. "Wait, I want to look a minute."

"Didn't you once tell me I'd ruin my eyesight by reading too much?" Zdenka asked.

"That's only if you read the newspapers. It doesn't happen if you read romances," Arabella responded. She picked up a leather-bound book and waved it at Zdenka. "Look, *Maria Stuart in Scotland*, a play by Maria von Ebner-Eschenbach."

"A romance? We'll be here all day," Zdenka groaned.

The bookseller, a fat man with sausage-like fingers said, "That's all right, miss. You read as much as you want." When Arabella flashed him her radiant smile, he looked faint.

A fiddler playing an Offenbach tune from *Il Signor Fagotto,* an opera where the heroine wore pants, caught Zdenka's ear. She drifted out of the bookseller's booth and found the fiddler between the candle seller and the apple vendor. She tapped her foot to the song, wishing she had a coin to toss in his hat. When the fiddler was done, the crowd applauded. Zdenka glanced around.

Where was Arabella?

Her muscles tensed. She spun this way and that, looking for Arabella. Her panic redoubled. How irresponsible to have left her alone. Arabella could easily be compromised if someone approached her. One of the Grafen might claim she'd made an agreement with him and force her choice. Worse, one of them might say they'd seen her flirting and withdraw his offer.

Zdenka raced back to the booksellers, but Arabella wasn't there. Her throat tight with panic, Zdenka elbowed her way through the surging crowd, ignoring the irritated glares. Her boots pounded the pavement as she dodged between stalls. Not at the lace makers, the perfumers, the bootblacks, or the hat makers. She leapt on top of a barrel and scrutinized the crowd.

Panic gave way to relief when she caught sight of Arabella's fox fur hat, her russet curls flowing from beneath. Zdenka jumped from the barrel and wriggled and bumped her way through the shoppers to Arabella.

In front of the sewing lady's stall, Arabella and the hulking man stood only an arm's length apart, their eyes locked on one another. Neither of them moved or spoke. The man gazed at her with something between drunken intoxication and wonderment. Arabella's hypnotized, gleaming eyes spoke a world of passion and hope. Her smile was the most content Zdenka had seen since they'd come to Vienna.

Dread swept through her. Her stomach clenched. Should she call out a warning? Step between them?

"Arabella?" Zdenka said.

The stranger's gaze didn't move from Arabella's face. "Arabella? What a beautiful name." He took Arabella's dainty fingertips in his saucer-sized hand and kissed the back of her hand far too long. "My name is Mandryka—"

Before he could finish, Zdenka grabbed Arabella's elbow and dragged her away. "What were you doing?" Zdenka bustled through the crowd, towing Arabella down the aisle. "I'm sorry I wandered off, but I didn't think you'd do anything so foolish as to stop and stare at some stranger. Did anyone see you with him?"

Arabella stopped short and wrestled her elbow from Zdenka's grip. "I think he might be the one," Arabella said, her voice rising in pitch.

"You're reading too many of those Jane Austen romances." Zdenka knew she sounded snappish, but someone had to put sense into Arabella's head. "He could be a murderous kidnapper or a Prussian spy, for all you know."

Zdenka stepped off the curb, but Arabella was frozen in place. "I know my instincts. My heart actually fluttered when he looked at me." She put her palm on her chest. "I felt lightheaded."

"You're probably hungry." Zdenka took her hand and pulled her across another aisle.

"I couldn't look away from him." She tugged her hand out of Zdenka's. "His eyes were so kind and gentle. When other men look at me, it's as though they want to eat me for dinner."

"Maybe he has bad eyesight."

How had the two of them been born of the same parents? Arabella could have any man in Vienna, but she wished for some fantasy man, while Zdenka loved the only man she couldn't have. It seemed utterly cruel.

"I think he's the man the fortuneteller spoke of." She closed her eyes and murmured, "Mandryka."

"Pfffft! Do you really believe in that old crone with her deck of cards? He looks like he's from the hinterlands."

If Arabella didn't give up this fantasy, she might bring about disaster. Then her engagement, the farm, the finances, the family, helping Matteo, would all go up in flames.

Arabella's voice was feathery and soft. "When his coat blew open, I thought his was the kind of chest I could lay my head on night after night. His were the kind of arms I want to be held by. Those were the eyes I've dreamed of looking into."

Arabella started walking again and she gave a little hop-skip-jump, like she did when she was particularly joyous. It was an action she'd scrubbed from her movements since coming to Vienna because it was undignified.

Right then, Zdenka knew Arabella was in love, and her decision to wed had taken an unexpected turn.

♫

Matteo dropped the cravat he was looking at for when he spotted the massive man kissing Arabella's hand. She looked rapturous, but the man had a dazed look on his face, like he had just awakened from a fevered dream. Or risen from the dead.

When he looked at Arabella, did he look so stupefied? Was she such a flirt as to let any man in the *Freyung* market kiss her hand? And where did the fellow get that coat? It made him look like a bear.

Matteo would have to press his case harder. Tonight, at the Coachman's Ball, Arabella would make her decision about whom to wed. Her letter had been passionate, forthcoming, but they had never had any time alone. Perhaps now he might walk them to their hotel. Anything so he might be in the warmth of her gracious presence.

And he would ask Zdenko about this interloper, and if he was a serious contender for Arabella's hand.

Disregarding the new cravat, Matteo dashed between two stalls and around the corner so he might 'run into' Arabella and Zdenko. He had to find a way to slip the letter from his pocket into Zdenko's. It was his final chance to let Arabella know he was serious about asking for her hand before she made her decision whom to marry.

Arabella turned the corner and nearly bumped into Matteo. Her skin was pink as a dawn sky, and she carried a small paper bag.

He smiled down at her, expecting the sort of look she'd bestowed on the massive man, but her face smoothed into a placid, meaningless smile that made him feel invisible.

"Gräfin Arabella." Matteo bowed. "Zdenko."

Zdenko jerked back as if he'd run into a madman.

"Herr von Ritter." Arabella acknowledged him by tilting her chin, but her eyes searched the space beyond him.

Was she looking for the man he'd seen her with?

Zdenko's face went pale. "M...m...Matteo," he stammered. "What are you doing here?"

"Everyone's here. It's a lovely day. I was searching for a new cravat for this evening."

"Did you find one? If not, I can take Arabella home and come back and help you," Zdenko said.

Why did his voice have a strange tremble?

Matteo said, "I'd rather walk with the two of you. Would you like to stroll along the Danube?"

"It's too cold for a walk on the Danube," Zdenko said. "And... and it smells of fish."

Matteo offered his elbow to Arabella, but Zdenko snatched Arabella's other arm and jammed it beneath his own. Arabella looked from Matteo to Zdenko and settled on her brother's arm.

Matteo shot Zdenko a glare over Arabella's head. "Then perhaps a hot chocolate at Dehmel's?"

Arabella glanced up at Zdenko, as if asking permission. She was as chilly as snow on the Alps. Had his last letter gone too far? Had he offended her? If so, he must have a chance to apologize, to tell her in person how he felt about her. He wasn't a romantic, but he did know how to storm the battlements.

Zdenko said, "We really must get those sewing supplies home to Mama. I'm sure she's eagerly waiting to do her mending."

Eager to do her mending? What was that about?

Zdenko pulled Arabella along so fast that she tripped on a curb. Matteo caught her arm as she was about to fall. He said, "Be careful. You don't want to twist your ankle before the biggest and final dance of the Season."

"Thank you," she murmured, and extricated her hand from his grasp.

He was at a loss as to what else to say and still remain proper. How did Edward manage flirtation and seduction with such frequent success? After the passionate letters they had exchanged, why was she so distant?

Taking a chance and feeling foolish, uttering the sort of romantic words Edward might spout, Matteo said, "I recall spring is your favorite season. It is said that spring is the season of love."

Arabella's sideways glance indicated she thought he'd grown another head. God, he sounded like a lovesick idiot, but if she didn't want him to pursue her, why had she written back? It was so much easier to write to her. Being near her made him tongue-tied.

Her diffidence was confounding. Women were infinitely complex. Hot one moment, cold the next. He looked at Zdenko for support, but his friend's face was a mask of fear.

Matteo bent down, and so no one else but Zdenko could hear, said, "Arabella and I have had no time alone, away from the crowds. Is there someplace we might speak privately for a moment?"

Zdenko stopped and gave a hacking, loud cough. He covered his mouth with his fist, doubled over and coughed so he sounded like he had consumption. People turned to stare. He turned red in the face. His eyes watered, so Matteo pounded him on the back and slipped his letter into his young friend's pocket. Finally, Zdenko ceased his coughing and stood.

"Are you all right?" she asked Zdenko.

Matteo didn't know what to make of the woman to whom he'd written love letters. She had seemed so guileless, but now, it was as if she were someone else entirely. He had to remind her that he was willing to do whatever it took to win her heart.

"Tonight, at the Coachman's Ball, I can't wait to hold you—"

"Oh! The Coachman's ball!" exclaimed Zdenko, practically shouting. "It promises to be a grand occasion. Now that you've given me some waltz lessons, it should be fun."

Matteo answered through clenched teeth, "Not the way you dance." Then he said to Arabella, "Who is escorting you tonight?"

"I'm attending the ball with Count Elemer and my parents. Mama has been looking forward to it all Season. It is to be her only ball." Arabella tucked a strand of her russet hair behind the curved pearl of her earlobe and Matteo caught sight of the underside of her wrist.

His breath tightened. Why didn't she acknowledge her affection for him? They were only in front of Zdenko. Just a word, a sweet smile, a lingering glance, the brush of her hand against his arm. Anything to acknowledge the mutual depth of their feelings as shared in their letters. He glanced at Zdenko, who seemed poised to run.

"Mama's waiting. I'll see you tonight. Come a little early if you can," Zdenko called over his shoulder as he rushed his sister down the street.

Matteo watched Arabella's narrow back retreat, her slender waist, the sway of her hips as she disappeared into the crowd.

CHAPTER 15

L ightning crackled through Zdenka's body as she read the letter Matteo had given her at the market. She had waited all day. Her fingers shook as she tore open the envelope.

Dear Arabella,

(In her mind, she replaced it with Zdenka)

My hunger for one tender glance from your eyes drives me mad. Your letter has made me fall deeply in love with you, I can't think of ever loving anyone else. I know your commitment to your family makes the chance of our love seem impossible. I assure you that I will do anything to a win your affections for eternity. If I could take you in my arms and whisper the words of my devotion in your ear, you would know the depth of my love and respect for you. One hour is all I ask to persuade you.

Your devoted servant,
Matteo

Here Zdenka replaced his words with one night.

Her breath caught to think of what one night might be like with him. Spurred by her "tender glance," his hands would roam freely over her body, his fingers burning on her virgin skin. He would nuzzle kisses on her eyelids. She would taste his lips. Her hands would glide over his sculpted chest, and his touch would set free the want she had been holding back like a dam about to burst. Just thinking about their assignation made her body prickle as though her veins were filled with sparks.

The raw, naked, gnawing desire didn't embarrass her because, with him, satisfying her desire seemed perfectly natural. He liked independent women who made their own decisions and choices. Those sorts of women were allowed to be lusty and forward, weren't they?

The Coachman's Ball was tonight, and Arabella would choose a husband. Matteo would be devastated it wasn't him. He'd stop writing to her. He might look for another young lady who struck his fancy. He might depart Vienna. There was no telling what, with his erratic moods, he would do.

Zdenka's stomach twisted at the thought of losing him. Tonight was her last chance to tell him she was in love with him. One night for him to cast her off for lying to him.

That fear made her sit bolt upright.

She didn't know how, but she had to convince him of her love, that she understood him better than anyone. That he needed her. That she could help him.

She couldn't very well march up to him tonight, plant a kiss on his lips, rip her bodice open, and hurl herself upon him. No. That would not do. She sat on the edge of the bed and racked her brain for a solution.

If she confessed she was a girl, he would be shocked and

angry. He thought of her as his pal, his friend, a young man, he and Arabella's messenger, nothing more.

She rose and paced the floor of her room. Three steps this way. Turn. Three paces back.

It wasn't merely enough to *tell* him she loved him. She had to *show* him. To prove it.

But how?

A gust of wind whistled through a crack in the window frame, blowing out her oil lamp. Darkness swept into the room. She sighed. They'd run out of lamp oil again.

The thought arrived like a shooting star. She froze, her hand in mid-air, letting her thoughts muster into one daring idea.

The ball tonight.

A message. From 'Arabella'.

A key.

The dark.

Her bedroom.

Just one night.

It was his idea, after all. He couldn't blame her. She was only giving him what he wanted.

She would grant his wish. Tonight, she would invite him to meet Arabella in her room.

But instead of Arabella, she would be the one waiting for him.

CHAPTER 16

Zdenka wound her way around the perimeter of the Hotel Prinz's ballroom, searching for Matteo. Even the sound of Maestro Johann Strauss the Younger's orchestra playing *Wienerbonbons* couldn't distract her from her worries. For the hundredth time since securing the key, Zdenka patted her pocket. If her plan came off, in a few hours, she would give Matteo her key and the note granting his wish of one night.

With her.

She could reveal her true self and how much she loved him, and he would return her love.

The Coachman's Ball was the most extravagant and anticipated social event of *Fasching*. Nobles and commoners all danced together to support the coachman's pension fund, and every Viennese who could afford a ticket crowded the ballroom. Thanks to Graf Elemer's generosity, Mama and Papa were able to attend the final ball of the season, where Arabella would make up her mind and put all their worries to rest.

Zdenka completed her circle of the ballroom and returned to Mama and Papa. As guests of Graf Elemer, they had the privilege of a sitting at one of the marble-topped café tables. She leaned against one of the pillars encircling the ballroom and let Strauss' polka wash over her.

"Zdenko, are you feeling all right? You seem out of sorts." Papa asked, remembering to use her male name. She hoped her face didn't betray the anxiety bashing against her breastbone.

"I'm nervous about Arabella's decision," she said. "So much depends on her."

Papa's lips stretched into a grimace, and he rested his chin on his hand.

"Look how the new gaslight crystal chandeliers glitter," Mama said, trying to cheer them. "It was never so beautiful when we were young."

"*Ja,* and the silver bowls of champagne are the size of bathtubs." Papa rose. "I think I'll have another glass."

Mama put a firm hand on his shoulder and pushed him back into his chair. "No, my dear," she said with false sweetness. "You have already had one drink. You must not get drunk tonight, of all nights."

When did husbands go bad? Were they like fruit that spoiled or bread that went stale? Could you know in advance which ones were good until the end or would turn belly up somewhere along the way? And even after all the years of financial hardship, Papa's gambling and drinking, still, they loved one another. She hoped that Matteo would be as forgiving of her as Mama was of Papa.

Papa scrubbed his face with his hand and turned to Zdenka. "Has Arabella shown preference for one over the other?"

Zdenka remembered Arabella's reaction to the stranger in the market. What if he was the man the gypsy predicted would be Arabella's husband? What if Arabella's instincts were right, and he was the man for her? Zdenka had dragged her away from her happiness, stealing her sister's future so she could have the farm. "I don't think she cares for any one of the Grafen in particular."

Mama's hand fluttered about her lace collar. "There's Lamoral and Elemer, waiting their turn to dance with Arabella. Just a few more hours until Arabella makes her decision. Then, I will rest easy." She glanced at Zdenka. "Until next season."

Through the fabric of her coat, Zdenka patted the key again. If everything went according to plan, no one would have to look for a husband for her next season. Or ever.

"I hope she chooses Elemer," Papa said as Graf Dominik, with Arabella in his arms, danced by like a man with his feet on backwards. "He's reputed to be the wealthiest. Arabella will want for nothing."

And neither would they.

"Have you heard from your old Army friend?" Mama asked, sipping her cordial.

"No," Papa said, looking longingly at Mama's yet unfinished cordial. "If he granted me a loan, then Arabella could have a little more time to make up her mind."

"It's too late," Mama said, her brow wrinkling. "Fitznagel accosted me in the lobby as we were leaving and insisted if we didn't pay our hotel bill tonight, he would throw our baggage out on the street."

Papa's face sagged. He rested his forehead in his hand.

Zdenka found it difficult to have any sympathy for him. Their situation was, after all, his fault.

The orchestra struck up *The Blue Danube* and dancers whirled by in a kaleidoscope of colors. She imagined herself waltzing with Matteo, caught up in his muscular arms, the music lifting every care.

From the top of the stairs, the liveried, white-wigged footman chimed out, "Matteo von Ritter."

Tension in Zdenka's shoulders eased. Her cheeks tingled,

and her heart did the same little whiz-spin it did each time she saw him.

Matteo strode down the stairs, back erect, eyes sweeping side to side as he took in the room. Since he'd turned in his commission, he no longer wore his uniform. In his black swallow-tailed coat and light grey slacks, he looked as dashing as ever. His white shirt strained across his broad chest, and she envisioned running her hands over his bare chest, his broad shoulders. What would it be like to kiss the scar at his temple, to feel his weight on her?

Her body flushed at the thoughts, and she breathed deeply, pushing against her bindings to remind herself she was still, for a few more hours, a man.

Matteo paused on the staircase. She recognized his discomfort at entering such a crowded, noisy room.

He needed her.

"I'll be back in a bit," she said to Mama and Papa then pushed through the throng of people.

When Matteo spotted her at the bottom of the staircase, his brow smoothed, and he smiled.

Warmth spread throughout her, right down to her toes.

He turned to take in the ballroom. His eyes narrowed, like a man taking aim with a gun. She followed his gaze. He was watching Arabella waltz off with Elemer. Despite the energy and merriment of the waltz, the frolicsome music and the celebratory mood, Arabella's face was still frozen in her placid, imperturbable smile.

"When can I dance with Arabella?" Matteo asked.

His black tie was slightly askew. Zdenka, without thinking, reached up and straightened it. She felt a sort of zing in her fingertips as they brushed against his chin. He must have felt it, too, because he stared down at her, confusion in his eyes.

She stared over his shoulder, so she didn't have to see the hurt in his eyes. "Her dance card is full."

"But I thought she would save at least one dance for me." His voice had a low, scraping quality.

Taking an overly enthusiastic tone, Zdenka said, "There are hundreds of young ladies here tonight who would love to dance with you."

Her among them, but that would have to wait.

"I'm not interested in any of them. I'm interested only in Arabella." He shot his cuffs and smoothed his shirtfront. "I think it's time I met your parents. Would you introduce me?"

She gulped.

And at that moment, Mandryka, the stranger from the market, galloped down the stairs, his wild hair flaring behind him, log-like arms pumping.

Her heart stopped. All thought flew from her mind. Her feet wouldn't move. Her necktie felt as though it was strangling her, and she couldn't speak.

This was the man Arabella had fallen in love with at first sight. She was a featherhead, but the one idea she had held onto for her entire life was that the right man would come along and she would recognize him. After all the suitors she had turned away in Vienna, after offers from three of the richest men in all of Austria, after weeks of being wooed at parties and events, Arabella had found the right man at the last minute, in a bookstall in the *Freyung* market.

It was too fantastical to be true, but here he was.

She had to give Arabella the chance to speak to Mandryka, to see if he really was the right man for her.

Across the room, Arabella waltzed with Lamoral. Dominik and Elemer awaited their turns to waltz with her. Zdenka had to get Arabella alone with Mandryka, give Matteo the key and note, and meet him in Arabella's bedroom.

How was she to do all that?

Mandryka plowed through the crowd towards their parents. She felt faint.

Matteo put his hand on her arm. "Is anything the matter? You look as though you've seen a ghost."

She blinked, trying to think of something, anything. "Mama and Papa asked me to bring some champagne," she fired off. "Let's stop by the champagne table first."

Matteo frowned but nodded and started toward the champagne table. The crowd surged around them. Zdenka slipped away, navigating back to her parents. If Matteo asked, she would tell him she hadn't been able to get to the champagne.

Back at the table where her parents sat, Mandryka bowed to her parents.

Perspiration broke out on the back of her neck. Zdenka stepped into the dim alcove to eavesdrop.

Mandryka pumped Papa's hand, which disappeared into the man's grip. "Mandryka was my uncle. I, too, am named Mandryka."

Papa's looked more confused than when he was drunk. "You've...come. But I expected only to receive a letter from your uncle. How is he?"

"He is dead now these ten years," Mandryka answered.

Papa blanched and sat hard in his chair. "Oh, how dreadful."

"May I?" Mandryka asked and pulled up a free chair and took a place at the table. "When I got the letter and portrait you intended for him, I came straightaway to ask for her hand." He glanced from Mama to Papa. "Am I too late?"

The man from the market was Papa's friend's nephew? *This* was the man Arabella thought was the right man?

"Can you tell us something about yourself?" Mama asked.

"When my uncle died, he left me everything. His fields, tenants, forests, livestock, houses, and barns. I live in the valley of the high-shouldered mountains of the Slavonichka range. My country is beautiful, and I want to show it to Arabella."

At every word, Mama and Papa leaned closer and smiled, their faces filled with hope.

"My dear wife died in childbirth three years ago. My child died also."

He pulled a small round portrait of Arabella from his pocket —no doubt the one Papa had sent to his Army friend. Mandryka gazed at Arabella's portrait so lovingly, Zdenka was touched to the core.

"I have not found a woman her equal, until now. I can tell by looking at her portrait that Arabella is the angel I have dreamed of finding." He took a deep breath and his barrel chest ballooned. "If she will have me, she will be the Empress of all I possess. I will give her everything she wishes and make her the happiest woman alive."

Mandryka was warm and unpretentious, not like Viennese Society. He cared nothing for appearance. He had changed his suit and shaved, but aside from that, he was the same man Zdenka had seen in the market. No wonder Arabella fell in love with him. His eyes spoke of pain and longing. Longing for Arabella.

Zdenka knew all about longing.

At that moment, Lamoral swanned by with Arabella in his arms. Zdenka dashed from her place in the alcove and caught Arabella's arm. Lamoral stopped with a jerk and a scowl.

Zdenka pulled Arabella aside. "He's here."

"Who?" Arabella asked, panting from exertion.

"Couldn't you wait until we were finished dancing?" Lamoral asked.

Zdenka whispered in Arabella's ear. "The man from the market."

"Here?" Arabella's brows winged up.

Zdenka pointed to where Mandryka sat with her parents.

"What is the matter?" Lamoral said, sounding like a five-year-old who had been denied ice cream.

Zdenka led Arabella from the dance floor, and she gave a little skip. Lamoral followed, but when he saw Mandryka, his face grew thunderous. Arabella didn't give him a second look as he stomped off.

Arabella only had eyes for Mandryka. She seemed to thaw as all the anxiety which had tightened her smile and nested in the tiny wrinkles between her brows, disappeared, replaced by a smile that outshone all the chandeliers.

Mandryka stood and held out his work-roughened hands. Arabella smiled at them for a moment, then laid her hands in his.

Mama and Papa stared, openmouthed. For once, they said nothing.

Mandryka *was* Arabella's right man.

Zdenka's chest filled with a cloud of warmth. Now she had to get rid of the Grafen. As forthright and independent as Zdenka was, it was daunting to ward off three men who had spent the Season paying suit to Arabella. Her parents might prefer one of them, but Zdenka owed it to Arabella to give her every chance at love with Mandryka. He was kind and truly in love with Arabella, and she with him. If it meant sacrificing her dream of the farm, then so be it. Arabella's happiness counted for more than hers.

Zdenka stiffened her back and beat through the crowd where Graf Lamoral, Elemer, and Dominik stood, each one fuming in his own way. Her heart climbed into her throat, and she jammed her shaking hands into her pockets. As kindly as possible, she explained Arabella would spend the remainder of the evening with Mandryka. With scowls, glares, and growls, the three melted into the crowd.

When they had departed, Zdenka slumped against a pillar. It hadn't been as bad as she'd expected. Matteo was within a few feet of their table, holding two glasses of champagne. His face was tight, and his dark eyes bored into Mandryka. Zdenka sprang to attention.

A lump of panic rolled up her throat. Sweat gathered in her collar as she dashed through the crowd. She crossed Matteo's path within a few feet of her family. Their eyes locked on one another. Mandryka and Arabella sat at the table, and her parents hovered a short distance away, observing. Mama's perpetual scowl was gone, and Papa grinned as though he'd pulled off a victory of some sort.

"Who is that?" Matteo glared, as he gestured at Mandryka with one of the champagne glasses. "I saw him this morning at the market, speaking with Arabella."

Hurt rolled off him like steam. The letter and key would salve some of his insult. Zdenka swallowed hard. "He is the nephew of a friend of my father's. He's come to visit Vienna."

"He seems quite taken with Arabella. And she with him." Matteo stiffened. "He's holding her hand." He glared down at Zdenka. "Did you give her my last letter?"

This was it. The moment upon which her life hung.

"Yes. I did give it to her. And she gave me one for you." She took the glasses from him. "Let me give these to my parents. We can go outside to the balcony where it's quieter, and I will give it to you."

At that moment, Mandryka rose from the table and escorted Arabella to the dance floor. He gathered her in his arms. Rather than holding her discreetly at a distance, he pulled her close. She laid her head against his vast chest. With their bodies pressed scandalously close, they swayed—more than waltzed—to the music. Other dancers stared and whirled around them, but the two lovers were oblivious to everything. Arabella was more content than Zdenka had ever seen her. Indeed, her sister knew her own heart.

Zdenka dug into her pocket and fingered the metal key and note. Soon, she would place them in Matteo's hands.

Along with her virginity.

CHAPTER 17

Headed for the balcony, Matteo stalked through the crowded ballroom, not caring who he bumped into, whose gown he stepped on. Zdenka followed close on his heels. The balcony would not be much quieter, but at least it was dark. Inside the ballroom, the flickering gaslights made his scar throb, and the press of the crowd made him tense and uneasy. He felt like he'd been run through with a bayonet and the job left unfinished. In the dim moonlight, couples moved arm in arm across the balcony, resting in the cool night air. Matteo suppressed disappointment that he and Arabella weren't among them.

"I'm sorry," Zdenko said. "I wanted to tell you earlier."

Fury rode up his throat and burned like acid. Matteo rounded on his friend. "How long have you known?"

With a small gasp, Zdenko stumbled back and bumped into someone. "Papa wrote to him a while ago and Arabella and I saw him in the market today, but I only realized the two men were one and the same when he appeared tonight."

The orchestra struck up the *Thunder and Lightning* polka. Looking forward to holding Arabella in his arms had made him feel almost normal, but now, every cymbal crash made Matteo's skin jump.

"Who is he?" The question left a bitter taste in Matteo's mouth. He wasn't sure he wanted to know.

"A wealthy landowner and farmer. His name is Mandryka. He's from Slavonia." Zdenko peered into the ballroom. "I expect her to reach some kind of understanding with him tonight."

"Tonight? Impossible," Matteo snarled. "So quickly? Why are you lying to me? You know how I despise lies. She must have known him for a while."

Zdenko rested a hand on Matteo's shoulder. Despite his anger, the gesture felt warm and comforting. "I'm not lying. I swear to you on my grandmother's grave. Arabella always said she was waiting for the right man, and...I thought it might be you. We assumed it was a romantic delusion, but Mandryka appeared."

"Was she leading me on with the letters? Toying with me? Making a fool of me?" Matteo gripped the stone balustrade so tight, his knuckles hurt. The scar on his back felt tight as a violin string. "All her talk about being a woman of self-determination was nothing more than talk. She is following your parent's expectations."

"Mandryka's arrival surprised us all. She meant every word she wrote." Zdenko's voice trembled. "But you know she was never free to make the decision. She had to think about the family, not just her happiness."

"I always knew Arabella might not accept me, but I fell in love with the girl who wrote me." He straightened up and stared up into the star-dusted sky.

Zdenko's lips—lips like his sister's—parted in a soft gasp. He turned away rapidly, as though to hide some reaction.

Amorous couples hid in the balcony shadows. Matteo wanted to be away from every coupled creature on the earth. He was relieved when a hulking figure, single and alone like himself, positioned himself on the other side of a nearby pillar. Matteo wouldn't have noticed but for the man's size.

Zdenko's hand worked in his pocket. "In your last letter, you asked Arabella for one hour to persuade her of your love."

Matteo snorted. "That was stupid. I let my heart get ahead of my common sense." He was glad it was dark because his face burned with humiliation.

"But ... what if she agreed to your request?" Zdenko's voice wobbled. He shifted his feet. He clasped and unclasped his hands.

What was he so nervous about?

"Why would she do that?" There was no use belaboring this conversation. What he needed now was a drink stronger than champagne punch.

"Arabella sent this note." Zdenko handed him a folded piece of manuscript paper that smelled not of Arabella's usual lavender scent, but of vanilla.

Matteo held the letter in a spot of moonlight and read. It was unbelievable. Something hot and potent sizzled under his skin. He lowered the letter and stared hard at Zdenko. Even in the dim light, with his bad eyesight, he could tell his young friend's face was white. "She's asking me to meet her in her room at one o'clock."

Someone, obviously drunk, guffawed too loudly. A man swerved into him and Matteo righted the fellow before he plastered his face on the pavement. The man on the other side of the pillar muttered curses. Matteo hoped he wasn't so ill-behaved when he was drunk.

Zdenko chewed his lower lip. "She wished to spend the rest of her life with you, but she cannot. Tonight, her life as a girl ends. This is the final decision she will ever make on her own.

She trusts you will not make undue demands and that you will keep this hour a secret forever."

Zdenko pressed a key into Matteo's palm. "This is the key to Arabella's room. The entrance on the top floor of our hotel. The second door is her room. You can go up the back staircase, so you won't be seen."

The moon dodged behind a cloud, throwing the balcony into deeper darkness. The mountain of a man standing near them growled. The sound raised the hairs on Matteo's nape.

"But if I take this key, I am going to compromise the purest, most intelligent and unique woman I've ever met. We didn't spend much time together, but through her letters, I feel we know one another intimately. I cannot dishonor her." He held out the key to Zdenko.

His friend shook his head and refused it.

"There is no dishonor involved. You haven't forced yourself on her, tricked or deceived her. I've seen how happy she was when she got one of your letters. You gave her permission to be herself. She only wishes to say farewell. Nothing more."

The man in the shadows doubled over as if he'd been punched in the gut.

Protectiveness for Arabella gave Matteo pause. "This is too rash. I cannot go to her. It's my duty as an officer and a gentleman. To do otherwise would be dishonorable."

Zdenko made a noise of impatience and threw his arms wide. "Are you sure it wasn't you lying? Maybe you don't really believe a woman has the right to decide who to love. Maybe it was all talk on your part to flatter and impress her."

Zdenko's accusation stung. Matteo hated lying and being accused of lying was equally bad. "Why didn't you try to talk her out of this?"

"I did, but she is impulsive. Stubborn." Zdenko tugged at his collar. "She, too, fell in love through your letters, but marriage is impossible. You convinced her to listen to her heart, even if circumstances require compromise."

"I believe every word I wrote, but I also believe in being decent. I'm not like my cousin, who takes his pleasure, regardless of the lady." Matteo loved Edward, but he was a scoundrel.

For some reason, Zdenko's hands shook. "I don't think you're like Edward, either. Can't you go and wish her farewell? Give her an embrace and a kiss goodbye?"

Perspiration shimmered on Zdenko's upper lip, and he drew the back of his hand across to wipe his mouth. It seemed odd, because it was quite cool and breezy outside.

"Please don't disappoint her," said Zdenko. "She ... loves you more than you know."

Matteo's resolve weakened. It was a small concession. Zdenko made the request at the behest of Arabella, and Matteo didn't want to disappoint or insult her, even though she'd run a stake through him. "I will not compromise her."

Zdenko's chin trembled. "Arabella is loyal to our parents. She honors the ideals of obeying her parents while secretly following her heart. Tonight, she gives you the gift of her trust. She wishes only to say goodbye."

Moonlight fell across Zdenko's face, highlighting the contours of his feminine face, the luminous quality of his skin. Reminded of Arabella, an unexpected ache of physical need swept over him.

"Please don't disappoint her," Zdenko said. "She'll be waiting for you in her room."

The realization hit Matteo like a bullet. Why hadn't he understood before? He unfurled his fingers and stared at the key. "She is making not one, but two great sacrifices for love. One for me and one for your parents."

He threw an arm over Zdenko's shoulders. A bolt of heat shot through his body. As though he'd touched a hot flame,

Matteo stepped back. He put his hands on Zdenko's shoulders and held him at arm's length. "I didn't get a wife, but I did get a great friend."

A curse from the man in the shadows rattled the air. What was bothering that poor man? When Matteo had seen Arabella with the man she'd chosen for her husband, he'd bit back such a curse.

Now, she was offering him a compromise, and he seized upon it. He questioned his ability to control himself around Arabella, but honor dictated he protect her, even from himself.

He grinned at Zdenko and slipped Arabella's key into his pocket. "I will return this to you in one hour."

Mandryka watched as the two men departed. He didn't recognize either of them, but the intent was clear. He was glad it was dark because his body was shaking with rage. Only moments before, happiness and joy had sung in his breast, but now, his chest felt like the time he'd been kicked by a mule.

He had fallen for Arabella's enchanting eyes, her grace and the way his once-dead heart revived when she smiled at him. But Waldner had lured him to Vienna for the purpose of entrapping him in Arabella's charms. Charms she freely gave away. Mandryka clenched his jaw and beat his fist against the marble pillar. He must take his revenge against Graf Waldner tonight for this cuckolding. Then tomorrow, he would board the first train back to Slavonia, where he should have stayed. This was what came of a simple man coming to a dung heap like Vienna.

Inside the ballroom, guests waltzed to the merry music, drank, and laughed. He would never again laugh or feel joy like he had in the few moments he'd held Arabella in his arms. Clearly, she had planned to ensnare him, then give herself to another. He might love Arabella, but she would never love him.

Happiness had escaped him because of his gullibility and the avarice of Waldner.

Through the starlit night, the bells at St. Stephan's pealed midnight. The orchestra went silent right in the middle of a waltz. A drum roll split the air. Everyone turned toward the staircase and stared and held their breath.

To wild applause and cheers, Fiakermilli, the flirtatious troublemaker, appeared at top of the stairs. As the coachman's mascot, it was tradition that she arrived promptly at midnight, escorted by her brigade of whip-cracking, mask-clad coachmen. Every year, the Fiakermilli capered about the ballroom, embarrassing men, scandalizing the ladies, creating chaos, flirting and making risqué jokes. Tonight, she was dressed in a garish black and red striped dress which showed her black-stockinged calves. Her waist cincher pushed up her breasts to the point of spilling out of her dress bodice.

Even in Slavonia, Mandryka had heard how, over the years, various lascivious Fiakermillies had caused ruptures in relationships during her outrageous appearances at the Coachman's Ball.

When Mandryka saw the wanton Fiakermilli, a mirthless smile came over his face as he devised a plan. A mirthless smile lifted his mouth. By creating a sordid scene with Fiakermilli, he would avenge being made a cuckold, and all Vienna would witness Arabella's downfall.

CHAPTER 18

Panting from her sprint back to the hotel, Zdenka's hands shook as she tried to fit the key in the lock of her bedroom door. Her heart jammed against her ribs. Blood thundered in her ears. She gulped air. After what felt like hours, she turned the key and slipped inside. She leaned against the door, trying to slow her panicked breathing.

In minutes, he would be here. In her room. And she would be in his arms.

She turned up the wick and lit the oil lamp. A warm buttery glow filled the room. She struggled out of her evening jacket and hurled it in a corner.

He had agreed to come for a kiss and an embrace. This one time, she damned honorable men.

Matteo would whisper her name.

Well, Arabella's name.

She tugged her shirttails from her pants as her mind whirled.

His arms would encircle her waist, and he would pull her to his strapping chest. She would smell his scent of rosemary and juniper, feel the brush of his stubble on her cheek. His lips would brush lightly against hers and she would part her lips, letting him taste her mouth. Their kiss would be as sweet as a summer peach, and she would be breathless, dizzy with delight.

The mattress groaned as she sat and tugged off her boots. She flung them in a darkened corner where they landed with successive *thunks.*

She never meant to fall in love. She hadn't intended to deceive Matteo but when she saw him, read his letters, it was as if she'd tumbled from a great height and she could only see his face above her. Day and night, he had crowded her mind, blotting out all other thoughts so she sometimes felt as though she stumbled about, blind.

Was that how he felt about Arabella? She reminded herself that she was the girl in the letters. He loved her. He just didn't know it yet.

Pale moonlight streamed through the tiny window. The cot sagged. Cracks spider-webbed the low ceiling, and the bedside table teetered with a book under one leg. Not at all the bower of roses and soft bed which she'd fantasized about.

Were those footsteps on the stairs? Her pulse raced. She yanked off her socks, balled them up, and threw them on top of her boots.

Zdenka sprang off the bed. The pads of her fingers tingled as she fumbled to unzip her pants. She wanted more than an embrace and a kiss. She wanted him to trace a finger down her neck, trail his fingertips across her collarbone, tease the cleft between her breasts. Beneath her bindings, her nipples hardened. Her pants landed on the bottom of her armoire.

Flames snaked through her limbs. If imagining was even near to the act, she might lose her mind once she was in his arms.

She yanked at the placket of her shirt Her fingers were too

slow to work the buttons. Be still and stop trembling, she commanded them. The shirt joined her pants in the armoire.

Wearing nothing but her pantalets and bindings, she stilled in the dark to listen. The whiz-spin she usually felt in her heart was a flock of mad birds trying to escape. Her fingers searched along her side until they found the pin which held her bindings. Though he'd agreed to come for only a farewell, she intended he would receive more. Scandalously more. Tonight, he would touch her breasts, and by so doing, she would be a woman. The kind of woman she wanted to be.

The binding pin pricked her finger. She muffled a cry and sucked her fingertip for a moment. As she unwound her bindings, the ribbon of fabric pooled at her feet. Without clothes, gooseflesh rose all over her skin.

Would he figure out it was her? Would she tell him it was her who wrote to him? That it was she, not Arabella, with whom he was in love? He might be repulsed, furious at being deceived, confused. Would he understand she had dressed as a boy to help her family?

Her heart clawed up her throat, and she could barely swallow. She wrapped her arms around herself and padded across the cold floor to her armoire. Inside hung a filmy, white muslin nightgown trimmed at the neck and wrists in Belgian lace. Arabella had given it to her for Christmas, and she'd been saving it, though she didn't know why. She slipped it off the hanger, lifted it over her head, and let it float down over her breasts, hips, and belly as it wafted around her like a cloud.

In the mirror, the lamp's flame flickered. She caught a glimpse of herself. The nightgown did a great deal to hide her knobby knees and pointed shoulders. It would be dark, but he would feel her body beneath the slick fabric. Moonlight shone through the gauzy nightgown, outlining her figure so she appeared to be an angel.

Soon to be a fallen angel.

But her hair was the devil. Poking out from her head like a mad haystack, it would give her away. She raked her fingers through her hair until it fluffed out around her head in a nimbus of ginger curls.

Matteo was determined to protect Arabella, but Zdenka didn't want to be protected. She wanted to be touched, caressed, to give herself to him. She was mistress of her own life. It was her decision. This is how independent women lived. How Viscomtess Dorothea Prokovsky lived.

A key rattled in the lock.

Adrenaline seared her veins. For one panicked second, she nearly lost her nerve.

Her breath abandoned her as she tried to blow out the lamp. She huddled, quaking, in a shadowy corner. Was her trembling from fear or desire?

Matteo opened the door and paused.

Backlit by light from the hallway, his vast body filled the doorframe. Powerful shoulders rose and fell with quickened breath. He stepped into the room. The air hummed with masculine vitality.

"Arabella?"

Her lungs fought to hold breath.

He closed the door behind him.

The latch clicked loud as a crack of lightning.

CHAPTER 19

Matteo paused in the doorway of the darkened room and held back his desire, straining like a horse against the reins. He'd waited, wondered, wanted Arabella ever since he read her first letter. A kiss and an embrace. Then he would take his leave. Holding her in his arms and tasting her lips would be a memory he would carry with him forever.

He closed the door. The night was cloudy, the stars dim. A glow of meager moonlight illuminated a patch on the floor. With his compromised vision, he could barely make out the shapes of a narrow cot, a boxy armoire, and next to the cot, a table.

Where was Arabella?

He inhaled. The sweet fragrance of...vanilla? He frowned. The scent was new. Arabella usually wore lavender. Perhaps she'd chosen something special for him? In the near silence, her soft, rapid, breathing.

His cock ignored his conscience and hardened with expectation.

A rustling in the shadowy corner revealed her location.

Despite her independence and bravery, she was timid. Determined not to scare her, he stepped slowly in her direction. Even so, the floor creaked underfoot.

"I came as you asked. To bid you farewell." Matteo kept his voice low, gentle. He extended his hand, searching in the darkness for her. It made him feel silly. Like a child playing hide and seek. Did she mean to have him on?

"Arabella?"

The shuffle of her feet answered him.

His body tightened. Heat flooded him in a way he hadn't anticipated. He must be careful not to let things get out of hand. It had been so long since he'd had a woman, but protecting her honor surpassed his raging need.

"You have me at a disadvantage. I cannot see well in the dark since my head wound."

Bare feet padded across the floor. As she drew close, the air vibrated. Warmth radiated from her, and he experienced a sense of being more alive than he'd been since returning from König-gratz. In this darkness, in her room, did she intend more than a kiss and embrace?

Mustn't assume. Don't take liberties you don't deserve.

She pressed her hands to his lapels of his jacket. He clasped them to his chest, drinking in her aliveness, feeling his body quicken. He raised her fingers to his mouth and kissed the tips.

Her quick inhalation let him know the sensation pleased her.

Why were the pads of her fingers callused? Women like Arabella always wore gloves. He didn't think he had ever seen her without gloves.

She rose up, and her breath feathered his lips. He inclined his head so she could reach him more easily. Like ember to tinder, their kiss caught fire. Heat coursed through his body. Her kisses grew hungrier, more insistent.

He flicked his tongue on her upper lip. Her lips parted, and he tasted her mouth, traced her lips, until her tongue explored his mouth. She tasted of vanilla, and her lips felt like heaven. It was more than he could have hoped for, such a luscious, indescribably enlivening kiss. Where had she learned to kiss like this? He couldn't imagine her letting Dominik slobber over her or Elemer's sandpaper lips inspire her, or Lamoral stop talking long enough to kiss her.

She guided his hands to her waist. A thin garment was all that lay between his hands and her milky skin. He nearly stopped breathing.

If only he could see her. Were those delectable lips smiling? Were her cheeks flushed? Were her eyes half-closed?

Her hands, sure and strong, slid up the front of his jacket to his cravat and worked the knot free. With a fingertip, she traced the edge of his jaw from ear to chin then down the side of his neck where a vein pulsed with heated blood.

He allowed his hands to drift up her torso, to feel every rib, the ribbon of her spine, the narrow slope of her hips. His hands drifted to cup her backside. It was ... a little flat. Rather like a boy's arse. He glided his hands back to her waist and felt the rise and fall of her breathing.

She tugged at his collar button until it opened then licked the small triangle at the base of his neck.

His cock responded in salute.

This was more than the kiss and embrace he'd expected, but he wasn't sure how much to respond, how much to let go. He didn't want to debauch her. "You needn't be afraid. I haven't come to dishonor you."

A finger pressed his lips silent. He kissed her palm then pushed up her sleeve and kissed a trail up the inside of her arm until he reached her elbow.

She gave a tiny squeak of pleasure.

Her aggressiveness was a surprise but not unwelcome. It would take a mountain of resolve not to take what she offered so willingly.

She worked the buttons of his jacket open. Life surged into his body like a gust of air through an open window. The scar on his shoulder loosened. His mind quieted. Her touch tore away the bonds knotting him to bitterness and self-loathing.

Like a sleeping leviathan, his heart revived. Every sense was heightened by her touch, her nearness, by her.

He clasped her hands to still them. "Sweet ..."

His words died as she pulled off his jacket and dropped it to the floor in a heap.

He must protect her from the gunpowder that was his lust. Riding into oncoming rifle fire was easy compared to stopping her passionate abandon.

She jerked his shirt from his pants and worked her way down the clasps. Several buttons popped and skittered across the wooden floor. Cold air hit his chest, but she warmed it by rubbing her cheek against the dusting of hair. Her hand slithered inside his shirt, and somehow, she knew to find his nipples and tongue each one until he was in exquisite agony. He would go mad if she kept this up. Already, his control hung by a piano wire.

"I mustn't ..." He bit the end of his tongue to focus his mind, but his penis strained uncomfortably in his fitted trousers.

Again, she silenced him with a finger to his lips.

He stepped back, but she moved into the space he'd vacated and pressed her body against his. Matteo's threshold gave way. He rummaged through his mind to think of an erection discourager, but it was no good. He was too far gone.

She fitted his hands to the curves of her breasts. Beneath her chemise, her nipples were taut, her breasts firm and up-tilting. As he rubbed a thumb over her nipples, she gasped, sounding at once surprised and carnal. He gave himself over to the pleasure. It was like falling into the sun: a hot brilliant want he'd not known he had. How amazing she was to give herself to him, to ask for what she wanted.

"Are you sure this is what you want?" he asked.

"Yes," came her response in a low timbre he'd never heard before, no doubt attributed to the intensity of her desire.

He forgot his disconcerts as desire diluted every ounce of his fortitude. At least if they were standing, the tryst would go no further than naked caresses.

She took his hand, led him to the narrow cot, and pushed his shoulders so he sat on the edge. Palms on his shoulders, she silently urged him to lie back.

"Are you sure?" he asked again.

"Yes, yes, yes," she said, the timbre of her voice now light and girlish.

How changeable women were.

He lifted his legs onto the bed and lay back as her busy hands demanded. She made a movement, and he felt a gust of air as she pulled her nightdress over her head. How he longed to see her naked body, which had been encased in corsets, petticoats, gowns, and capes. The forthrightness revealed in her letters extended to exuberance in bed as she straddled the pinnacle of his thighs.

Matteo grasped her around the waist and allowed his hands to roam over her firm stomach. He thumbed the crevices of every rib, pressed his fingers into the tendons on her back. When he reached the infinite softness of her breasts, she sighed and made a purring noise.

Having seen her clothed, her breasts were more generous than he'd expected. Her breasts inspired a new and wondrous tenderness in him. What was she awakening in him?

He pulled her to his mouth to suckle her nipples as she

braced herself up with one arm. A throaty gasp escaped her, and he wished he could watch her dissolve into desire.

She drew away from his greedy mouth and fumbled at his zipper.

"Oh, God," he said, the ragged voice not his own.

At last, his penis pushed free as she drew down the waist of his small clothes. The back of her hand stroked up and down the shaft. A single finger circled the engorged head. He reached down and stroked himself once or twice and she repeated the gesture, making him chew the inside of his cheek to keep from coming.

Strong thighs flexed as she rose on her knees and rode his erection. Dampness slipped over him. He strove to not enter her, but she rolled her hips over his erection, intensifying his urge to thrust up into her. His body was a lit cannon. It would be impossible for him to stop now. Blood surged through his thighs. His balls ached. His penis took over his mind as raw need overran his desire for honor. He thumbed her thatch of hair until he found the center of her and rubbed until she shuddered and bucked, once, twice, three times.

"Matteo, take me," she murmured.

Her climax made her lose her mind. It sometimes made women say things they didn't mean. The request startled him, and he fought his instincts boiling out of control. "We cannot."

"I want you. I've wanted you since the first night I saw you at your aunt's. The time we rode together, and you tried to teach me how to waltz—"

She froze. A gasp.

Cold, like a dash of ice water, washed over him.

His erection lost all impulse.

"We never rode together ..." he said, suspicion dispelling his lust-filled daze.

She leapt off of him and scrabbled about on the floor.

"Where's my nightgown?" she said, her words a fast and tremulous squeak.

"What the devil?" He sat up and reached for her. His hand found curls... soft...*short curls.*

She recoiled from his touch.

Clouds whisked off the moon. Brilliant moonlight bathed the room and lit the outlines of her face. Clutching her nightgown to her chest, she gave a frightened cry and turned her back.

Before she hid herself, he'd glimpsed large breasts.

Solidly muscled body.

A head of ginger curls, badly cropped.

Zdenko?! My friend?

Filled with mortification, he scrambled out of bed. His mind stumbled for coherence. Was his wounded head playing tricks on him? Had he stumbled by mistake into the wrong room? Was this a cruel joke?

Words choked in his throat, tumbled out nonsensically. "What? Who are—Where—Who? Zdenko? Did I just make love —." *Holy Hell!* He put himself back together and zipped his pants. "This can't—What is the meaning? Impossible—all this time?"

In two paces he loomed over the crouched figure. He hoisted her up by the armpits and dragged her fully into the glare of the moonlight.

Before him, hair wild, eyes filled with terror, his friend, Zdenko, grasped a nightgown in front of his naked body.

His naked body?

Her.

Her naked body.

CHAPTER 20

Zdenka's entire body flamed. Humiliation clutched her throat in a stranglehold so she couldn't catch her breath. A cold slap of shame hit her. She wished she could melt into the floor. The magical tingly thing which Matteo's touch had elicited within her body now turned to black mortification.

She hadn't worked out when to tell him she was a girl, that he was making love to her, not Arabella. She had expected to have the chance to show him how much she loved him first. Now, it was too late.

He turned his back to her and covered his eyes with his hand while she pulled her nightdress over her head. He snatched the thin blanket off the bed and tossed it behind his back in her direction.

At least he was gallant.

She draped the blanket about her shoulders.

"Who, in God's Holy name, are you?" Each word was like a bullet aimed at her heart.

Her tongue stuck to the roof of her mouth, and her voice came out in a croak. "I'm Zdenka."

"As in Zdenko?"

She lit the oil lamp. The room filled with exposing light. "We are one in the same. I am your friend."

His finger stabbed the air. "You are *no* friend of mine."

Matteo hauled his shirt over his head, snatched his jacket from the floor, and jammed his arms through the sleeves.

She reeled back. It would have hurt less had he slapped her in the face. Were all the hours they'd spent together worth nothing because she'd turned out to be a woman? And to think his fingers had butterflied along her inner thighs.

"I ... I have been your best friend. You've told me secrets. I've shared my mine with you."

His tone was biting. "I shared them with the person I knew as Zdenko."

The air in the room was as cold as a snowstorm.

"Are you decent?" He snapped, his back still turned to her.

"Yes."

Slowly, he turned, his gaze scalding so she felt her skin go hot again.

"How could you do this?"

"Because I love you."

How foolish she was to think her love could outweigh her deceit.

"How could I have been such an idiot?" he muttered to himself.

"Everyone has been so preoccupied with Arabella, no one in Vienna knows I'm a girl. Only you."

As he paced the tiny room, the gleam of moonlight gave his face a spectral aspect. A ghost of the man she knew. The loss made her heart feel as though it had been hit by a sledgehammer.

His face was stony. "Did Arabella put you up to this because she wanted nothing to do with me? To humiliate me?"

"No, no, no." She waved her hands back and forth and the blanket slipped from her shoulders to the floor.

His eyes skimmed her body, and despite himself, she noted a certain stunned appreciation in his face. "How ...? I ..." He frowned at her again and shook his head.

She pulled the blanket back around her shoulders.

"And what of the letters she wrote?"

"I wrote the letters."

"You? You wrote them?"

"And you said you fell in love with the girl who wrote the letters. That's me."

His eyes narrowed. "I thought they were from Arabella, not you. All this time, you lied to me. Why didn't you say you were a ... a ... ffffemale?" He dragged the *f* so it sounded like a hiss or a curse.

"Please give me a chance to explain."

His jaw worked as he buttoned his shirt.

"I've always worn pants at home on the farm. My dresses were forever torn, dirty, missing buttons. Papa's a drinker and a gambler. The farm is mortgaged to the hilt. Soon, the creditors will take over. If we're to save it, Arabella has to make a good match—"

When she said Arabella's name, he shuddered ever so slightly.

"Not a match with a mere soldier," he said, his voice bitter as coffee dregs.

His cruel tone revealed the extent of his hurt. Hurt she would have taken on herself to spare him.

"I didn't mean to hurt you." She reached out a hand.

He stepped back.

She let her hand drop to her side.

"So how does your parading about as a *boy* come into this?"

She took a steadying breath, which did no good. Her insides

were still a knot of stone. "There wasn't enough money to bring both Arabella and I out. I didn't want a debut. I've told you how I long to return to the farm and make it profitable again. I *love* the farm. It's my home. It's where I belong. I promised my Grandmama I would never let the farm leave the family. My ancestors are buried there. I *have* to save it. It's the one place I feel free to be myself."

"I can imagine." He flicked his fingers at her. "If you're dressing up like a male."

"It's not that," she said, angry now. "I did it for Arabella. For my family. They come first, even if it meant lying to you."

"You could have stayed home and not come to Vienna. Then there would have been no need to masquerade as a boy."

"I chaperoned Arabella as her brother because there wasn't even money to buy Mama more than one decent gown. Everything has been invested in Arabella making a good match." She jutted her jaw at him, *damn him.* "I'd do anything for my family."

"Which includes lying." He stepped across the room and brought his face close to hers. "Which I despise." She smelled his scent. His heated breath skimmed her lips. The fire in his eyes threw sparks she could almost feel on her cheeks. Clouds drifted back over the moon and the room lost all trace of romance.

She stood her ground, but her voice trembled. "I never meant to lie. But I fell in love with you, and I couldn't tell you the truth. I had to protect my family."

There was the tiniest hesitation, a tick of his head before he gave her his back. "Why didn't Arabella marry one of the Grafen and be done with it?"

She sighed. "You don't know how many times I've asked Arabella the same question. I've always wanted her to marry for love. She was waiting for the right man to show up. At first, I tried to convince her that *you* were the right man. Then

Mandryka came and she declared him the right man. You saw how besotted they are."

"So, you decided to play a prank of magnificent proportions on me?" He sounded like a snarling animal, ready to attack.

"No. It was never a prank." She took two steps toward him. "Don't you see? I'm in love with you."

"I cannot return your love. You are a liar and ..." He backed up and gave his head a quick shake. "A man."

"After what we just did, you still think of me as a man?" She pointed to his now-resolved crotch. "That part of you didn't think I was a man."

He pulled his jacket shut and buttoned it. "You were the fellow I drank beer and rode with. Oh, God." He rolled his eyes and threw his head back. "The fellow I tried to teach to waltz."

Those moments in his arms had been, until tonight, the most intoxicating of her life. His revulsion over having held her in his arms hurt like skin tearing from bone. She took another step toward him.

His body tensed. His eye twitched.

"When I was in your arms in the woods, I saw the look in your eyes. In the deepest part of your heart, you sensed the real me."

"I did no such thing," he said, his words bumping together, so anxious was he to get them out. "We have nothing more to say."

"But I do." She stepped in front of him and leaned back against the door, blocking his way. "I fell in love with you when I saw how kind and compassionate you were to the soldier who stumbled on the stairs of your aunt's house. I love you even though you startle at loud noises. When you're grumpy and unpredictable. I know it's hard to understand, but I lied *because* I love you. I invited you here because I thought if you spent one hour with me, you would see I'm the same person as a girl that I am as a boy. You'd see how much I love you, that I'm willing to sacrifice my reputation, my future, the farm, all for you."

He straightened his shoulders with military precision. The wall of his fury made the corners and edges of the room seem sharper, harder, inescapable.

"This must *never* become public, you understand," he whispered, his tone so acidic it burned her right to the breastbone.

She sagged against the door, her heart desolate and scorched. "I would never tell anyone."

"You'll understand if I don't believe you," he said with a snort. He pried her off the door and opened it. Turning back to her, he said, "I can't bear liars."

The slam of the door made her jump. As he descended the stairs, his boots thudded like doom marching into hell. She slipped down the door until she met the floor, tears wetting the front of her beautiful nightdress.

♫

Matteo supposed anyone seeing him stomp down the hotel stairs would see yellow and orange flames shooting out of his nostrils. What a damned blasted fool he'd been not to realize Zdenka was a *girl*. Never again, as long as he lived, would he ever speak to another duplicitous Waldner.

Arabella's distressed voice rose from the lobby. "Why did you make such a disgusting scene with Fiakermilli, flirting and carrying on like you did?"

Matteo should have taken the back stairs. The last thing he needed was to run into Zdenka's co-conspirator.

A man's voice answered, "Because you made a fool of me."

Matteo arrived in the hotel lobby to find Graf Waldner leaning weakly against the fireplace mantel. Arabella sat on the sofa, sobbing on her mother's shoulder. Arabella's intended,

Mandryka, with his mountainous bulk, all but blocked the door to the street.

"You humiliated me in front of all Vienna," Arabella blubbered. "How could I have been such a fool?"

"Now, now, dear," Gräfin Waldner cajoled as she patted Arabella's back. "We must forgive men their bad behavior now and then. Amends can be made. Love makes fools of us all."

A shared sentiment, that.

Matteo remained out of sight and judged the distance to the door. His escape would be overlooked in this madhouse.

"You deceived me," Mandryka said. "It is you who made fool out of me."

"We had reached an understanding. Then you paraded around the Coachman's Ball with Fiakermilli on your shoulder, threw her in the air, and kissed her on the *mouth* when she dropped back into your arms," Arabella said.

Gross Gott, the man was a fool.

But not the only fool here tonight.

Graf Waldner mumbled, "You have ruined my daughters' chances. I demand satisfaction."

Even from across the room, Waldner smelled like a schnapps brewery.

Mandryka glared down at the diminutive Waldner, whom he could have squashed under his boot. "Less than an hour after I offered for her, I saw a young man give her key to another man and tell him Arabella requested him to meet her in her bedroom."

Had Mandryka overheard Zdenko—*Zdenka*—give him the key?

Arabella glared at Mandryka. "What are you going on about? I told no one to pass along my key, and I would never invite anyone to my room."

Graf Waldner weaved unsteadily on his feet. "No, no, no. Arabella is no *fille de jolie*. She will make you a fine wife."

This was getting out of hand. Let these treacherous frauds unravel this. The only way out was a direct charge across the lobby. Striding toward the door, Matteo angled to outflank Mandryka, but Mandryka caught sight of him, snatched Matteo by the arm, and spun him around.

Mandryka poked a beefy finger in Matteo's chest. "*This* is the man who received your key. He's the one you arranged to meet."

"Herr von Ritter?" Arabella's forehead wrinkled "I did nothing of the sort. He wrote me a letter several weeks ago, but I never responded because I had no feelings for him."

Mad as they all were, Arabella's words stung.

Arabella narrowed her eyes at Matteo. "Herr von Ritter, what were you doing upstairs?"

"Looking for you, most likely," Mandryka said.

"It would be highly improper for a young lady to meet a man in her *boudoir*," Gräfin Waldner said, puffing up like an angry cat. She turned to Matteo. "What were you doing upstairs, Herr von Ritter?"

"I must be going," he said, yanking his arm out of Mandryka's iron paw. Matteo might be a fool, but he was not going to expose Zdenka's secret to this bunch of lunatics.

"Not until you tell me who gave you the key to Arabella's room." Mandryka gave Matteo a tooth-rattling shake. "You were upstairs waiting for her, weren't you? Admit it."

Graf Waldner staggered toward Matteo, waving his arm so he nearly toppled over. "Von Ritter! Choose your weapon. Pistols. Swords. Knives."

Waldner was so drunk he probably couldn't hold a gun. And it wasn't gentlemanly to accept a challenge from a lunatic anyway.

"I will kill him first," Mandryka said with a snarl. He hooked an arm around Matteo's neck.

Mandryka squeezed his forearm against Matteo's Adam's apple. He gasped for breath.

"Stop it! Stop it, all of you," Zdenka's voice called from the stairs. "It was me. It's all my fault."

Her voice shot up Matteo's spine like a rapier. Had she come down to mock him? To watch this monster of a man choke him to death? Or worse, to entrap him into marrying her?

Everyone froze.

CHAPTER 21

S till in her nightgown, trailing the blanket she had thrown over her nightdress, Zdenka flew down the stairs. "Stop! It was me. I gave him the key and invited him to Arabella's room."

She arrived in the hotel lobby, panting, her hands shaking. Never could she have foreseen such a disaster. Her lightweight nightgown and blanket around her shoulders did nothing to stop her shivering. Cold penetrated her bones.

Matteo elbowed Mandryka to no effect. Mandryka lifted Matteo off his feet, preparing to throw him across the room.

Zdenka screamed, "Take your hands off him!" She struggled to hold back sobs. Why had she let herself fall in love? Why?

Matteo glowered at her.

Arabella's eyes widened at her sister then flooded with tears. Arabella's entire body seemed to deflate. "You?"

Zdenka nodded. "I gave him the key and asked him to meet you in your room. I was ..." she swallowed. "I was waiting for him."

"Who is she?" Mandryka asked.

"My sister, Zdenka," Arabella said.

"Impossible. A young man gave him the key," Mandryka said.

Matteo chimed in, his voice hard-edged. "Until an hour ago, Zdenka was Zdenko. Arabella's younger *brother*."

Heat flamed Zdenka's cheeks. Was he going to disgrace her more than she had already disgraced herself? God help her if Matteo revealed what had happened upstairs. She drew the blanket closer around her shoulders. Her bare feet felt like ice.

Mandryka frowned. "She looks like a girl to me."

"I am a girl." Zdenka said.

Even with all the trouble at hand, admitting the truth was akin to shedding an impermeable coat of ice. She was herself again. Not somebody created to save her family. She could once more be a girl who wore pants to work on the farm, not to deceive others. But in helping her family, in trying to prove her love to Matteo, she had caused irreparable harm to everyone.

"What have you done?" Arabella said in a hushed voice.

"If she's a girl, why was she dressed as a boy tonight?" Mandryka said.

"It's not just tonight," Arabella answered. "Zdenka wears pants to work on the farm. She's been masquerading as a boy since we arrived in Vienna because we haven't enough money to bring the two of us out. She chaperoned me as my younger brother because there wasn't even money to buy Mama proper attire. It was easier to let her pretend to be a boy. We didn't intend to hurt or deceive anyone."

"And she gave you the key to Arabella's room and told you to meet her there?" Mandryka asked Matteo.

Matteo responded with a sharp nod.

With a groan, Papa flopped down onto the sofa, let his head fall back against the cushions, and closed his eyes.

Mama tried to appear calm, but her neck blotched red and her cheeks trembled. "Oh, you impulsive, headstrong girl. What have you done?"

"Why did Matteo even think I would meet him in my room?" Arabella asked.

"Because she's been writing me letters saying they were from you," Matteo said. "They said you loved me."

Arabella's jaw dropped, and she stared at Zdenka.

Mandryka turned to Zdenka. "Why did you write him letters saying they were from Arabella?"

"Because she's in love with him, but she was a boy, you *dumkopf!*" Arabella said.

Mandryka rubbed his forehead. His wooly eyebrows bobbed up then down. To Matteo he said, "So you were upstairs with the sister, who was dressed as a boy and wrote you love letters and gave you a key to Arabella's room because she's in love with you?"

"It appears so, yes," Matteo said.

The bitterness in his voice sliced through Zdenka. How had she let things get so out of hand? Did love do this to everyone? Was it like a sickness where you lost your mind entirely?

"Zdenka was upstairs....oh dear." Arabella gasped and raised her hands to her cheeks.

"Nothing happened," Matteo said. "Her honor is entirely intact."

Mostly intact, and not for lack of trying.

Never again would she feel his heart beating beneath her cheek. Never hear him whisper to her. Never feel the flutter of his breath on her lips before he kissed her.

Arabella pointed. "Then why are there buttons missing from your shirt?"

At the suggestion of scandal, Papa revived and struggled to his feet. "You have been in my daughter's rooms upstairs. You are a rapscallion. A rake. A scoundrel. You courted my first daughter without my consent then ruined my second daughter."

"Zdenka, you have destroyed all my prospects," Arabella said, her eyes filled with anguish.

"And you intended to take advantage of my Arabella. To make a cuckold of me," Mandryka snarled.

Arabella stiffened and said tartly, "I am *not* your Arabella."

Mandryka seemed to shrink slightly.

"I intended only to bid her farewell with an embrace and wish her well," Matteo said.

"My daughter is wearing only a nightgown. Did she disrobe to say farewell?" Papa said.

"Embraces, sir, do not cause button malfunctions," Mama said.

Zdenka squeezed her eyes shut and tucked her chin to her chest. She had made a catastrophe of everyone's life. She raised her eyes to Arabella. "Don't let me ruin your happiness. I've made a terrible blunder. You've waited for him all your life. You fell in love immediately, and I can tell he loves you beyond all sanity."

Zdenka crossed to Mandryka. "You traveled all this way to meet the woman you fell in love with. I've never seen her as happy as she was tonight in your arms. Please don't lose her because of something reckless I did."

Papa plopped on the sofa again, his eyes barely open. "No one in our family has ever done anything so stupid."

Though Matteo would never forgive her, Zdenka held out hope that Arabella and Mandryka would forgive one another.

And her.

Arabella cocked her head at Mandryka, and her features softened. She pursed her lips the way she did when she was thinking.

"If you never learn to forgive, you will not be happy in any marriage." Mama laid her hand on Papa's shoulder.

He let out a snore. He'd dropped off to sleep.

Mandryka's face sagged like a dog who'd gotten a terrible scolding. "My dearest, I am a stupid man. A proud man. When I thought you'd wronged me, my heart was smashed into a thousand pieces." He shuffled to Arabella's side and knelt before her. "Forgive me."

Arabella's fists unknotted. A soft smile spread across her face. Mandryka took her hand, kissed her palm, and enclosed it in his gigantic hand. He stood, gathered her to him and kissed the top of her head.

"To think I almost lost you," Mandryka said.

To witness their affection splintered Zdenka's heart. If only Matteo could be as forgiving as Arabella, they might have a chance. She was the same now as she had been in pants, but he wouldn't give her a chance to prove it. "At least I haven't caused any permanent damage to you two," Zdenka said to the two lovers. "I'm sorry."

Arabella lifted her head from Mandryka's chest. "Why didn't you just tell Matteo you were in love with him?"

Tears stacked up in Zdenka's throat. "I couldn't tell him until you were betrothed, and you wouldn't make up your mind. Everyone had to still think I was a boy. And Matteo was in love with you. I didn't want him to be hurt."

"What we do for love," Mandryka said, his tone one of simple wonderment.

The kindness in Mandryka's coffee-colored eyes made Zdenka understand how Arabella had fallen in love with him instantly. He was like an older brother who understood Zdenka without her having to explain.

Mandryka chided Matteo, "She loves you very much to take such a chance in the hope you would return her affection."

Matteo's lips twitched. "How can I be expected to fall in love with someone who was supposed to be my friend—my gentleman friend—but lied to me for weeks? I loathe liars."

Zdenka fought the impulse to reach out and take Matteo in her arms. Because of her deceit, perhaps he would never trust again, and his future would be bleak and loveless. He would be alone in his disquiet and dreams. She had destroyed everything she wanted, and, very nearly, everything Arabella, Mandryka, and her parents wanted. She brought calamity wherever she went.

Mama crossed the lobby and patted Zdenka on the back. "There, there, my dear. We will leave for the farm at first light. No one need know you were masquerading. No one will know you were alone with," she sniffed in Matteo's direction. "Him. Everything will remain a secret."

"No more charades, Gräfin Waldner," said Mandryka with the air of someone accustomed to running things. He turned to Matteo. "So, were you just in this lady's bedroom?"

Matteo nodded and slid Zdenka a sideways glance, which she took and heeded as a warning.

"But her honor is intact, and no one need know how, er, it came about," Matteo answered.

"Her secret is not intact." Mandryka nodded toward Zdenka. With utmost kindness, he added, "Nor is her pride or heart. You must do the honorable thing, sir."

At the word 'honorable', Matteo locked his hands behind his back. Zdenka knew he *lived* for the purpose of honor. It was as if he didn't know what made life *worth* living was being *loved*.

Mandryka covered the distance to the sofa and shook a snoring Papa awake. "See here, Graf Waldner. Your attention is needed."

"I'll take a card." Papa snorted awake and rubbed his eyes. "Is it my bid?"

Mandryka locked his hands behind his back and

pronounced, "Graf Waldner, Herr von Ritter, of the *Kaiserlich and Königlich Kavallarie,* has compromised your daughter by going to her room."

Matteo's eyes glowed with fury, but he didn't flinch.

Really, it had been Zdenka who had compromised him. She'd led him on, deceived him, but for love. For adoration. Wasn't that worth forgiving?

"While, by both their admissions, nothing improper happened, she is compromised." Mandryka addressed Matteo. "You must do the honorable thing and marry her."

Zdenka's heart lurched once, twice, then resumed its normal rhythm. She caught her breath.

Matteo fixed her with a distasteful look, indicating he'd prefer self-immolation to marriage.

His chin jerked sideways, ever so slightly. "Zdenka Waldner led me on, pretended to be my friend, lied about Arabella, gave me forged letters, and pretended to be a boy. I hardly think I owe it to her to marry her."

Her worst fears had come to pass. Matteo hated her. With each condemnation, Zdenka felt herself whittled smaller and smaller. To him, everything they had shared was sickening and disgusting. For her, it only confirmed she could never be a wife. She'd thought she might have a chance of being authentic with Matteo, that he might accept her independent, headstrong ways. How wrong she had been.

"He doesn't love me." The words burned like a red-hot poker in Zdenka's throat.

Matteo glared a hole right through her. He thrust his chest forward. "Mandryka is correct. Marrying ..." tendons in his neck bulged. "Zdenko...*Zdenka* is the honorable thing to do. I went to her bedroom. I owe her an unsoiled reputation, and she owes me my future, which is built on my good name."

"Your ... future?" Zdenka stammered.

Matteo strode to her side. He loomed over her. In a low voice only she could hear, he said, "As I said upstairs, I don't dare have this scandal revealed. I would be a laughingstock."

She could hardly blame him for not trusting her.

"What a marvelous solution." Mama clapped her hands.

Arabella threw their mother a withering glance.

Mandryka stepped to Matteo's side and laid his hand on his shoulder. "You are a true gentleman."

Matteo ground his teeth. He wiped his palms down the front of his jacket. She'd seen his agitation, the way his anger seethed when he was irritated so she took a step back from him.

His mouth pressed into a grim line. He lowered himself to one knee. Without a trace of affection in his voice, he said, "Will you, Graf Zdenko—" He put his fist to his mouth and coughed. "Gräfin *Zdenka*, accept me as you husband?"

He might have been reading a child's primer for all the emotion he put into it. He had disappeared into himself again, the way he had when they'd first met. His empty eyes didn't see her.

The blanket of ice she'd thrown off when she'd admitted she was a girl descended on her again, wrapping her tightly, chilling her soul.

In the years ahead, she would be invisible to the man she loved. Marrying for the sake of his bloody honor wasn't what she wanted. She loved him enough to do anything for him but to marry him and yet be unloved by him. That sort of marriage was a death sentence. Being his wife would mean giving up every dream of being independent, of returning to the farm and making her own decisions.

Years in the future, she would be an old, white-haired lady, leaning on a cane and tottering around the farm. Lonely, yes, but not as bad as marrying a man who despised you.

Her mouth was dry as hay dust. "I must refuse you. I will

only marry for love, not honor. Therefore, I must ask. Do you love me?"

CHAPTER 22

Matteo rose from bended knee. The scar on his temple hurt from clenching his jaw. He strode across the threadbare carpet of the hotel lobby, then back to Zdenka, trying to quell his temper. Her refusal to marry him was akin to her dashing ice water in his face.

As much as he thought he understood his young friend, Zdenko, the female version flummoxed him.

"You went to such great lengths to deceive me, you claim to love me, to have been my friend, and now you refuse to marry me?"

"What kind of life would I have if I married you only out of duty?" Zdenka asked.

He swallowed hard. "I'm aware I'm not a great catch. I have no title, money, or position, and only my good name to recommend me. If you refuse to marry me, once all of Vienna hears of this debacle, you'll cost me my name, my honor, and my pride. Perhaps that's what you and your sister intended all along."

Zdenka shivered but stared back at him with bullish defiance in her eyes.

As a woman, she was twice as formidable as she'd been as a

boy. This was the woman who had bewitched him, dissolved his self-control, and stoked his need with the intensity of her desire. He owed it to her to marry her. It wasn't as if *nothing* had happened upstairs.

"Forget me." Zdenka's voice quavered. "Forget I was your friend. Forget the things I shared with you. Forget what we know about one another."

Gräfin Waldner leaned forward on the sofa. Palms together, she pleaded, "Zdenka, be reasonable. You have made a mess of things, as the fortuneteller predicted. You will never get another offer of marriage. Think of Arabella. Of Papa and me. We will all be humiliated."

Zdenka stood taller. "I never wanted to be bound to anyone, and I certainly don't wish to be married to someone who doesn't love me. I'll do what I've always intended. Return to the land of my birth. To the farm."

Graf Waldner squirmed as though his suit had suddenly become too tight. Like a hunted man, his glance darted around the room and settled on the door. Was he intending to bolt?

Arabella left Mandryka's side and put an arm around Zdenka's shoulders. She gazed at Matteo. "Isn't marrying Matteo what you wanted?"

Arabella's gaze left him entirely cold. Not angry, not resentful or feeling thrown over. Just lifeless. How could he have thought himself in love with her?

"I want to be loved, not treated like a captured animal," Zdenka said.

Zdenko, his boyish friend, had banished the loneliness Matteo had felt since returning from the war. But with her lies, that was over. Even if a marriage to Zdenka would be nothing but a cold and distant acquaintanceship, Matteo refused to be like his philandering, dissolute father. Matteo owed Zdenka his protection, and she owed him the chance to maintain his honor.

"You deceived me. At the least, you owe me the redemption of my honor by marrying me," he said.

"Why do you care what other people think?" Zdenka said.

"I don't care, but I have standards for myself."

"And what are those?" Gräfin Waldner said. "Not to get caught sneaking into the rooms of young ladies?"

He fixed her with a glare. "At a minimum, to be honest and honorable."

"And you insist on marrying me to maintain the latter?" Zdenka said.

"You will have the freedom to do as you please. My only request is that you don't take chances with your safety."

"You see? You can go back to the farm as you wish," Arabella said.

Graf Waldner's voice shook. "I ... I'm very thirsty. Is there some schnapps about?"

Gräfin Waldner scowled at him, and he shrank into the corner of the sofa.

Zdenka said to Matteo, "Is that all? No more demands, such as produce an heir?"

There was rebellion in her voice and fire in her beautiful green eyes. Why hadn't Matteo seen that rebellion when *she* had been a *he*? Her white nightgown rippled around her long shapely legs. Her body was utterly, irrefutably, feminine. A body that had pleased him unimaginably. But if she agreed to marry him, he did not want to be constantly reminded of having been duped. That he'd married a liar. "I ask that you only wear pants when you ride. Aside from that, do whatever you wish, so long as you use discretion."

"How generous of you. You'll understand if I refuse your enticing offer. None of this matters because I'm going back to the farm. There, no one cares if I wear pants."

Graf Waldner levered himself off the sofa. He grimaced and sucked air through his teeth. "No, no. That's no longer possible."

Everyone stared at him, waiting.

Mandryka broke the silence. "What is not possible?"

"For Zdenka to return to Friedenheim."

Waldner's voice came out a shaky whisper. "I ... lost the farm last night to the Argentinean in a card game."

Arabella gasped.

Mandryka murmured some imprecation in his native tongue.

Gräfin Waldner's jaw dropped. "You played the Argentinian? He's one of the most dangerous men in Vienna."

One glance at Zdenka told Matteo she might drop in a faint. She swayed and tipped.

"How could you?" she said on an exhale.

"I thought I could win back the money I'd lost."

Waldner's voice rang in Matteo's memory. His father often used the same voice when begging his mother to take him back after an incidence of his philandering. Zdenka needed protection from her father's betrayal of his family responsibilities.

Zdenka's knees buckled, and she sank. Matteo caught her before she hit the floor and eased her into a chair.

"It was to be mine," she said. "I promised Grandmama I would take care of the land."

Waldner reached out to pat her arm, but she turned her back on him.

"The deed to the farm was all I had left. You understand, don't you?" Waldner pleaded. "I had to try to win back the money. I was only doing it for you."

Matteo knew how life could be ripped away suddenly, leaving nothing but a scorched wasteland. His anger at Zdenka retreated, knowing the devastation she must be experiencing.

All the time she'd spoken of the farm, she—he—always said it was where she felt most herself.

Gräfin Waldner straightened herself. "Now there is no choice but for you to marry Matteo."

Tears flowed down Zdenka's cheeks. Her shoulders curved inward as though to protect herself. He wished he could have protected her from such disappointment. Wordlessly, he handed her a clean handkerchief, and she took it.

In the background, the Waldners and Mandryka hurriedly made plans. Secrecy had to be maintained, therefore they would marry in the *Schubertkirche*. No invitations. The license would cost extra so they could marry without the banns being read. No traditional celebratory breakfast. Matteo and Zdenka would reside with Thea. The wedding was to be in two days, but all he wanted to do was to gather Zdenka in his arms and reassure her everything would be all right.

Except, he could not say that because had no illusions.

CHAPTER 23

The morning of her wedding—a wedding she had no intention of attending—Zdenka lay in bed and pulled the covers over her head. She'd eaten nothing in the last day. Her head hurt, her eyes burned, and her lips were dry and cracked. Her heart was hollow, and her mind filled with black images Matteo's angry glare, a cold bed, day upon day of an empty life here in the drawing rooms of Vienna.

How could the farm be gone? She had to find a way to get the farm back, no matter what. Then, she could take Matteo there, married or not. He would heal there, feel safe. At Friedenheim, he could forget the war.

On the farm, she had helped the ewes birth lambs on the bright green grass. Hawks wheeled on winds blowing down from the mountains. The scent of ripening apples, crisp and sweet, perfumed the air. Horses galloped across the meadow, their hooves like drumbeats. The land gave her strength to be wild, independent, courageous.

She didn't want to get out of bed. In this room, Matteo had taught her about being alive, and she didn't want to forget his hand on her thigh, his tongue tasting her lips, his murmurs of desire. If she could stay in this bed forever, the memory would never fade.

Arabella knocked on the door. "May I come in?" Not waiting for an answer, she let herself in.

Zdenka rolled on her back and peeked out from the covers at her sister. Every movement made her bones ache.

Arabella's brows drew down. "Oh, dear," she whispered. "You don't look well."

Zdenka croaked, "I'm not going to the church."

"You have to get up." Arabella tugged Zdenka into a sitting position at the edge of the bed and sat beside her. "I'm so sorry about everything. Sorry I was so wrapped up in myself. If only you'd have told me, perhaps I could have done something to help you." She pointed across the room. "Mandryka sent something for you."

Zdenka rubbed her eyes. In her armoire hung a lacy, cream silk gown. A pair of fine silk stockings and satin shoes occupied her dressing table. They were beautiful, but to Zdenka they looked like handcuffs, leg irons, and a shroud.

She clutched Arabella's hands. "Will you help me now?"

"Let me get the hairbrush. We've prepared a bath in the other room."

"That's not what I mean." Zdenka's legs seemed so heavy, she could hardly muster the strength to stand. She went to her armoire and rummaged the shelves and drawers. "Where are my pants and jacket? The evening scheme Edward bought me? My boots?"

Arabella tilted her chin. "I don't know." She stood and crossed to Zdenka's side. "But you don't need them this morning. Perhaps Mama packed them to send to Viscomtess Dorothea Prokovsky's house."

"I need them. I'm leaving."

Arabella's eyes widened. "You can't be serious. The farm is

gone. There's nowhere to run. The wedding is set. Matteo will be waiting. You can't humiliate him further. Everyone is talking of your masquerade. He'll be the subject of ridicule. A drawing room joke if you don't go through with the wedding."

Zdenka dropped to her knees and looked under the bed. Nothing but a ball of dust. Where were her clothes?

"I can dress as a man again. No one knew the first time, and they won't know now. I'll find work. I have to leave." She stood and swayed, lightheaded. Arabella gave her a steadying arm.

Zdenka sat back on the edge of the bed. "Why should I marry him if he doesn't love me?"

"You were rather eager for me to marry someone I didn't love," Arabella chided gently.

Her sister's words hurt like a thumb pressed to a bruise. Now that Zdenka knew love made a woman feel as though she'd awakened from hibernation, she realized how selfish she had been.

Remembering Matteo's stony stare sent a shudder through her. "He hates liars."

Arabella stepped to the armoire and smoothed the folds of Zdenka's wedding gown with her palm. "I've never seen anyone as determined as you. You can convince Matteo how much you really love him."

"Why can't I come live with you and Mandryka in Slavonia?"

"Because if you don't marry Matteo, this dreadful scandal will follow both of you the rest of your life. He will never live it down. At least if you marry him, there is a chance he'll come to love you."

Zdenka leaned forward and rested her head in her hands. "What if I wear the evening suit? He'd never marry me then."

"You wouldn't."

Arabella patted her on the back. The gesture had always made Zdenka feel better when she was ill as a little girl. Arabella always tried to soothe her. They always watched out for one another. Now it was Arabella's turn to help her.

"Can you get my clothes back?" she asked Arabella.

"Are you sure it's what you want?" Arabella's brows furrowed. "It's dangerous."

Hope stirred. If Arabella would help her escape, she would have a chance. They would have to hurry. "I'm not afraid."

"You should be." Arabella stared at her hands. "If I send for your clothes at the Viscomtess Prokovsky's, Matteo will know something's amiss."

Zdenka paused and sniffed an acrid odor. "What's that smell?"

Arabella sniffed too. "Fire in the fireplace, I guess, but...it does smells strange. Like burning leather."

Oh no! Zdenka jumped to her feet. Her nightgown flapped behind her as she raced to the drawing room.

Mama tossed her beautiful evening suit into the fireplace.

Behind Zdenka, Arabella gasped.

Zdenka blinked, not believing what she was seeing. Her heart leapt to her throat. She couldn't catch her breath. Her head went light.

Her entire wardrobe was burning. Flames ravaged pants, shirts, bindings, vests, even her overcoat. Her boot dissolved in flames as Mama poked it deeper into the fire.

Zdenka leapt to the fireplace. She snatched up the poker, jabbed it into the fire, and tried to rescue her clothes from the leaping flames. Ashes of her jacket fell through the grate. Orange embers snapped onto the carpet. Yellow blazes devoured the legs of her pants. The inferno devoured every shred of her past identity.

No escape remained but to marry a man who hated her for lying to him simply because she loved him.

CHAPTER 24

M atteo's eye twitched as he paced back and forth at the rear of the chilly *Schubertkirche*. Pale morning sun streamed through the tall, clear windows, giving the space a cold, harsh look. Candle smoke blackened every surface, and incense barely masked the stone floor's damp, moldy odor. Wheezy Father Bartolomeo slumped on a chair, snoring.

An appropriate venue for a wedding no one desired.

"Why did you choose this dreadful church?" Matteo asked Edward.

His cousin sat on the last pew, swinging his leg back and forth. Matteo knew weddings made Edward nervous because they reminded him of how frequently he had narrowly escaped the institution of marriage.

"Because it's slightly out of the way." Edward nodded to the priest. "And for a rich price, he was willing to do it without the banns being read."

Matteo checked his pocket watch. "She's late. I want to get this over with."

Tired of trodding the same path, Matteo meandered up the

center aisle and stared at the altar painting of the *Transfiguration of Christ* by Franz Zoller. In the lower left corner of the painting was the Centurion, his face contorted in grief as he stared up at the risen Lord. The Centurion had done his duty, and so would Matteo. He set his shoulders back, returned to Edward, and leaned against the last pew.

"You know you don't have to go through with this, don't you? She trapped you and nothing happened. I've had several romantic misadventures," Edward said. "Neither the lady nor I felt compelled to rush to the altar."

"My sense of honor and duty compels me to the altar."

The Centurion reminded Matteo that he had heard another group of soldiers had returned from the Front. Hopefully, Luther was among them. He also wanted to check on how Kurt was progressing in the hospital. Helping Kurt, Luther, and the other soldiers gave him purpose and, even if no one spoke of them, Matteo knew he shared the unspeakable memories of war with these other soldiers.

"I wish you'd have let Mama come," Edward said. "She'll be sorry to have missed your nuptials, since it's likely the only family wedding she'll ever witness."

"No need for everyone in the family to be dragged into this mess."

"You had no problem dragging me into it," Edward said with a laugh.

"You're no stranger to messes," chided Matteo. "And thank you for taking care of getting the banns waived. Was it much trouble?"

"Only expensive," Edward responded. "The judge wasn't terribly happy to be awakened so early, but I made it worth his while."

The massive double doors of the church creaked open, and Graf and Gräfin Waldner bustled in. The stubby Graf took long strides, reminding Matteo of an old rooster trying to look as though he owned the barnyard. The Gräfin's lips pressed into a thin, determined line, and she spewed an attitude of righteous indignation.

Matteo had forgotten he would have in-laws. As long as he didn't lend Waldner any money, and they never saw one another, they would get along.

The massive wooden door opened again and Mandryka, smiling, immense and shaggy as a tree, entered. He held the door open wide and a shock of sunlight momentarily blinded Matteo. He hated Mandryka's smile. It was as though he had been crowned Emperor. Arabella entered next. She might as well have been one of the stone statues for all the effect she had on him.

Then, Zdenka stood before him. Her presence struck him with the force of a freezing gale in the face.

With tentative steps, she moved into the space and gazed around. A lacy veil crowned her head and a nimbus of ginger curls framed her sad, pained face. A cream, silk gown flowed over the bosom which had driven him to the edge of sanity. Still tall and slender, her figure was no longer boyish but curved in all the right places. In trembling hands, she carried a nosegay of wild violets. Zdenka's eyes had never failed to telegraph her thoughts, but she kept her gaze downcast. She glided down the aisle as though she was an angel escaped from the frescoed dome of the nave.

Matteo inhaled and held his breath.

He had half-expected his bride to show up in trousers, a coat, and boots, swaggering confidently down the aisle. This exquisitely beautiful woman confused him. Every angry word he'd thought to spit out dribbled from his brain, leaving him mute and dumb.

Matteo felt Edward at his elbow.

"I say! She's quite gorgeous," Edward said in a mix of admiration and barely-disguised lust.

Matteo jabbed his elbow into Edward's rib, and he grunted.

"Graf Waldner, Gräfin Waldner, Ladies, Herr Mandryka," Matteo managed.

Mandryka held out his hand and greeted him with the traditional wedding congratulations. "*Herzlichen Glückwunsch.*"

No amount of heartfelt good wishes could make Matteo feel joyful on this day.

"Good morning." Arabella dipped a curtsy.

A bit clumsily, as though out of practice, Zdenka followed suit.

Not his pal, Zdenko. Definitely not.

"Glad to see you haven't changed your minds regarding our..." Matteo paused and ground his teeth. "...nuptials."

The Graf jammed his hands in his pockets. "No, we have not changed our mind," he grumbled, barely intelligible.

Had he been drinking already or was he still drunk from the previous night?

Gräfin Waldner drew herself up, hands clasped under her bosom. She narrowed her eyes at Matteo. "You must do the honorable thing and marry our daughter."

Had she been a man, the Gräfin could have been a general. Matteo's eye twitched. "That is why I am here, Gräfin. Even though I was tricked into going to her room and nothing happened." Although, what *had* happened was quite memorable.

Arabella peered about the church. "Is the priest here?"

"Somewhere," Edward muttered. "And sober."

Father Bartolomeo's long snort echoed throughout the church. Edward went to fetch him, and the others clustered in a group a short distance away.

Zdenka stepped to Matteo's side and spoke softly. "We took a roundabout route to get here because my family wishes the wedding to remain as quiet as possible. That's why we're late. Forgive me."

He wanted to tell her it was all right, but he was distracted by the scent of vanilla and the arc of freckles on the bridge of her nose, by her plump lower lip. Her green eyes reflected the flames of the votive candles. Had her dark lashes always brushed her cheeks? Her soft, curly locks accentuated the curve of her cheekbones and gave her the appearance of a delicate baby bird.

No wonder kissing her had been so fascinating. How could this lovely creature have hidden her gender? This alluring woman couldn't possibly be happiest working on a farm.

Zdenka lifted her chin. Her eyes searched his face as they had a thousand times before. As his trusted friend, Zdenko, he had welcomed the direct gaze, which had always made him feel known, relieved, comfortable. But at this moment, he drew back, sensing she recognized things in him he wished to keep secret.

He took a deep breath and reminded himself she had lied to him. Duplicity was her forte, and he would have none of it. This was a marriage of duty and honor. Nothing more. And forever it would remain nothing more.

"How could wearing pants end up like this?" she murmured under her breath, blinking furiously.

He found it disconcerting to glare into her green eyes, shining with unshed tears. "Shall we be done with this business?"

She flinched when he said the word *business*.

"I think you have something for your bride," Edward said with a charming lilt. He pushed a parcel into Matteo's hand.

"Ah yes." Matteo, in turn, thrust the parcel into Zdenka's hand "I bought you this as a wedding gift. Please accept it as a token of my ... my." He cleared his throat. "Anyway ..."

Her eyebrows rose. Gingerly, she took the gift in her gloved hands and pulled away the tissue paper. He'd had to bang on the shop window to procure the gift, but, angry as he was, he had to have something for his bride. He settled on a carved wooden music box with a picture of a rose on the lid, chosen hurriedly so he hadn't taken time to listen to the tune.

"How ... lovely." She turned the music box over, wound the key, and opened the lid. The sweet, cheery music that tinkled out juxtaposed with the bitterness surrounding the wedding.

The tune turned out to be his favorite. It was from Mozart's *Die Zauberflöte, Bei Männer welche Liebe fühlen,* and was all about the joys of married life. It would never again be his favorite tune.

One corner of Zdenka's mouth twisted up in an ironic half-smirk. She clapped the lid closed and handed it to Arabella.

"Shall we?" He winged his arm to her, and she took his elbow.

An unexpected heat traveled to his shoulder, spread across his chest, webbed through him.

"Why do you insist on going through with this?" She pulled him around to face her. "You never wanted a marriage that was strictly a business transaction."

He forced himself to stare over her head so as not to be distracted by the slope of her jawline or the elegance of her neck. He lifted a single eyebrow. "No, madam, I did not. Nor did I ever intend to be taken for a fool."

"I never intended to make a fool of you," she said.

He glowered at her, willing her to stop making him *feel* things.

"What did you intend to happen? You knew Arabella had no intention of marrying me, yet you wrote to me and led me to believe she did." He ticked off his fingers one by one. "Then, you presented yourself as a boy. Next, you lured me to her room with the promise of a farewell kiss and instead ..."

The weight of shock and humiliation slammed into his chest

again. He grimaced. "Well, we both know how that ended, don't we?"

Although much of what had happened was quite pleasant, actually.

Zdenka laid her hand over her heart. "Those were my letters. Those were *my* thoughts and opinions, *my* hopes and dreams. You always said you believed in a woman's right to choose her destiny, but it seems you really don't, do you? If you don't love me, why must you take my life from me as payment for your honor?"

"It seems we must both make accommodations to the situation *you* have put us in. I trusted you, and you betrayed that trust. Was entrapment your aim all along?"

She tore the veil from her head and flung it on the ground. "How vain to think I would entrap *you*. I don't need you, and you don't want me. Let us end this farce and part as sworn enemies."

♫

Matteo straightened his spine like the soldier he was. Zdenka had never seen him so severe, so militaristic. It made her blood run cold to think she had to marry such a hard, angry man. Surely something would stop this madness.

He offered her his arm, but she held her ground, staring at him. The pulse on his neck ticked rhythmically. The heat of his body threw her mind back to the bedroom and the tingling of skin to skin. She tried to hold on to the anger, but the recollection of his fingertips grazing her collarbone drove her thoughts into a fog. She wanted to throw herself on his mercy, plead his forgiveness, and beg him to let her go. If only he'd take her in his arms and bury his face against her neck. If only he'd press his lips to her ear, swear his eternal faith, confess how much he needed and wanted her, it would be all right.

But she did not. And he did not.

She scooped the veil from the floor and followed him. Despite feeling as though a gravestone sat atop her chest, she would not, absolutely would not, cry.

"Everybody here now?" The rotund priest asked, as he waddled down the aisle towards them, rubbing his hands together. "Shall we perform the ceremony? Mass begins in fifteen minutes. We must hurry it up." He gave a little clap as if to speed them along like a flock of chickens.

Matteo's answer was brisk. "We're ready."

With her arm in his iron grip, Matteo strode down the aisle, his long legs outpacing hers so she had to take two quick steps to his one. His every step resounded in the church like a hammer driving nails into her coffin. Her family and Edward followed. It was more like a funeral procession than a wedding.

When they stood before the altar, the truth came to Zdenka with the force of a well-placed boot to the seat of her pants. Or skirt, as it were. She wasn't the iron-willed, independent woman she thought she was.

Neither, it seemed, was Matteo who she thought *he* was. What he really wanted was a docile, mindless, malleable show-piece, not a woman who could manage a farm, make her own decisions, and think for herself.

This marriage was going to destroy every shred of her spirit. Collapsing under the weight of everyone else's expectations was weak and spineless. No woman could be her best when dragged into a marriage of duty and convenience. A loveless marriage was degrading.

Zdenka remembered that this was the church where Franz Schubert had been baptized, the church where he had composed several Masses. The melody to Schubert's plaintive song, 'Death and the Maiden', slithered through Zdenka's mind.

The Maiden:

"It's all over! alas, it's all over now!

Go, savage man of bone!

She stared up at the painting of the *Transfiguration and the Fourteen Helpers*. Would no one help her?

I am still young - go, devoted one!

And do not molest me."

Everything happened around her as though her feet were chained to the spot. Arabella straightened her veil. Mama dabbed her nose with a handkerchief as though she was crying. The priest shuffled nearer. Matteo took her hand in his. How she'd longed for him to hold her hand, but now, his hand felt like a ghoul's grip, dragging her to her death.

Death:

"Give me your hand, you fair and tender form!

I am a friend; I do not come to punish.

The air closed in around her.

Be of good cheer! I am not savage.

You shall sleep gently in my arms.

How could she ever find her way back to herself again? Who would she be as a woman, married against her will to a man who didn't return her love?

He doesn't love me were the last words that crossed her mind before she said, "I do."

CHAPTER 25

After the wedding, Matteo and Zdenka took up residence with Thea, on what was to be on a temporary basis until Matteo found a suitable position. Until he found a job, he would continue his search for Luther and make sure Kurt had whatever he needed. These things were his first priority and would remain so until he felt he'd redeemed his honor.

They kept separate sleeping quarters and there was no wedding night. He hadn't expected one. He'd forced her to marry him, but he had no intention of forcing himself on her. He would not be the sort of man his father was, a man who took his pleasure as it suited him. Women were, after all, entitled to ownership of their own bodies, for God's sake.

When he was at home, Matteo did his best to keep occupied and to steer out of Thea and Zdenka's way. He couldn't help noticing how Thea took to mothering Zdenka. After raising two hellions, clearly Thea was pleased to have a daughter-in-law to dote on, shop for, and show off. He thought perhaps Thea even relished the novelty of Zdenka's previous identity since it gave Thea a good chance to throw convention in the face of the staid

Viennese. There had been no way to keep things quiet, but Zdenka, stalwart that she was, hadn't let it bother her in the least.

He was also secretly grateful to Thea because he hoped Zdenka was less lonely. In time, he expected his wife might grow used to their arrangement, even though he found he could not. Every time he looked at Zdenka, he recalled how their bodies had fit so perfectly together, her fragrance, the soft hush of her breath against his cheek, the springiness of her hair, how he lost himself in her arms.

Zdenka also spent a good deal of time preparing for her sister's wedding, two weeks after theirs. It was a wedding he dreaded attending. Mandryka, unlike him, would be deliriously happy about his nuptials, reminding Matteo his vows had been conducted as a means to keep his name and honor intact. His drunken father in-law would most likely show up drunk and embarrass his family. His mother in-law would narrow her suspicious eyes at him. Guests would recognize Zdenka as Arabella's brother and, by association, him as a fool.

As his concern for Luther mounted, Matteo redoubled his search efforts. Some evenings, Matteo met Father Benedict at St. Stephan's and gave him food, paper, and pen and ink to pass on to Kurt. He searched for other soldiers who might be living in cold, damp hovels in the poorest parts of town, and did what he could to help them. He spent only a few evenings with Edward playing cards, at the opera, or drinking. Most days, he fenced at the Academy or rode in the Prater.

Still, he was lonely without his friend *Zdenko*.

Worst of all, Matteo struggled beneath the black loneliness that had plagued him since returning from the war. It hung about behind his eyes, darkening his view of everything around him. He was perpetually wary of impending catastrophe. A particular shade of red brought on a wash of nausea. The scar on his shoulder tightened and burned. His eye twitched at the most inconvenient times. He woke from a recurring nightmare, drenched in sweat, tangled in his bedsheets. He lost his temper at the smallest provocations, such as when a passing cart splashed water on his pant leg. The clattering of the streets made the tendons in his neck tighten so that his jaw hurt.

Strangely, he had not been so testy or irascible when his friend *Zdenko,* had been at his side. Now, relief came when he sat next to his wife. Then, he noted, the loneliness ebbed, like dust settling after a gentle rain. Her alluring voice, more feminine than before, calmed him. Sometimes, when their hands accidentally touched, muscles and tendons in his forearms relaxed. If he knew he would be seeing her, expectation thrummed in him and he paced about until she arrived. But as before, their coupling would have to be her choice, not his.

When Zdenka engaged in discussions of a political or social nature with Thea or some guest, Matteo watched Zdenka from a distance, curious, freshly intrigued, even charmed at her liveliness, her willingness to speak out, and her quick mind. Her hot skin. Her searching mouth. Her thrusting hips. Her hungry hands.

She had made him lose all control, so the world fell away, their two bodies made more alive by one another's.

But his mind returned to her deception like a dog to a bone. No matter what it cost others, liars always lied. Trust was something they would never share. Just as they would never share love.

CHAPTER 26

The Vienna South Train station was crowded with people waving goodbye to loved ones and porters pushing luggage to waiting trains. Cinders whipped about, smoke chuffed from train stacks, conductors shouted, whistles screeched arrivals and departures.

Zdenka could hardly gather her thoughts as she huddled next to a pillar. In a few minutes, she was to be alone, in Vienna, with her husband, a man who did not love her.

Arabella held her nosegay, her cheeks flushed with excitement. She was starting off on a whole new life. One that didn't include Zdenka.

"Goodbye, my dear," Mama said to Zdenka.

She let herself be embraced, anger fighting with love and devotion, with a sense of abandonment and dedication, to the two people she loved most after Arabella.

Papa said, "I'm sorry ..." He smoothed his mustache with his fingertips. "Things might ... well, I wish ..." he stopped short and finished by patting Zdenka's shoulder. He turned away, red-faced and damp eyed.

Papa helped Mama into the train carriage and climbed in

beside her, quietly bickering about how long they were to live with Arabella and Mandryka. Matteo and Mandryka helped load trunks, valises, and crates onto the train in preparation for the departure to Slavonia.

The past two weeks had been busy with fittings for Arabella's wedding gown, inviting guests, and packing Arabella and Mama and Papa's belongings for the trip. Arabella skipped every few steps when she walked alongside Mandryka. He bent his head to listen to her, and his eyes glowed like a man who had drunk too much champagne. They shared their meals with one another, holding a bite on their own fork and popping it into the other's mouth for a taste. His laugh boomed as Arabella threw her head back, her belly-laugh joining his. They sat together and pretended to read on the sofa in her parent's apartments, which were now much improved thanks to Mandryka's generosity. Dressed as a girl, Zdenka chaperoned, lagging further and further behind to allow them some privacy.

And to save her heart from breaking.

Arabella and Mandryka had everything she wanted with Matteo, but she doubted he would ever forgive her. Witnessing every stolen kiss, each hug, the way the two lovers gazed at one another, made her realize she had lost all she'd hoped to gain by inviting Matteo to her room.

The wedding had been beautiful and solemn, the *Pummerin* bell of St. Stephan's pealing joyfully. Arabella wore a cream satin gown, and big Mandryka looked about to cry when she appeared. Zdenka's heart squeezed, knowing her marriage had been, and would probably remain, a sham.

Like her.

Arabella laid a hand on Zdenka's forearm. "You've been so sad since your marriage. I thought you would be happy. What's the matter?" She handed Zdenka a lace trimmed handkerchief with her monogrammed initials. It had been one of many wedding gifts from Mandryka.

Zdenka didn't want to spoil her sister's wedding day, but she couldn't hide her disappointment at her own marriage, such as it was. "I want what you have with Mandryka. I want Matteo to look at me the way Mandryka looks at you. I want him to love me."

Matteo stood against the wall with his knees locked, his hands behind his back, a stern expression on his desperately handsome face. His narrow-eyed gaze swept up and down the length of the platform, as though he was watching for someone.

"He does look a bit chilly," Arabella said. "Has nothing changed?"

Zdenka shook her head. "I want my friend back. I want to ride, to walk and talk, to laugh with him. I want to attend the opera and have him hold my hand in the dark. To look at me as if I mean something to him." Zdenka slumped against a cold, hard stone pillar.

Cold and hard as Matteo.

Arabella pulled her away from the pillar. "You'll soil your dress." Arabella brushed the back of Zdenka's skirt. "You've been married for several weeks now. Living in the same house. Hasn't he come to realize you're the same now as before?"

"I wish he would. If he'd only give me a chance to prove I'm the same, he might be able to love me. He still blames me for dressing as a boy to help my family. It's as though he thinks that is the sum of my personality. He's forgotten everything he knew about me. He still thinks I'm untrustworthy."

Arabella's eyebrows rose. "Do you blame him?"

Zdenka kicked at a stone. She did have a point.

"Eventually, he'll realize you're the same in trousers as in a bonnet."

With tears streaming down her face, a woman ran alongside

a train, blowing kisses to a man sitting at a window as his train pulled out.

"He doesn't want me." Bitterness bunched in the back of her throat.

"But you want him, yes?" Arabella asked slowly.

Oh, dear God, how she wanted him.

Zdenka couldn't admit even to Arabella how much she wanted him. She recalled how his touch made fireworks burst inside her. How, when she sat by him at dinner, the scent of his cologne made her want to bury her face in the crook of his neck. The way she cried at night for the absence of his weight pressing down the other side of the mattress.

"I know he still feels something for me because I catch him staring at me and his glance sends a shiver through me. But I don't know how to ..." Her cheeks flamed. "To encourage him."

Arabella stared at Mandryka lifting the heavy trunks onto the carriage. There was a look that could only be described as hunger in her sister's eyes.

"I was counting on you telling me what to expect tonight." Arabella's voice was tight with anxiety.

A train whistle blew. Zdenka clenched her hands together, remembering her night with Matteo. How much more she wanted to give him. Wanted of him.

She stared down at her hands and her ears grew hot "I can't tell you. We still haven't become ... man and wife."

Arabella's eyes widened. "Not at all?" Then, a murmur. "Oh, dear."

Overcoming her shame, in a whisper, Zdenka confessed her living arrangements. Then she admitted the worst of it. "I can hear him when he has terrible nightmares. He drinks too much and ... he goes out at night." This last came out as a choked sob or a cough.

"What?" Arabella's brows shot to her hairline.

"He goes out many nights. Alone. He leaves by the back stairs and stays out quite late and sometimes, not always, comes home drunk." Zdenka chewed her lower lip.

"Where does he go?"

Desperation flooded Zdenka as she finally allowed herself to speak of her worst fears. "I ... I don't know. Do you think he has a mistress?"

"Matteo?" Arabella gasped. "It can't be."

"Or maybe he goes to opium dens. Or ..." Zdenka shuddered and swallowed. "To brothels."

Arabella grew as pale as the ivory of her wedding gown. "Why would he ever do that?"

"He doesn't want me."

The corner of Arabella's lip turned up. She looked down the train platform at Matteo standing near the soot-blackened wall. "Have you told him you love him? That you ... want him?"

Zdenka frowned. "He won't speak to me. Maybe he still thinks of me as a boy, and he's not attracted to me."

Arabella laughed. "Have you looked in the mirror? He'd have to be blind to think that. You're lovely. So feminine. Even I'm surprised by your transformation." Arabella leaned closer and whispered conspiratorially, "If he won't talk to you, then you must show him."

"How?"

"Flirt with him. Smile sweetly when you catch his glance. Brush against him. Touch his hand at dinner. Lean close and allow him to smell your perfume. Nuzzle his ear. Straighten his hair or cravat. Look deep into his eyes when he's speaking."

"But what about his sneaking out at night?"

"Don some trousers and follow him and see where he goes. You must know what you're up against." Arabella squeezed Zdenka's forearm. "I know you're stronger than whatever calls him out at night."

Mandryka stood at a short distance and caught Arabella's eye. He nicked his head toward the train, indicating it was time to depart.

Arabella's eyes glowed when she looked at her husband.

Zdenka hugged Arabella's neck. "I'll miss you so much. Please promise you'll write."

Arabella returned the embrace. "Of course, I will. Thank you for everything you've done for me. I wouldn't be so happily married if it hadn't been for you."

With those words, Zdenka knew her sister forgave her for nearly ruining her future. A weight of guilt dropped from her shoulders.

Mandryka handed Arabella into the train carriage and the conductor slammed the door behind them. Arabella lowered the window and leaned out and motioned Zdenka closer.

"Remember. Men fight wars with weapons. Women fight with our minds and our hearts." She tossed Zdenka her nosegay. "To battle!"

CHAPTER 27

The morning after Arabella's wedding, Matteo, Thea, and Prince Dimitry sat at the dining table, reading the morning newspaper, *Die Zeitung,* and finishing their breakfast.

Prince Dimitry scowled at the newspaper. "There's been another attack by one of the soldiers living in the Prater and the Wienerwald. They're trying to clear them out."

"Oh dear," Thea murmured, glancing at Matteo. "And they're blaming the soldiers for the escalation in petty thievery sweeping the city."

Several nights ago, Matteo had been to this same lair, taking food, clothing, and blankets, and asking about Luther, but no one knew anything. "Where did they take them? Did they give their names?"

"To the soldier's hospital, the *Allegemeines Krankenhaus.* There are no names." The Prince lowered his paper and stared at Matteo.

Matteo turned his cup around in the saucer. He would ask at the hospital this afternoon if Luther was among the men taken prisoner. "They aren't dangerous. They're confused. Battle-shocked. They simply cannot readjust to coming home. War ruins some men. Others escape with only a few scratches."

"Can't these men return to their families?" Thea asked.

"Some of them have no families. No where else to go. They've fought a losing battle and saved Vienna but are now tossed aside like table scraps. The Emperor owes these soldiers. The whole of Vienna owes them." His head pounded like the drummer boy rat-a-tat-tatting on his scalp. He would see to it that something was done for them, even if he had to do it himself. Matteo softened his tone. "After what they've been through, they need care. A chance to heal."

Zdenka sauntered into the breakfast room wearing brown checked wool trousers that snugly outlined her derriere and showed slender, impossibly curvaceous legs. Beneath her vest was a cream silk blouse with a ruffled neckline. Her waistcoat flowed over her breasts, nipping in to an un-cinched yet narrow waist.

Matteo coughed and blew tea out his nose.

"*Mein Gott!*" the Prince exclaimed.

Zdenka had a gentleman's coat slung over her shoulder. She wore riding boots, and she carried a cap to hide her lush cloud of her ginger curls.

Curls perfect for running his hands through.

Her impish grin dared him to object.

He'd seen her in pants before, of course, but never looking so damned ravishing. Before, she'd dressed to hide her feminine curves, but this outfit had the opposite effect.

He sopped up the tea and wiped his face, trying to hide his stunned reaction.

Aunt Thea exchanged a sly smile with the Prince. "Ah, good morning, my dear," she said to Zdenka. "Those trousers were an excellent choice. I quite like the color on you."

"Quite fetching." Prince Dimitry refolded his copy of *Die*

Zeitung and laid it beside his plate. "I think I might order a pair of those trousers for myself."

"Don't bother, my dear," Thea chuckled. "They won't have the same effect on you."

"Good morning, everyone," Zdenka said, and the whole room seemed to brighten.

Matteo rose and held his wife's chair.

"Thank you." Enchanting green eyes glanced up at him from beneath long, dark lashes.

Her scent of vanilla jolted him back to the night in her bedroom. A shock of need ran through him.

Addle-minded, Matteo resumed his seat. It took him a moment to formulate a sentence. "You're going riding?"

"Yes, in the Prater. Prince Dimitry lent me his horse, Schwartzkönig." She lifted her teacup to her plush lower lip and sipped.

"The stallion?" Matteo said, a sense of protectiveness and concern flaring in him. He couldn't let her get hurt like everyone else he'd ever been close to. They were mere acquaintances now, but still, as her husband, he owed it to her to protect her.

He scowled at Prince Dimitry. "Why would you allow her to ride Schwartzkönig? He's unreliable."

Thea answered for her lover in a reproving tone. "And why not? She's a grown woman. She knows what she can do."

Prince Dimitry glanced up from his newspaper, raised his eyebrows, and cocked his head towards Thea as if to say *she's got the last word.*

Matteo said to Zdenka, "He's nearly seventeen hands, and a *Kisber Felver.* A lively and spirited breed. Perhaps you should ride Reinhold. He's a *Trakehner* breed, so he's a bit smaller, and he's been through battle. Very steady should anything startling arise."

She said, "I rode Kessler from the time I was twelve, and he was a seventeen-hand stallion. I like Schwartzkönig. I can handle him."

Had she always been this overconfident? He was concerned for her, and that irritated him. He wanted to remain distant, but her presence these weeks was slowly undoing him. One reason he drank so much: to deaden any feelings she stirred in him.

"There have been reports of attacks in the Prater. It's not safe to ride alone, even dressed in pants," Matteo said, aware he was becoming growly.

She laid a hand on his arm.

Hairs on the back of his neck prickled.

"If you're worried, perhaps you'd like to come along." She took several lumps of sugar from the sugar bowl and slipped them into her pocket. "Remember how much fun we used to have riding together?"

She was lovely. Charming. Alluring. Well-endowed. Luscious. He wanted to cup her soft, round, delectable bum in his hands the way he had the night in her bedroom.

The night she had revealed herself to be a girl, not his pal, and not Arabella, but Zdenka.

"Yes," he found himself agreeing. "I can keep an eye on you and make sure nothing happens to you."

"I would like that." She ate her breakfast with the gusto of a farmer. He liked that about her. No picking and poking at her food. She ate like he remembered her making love, hungrily and without restraint. It had been thrilling, he had to admit.

Thea hid her smile behind her teacup, but the crinkle lines at the corners of her eyes betrayed her.

The Prince chuckled behind the newspaper lifted high in front of his face.

Zdenka froze, her teacup in mid-air. Matteo followed her gaze. She stared at the back page of the Prince's newspaper at an article about a man known only as 'The Argentinean.'

Her eyes moved from side to side as she read the article. The Argentinean had been accused of pulling a knife on a man at Dommayer's, a notorious casino with food, music, and dancing, located in the district of Hietzing.

Zdenka's face was white, her lips a straight stripe of pink. Two red spots appeared on her cheeks. Oddly, he found that he wanted to be the one to comfort her. It tore at him to see how shattered she was at the loss of her farm to 'The Argentinean.'

"The man who won the deed to Friedenheim?" Matteo asked her quietly.

"He must be. Not many Argentineans in Vienna." She stared at the paper then narrowed her eyes and jutted her chin.

Zdenka laid her napkin beside her full plate. "I'm ready to ride. Are you?"

"But you're not done."

"I've lost my appetite." She pushed back her chair and strode from the room.

♫

Zdenka and Matteo strolled into the stables. Immediately, she was overcome with homesickness for her barns on the farm. The smell of hay dust, the sun beaming in the open door, and the warm, pungent odor of the horses transported her back to Friedenheim, a world away from the crowded, noisy streets and the rigid social expectations of Vienna.

A pigeon cooed overhead in the hand-hewn roof timbers. Her boot heels made a scraping noise on the cobblestone floor. Polka, the horse she'd ridden last week, munched his oats in the first of six stalls. Thea's matched bays occupied the next two stalls. Zdenka inhaled the scents of leather, brass polish, and oats. Harnesses, saddles, and bridles hung on the walls, and boxes held grooming brushes.

The two stable boys, Fritz and Albert nodded politely to her. Having already seen her several times in her trousers, they were no longer surprised to see her in them today.

The horses were saddled and ready. Matteo's mount, Reinhold, a bay with a white mane and tail and white socks, was a fine horse. Steady and handsome, he was still modest compared to the gigantic *Kisber Felver*, Schwartzkönig, who held the allure of a challenge.

Schwartzkönig's nostrils flared, and he snorted.

Matteo frowned at her.

She said, "Last week, I rode Polka here. When I came back, I curried and groomed him and afterwards, I did the same for Schwartzkönig. He knows me."

"Give him to me," Matteo commanded the stable boy.

The boy stepped back, and Matteo took hold of the bridle.

Schwartzkönig jerked his head at the bridle and shied sideways.

"For the love of God, Zdenka. Please don't ride this horse. You could get hurt." Matteo's brows drew together.

His concern for her safety reassured her that, somewhere in his angry heart, he still felt something for her. This gave her hope that her plan would have the desired effect.

She had not known when she might bring the plan about, but everything fell into place today. Last week, she had discovered a secluded spot in the Prater. This was where she intended to seduce her husband in an amorous ambush.

She laid a hand on Matteo's powerful fencing arm. The tendon along his upper forearm jumped. Trying not to sound arrogant, she said, "It's all right. I know what I'm doing."

At her touch, his face softened, but there was an old, unidentifiable fear in his eyes.

She produced two sugar cubes from her pocket and held them in her palm. The horse snuffled her hand and picked up the lumps between his soft furry lips. She caressed Schwartzkönig's nose and spoke softly to him. In response, the stallion rubbed his big head against her cheek.

"She's a natural with this great devil of a horse," Albert said admiringly.

Matteo swiveled around and glared at the boy.

Albert's face looked like it was on fire, and he took a few steps backwards.

Matteo turned back to her. "Please, Zdenka," he pleaded in a low voice.

"I'll be fine." She held out her hand to Matteo for help stepping up on the mounting block. He obliged and her breast brushed lightly against his solid upper arm. He drew a hand down her leg as he settled her boot into the stirrup. His touch sent waves of heat through her.

She had to find a way to get Friedenheim back. She had to come up with a plan to gamble against the Argentinean. At Friedenheim, Matteo could rest and forget what he'd experienced in the war. He would recognize how resourceful and clever she was, see to what lengths she was willing to go to help him. He would see how much she loved him.

In return, he would love her forever.

CHAPTER 28

Matteo and Zdenka entered the Prater at the Stern, so called because seven of Vienna's streets converged into the shape of a star. From there, the *Hauptalleé*, or Main Street, ran into the deepest parts of the park. Once the Imperial hunting grounds, the Prater had been turned into a public park. All of Vienna enjoyed the wide carriage lanes, lush meadows, skating ponds, thick forests, and riding paths.

Matteo rode behind Zdenka, hypnotized by the way her perfect behind swayed in the saddle. How he would love to cup her lovely arse in his palms again. In the sunlight, Zdenka's hair was even more ginger. Her creamy skin and apricot-tinted cheekbones glowed with exertion.

"Let's ride down the *Hauptalleé*," she said. "The chestnut trees are in bloom."

He nodded in response and followed her. She rode tall in the saddle, ignoring stares and pinched looks. Her confidence made him proud.

He'd always wanted a woman like his Aunt Thea. How many women would have dressed as a gentleman to help their sister?

Was Zdenka the same person now as when she wore pants? It had been easy to talk to her when *she* was *he*. Men and women were so different; and aside from Thea, he had never met a woman as independent and forward-thinking as Zdenka. How would they form a relationship now?

There was no need of a relationship in any sense. This was a marriage of honor, not love. Not even lust. Merely to redeem his family name. To do what was right.

Even if she was as luscious as chocolate-covered cherry.

The Prater was filled with other couples riding, families strolling, nannies pushing prams, children running, old people sitting on benches, and nurses pushing soldiers in wheelchairs. The chestnut trees gave off a sweet aroma and sprinkled petals like spring snow.

A way down the *Hauptalleé*, they arrived at the busy outdoor cafes and stalls selling spiced wine, cookies, and warm buns. The aroma of freshly baked gingerbread wafted from stalls of the cookie-sellers.

Zdenka closed her eyes and inhaled deeply. "Oh, a *lebzelter*," she said on softly sensual sigh.

His mouth watered at the possibility of tasting her plush lower lip.

"Let's stop, and I'll buy you a gingerbread," he said.

They dismounted, and he bought her the freshest, biggest *lebzelter* he could find. When she held the cookie to his mouth to take a bite, he placed his hands over hers.

It was as if a cinder had singed his fingertips.

She looked up from beneath thick lashes. "I love gingerbread."

"Really? I never knew that about you." He handed her the cookie. "I thought I knew my friend, Zdenko, fairly well, but my wife continues to surprise."

"Every word I ever said, what I wrote, every feeling, memory, dream, hope, was me."

"And how am I to trust that is true?"

"I held nothing back." She handed him the cookie. "You, on the other hand, won't tell me what happened in the war that makes you drink so much, that makes you startle so easily and get angry."

"Men don't tell women those sorts of things, just as women have secrets they only divulge to their women friends." He took a bite of cookie and tossed a bit to a squirrel scampering nearby.

No one talked about the war and neither would he. Especially not to her.

She said, "I miss talking to you. Hearing what you have to say. Your ideas and hopes. Isn't it me who should be wary of you not being truthful?"

The gingerbread in his mouth tasted like tree bark. He tossed the rest of the cookie to the squirrels.

She stared at him amidst the chaos of the park, the noisy families, the carriages trundling past, waiting for an answer. When he didn't speak, she sighed and said, "Let's go on."

Leading their horses, they strolled down the *Hauptallée* until they came to a footpath leading across a meadow. She paused and bent to smell a wild, purple flower.

Her movements were feminine but free. Her mind, her boldness, her ability to toss convention, drew him inexorably like a bee to the throat of a nectar-filled bloom.

He licked his lips reflexively, recalling the night in her bedroom when he had tasted her nectar. He wanted to clutch her hair in his fists, run his tongue along her curves, cup her breasts. What did she look like out of her well-fitting clothes, her mass of hair spread across a white pillow?

His cock stirred.

This was not the time to admire the swell of her breasts and breadth of her hips. He still had to find Luther and make sure Kurt's hand continued to heal. Matteo had to find him work. And there were so many other soldiers who needed help. He couldn't fathom a way to reach them all.

She rose and gazed at him. "What are you staring at?"

"A most beautiful woman." He pretended to straighten the bow of her silk blouse and let his hand drift downwards to slowly brush his knuckles against the top of her breasts.

With the same boldness she had shown that night in her darkened bedroom, she took his hand and slipped it into her jacket, cupping her hand over his so he held her breast. She inhaled sharply. Her eyes closed, and she bit her lower lip. For a moment, there in the open meadow, they shared a moment of promise.

Two screeching children ran by. Her eyes flew open and she turned away, two bright pink circles on her cheekbones. She inhaled deeply as she watched the children race away across the meadow.

"Let's ride again. I have something I want to show you." Her smile held a hint of wickedness.

"I can't wait to see it." He interlocked his hands and boosted her into the saddle. Her thigh muscles flexed when she swung her leg over. Those thighs locked around his waist would be delightful.

"I'm getting quite used to the idea of you being a woman." How was it, that around her, he felt both heavy with lust and light as a winged bird?

"Don't get the idea that I'm some weak woman who needs to be rescued." Her eyes flashed, and she jutted her chin.

He dropped his hand. "Not at all." He mounted Reinhold and said, "Lead on, *mein General*."

Without warning, she dug her heels into Schwartzkönig's

flanks and shot across the meadow. The horse's long strides ate up the earth as if he were flying.

His chest tightened. She shouldn't ride so fast. The horse was unpredictable. She'd never jumped him. What if she wanted to stop and the horse wouldn't heed the reins? He ground his heels into Reinhold's flanks and raced after her.

Zdenka raced over a hillock, up a long incline, leapt a stream and, a bit further on, a hedgerow. His heart clawed into his throat, as he tried to keep up with her. If only she'd have let him ride ahead to make sure everything was safe.

Reinhold strained to keep up. Matteo stood in the stirrups and leaned forward. At a copse of trees, she pulled up and slowed Schwartzkönig to a walk. Matteo caught up with her.

"Someday, I'm going to buy a horse just like this one." Her eyes glowed with excitement.

"Over my dead body."

Her eyebrows shot to her hairline.

"How can you be so reckless as to ride terrain you don't know? You could have been thrown or lamed the horse." He knew he sounded angry, but really, he was afraid for her.

She responded in a voice as cross as his own. "What makes you think I've never ridden here before?" Snapping the reins, she rode off at a trot.

Left without an alternative, Matteo rode after her.

Soon, she left the narrow path. He followed as she ducked beneath tree branches and navigated between close-growing trees, around fallen branches and rocky outcroppings. The density of the woods and unfamiliar terrain made the hair on the back of his neck prickle. Thoughts of lust evaporated as his vigilance kicked on. "Where are you taking us?"

"You'll see. Trust me," she called over her shoulder.

Not bloody likely.

When there wasn't even a hint of the footpath, she halted and dismounted. "We have to continue on foot from here."

He followed on foot as she kicked through underbrush and held branches out of the way. Schwartzkönig shied, but she spoke low to him and pulled him along. The dense woods created a shadowy world that smelled of moss, pines, and damp foliage. Sun peaked through the silver-gray branches. Snatches of birdsong accompanied them. Deeper and deeper they trudged into the forest, and the air became cool and dank.

"It's as if we're in some primeval forest," he marveled.

Something rustled in the underbrush.

Matteo whirled then silently cursed his weakness.

"Don't worry," she said, gently. "We're far away from everyone. No one will bother us here."

His chest relaxed and he found himself able to breathe again.

She pushed her way through a thicket of bushes. Before them was a lush meadow about the size of the fencing ring at the Military Academy. Pines ringed the perimeter and wildflowers in blue, red, and yellow speckled the bright green grass.

For a moment, all Matteo could do was stand and gaze. The last time he'd seen a meadow, it had been littered with bodies.

She gazed up at him and took his hand in hers. "Isn't it magical?"

He nodded. "I've never seen this, and I thought I knew the entire park."

On the far side of the meadow, a stone outcrop jutted high above the treetops.

He tensed. Just like the stone wall at Königgratz. Muscles in his upper arms tightened. Instinctively, he reached for the sword he wore at his belt, but it wasn't there. His alertness spiked. His back went rigid. Stepping protectively in front of her, he scanned the trees, looking for signs of Prussian attackers.

"Back up, slowly. Do exactly as I say, and we'll be all right," he said, keeping his voice low and steady so as not to alarm her.

From behind him, she laid a hand on his shoulder. "Take a deep breath. It's all right. I'm here." She turned him to face her. "Look at me."

Her gentle voice tripped a release valve inside him. Tension flowed out like the poison that it was. To regain his equilibrium, he focused on the details of her face, the tiny dip above her upper lip, the freckles dusting her straight nose, the pale hairs of her eyebrows.

She took his face in her two hands, drew him to her and kissed the scar at his temple.

His breath steadied, and he managed a half-smile.

What a fool he was, thinking *she* was the one needing care when she could turn his mood from wary to want in a heartbeat.

"Come on. There's more." She hummed the Mozart song about husbands and wives and how happy they made one another. Everything here was so beautiful and peaceful, he almost believed the sentiments of the song.

Hand in hand, leading the horses, they waded through the spiky grass to the far side of the meadow. A spring burbled from a fissure in the rock wall and created a pond where glints of sunlight sparkled on the water's surface. A hedge of wild rose bushes, laden with blossoms, encircled the pond and perfumed the air.

"The water is so clear you can see the bottom." Her lips curved into an entrancing smile.

"It seems you've found your own garden of Eden," he managed.

She bent to sniff the roses. Straightening, she said, "These were my grandmother's favorite roses. They're called *Mein Liebling*.

My beloved.

He plucked a rose and poked it behind her ear.

She said, "Thank you. I'll take it home and put it in my music box."

In turn, she chose a fat blossom and tucked it into his buttonhole. "You didn't have one at our wedding."

Tiny lines appeared at the corners of her eyes, and he wondered if they indicated the pain at his insisting on their marriage.

He determined, at that moment, to erase any regrets she harbored.

"We can tie our horses here." She tied Schwartzkönig to a tree. The stallion bowed his sleek, black head and drank from the pond.

He looped Reinhold's reins over a low branch.

When Matteo turned back to her, she had unbuttoned her jacket and dropped it onto a pile of pine needles. The bow at the neck of her silk blouse made a slick sound as she untied it. She thumbed open several of the top buttons on her blouse to reveal a tissue-thin chemise and the tops of her creamy breasts.

His breath caught at the sight of her skin, delicate as a rose petal.

Her lips were parted, her eyes daring with invitation.

"So, this is why you brought me here," he said, delighted he'd come along for the ride.

CHAPTER 29

With the tops of her breasts bared, Zdenka held her breath, waiting to see how Matteo would react. She kept her eyes riveted to his. Her desire for him had jammed up inside of her these past weeks, being near to him.

But did he want her?

"Let me help you with that," he murmured, with a low seductive laugh as he slipped her blouse from her shoulders and let it flutter to the ground.

That was the answer she sought. Despite her muddled mistakes, her necessary deceptions, her independent ways, he still wanted her.

Lines at the corners of his eyes tightened. His nostrils flared, and his pupils dilated. The way his eyes lingered over every inch of her body made her nervous. But she was also filled with desire. The air between then crackled like ice melting in the spring thaw.

"One good turn deserves another." He licked his lips and pressed them together. In a moment, he'd shed his jacket and shirt and stood bare-chested before her.

She wanted to comb her fingers through the dusting of hair on his chest, but she didn't know if it would please him. She had expected Arabella to tell her how to go about love making. What if she bumbled about and he laughed at her? What if she made a mistake and he thought her distasteful? Would it hurt or would he be rough? Of course, on the farm, she'd seen animals go about procreating. With humans, there had to be more to lovemaking. He would know what to do and show her. How many women had been in his arms before her? She didn't feel jealous, but she wondered if she would be their equal.

He took her hand and drew her to him. Her breasts pressed against his hard, sculpted chest. His erection pressed against her abdomen. She tingled from head to toe. He was so vast, so solid. Bare-chested, he seemed vulnerable and yet invincible, like an ancient warrior lord come to conquer.

He kissed her palm, up the length of her arm to the soft spot at her elbow, and murmured, "How delicious you are. I can't wait to taste every inch of you."

Goosebumps rose on her arms.

With one arm around her waist, he brushed his thumb against her lower lip. She took his thumb into the wet warmth of her mouth and sucked. She was mad with excitement at the prospect of his being inside her, of their bodies finally merging as one.

His lips brushed hers, lightly at first, then with more insistence. She tasted the gingerbread and a hint of sugar on his lips. His tongue darted and flickered inside her mouth, increasing rather than satisfying her want. He pulled back, and she wasn't sure she could remain standing without support. Fire raced through her entire body, from her toes to her scalp.

He spread their jackets atop the grass. "It's not the softest of beds, but I believe it will do."

"It is a bed fit for a queen," she said and lay down. They both doffed their boots into a heap.

Hunger burning in his eyes set her blood to thrumming. With infinite gentleness, he caressed her shoulders, the line of her jaw. She looped her arms around his neck and tangled her fingers in his hair.

"Turn around," he said.

She did as he asked, and he worked the pins from her hair. The roots of her hair tingled as he combed out her curls with his fingers. He lifted her hair and kissed the nape of her neck. Any attempt on her part to get control over her rampaging blood was useless.

He tucked a few wild curls behind her ear and explored the outer shell with the tip of his tongue. She leaned her head back against him. The least brush of his chest against her bare back sent a hot shiver up her spine.

Taking her sensitive lobe in his mouth, he sucked and nibbled. Warmth swelled in her pelvis as husky, wordless murmurs rose from the back of her throat.

Still kneeling behind her, he encircled her waist with one strong arm. He picked a bachelor button and stroked the bloom down the front of her neck. She purred and moaned as he slipped his other hand into the top of her chemise, squeezing her nipples, until she couldn't hold still any longer.

"I want to touch you," she rasped. As she pivoted to face him, pine needles crushed beneath her knees released an earthy fragrance. Sun made his skin glisten as her hands roamed his chest, his broad shoulders, his iron arms.

"You are magnificent. Even more than I dreamed," she whispered. Her fingers trailed over his back and encountered his scar, which she had noticed the day in the fencing hall.

"How did you get this?" She caressed the scar's length.

His eyes darkened. He took her hand and kissed each fingertip. "That is best left in the past, as are our distrust and resentments."

Did he not trust her to tell her the truth? Why was he withholding a secret from her?

His eyes lingered on her breasts, visible through her sheer, lacy chemise. "How could I have wasted so much time missing my friend Zdenko, when you were right under my nose?"

"Can you forgive me for masquerading as a boy?" she asked.

He put a finger to her lips. "Let's not talk of that now. There are more important considerations."

She had a moment's hesitation. Did he forgive her? Was he simply satisfying his physical desires? Would he go back to being angry and cold when this was over? She didn't think she could stand that.

Sensing her pause, he moved her down on her back and laid next to her. His erection prodded her hip, at once thrilling and dangerous.

He cupped one breast and squeezed an already-hard nipple between thumb and forefinger until her breath went ragged.

"To think you were hiding these lovelies beneath a binding," he whispered.

Through her chemise, he alternated sucking one nipple then the other. Even as the roughness of the wet lace made her nipples raw and more sensitive, she wanted more. The breeze blew across her nipples. A spark shot from her breasts to the dampness between her legs.

Seeking more sensation, she tugged the ribbon and opened the top of her camisole so that he might have full access to her breasts. With his tongue, he circled and flicked each nipple until she scratched and clutched at the coats upon which she lay.

"I ... I can't ... I must," she gasped. Panting, she rolled away from him and saw his bulge.

She made to unzip his trousers, but the zipper caught the fabric. She pulled and worked at it for what seemed an eternity.

"Pants seem to be in the way of everything between us," she said.

He laughed.

At last, the zipper gave way. She tugged off his trousers and his small clothes, exposing him. His penis stood strong, its pink head glistening, its veins tracing down his shaft into a pouf of dark hair.

Robins winged from branch to branch. The spring burbled from the rock into the pond. Here in nature's temple, they were doing what nature intended. He lay before her, naked, like Adam in the beginning of the world.

The world of their true marriage.

Taking his penis in her hand, she stroked up and down. She marveled at how such a hard part of the body could be so silky.

His eyes closed and he sucked air between his teeth. He put his hand over hers and guided her movements. She let him direct her, lightening the pressure up, increasing pressure down.

Just when something seemed about to happen, he put his hand over hers and made her stop. In a voice gravelly with lust, he said, "If you're not careful, I'll come, my beauty. I want to taste you first."

"What does that mean?" she said.

He grinned. "You will see soon enough."

He drew her back down onto the coats and with gentle pressure on her shoulder, urged her onto her back. "If I do anything you don't like, tell me and I'll stop, all right?" His warm smile reassured her that whatever he did, she would enjoy.

"I can't imagine anything you could do that would make me stop," she said, intoxicated by his bare skin, his touch, the raw, male scent of him.

He unbuttoned and unzipped her trousers, this time,

without a hitch. "What a revelation you are, without your trousers."

She laughed as he wriggled her pants off and tossed them in the heap with his.

As he kissed down her belly until he reached the secret place between her legs, his sure strong hands cupped her behind. His tongue found her outer lips and licked until they were swollen and hot. She raised her head to watch him, but when his tongue flicked the nub of her sex, she could do nothing but throw her head back and close her eyes, giving in to a sense of floating and plunging all at once.

His tongue fluttered like the wings of a hummingbird, fast and light, but insistent, urging her toward some distant sun. She pushed up against his mouth, her body arching upwards. Stars sparkled on her skin and nothing existed but his dark eyes watching from between her legs. She hissed his name and moaned wild words that had never before crossed her lips.

A winding up, a tautening between her legs, something irreversible built in her. Then, her head snapped back, her legs quivered, and falling stars cartwheeled through her mind. Her small, shrill scream ripped the air as wave after wave quaked her body. Her hips bucked, but Matteo kept on and she took from him greedily. Twice more, she experienced the same building, the rush of release, until she lay exhausted, panting and amazed.

She opened her eyes to find him smiling in a way that was unfamiliar—one of intense self-satisfaction. She wrapped her arms around his neck and drew him down on top of her.

His erection prodded between her legs, softly, an inch in, then out, then a little deeper, then withdrawing.

"Is this all right?" he asked with a tenderness of which she never thought him capable.

"No, I want it. All of you."

"Slowly, my beauty. I don't want to hurt you."

Inside her body, she sensed the resistance that made him so careful. She breathed deeply and relaxed her body to receive him. He pushed into her, and was about to pull out again, but she couldn't bear not having him, filling her up, so she wrapped her legs about his waist and pulled him into her. With a hard thrust, the barrier gave way with a short, sharp pain. Then he was inside her, thrusting, pushing, filling her.

Never had she felt more alive, more thrilled than this moment. He closed his eyes and thrust into her, experiencing the satisfaction of her longstanding craving for his body.

He panted through parted lips. His movements increased in depth and speed, until, with a great gust of breath, he swore. His penis throbbed inside her, and he thrust once, twice more, then lay down quietly on top of her. His heart pounded against hers, his breath was hot against her temple. He rolled off her, smiled, and pushed the hair out of her face.

"That was," she searched for a word, but none seemed expansive, deep, or colorful enough. She settled on, "Perfect."

"It was, wasn't it?" He kissed her forehead. "You are perfect, in trousers and most definitely, out of them."

Zdenka felt replete, filled with a new kind of vibrating energy. His desire made her the woman she had always been without changing who she really was. She was changed, and yet, more her than ever. For loving him, she was better. Whole.

If this was what happened when women married, she could see why it was such a venerable institution.

♫

Out of the corner of his eye, Matteo watched Zdenka riding beside him. Her nectar was still on his lips, her scent in his nostrils. Her skin had been gloriously satiny, unlike the reins now chafing his palms. He smiled at how she had greedily arched to his mouth. She was no shrinking violet.

He was awake with an aliveness he hadn't experienced in ages. The tight band of scar on his shoulder seemed to loosen, and a calm serenity enveloped him. Overhead, the sky was so blue as to seem an imitation. Sun-shot clouds scudded overhead. Meadow grass eddied around the horse's legs. Breezes danced among the new leaves. How had he missed the world's beauty until now?

The world wasn't beautiful. Not really. It was the afterglow. It would pass. This marriage was about honor, nothing else. It certainly wasn't about trust and love.

He tightened his hold on the reins. How could he have been so idiotic as to let things get so out of hand?

He'd gotten her to marry him to save his honor, and never considered the fact that he might one day actually *love* her. His honor demanded that he make amends to Luther and Kurt after having abandoned them on the battlefield. Once that was done, he would feel worthy of Zdenka's love and respect. Letting her love him, returning her love, meant lying to her. She didn't know everything about him. If she did, she would push him away in disgust.

The thought of her rejection cut him like a knife and focused his thoughts on the present.

A small animal startled Schwartzkönig. The massive stallion sidestepped off the path.

Matteo's chest clinched.

Zdenka spoke quietly and redirected the horse. Schwartzkönig cantered back to the path.

Matteo's breathing slowed. He needn't have worried about Zdenka's ability to handle the horse.

Zdenka turned to him and, with a mischievous smile, said, "Race you to the Kaiser Josef's Bridge."

Without waiting for his answer, she kicked her heels into the horse's flanks and shot ahead.

His belly twisted and gripped the reins tighter. This morning, Prince Dimitry had read in *Die Zeitung* about the homeless soldiers in the Prater. It wasn't safe for a woman to be alone in the Prater. Not even one as bold as Zdenka.

"Let's stick to the *Gürtel* Road," he shouted after her.

But she was already out of earshot. Hellbent to run, Schwartzkönig's legs took great earth-gulping strides.

Matteo whipped Reinhold to a run, but Zdenka was far ahead.

The Kaiser Josef's bridge was in sight. Something like a pile of rags lay in the middle of the bridge. Zdenka glanced back over her shoulder with a devilish grin. She didn't seem to see the rags.

"Wait!" he called, but she urged her horse on.

The pile shifted. Among the refuse stood a man. A tattered soldier's coat. In the colors of Matteo's regiment.

Matteo loosened Reinhold's reins and urged him on.

Zdenka's jacket flapped behind her as she gained speed.

The man shouted curses, waved his arms and blocked her path.

Schwartzkönig's hooves thundered onto the wooden bridge.

She looked back at Matteo; terror etched on her face.

She couldn't stop.

Matteo shouted, but the wind carried his voice away. Why didn't she pull the horse up?

The man swung a club through the air in a great arc.

With a scream, Schwartzkönig reared on his hind legs, his powerful front legs pawing the air.

Matteo's blood froze.

CHAPTER 30

Terror, cold and sharp as a sword edge, pierced Matteo. He dug his heels into his mount, but Zdenka was so far ahead of him he would never reach her in time.

"Leave her alone!" Matteo shouted, but the vagabond didn't react to him.

Schwartzkönig's hooves crashed down on the attacker, knocking him down. The attacker scrabbled away and dropped the lethal club. The horse reared again and again.

Why had Matteo let her ride the damned horse?

Zdenka reined in Schwartzkönig to keep the horse from stomping the demented man, but he'd gotten ahold of the bridle. The horse screamed and jerked his head against the stranger holding his bridle.

Matteo bellowed, "If you her touch her, I'll kill you!"

Schwartzkönig bucked. Zdenka catapulted through the air.

Fury fired in Matteo's blood.

The man scrabbled to retrieve his club and ran at Zdenka.

"Stop it, you fool," Matteo shouted as he leapt off his horse and threw himself at the man, heedless of the swinging club.

"Look out!" Zdenka screamed.

The club brushed the hairs on Matteo's head. He dove for the attacker's knees and knocked him off his trajectory. The man landed on his back with a grunt. Matteo wrenched the club from his grasp and straddled the wretch's chest. The man's eyes were wild as he twisted and writhed, but he seemed weak and more bluster than strength.

With a lion's roar, Matteo cocked his fist back.

The man's tortured eyes locked with Matteo's. His fist froze in mid-air. Leaning forward, Matteo peered at the man pinned beneath him.

It couldn't be.

Luther.

Though dirty, reeking, disheveled, and bloody, Matteo recognized the attacker. Guilt exploded through him with the force of a cannon blast. After all this time searching for his comrade, here he was, a miserable wreck of a man, living in the Prater.

Zdenka struggled to her feet and dusted herself off. She appeared shaken but only slightly bumped up. If she was hurt, he didn't know if he could restrain himself from killing Luther.

Even though it was his fault Luther had lost his mind.

Matteo called to Zdenka, "Are you all right?"

She stretched her legs and arms. "Nothing broken. What about you?"

"Not a scratch."

Rubbing her hip, Zdenka limped over to Matteo. "He must be one of the soldiers Prince Dimitry read about in the paper this morning."

Luther squirmed.

"Stop fighting, Luther," Matteo warned.

Luther stilled and squinted up at Matteo.

"Lieutenant ...?" Luther croaked.

"You know him?" she asked, keeping her distance from her would-be-attacker.

"Yes. His name is Luther Klesper," Matteo choked back the guilt and rage crashing against one another in his mind. "He's from my regiment."

It was the truth. Just not the part that would make her despise him.

Tattered remnants of his Fifth Regiment uniform hung on Luther's bone-thin frame. His hair was filthy, matted, and over-long. A blood-soaked bandage had slipped from his forehead to reveal a gash oozing pus. Bits of leaves and sticks clung to his scraggly beard. To top all, he smelled like a privy.

Luther's eyes, vacant as a dying animal's, sent a chill through Matteo. Sometimes, eyes just as vacant looked back at him from his own mirror.

Luther's breath was labored, and his pale face had turned a sickly shade of scarlet.

Zdenka tapped Matteo on the shoulder. "He'll have survived Königgratz only to die from you squeezing the breath out of him. Let him up. He doesn't have the club anymore. Without it, he's harmless." She crouched next to Luther. "You must be scared."

Luther blinked mutely, his lips moving silently.

Alert to further violence, Matteo rolled off of Luther and stood. "He may have a knife or pistol hidden in his clothes. Be careful."

Luther had begun to wind down, but he kept muttering. "Prussians riding us down. Dead men everywhere ... downed horses kicking in the mud. Arms and legs...mixed with horse guts..."

He covered his ears and squeezed his eyes shut. "Make them stop screaming."

"What are they screaming?" Zdenka said, clearly recognizing the more guttural German accent of Schleswig.

"For us to kill them," Luther whispered.

"What does he mean?" she asked Matteo.

Matteo's mouth felt filled with stones. "Our fellow soldiers begged us to end their suffering."

Zdenka paled and touched her fingertips to her lips. She stared, wide-eyed at Matteo, her mouth open in disbelief.

Matteo's heart clawed up his throat. His scalp crawled. Sweat rose on the hairline at the back of his neck.

He had dreamed about those same visions, night after night. Of the gigantic black horses riding them down. Of the blood and smoke. Of the metallic taste of gunpowder and the stench of bodies. Of the drummer boy's blue eyes staring up at a blue sky.

A breeze brushed Matteo's cheek and brought him back to the sunlit meadow filled with grass instead of corpses.

Get ahold of yourself, man!

Matteo forced himself to suck air into his lungs. As she had taught him, he fixed his eyes on a ringlet curved around Zdenka's ear until his breathing returned to normal.

The thought tore through him like a bullet: if he hadn't abandoned Kurt and Luther on the battlefield, Matteo might be the one living under a bridge. Somehow, he had ended up in the field hospital, cared for and returned safely to Thea. He'd only been left with the sweaty nightmares, the way he startled, the throbbing headaches, the scars. Minor irritations. Nothing a strong will couldn't quash.

He wished it was him dressed in rags, not Luther.

"Dead men ... horses ... the horses ..." Luther mumbled.

"Quiet, now, Luther. She's not used to hearing such gruesome things," Matteo said.

Zdenka's hand trembled slightly as she moved closer to Luther.

Matteo laid a hand on her shoulder to pull her back. "I don't want him to hurt you."

She turned to Luther, who twitched and trembled. "You won't hurt me, and we won't hurt you."

She whispered the words over and over until Luther's eyes focused on her face.

"Will you let us help you?" she asked.

"Help? You've come to help? Not to kill me?" Luther rasped. It was not a question, but the plea of a damaged man.

"Your mind is only a little muddled. Let us take you to the hospital where they can help you and feed you. You can have a hot bath, warm clothes, and a soft bed."

Under his breath Matteo said, "Going to take more than a warm meal and clean sheets to set him right."

"It's a start," she said.

"It is that." Matteo helped Luther to his feet. "You must be starving. Come along, and we'll take you to the hospital."

"How long have you been out here?" Zdenka asked.

Luther wavered unsteadily on his feet. "Don't know." Slowly, he raised his haunted eyes to Matteo.

They were the eyes of a man who had seen too much, who remembered it all, who wanted to forget, but couldn't.

Matteo felt the same way.

"I think ... I know you, but ..." Luther trailed off as if his lieutenant's name had slipped through the cracks in his mind.

In his confusion, perhaps he had forgotten the ambush. Then, there would be no danger of him revealing the truth to anyone. Matteo would have to keep Zdenka away from him, lest Luther divulge Matteo's cowardice.

Matteo turned away, unable to see what seemed like an accusatory stare. To Zdenka, he said, "I'm sorry."

"For what?" she said.

"I'm your husband and I'm supposed to protect you and I failed miserably. Go home, and I'll take him to the hospital."

With her maddening bravado, she said, "I don't need protecting."

"You're independent and brave, but you're reckless and impulsive too," said Matteo. "He could still be dangerous. I want you to go home."

Matteo had to keep the two of them apart. If she knew how Luther had come to be so injured, she would never forgive Matteo.

Just as he couldn't forgive himself.

CHAPTER 31

Matteo left Luther at the *Allegemeines Krankenhof* and took Zdenka home. He breathed a sigh of relief that a few bumps and scrapes were the only injuries she sustained in the fall. Once he was certain she was all right, he left her in the care of one of his aunt's maids.

He wanted to return to the hospital to discretely pay Luther's bill and ensure his comrade was well cared for. Matteo would leave nothing to chance again.

The sun dipped into the darkness as he made his way along the streets. He hated leaving Zdenka, but Luther and Kurt were still his men. They had marched into battle together. Fought side by side. Faced the enemy. They were as much brothers to him as Edward.

On *Alser Gasse*, the grey stone monolith of the hospital sprawled over an entire block. The building was two stories high, with long horizontal bricks, high windows, and arched doorways. Hospital walls formed a courtyard with a fountain, wide walkways, and gardens. This was where soldiers who were lucky enough to have survived the battlefield hospitals were sent to recuperate.

Or die.

Matteo found Luther on the second floor in a high-ceilinged ward. The smell of blood made Matteo's stomach rise to his throat. Rows and rows of cots with a small table between lined both walls. Nursing Sisters in their long white, starched gowns and caps floated like silent angels about the ward as they cared for the sick men.

A nurse with kind, patient eyes glided up. "May I help you?"

"I've come to check on one of my men, Luther Klesper. I was his commanding officer at Königgratz. I left him here several hours ago. I wondered how he was faring?" Matteo reflexively touched his throbbing temple.

The nurse's face was grave. "The surgeon removed a piece of metal embedded in his head."

"Will he be all right?" Matteo asked.

"Dr. Semmelweiss is treating the wound with a mixture of chlorinated lime water. We've seen miraculous results."

"Make sure someone sends me the bills. Please spare no expense on his care." From his pocket, Matteo withdrew a scrap of paper upon which he had written his name and Thea's address.

"He's down here," she said, floating down the aisle between the cots.

He tried to hand her the slip of paper, but she was already halfway down the aisle. Reluctantly, he followed.

Walking between the rows of narrow cots filled with wretched men, Matteo imagined their haunted eyes condemning him for being whole, uninjured. Bandages swathed heads and covered blinded eyes. Sheets lay flattened where there should have been an arm or a leg. Men moaned in pain and rolled their heads from side to side.

Matteo's chest was hollowed out, like an empty eggshell.

He felt the weight of responsibility for each and every man, despite not knowing any of them. These were the soldiers who received medical treatment. Hundreds, perhaps thousands more, weren't able to seek help.

The conversation he'd had with Zdenka, then a boy, in the beerhall came to mind. How she had changed him, helped him look into the future. It was she who had suggested he establish a veteran's association. She had encouraged him to follow his heart, and she was right. He would find a way to help. He didn't know how yet. Perhaps raising funds, organizing benefits to establish some sort of special hospital. No one had made healing soldiers a priority. He would make it his life's work to help as many of these men as he could.

"Here he is," the nurse said.

The man she indicated couldn't have been Luther. Where was the jovial, good-natured man who always had a joke? The man whose sense of humor had made the rain, mud, and boredom of war bearable? He looked withered. Wrung out. His shoulder and knee bones formed sharp peaks beneath the thin blanket draped over him. His chest rose and fell in an irregular rhythm, and a clean white muslin bandage wrapped his head.

The nurse said something Matteo didn't hear. Luther's breathing sounded like the gurgling of a men dying on the battlefield.

Icy shards slipped through Matteo veins.

Remembering how Luther attacked Zdenka, Matteo shuddered. If Luther had hurt her, all debts would have been wiped out, and he would have killed Luther without a second thought. He turned away and focused on a spot of blood on the floor. The fierceness of his conviction that he would ever spill another drop overwhelmed him. To think he could kill another man for Zdenka. When had he come to love her so much? How had it happened?

He let out a long breath and his rage against Luther subsided.

"The next few days will tell us..." She left the words unspoken but glanced up at Matteo.

He took the glance to mean *whether he lives or dies.*

The nurse adjusted the blanket over Luther with gentle, efficient movements. His eyes flickered open. Matteo moved back into the shadows. If Luther knew he was getting help from the man who had abandoned him on the battlefield, he might refuse further assistance.

"They're coming! The horses!" Luther screamed. He bucked in his cot. His head slewed from side to side.

His words bayonetted through Matteo. He took another step back, unprepared to admit his guilt in a roomful of wounded men.

"Help me calm him," the nurse said with urgent sharpness.

Matteo gripped Luther's shin. His once muscular calves had shriveled to sinew and bone. He was so weak, it took no effort to keep Luther in bed. The nurse pressed his shoulders against the pillow and shushed him, but it only seemed to rile Luther further.

"They'll kill us! Where's the Lieutenant? Why did we come here?" Luther's hand shot out and clipped the nurse at the side of the head.

The rage Matteo had pushed aside surged, and he moved to Luther's shoulders.

"I must get some laudanum." The nurse rushed off.

Luther's sunken eyes focused on Matteo. "Lieutenant? Where did you go? Why did you leave me?"

It was as effective as a gut-punch. Matteo loosened his grip and stepped back. He wasn't ready to ask Luther what had happened. Wasn't ready to be accused. Wanted to help him. Make amends.

The nurse returned and jabbed a needle into Luther's arm. He stilled almost instantly.

"I'm sorry, but you must go. He needs rest." She exhaled and righted her cap. "You can come tomorrow." She tilted her head at Matteo. "Do you know what he's on about with the horses?"

Matteo didn't take his eyes off Luther but shook his head.

"When he wakes, I'll tell him you called." She took the slip of paper from her pocket, read it. "Lieutenant von Ritter."

He didn't even remember handing her the slip of paper. "No, no. It's not necessary. Send me the bills." He would worry about how to pay for them later.

She raised her brows in question. "As you wish."

With a nod, he bid the nurse goodnight and headed for the stairs.

Luther blamed him. Asked where he had been. Matteo had been right all along: he had abandoned his men.

Out on the street, Matteo felt as if wire knots were cutting into his chest, making it hard to breathe. He needed a drink. Several drinks.

Stopping at the first bar he found, he knocked back schnapps until he felt neither disgust nor hatred. Not even love.

♫

A loud thud wakened Zdenka.

Her heart jumped. She sat up in bed.

It was Matteo, drunk again.

She waited for a moment, listening closely as Matteo stumbled up the back stairs.

"When did they make these stairs so steep?" he mumbled.

This had to stop. *She* had to make him stop. Otherwise, he would kill himself, either from drink or falling down some stairs.

Slowly, because her body ached from the fall off Schwartzkönig, Zdenka climbed out of the bed and threw a shawl around her shoulders. She turned up the gaslight and opened the door. "Matteo?"

The hall mirror reflected the light and amplified Matteo's dishevelment. He leaned against the railing on the top stair, swaying precariously. His eyes were bleary, and his hair jumbled down over his forehead. He smelled of liquor and malodorous cigars. His cravat hung at his neck, untied, and his jacket looked as though he'd dragged it through the gutter.

She stole a glance at his crotch. At least his pants were buttoned correctly, which meant he hadn't taken them off to visit a mistress.

In his condition, he'd never have gotten them back on, let alone buttoned.

"It is I, your cavalier," he slurred, making a mockingly grand bow.

She grabbed him by the shirtfront and saved him toppling backwards down the stairs.

"Thank you for rescuing me." He yanked his jacket lapels back into place, which did nothing to improve his appearance. He added, "Again."

What did that mean?

"Where have you been? I was so worried about you." Which bierkeller in particular, she didn't need to know, but something told her he'd been out for some other purpose besides drinking.

"I paid a call on Luther." He rubbed the scar at his temple and winced.

This was the worst she'd ever seen him. "Is he all right?"

"No thanks to me, he'll make it."

'No thanks to me?'

"Was it visiting Luther that made you go out and get so terribly drunk?"

"I would not call this state drunk." He scratched his head. "Exactly." He stared in the mirror and fumbled at his cravat. "Sorry," he mumbled. "Did I wake you?"

"No more so than all the other nights when you go out carousing and come bashing home at nearly dawn," she said. The thought which had haunted her sprang to her mind again.

She jerked the belt of her robe tighter and pushed the question past the knot of tears in her throat. "Are you in love with someone else?"

He snorted and frowned. "Philandering was my father's pastime, but that is one evil I consider below me. You are the only woman I need."

She laid a hand on his arm, but he turned his back to her. His rejection of her touch was as brutal to her as kick in the stomach.

"If there's no one else, why do you avoid me? Why do you reject my overtures of love? Why won't you let me care for you?"

He shuddered. His voice was strangled. "You could have been killed today. Just like I almost let Luther die. I couldn't forgive myself if I let something happened to you like it did to my mother."

So that was it. He was afraid of loving her and of losing her. And what was this about letting Luther nearly die? He was no more capable of that than of hurting her. These were knots she didn't know how to untie. She spoke softly to him.

"It wasn't your fault your father tipped the carriage. That your mother died. You couldn't do anything about your father's philandering. You were too young to keep her safe."

He growled, "I should have stopped him. It might have saved her."

Even in the low light of the hallway, the dark torment in his eyes was evident.

"You can't keep everyone safe, my love."

"People around me aren't safe. What if I'm like my father? I might hurt you. Can't let that happen."

"I'll take my chances," she said quietly, speaking to his back.

"No," he said, emphatically. "No more chances. Never should have let you ride that stupid horse. Nearly killed you."

This last he said softly, sounding like a frightened little boy. He lifted his bowed head, turned to face her, and reached out. He lurched, pulled her to his chest and sank his hands into her mass of curls, clutching great fistfuls.

She gasped. Stopped breathing. Her scalp prickled.

He rubbed his cheek against her curls. "Zdenka, Zdenka," he whispered.

She burrowed close to his chest, feeling the architecture of his muscles beneath the fabric of his jacket, the rise and fall of his breath against the top of her head.

He rested his chin on her crown and inhaled deeply. "I can't measure up to your love."

"Love has no measuring stick. All you have to do is let me love you. Let me know what you're trying to forget when you drink."

He drew back. For the first time since staggering up the stairs, he looked into her eyes. Grief, anger, frustration and longing, passed over his face, like ghosts from his past. All these emotions came from a place inside of him she could not touch, because he would not let her.

His loneliness shredded Zdenka's heart.

"It's me. I was your friend as Zdenko, and I'm still your friend. I'm your lover, your wife. The friend who knows you best." She placed her hands on his chest and leaned her head there, listening to the beating of his broken heart. "Can you tell me why you're drinking so much?"

"I can't bear the thought of losing you. I lost you once when you became a woman. You are so reckless and hardheaded, I could lose you again, but this time, forever, because I can't keep you safe."

He stumbled into his cramped dressing room and left her standing alone, her heart aching, in the hallway.

If she was to keep him alive, she would have to uncover where he was going, what he was hiding, and why. If she took him to Friedenheim, he might forget what haunted him. Winning the farm back from the Argentinean would be the first place to start.

CHAPTER 32

*Z*denka laid in bed for the better part of two days, nursing her bruised arse. The spot marbled purple then plum, and it hurt to sit on one side of her bottom. An enormous vase of lilacs stood on the spindle-legged bedside table, filling the room with their heady fragrance. She had plenty of time to read and had the newspaper, *Die Zeitung,* sent up to her room.

On the second morning, she read an article about the Argentinean playing in a *Schwimmen* tournament at Dommayer's. The article stated he would play all challengers and board a steamer for Argentina the next morning.

Schwimmen was *her* game, and this was her opportunity to win back the deed. He had already knifed someone whom he had caught cheating. The Argentinean would turn murderous if he suspected her of card counting, but she would beat him at his own game.

For Matteo, for the promise she had made to her grossmutti, she would risk anything.

She slid painfully out of bed, padded to her dresser, and retrieved her deck of Skat cards, with which the game of

Schwimmen was played. She laid four hands out on the bed and pretended to play, counting the cards, sharpening her skills, making bids, taking another card. Giddiness bubbled inside her like champagne. Tonight, she would get the deed back. Tomorrow, she and Matteo would be on a train headed home.

She expected no trouble getting into Dommayer's because the owner would remember her from all the times she had dragged Papa away from the table in the back room.

Unlike Papa, this gamble would be one single time. Never again would she go to the table.

Her riding trousers and hat would provide a disguise. A 'bandage' of white muslin would disguise her lush red curls. She would wait until the Argentinean had beaten everyone else then ask for her turn to play. When it was her turn, she would claim Dommayer's house rule of 'new round, new stakes.' As a foreigner, The Argentinian wouldn't know or expect anyone to invoke the rule. She would ask if he had anything special he wanted to bet. Hopefully, he would put up the deed. It was a risk, but it was her only plan.

She frowned. To enter a game, she'd need a stake. Cash or valuables of some sort. She owned nothing of worth except the gowns Thea had given her.

Madame Bonterre, the dressmaker, might loan her money in exchange for the gowns. Zdenka would retrieve the gowns as soon as she won back some cash and the deed. She grabbed a quill and paper and penned a note to Madame Bonterre. Emphasizing the necessity for complete secrecy, Zdenka asked for a loan and promised to pay double when she retrieved her gowns. She rang for a footman and sent the letter off, straightaway.

A knock sounded on the door.

Her heart bumped.

"One moment." She scrambled to put the cards in her

dresser and the pen and ink back on her desk. She jumped back into bed and pulled the covers up. "Come in."

Matteo entered with bloodshot eyes and a haggard face, his skin the color of parchment. He was hungover again from last night's roaming. She would win that deed and get him to Friedenheim to keep him from drinking himself to death. He had not touched her in the last two days but maintained his habit of sleeping on the cot in his dressing room. She longed for him in bed with an intensity that bordered on a sickness.

"You look a bit worse for wear," she said.

"Mmm," he grunted. "How is your, um ...?" he flicked a finger in the direction of her behind as if he couldn't bear to mention that part of her anatomy.

After having been so eager to see all of her, why was he acting as if her bum was a diseased part of her body?

"It's sore, but healing. The ointment Thea gave me makes it less sore."

"Good, good." Keeping his eyes averted, his manner was taciturn at best.

"But I'm getting bored lying here." She lifted her hands and let them fall limply back to the bed. "I'd like to be up and about."

She patted the bed beside her, inviting him to sit.

He stalled, fumbling about in his jacket pockets as if looking for something. Giving up, he perched on bed as far away as he could get from her.

Did he not want to touch her again? She certainly wanted to touch him. What was bothering him, and why wouldn't he tell her?

"You seem out of sorts. Is everything all right?" She caressed the back of his hand with a finger.

He practically jumped off the bed. He didn't even look at her.

"No, no." He cleared his throat. "Perfectly fine."

Why was he acting if their lovemaking was a mistake he had to erase? Why was he so distant?

Arabella. What would Arabella do?

Zdenka pointed to her behind. "Would you like to see? The bruise is really a lovely shade of eggplant." She tossed the covers back and inched her nightgown up.

Matteo leapt off the bed and strode to the window, glaring out as if preparing for an attack by Attila the Hun. "No, no. That's fine."

Were those the only words he knew?

Heat raced up her neck. She dropped her nightgown and pulled up the blanket. An awkward silence fell over them. What could she say to draw him to her?

"Would you like to join me for a nap?" she asked. If they could lie together, perhaps he'd relax.

His voice was gruff as he spoke over his shoulder. "I can't. I must visit a sick friend."

Wasn't she sick? With his temperament, if he visited anyone, they would be glad to see his back.

"That's good of you." She plucked at the coverlet. "Are you going to visit Luther?"

"No. Luther's fine."

Why was he being so evasive? What was he hiding? Was there another woman?

Her heart twisted against her breastbone.

"It's odd, speaking to your back," she said. "Can you turn around and face me?"

Pivoting towards her, he inspected the mantle, the back of her chair, her hairbrush. He picked up her music box, opened and closed it, opened and closed it. Mozart's tune went on, off, on, off. He replaced the box on the dresser. "I'm glad you're improving. I must be going. Take care, and I'll check on you this evening."

He whisked out of the room.

'Take care?' A chill like an ice bath came over her.

The hour they'd spent, surrounded by roses, lying on a bed of pine needles, making love, was the most joyful memory she had. He, however, was acting as if their lovemaking embarrassed him. As though he had shown weakness.

What preoccupied him? If she could take him back to Friedenheim, perhaps whatever was bothering him would dissolve in the apple-scented air, mountain walks, and quiet atmosphere. He might even forget his experiences in the war.

And he might fall in love with her, once and for all.

The whole scheme was a risk, but she was nothing if not a risk-taker. Perhaps it was a characteristic she'd acquired from her father. Tenacity, however, she had gotten from her grand-mother. She remembered Grossmutti holding an apple from their orchard to her nose and inhaling. Then she had held it to Zdenka's nose. "This is what our apples smell like."

Our apples. Her apples. Her land. Her farm.

Zdenka had to save Matteo but she had also made a promise to her grossmutti. She wasn't about to let either of them down.

Tonight, she would be a gentleman once more.

CHAPTER 33

A t Dommayer's, the gaming room was a gloomy affair: smoky oil lamps, scarred wooden tables and chairs; the stench of cheroot smoke and the sweat of nervous, largely silent gamblers. Four men hunched over the table, playing *Schwimmen*.

The Argentinean wasn't difficult to spot. He was dusky skinned man in an odd hat with a tall crown and wide brim. The hat never left his head and, rumor had it, he only took off the hat to make love to his mistress. His manner was rough, yet the way his lids hung low over his eyes made him seem cool-headed and calculating.

Schwimmen was a point-trick game played by four players using a deck of thirty-two Skat cards. The objective was to accumulate as many points in hand as possible. Remembering how many cards had already been played was an essential part of the game; and, at this, Zdenka excelled. She had watched her father play—and lose—for countless hours.

Zdenka perched on a barrel and watched from a distance, waiting her turn at the tables. *Schwimmen* was ordinarily played for small change, but in this case, significant sums of money changed hands. The Argentinean always won. At least one man at every game was an accomplice. Signs of cheating, a glance to the left or right, a raised eyebrow, a scratched ear, a sniff, were barely noticeable to others. To Zdenka, the glances and facial tics were like torches on a moonless night.

After two hours of play and studying the men, Zdenka felt confident to try her luck. All she needed was a chance to enter the game.

At midnight, the stakes peaked and no one else stepped up. The Argentinean sat with a pile of *gulders* and a handful of gold coins in front of him.

Shaking inside, she clutched the *gulders* in her pocket with a sweaty palm and stepped forward. Careful to keep her voice manly-sounding, she asked, "May I play a round?"

The Argentinean slid a half-lidded glance at two other men around the table—a skeletal man with sunken cheeks and the other, a man with a mustache which made him look like a Schnauzer dog—before the Argentinean's hard stare landed back on her.

Zdenka gulped.

The Argentinean gave a silent nod. She was fairly sure both companions were accomplices.

Her hair grew damp beneath her fake bandage. She exhaled and sat in the vacant chair. Someone dealt. Bids were placed. She allowed the Argentinean to win, even when she was certain she had the best hand. It was important for him to see her money depleted so she would have an excuse to change the bet. She lost. And lost again.

Sweat dampened the insides of her elbows.

The Argentinean and his men were phenomenal cheats. Finally, she won the last game of the round. Now it was her turn to bid first. Her mouth was sawdust dry.

Schnauzer dealt. Zdenka's hand was excellent, but odds were that the Argentinean held an equally impressive hand.

Zdenka pretended a yawn. "It's boring only gambling for money. You have something besides money to wager?" She pointed to the Argentinean's hat. "I like your hat. How about that?"

The Argentinean scowled contemptuously. The two men stared at her as though she'd slipped her head through a noose.

Beneath the table, her leg jiggled wildly.

The Argentinean tapped his forehead. With a thick Spanish accent, he said, "That bump, it make you loco...crazy. We play for money."

Her heart lurched forward like a steam engine, but she forced her voice to be calm. "I guess you don't know, since you're a foreigner. New round, new stakes. Dommayer's house rules. First to bid sets the stakes."

A long, sinister silence followed. She feared the Argentinean might draw a knife.

"What you bet?" the Argentinean spat out.

Candlelight glinted on the wide, gold wedding band encircling her finger. This was the only thing she had left to wager. The ring meant everything to her: her marriage, the new trust her husband had placed in her, their future together, her commitment to him. The ring meant all those things, both on her finger and on the table as a bet. Losing the ring would shatter everything. Maybe even his love.

She swallowed hard and slipped off the band. It landed on the table with a light 'clink.'

Her blood went cold. Turn to ice. Congealed.

She could *not* lose. Matteo, her marriage, his life, the farm, her dream. Everything was riding on this one hand of *Schwimmen*.

"That's it?" The Argentinean raised a brow. "A ring?"

She locked eyes with him. "What? You don't like gold?"

He pushed his lower lip out and gave a nod.

Schnauzer pulled out a heavy silver cuff bracelet engraved with leaping stags out of his pocket and laid it on the table.

Skeleton pulled a gold pocket watch from his vest and dropped it with a *thunk* on the table. The Argentinean picked it up and held it to his ear to see if it worked. He opened it, examined the back, nodded, and returned it to the table.

The Argentinean shrugged and made a what-the-hell pout with his mouth. From his breast pocket, he drew a bulky packet of parchment bound in a black ribbon. He tossed it on the table. "I got this one," he said on a noisy exhale. "It's the deed to a farm near ... a village ... Hoho ... hupper ... daft or dorfs."

A trickle of perspiration ran down Zdenka's spine.

"Hohenruppersdorf?" Zdenka asked, keeping her eyes fixed on the table in front of her, even as blood pounded in her ears.

"Si. You Austrians. Such long words," the Argentinean said.

The room grew silent as each player laid down cards.

Schnauzer. Nothing.

Skeleton man, a losing hand.

Behind her, the door opened and closed but Zdenka didn't allow her attention to shift for a moment. She stared at the deed on the table. If only she could reach out, snatch it, and run like mad. It was hers, by all rights. He'd likely cheated her father to get the deed.

She laid down her hand. Three Queens. Thirty points.

The Argentinean fingers dipped out of sight for a split second.

He had a card up his sleeve.

The Argentinean laid his cards on the table and the corner of his mouth twisted up in an ugly, triumphant grin. He held, improbably an Ace and two Queens. Thirty-one.

Zdenka's vision narrowed to a tiny circle. A crushing weight squeezed her chest. Her stomach plummeted.

She had lost the farm. Again. Now there was no one to blame but herself. It had been within reach. She glared at the Argentinean.

He met her eyes.

Zdenka jutted her chin at him. "You cheated," she said low and evenly.

He rose slowly from his chair. Sitting down, he had seemed ordinary, but he towered over her—hulking shoulders, a neck like a tree stump.

"You accuse me, you little *mierda,* of cheating?" He reached for her neck.

A hand gripped Zdenka's shoulder and jerked her out of reach of the Argentinean's outstretched hand.

"My friend here made a mistake, sir," said a familiarly jovial voice. He shoved her behind him, and she found herself looking at a tall, broad back wearing a coat of luxurious fabric.

"You see the wound on his head has made him a bit irrational. Please forgive him."

"If I ever see him again," the Argentinean growled, "I'll kill him."

"Come along now, let's get you home and back to bed. We need to change that bandage immediately." The man in the fancy coat clapped her on the shoulder with a grip like a blacksmith's tongs and steered her toward the door.

She blinked. Edward smiled at her, but his eyes were ablaze with fury.

CHAPTER 34

Edward marched Zdenka outside to the alley and backed her up against a wall. Light from an upper window illuminated trash, barrels, and a drunk.

Holding her by the forearms, Edward loomed over her, his face even with hers. "What in God's name did you think you were doing? You could have been killed. You won't do Matteo any good if you're dead."

He stalked around the alley, huffing and swearing in French, Italian, and Russian.

Bricks dug into her back as she slid down the wall to rest on to her haunches. She squeezed words past the hopelessness constricting her throat. "I only wanted to win back the farm."

Edward whirled around. "A farm? A farm?" he barked and threw up his hands. "What good is a farm? And now you've gone and lost your wedding ring. Your father was a losing gambler, and now you've chosen to follow in his footsteps?"

"The Argentinian cheated."

"Of course, he cheated." Edward stomped up and down the alley. "You can't accuse a man like that of cheating. You have to out-cheat him."

"But I recognized the signals. I thought I could win. I knew what he was doing. I knew what I was doing."

"Then why, pray tell, did you lose?"

She was painfully aware she had overestimated the Argentinean, same as she'd overestimated her ability to handle Schwartzkönig. Maybe everyone was right. She was impulsive and headstrong.

Edward ranted on. "Being courageous and independent is one thing. Entering a card game against an infamous gambler and murderer is lunacy."

"I've studied books on card cheats. Watched them cheat my father. I knew what I was doing."

Hands on his hips, Edward glared down at her. "I assume Matteo knows nothing of this."

Zdenka couldn't meet his eyes. She shook her head. Edward had always been easygoing. His temper was a shock.

"Where did you get the money to wager?" he demanded.

She bit her lip.

He raked his hands through his impeccable hair. "Oh, good God! Say it. You just lost your wedding ring." He threw up his hands. "It can't possibly get any worse."

Zdenka had already *surpassed* worse. "I sold my dresses back to Madame Bonterre, the dressmaker. I expected to redeem them in the morning with my winnings."

"Gifts from my mother, weren't they?"

Zdenka shrank a little lower and nodded.

"Knowing my mother, she would have probably done the same thing." He shook his head and laughed. "Oh hell, then we have to retrieve your dresses as well." With a debonair smile, he said, "Madame Bonterre is a good sort. We have—how shall I say—a familiar acquaintance. She should be quite amiable."

That was the Edward she was used to. Her stomach unclenched slightly.

He jammed his hands in his pockets and returned to pacing. "How are you going to explain all of this to Matteo?"

"I didn't think that would be necessary, and I wouldn't have to if you would front me a stake, I could go back--"

"Do you think I'm mad? I would die before I let you go back in there, and that would make me very unhappy."

She leaned her forehead against her knees. "This was my last chance. I wanted to get the deed back so I could take Matteo to Freidenheim. At the farm, I'm sure he can forget the things he's seen, the things he's done in the war. I wanted it for him, because I lu ... lu ... love him," she sobbed.

"I know you do." Edward pinched the bridge of his nose between his thumb and forefinger. "Oh, dear God, don't cry. I hate it when women cry. It makes me feel so utterly helpless."

He squatted down and gave her his handkerchief. His face softened. "Promise me you'll never do anything like this again. Please, Zdenka. I know my cousin is oftentimes a perfect ass, but I do believe he cares for you."

"Then why doesn't he act like it?"

Edward stood and stared into a greasy puddle. "The war changed Matteo. He used to be such a happy man. So jolly and carefree. You would have liked him a great deal. Maybe even loved him. He never drank like he does now."

For the first time, Edward's voice pierced with grief. He had lost his friend, a man he considered a brother when Matteo returned a changed man. Would she have loved old Matteo? A man who didn't need her? A man whose heart had no cracks and whose mind was solid as a stone?

Edward continued. "He's never spoken to me about the war, and I don't think he will. Your desire to win back the farm is admirable." He stared down the alley, as if looking for someone. "But I doubt country life will make my cousin the sort of man he once was."

A brick jabbed at the base of her spine. Whether country life would help Matteo was now a moot point.

"I only want to help Matteo be the best man he can be. I had hoped that knowing I loved him would make a difference, but it hasn't seemed to."

Once he found out about her escapade, even that hope was gone.

"You do love him, don't you?"

"Enough to risk being killed," she said.

Edward gazed down at her. "Promise me you will never, ever, ever do anything so foolish again."

She felt like a naughty child getting a well-deserved scolding. Drawing a deep breath, she said, "All right. I promise."

"Are you going to tell him?"

"You take me for a tattletale? I wouldn't do that to you." He held out his palms. She put her hands in his and he pulled her up. "Come along now. Let's get you home where you won't get into any more trouble. This is no place for a lady like you."

She hung her head and let him take her by the elbow again.

They left the alley, and he hailed a *fiaker*. He handed her in, paid the fare, and closed the door. "Don't let her get out anywhere, you understand?" he said to the driver.

"Aren't you coming?" she asked in surprise.

Edward shook his head. "I have a few things to do. Go home. And no more stupid pranks." He banged a fist on the door. The driver snapped the ribbons, and the *fiaker* jerked on its way.

Zdenka watched out the back window as Edward opened the front door to Dommayer's and stepped inside.

CHAPTER 35

Zdenka trod out to Thea's garden, Edward's scolding from the previous night still stinging her ears. Stacks of silvery clouds hid the sun, and chilly gusts rattled the branches and shivered the shrubs. Back and forth, chilly and warm, calm and windy. It was as if spring couldn't make up its mind. She pulled on her gardening gloves. Inside the bulky gloves, she wore fancy dress gloves to hide her missing ring. But using a rash on her hand, a hangnail, a cut, fear of dirt as an excuse for wearing gloves would forestall Matteo's suspicion only so long.

And no one would imagine she was trying to be dainty.

To think she'd lost her ring in a card game! Had she learned nothing from watching her father dribble away their fortune?

Arabella's too-short, old dress hung on her slender frame. She didn't care if it got dirty, and she had to keep clean the single day dress still in her possession. On her knees, she hacked wretched weeds, beheaded spent daffodils, clawed dead leaves. Exhumed stones from the soil remained a temptation. Hurling them at something, anything, might satisfy her self-directed fury.

Trying to improve her mood, she hummed the Mozart tune, *Weib und Mann,* about happily married couples and marital bliss.

As if.

Despite the breeze, she had worked up a sweat with energetic gardening. A snarly weed behind a rose bush sneered at her. She dove at it with both hands. A needle-like thorn raked the underside of her wrist. Blood, dark as chocolate, soaked her sleeve. "Stabbed by a bush. Now I have a genuine reason to wear gloves inside."

She sat on the ground, splay-legged, and used a clipper to snip off a strip of her petticoat. Holding one end of the strip in her teeth, she wrapped the makeshift bandage around her bleeding wrist and tied it in a sloppy knot.

Blood soon soaked through the bandage. She jerked her gloves over her wrist and kept hacking away.

"Are you nearly done killing that dirt?"

She jumped. "Very nearly. I didn't hear you."

Matteo stood behind her, surveying her handiwork. "I didn't mean to frighten you."

"You didn't." She pushed her straw hat back on her head and gazed up at him.

His coat of fine grey wool outlined his muscular frame and black pants defined his legs. His waistcoat snugged over his flat abdomen.

Her blood heated.

"You must be tired. Would you like a bit of lemonade?" he asked.

To hide the bloody cuff, she tucked her hand into the folds of her dress and swiped her forehead with her other sleeve.

He chuckled and glanced away.

"What?"

"Umm, dirt." He bent down and pointed to a spot above her right eye.

"Oh, thank you." She swiped with her sleeve again.

This time his laugh made her throat tickle and her spirits lift. "Worse?" she asked with an embarrassed giggle.

He drew a finger across his forehead. "It looks like a giant eyebrow." His sensuous mouth broke into a wide smile that made her heart flip-flop.

Matteo extended a hand and helped her up. He took out his handkerchief and, gently, he held her chin in his hand and scrubbed at her forehead. "There." He returned his handkerchief to his pocket. "You look like your own beautiful self again."

Heat rose to her cheeks.

"Wait here. I'll bring out some lemonade." He pointed to a wrought iron bench which encircled the trunk of the towering cherry tree.

She rested back against the bench, surprised at how tired she was. As he walked into the house, the ease of his body fascinated her. Long, thick-thighed legs striding. Powerful arms swinging. Sculpted chest muscles rippling. Beneath those clothes were a lifetime's worth of mysterious joys.

He had seen every inch of her, but now, he barely looked at her. He had made her dream of a lifetime luxuriating in one another's arms. Why, after finding Luther, did he now find her as enticing as a cold cup of tea?

She cinched her gloves tighter and laid her straw hat on the bench beside her.

In a few minutes, Matteo returned, carrying two tall glasses of lemonade. He handed her a glass. "Do you want to take your gloves off? Might be easier to hold the glass."

Her heart hiccupped.

She avoided his gaze. "No, I can manage."

A breeze gusted, and a few leaves she hadn't captured scuttled around her feet. She shivered. From the breeze or fear of discovery, she wasn't sure.

He sat beside her. She took a long sip. Even though the air was brisk, the cool sweet-tart lemonade was refreshing and helped her relax. Another breeze caught her hair and blew out several strands. Without thinking, she brushed a strand of hair away with her left hand. Matteo caught sight of the bloody bandage.

He turned her wrist over and brushed his thumb on the soft skin near her pulse, making a sizzle run up her arm. Her heart flip-flopped twice.

"You've hurt yourself." He examined it closely. "Looks like a field medic bandaged this."

She drew her hand back and tucked it back in her pocket. "It's nothing, really."

"You think I'll faint at the sight of blood?" His tone was joking, but she could tell by the tiny lines at the corners of his eyes, he suspected something. "Take off your glove and let me take a look."

Slivers of ice pricked her chest.

"It's fine. Don't bother." In fact, the cut stung like fire.

She managed a smile, but he stiffened and shifted his body away from her.

Loneliness for him swept through her. How she wanted to caress his cheek and tell him the truth about her missing ring.

For once, her mind overruled her heart.

They sat for a minute more, quietly sipping lemonade, awkwardly silent, his suspicion hanging between them like smoke.

She peeked at him out of the corner of her eye. Dark circles hung under his eyes. His skin was pale and unhealthy. The previous night she had lain awake, listening to his broken mutterings as he suffered through another of his recurrent nightmares.

"You look tired," she said softly.

He sagged. "I am."

His broad back hunched as though protecting his midsection. It moved her that, in spite of his weariness, he had come to sit with her.

The breeze quieted, and the clouds thinned to wisps. Sunlight dazzled through the branches overhead. A ray lit the edges of his cheekbones, and it struck her how prominent they had become.

If only she could take off her gloves and rub his shoulders, lay her cheek against his back. "I do wish you'd stop drinking so much. It worries me."

His eyebrows winged skyward. "I'm fine."

She set down her glass. "Drinking yourself to death is not fine." Measuring her voice so it grew gentler and softer with each pronouncement, she said, "Going out late at night and stumbling home at dawn is not fine. Nightmares that make you shout and wake you are not a symptom of being fine."

"I'm ... sorry if I awakened you."

"I wasn't bothered. Only worried."

"I assure you, I'm fine." His voice was flat and emotionless.

"When we were in the *bierkeller* together, you said you wanted to start an association to help the wounded veterans. You must help yourself first before you help others."

Tendons in his neck tightened. "There's nothing wrong," he said, his tone more insistent.

"I can help you, if you'll let me." She didn't think he realized how hopeless he sounded. "Talking about them might help the nightmares."

He squinted. "I prefer drink to talk."

"The other night when you were drunk, you talked."

He stared at her, his eyes wide. "What did I say?"

"How people close to you get hurt. What did you mean by that?"

He gripped his glass so that his knuckles were bone white. "Obvious, isn't it? I nearly let you get killed on that damned horse."

"You didn't *let* me do anything. I insisted on riding Schwartzkönig."

"You're my wife. It's my duty to be responsible for you," he said with exasperation.

"You also said you missed your friend, Zenko." She leaned her cheek against his shoulder, lightly at first to see if he would pull away. When he didn't, she rested her body against his. He was so solid, so substantial, but he was spending so much energy holding something inside, something fragile, frightening, flawed.

"Here I am, same as always, just in skirts. I miss my friend too. I'm your wife. Married people share their worries, tell one another what they're thinking. That's what I want, and you said as much the other night."

He ground the gravel under his heel. "I didn't mean about everything."

She laid her hand on his thigh. Hard striations of muscle softened beneath her fingers. "I'm listening."

He exhaled with a weariness that made her breastbone ache. "War is not something men discuss. It's best forgotten."

"I'm strong enough to hear whatever it is you want to say." She kicked a pebble. "I'm no shrinking violet."

He scrubbed his face with his hands. "Drinking is the only thing that makes the images, the stink and ... shrieking voices stop." He cupped his hands over his ears.

"The sorts of things Luther babbled on about?"

Etched in the lines in his face, the painful grief he lived with like a second skin. He nodded. "Things that should never have happened."

"You needn't tell me everything. Start small. One thing." She reached up and brushed her lips against the hard edge of his jaw.

His Adam's apple bobbed. "When I try, I ... I can't remember what happened. Only colors. A flash of light. The pitch of a scream. But my nightmares are vivid. In the morning, I can't recall much."

After a long pause, she asked, "What do you remember from the nightmares?"

"Horses. Massive horses trampling us. Then ..." He touched his temple. "...I wake, and my head feels as if I've been kicked in the head."

"How terrible for you." She kissed the scar at his temple.

"My mind doesn't work right any longer. There are ... holes. I know I did ..." He gritted his teeth. "Things I should not have done. I think that's why I can't remember."

She stroked circles on his hunched back. He was so strong to keep everything to himself. Was it guilt and shame or fear that haunted him? His memories tore something in him apart. Or was it the *lack* of memories he found so painful?

"Maybe Luther remembers, and he could help you remember."

Matteo's shoulders went rigid, and he shrugged her hand off. "He's sick. There's no need to bother him."

She was taken aback at his sharp tone. Clearly, Luther was more than a fellow from his regiment. "If you don't want to, I could speak to him."

She'd hit a nerve.

"I could—"

"No. I forbid it." His eye twitched, and he stood and turned his back to her.

Rising slowly from the bench, she spoke sweetly. Softly. "Forbid? I've never let anyone tell me what to do before. What makes you think I'd let you do so now?" With forced calm, head held high, she stepped across the garden, up the back steps and into the house.

She would get to the bottom of his nightmares. His drinking. His going out at night.

By God, she would, even if *she* became the one to sneak out at night.

CHAPTER 36

Lying in bed, Zdenka held her hand in the pale beam of moonlight and stared at the naked finger. Tears leaked from her eyes. No wedding ring. No gowns. No farm. A distrustful husband. Edward furious at her. A bruised behind. The argument she had with her husband in the garden left the bitter taste of burnt coffee in her mouth.

Each failure clanged in her mind, loud as the *Pummerin* bell at St. Stephan's.

Beneath the fluffy eiderdown, she listened as Thea's servants closed doors. The fire snapped in the grate. A *fiaker* clattered by. She listened for his footsteps, a knock on her door.

When she heard him climb the stairs and the door to his dressing room close yet again, she turned over and sobbed into her pillow. That hour together in the forest had awakened her body to sensations and responses she didn't know even existed. She wanted to feel the icy-hot tingling on her skin, to launch untethered in the moment of climax.

And she wanted to give *him* those feelings as well.

Mostly, she wanted her best friend back.

During the day, he was kind, reserved, cool. At night, he retired to the tiny adjoining dressing room. It was as if he had forgotten they'd ever made love.

She plumped his pillow, lay down and, in soft murmurs, pretended to speak to him. About the dog she had seen while riding and how he reminded her of Harbin, her dog at home. How the sun made the gold on the *Pestsaule* monument gleam when it hit just so. About a concert led by Herr Brahms next week. Her eyelids grew heavy and she fell into a nightmare where she saw Luther, Matteo, and his horse, dead in a field of mud.

"Got you in. I'll ... I'll get you out!"

Her eyes flew open, body rigid, listening.

Matteo.

He shouted, "Honor over death."

She vaulted out of bed and went to the door to his dressing chamber. Pressing her ear to the door, she listened. Usually, he went quiet after a minute or so, but this time, his frenzied tone was different. It frightened her. The door was unlocked. She tiptoed in.

Feeble moonlight filtered in through a tiny octagonal window above his bed. He was on all fours, naked from the waist up, sheets twisted around his legs, his arms. His chest heaved with labored breathing as if he'd been running. Sweat beaded his brow and cords in his neck stood out.

His open eyes had the tortured look she had seen in Luther's eyes that afternoon.

"Luther!" he shouted.

She jumped.

"Follow ..." His teeth screeched as he ground his jaw.

How could she calm him if he was still asleep? What triggered Matteo? Made this nightmare worse than the others? The last time he'd visited Luther, he had come home drunk. Was Luther somehow a key to these nightmares? To his nightly roaming? Today in the garden, he refused to speak of the war, of how he knew Luther. This made her all the more certain she needed to pay a visit to Luther.

She glided silently to his bedside, pulled up a footstool, and sat to watch him. Perhaps he would reveal something in his nightmare.

"Run! Now! Get back."

His arm went rigid as he pointed at something in the distance that only he could see. "The horses ... through there."

The torment on his face cut her heart to ribbons.

"Trapped. No way ..." he panted. "Through. No way around."

His voice was commanding, even though his words broke and swam back together like ice floes on the Danube in winter.

Moonlight gave the ragged pink scar on his shoulder blade a ghostly glow, as though it wasn't really part of his body. He never mentioned or complained about it. The injuries to his heart, his mind, his soul were still open wounds, not yet scarred over, still festering. How could she help him heal those if he wouldn't let her love him?

He choked out, "Led my men ... trusted me. A culvert ..."

She wanted to speak calming words to him, to hold him, wake him, but would he know it was her? Would he be angry she had witnessed one of his nightmares?

"Matteo, it's all right."

He snorted like a bull. His arm swung and clipped her on the chin.

Her arms pinwheeled backwards and her feet left the floor. The footstool tottered backward. Her head connected with the corner of a table. Fierce pain rayed across the back of her head and down her neck. Stars wheeled before her eyes. She crawled away and leaned against the wall, gulping air. Warm liquid oozed from the back of her head, soaked her hair, dripped down her neck. When she touched the base of her skull, her hand came away damp with blood. Her mouth filled with the metallic taste of blood and her lower lip throbbed.

She hadn't even seen his fist coming.

Her head swam, but she was determined to stay awake.

"Culvert ... Prussians ... get out ... on my honor."

Again, the word *honor.*

"On my honor ... on my honor."

It was as though something was working itself out of him, the way a splinter eventually worked itself from beneath the skin.

When she stood, she braced her hand against the wall. Two steps, and the room started to go black. She grabbed the back of a chair and inhaled. When she could see the moonlight again, she wobbled over to his wash basin.

But there were two basins. No, one. Two again.

She squeezed her eyes shut for a moment. When she opened them, there was only one basin again.

He continued muttering as she soaked and wrung out a towel. When she held it to the back of her head, she grimaced and sucked air between her teeth. *Gottes im Himmel,* it hurt. Getting thrown from the horse and landing on your arse was child's play compared to this. She alternated holding the towel to her head and her lower lip, each one pulsing with pain.

She never took her eyes off him.

His pain was much greater than hers. Hers would heal, but his? She wasn't so sure anymore. Maybe even Friedenheim couldn't help him.

She slumped on the floor next to the washbasin and settled in to watch him all night, if necessary. The room canted from one side to the other. A drink of water was what she needed.

The pewter ewer balanced on the edge of the washbasin. She reached up to get it, but she bumped the wash basin. It tottered back and forth. Loud as a gunshot, the ewer crashed to the floor. Water sprayed her, the Persia carpet, the walls.

And Matteo's face.

CHAPTER 37

Blood stained Zdenka's robe. She held a crimson towel. Her lower lip was split and swollen. A smear of blood marred her cheek.

His loss of breath was like he'd taken a cannonball in the chest. He knelt beside her. "Did I do this?"

She shrank from his touch, raised a palm to ward him off.

That was all the answer he needed. "What happened?"

"You had a nightmare," she said.

Her voice had a timidity he'd never heard before. *Damn him. He made her scared.*

"Let me have a look. I promise I won't hurt you." Could he keep that promise? Forever? If not, they would have to stay apart. The thought that he might never again taste her, never feel the sweep of her curls against his cheek, hit him like a second cannonball.

He took the bloody towel and moved around her so he could see the damage he had inflicted. Her lower lip wouldn't be kissable for a very long time. With tentative fingers, he pushed aside her curls until he found the wound. She groaned softly. The gash was deep. Blood matted her hair.

"I'm dreadfully sorry. You know I would never knowingly hurt you." He positioned her arms around his neck, picked her up, and sat her on his bed. It reassured him that she let him help her. Some women would never speak to a man again after something like this.

He would rather have been run through with his own sword than hurt her even a little bit. He was turning into a violent, abusive brute, just like his father. No one was safe from him. He was a menace to everyone close to him. It was a mistake to sell his commission. The only place for him was the battlefield. "Are you all right otherwise?"

Her smile was weak, but he could tell by the tight lines around her mouth, she was still frightened of him.

"Why is everything wet?"

She pointed to the ewer lying on its side. "I knocked it over."

"I'll mop it up, but first, sit on the bed so I can look at the wound on your head," Matteo said. "Lie still. I'll get more water and a clean towel from your room."

In moments, he returned to her side with a basin, ewer of water, and a fresh towel. He took the basin and set it on the bedside table and poured water onto the clean towel. The water already in the basin swirled with blood.

He might have killed her. Shaken, he set the bloody basin aside and filled her empty one, taking his time until he could speak. He sat beside her on the bed and dabbed at the back of her head. "Tell me what happened."

"You sounded so scared. Frantic. I came in." Her voice quivered. "I was frightened for you. Afraid you might do something rash."

"It appears I did do something rash." He rinsed the towel, poured fresh water on it and refolded it. What had he said? Had he spilled his own secret? Did she know he was a coward?

"Stupidly, I tried to wake you, and you took a swing, but

really, the table was the primary attacker in this battle. Do you remember the dream?"

Matteo folded the towel to a clean side. What did he remember? Blurry images. Looming figures. The sense of inescapable doom. Not knowing where his men were. "I don't remember." He turned to face her. His eye twitched.

She fixed him with a look that could have sliced through rock. "I don't believe you. Today in the garden, you said you often have the same dream. Was this that same dream?"

Even injured, she was resilient and strong as iron. She knew him well enough not to let him get away with anything.

"And you talked a lot. It was as though you were watching something happen."

He turned to stone, only his heart in his chest moving. "What did I say?"

"You said the word, 'honor' several times. Once, 'death over dishonor.' What did you mean?"

His moods, his drinking, his nightmares, his secret about the botched mission, his quest to regain his honor. Damned fool that he was, he hadn't thought how it all affected her.

Matteo adjusted his position on the bed, leaving a space between them a chasm he couldn't cross.

"Do things that happened in the war return in your nightmares?" she prodded.

He owed it to her to tell her something. If only he could remember what had happened after they had gotten to the rock wall. Where were those memories buried? Had he so shamed himself that his mind forgot he had abandoned his men? He could not, would not, tell her of the men, screaming for wives, mothers, begging for someone end their lives. Not of the grey entrails unspooled like slick yarn. The metallic taste of gunpowder. The blood pooled in hoof prints. Acrid smoke stinging his eyes. Limbs without bodies and bodies without limbs. Blood spilled for the very dirt upon which they all lay dying. A colossal waste.

Her eyes searched his face, but he refused the comfort of love offered in those cool green pools. He didn't deserve love or comfort, and if she knew the truth about him, her love would evaporate. And that would kill him.

"The dreams are flashes. Sounds. Nothing specific. I suppose they have something to do with the war."

"Can you tell me what happened? In the war?"

He touched the scar with his fingertips. "I don't remember anything after I was shot."

"Nothing?"

"No. Not until I found myself in the field hospital."

She threw her arms around him and the room came back into focus. "I love you. Do you hear? You might never trust me because I deceived you, but I love you, and I will always love you."

She leaned her head on his chest. It was like being wrapped in a warm blanket, having her here, next to him. He permitted himself a moment to absorb her devotion, and the wall around his heart opened a crack.

"My mind is like a moth-eaten tapestry with holes in all the worst places. I'll never be a normal person again. I'll never have a normal life." He rested his head in his hands. "You have to leave me. I can't be the sort of husband you need."

She wriggled onto his lap and laid her head on his shoulder. "You may never be the man you were, but you will be a better man. And as for being the sort of husband I need, that's my decision. I've decided you are precisely the man I need."

He rested his chin on the crown of her head. Slowly, his heartbeat returned to normal. Good God, did he love her. Until Luther attacked her, he hadn't known how much he loved her.

How much he needed her. It was terrifying. More terrifying than facing the Prussians.

"Confessing one's shortcomings isn't very manly." He pulled her closer.

"Oh, I see. You think pretending those shortcomings don't exist or drinking them away is manly?" She nuzzled into the side of his neck. "It's quite difficult to pretend you're the only human being on Earth who hasn't any shortcomings."

Realizing how much she believed in him, he pushed through his distrust. His need for her love was greater than his need to keep his secret. "I can't bear knowing you might think I'm a coward."

Laying her hand on his cheek, she gazed into his eyes. Her touch reached down to his wretched heart, weary of carrying the burden alone for so long.

"You are the most honorable, bravest man I know. I love you. Nothing you say will change that."

Did he dare believe that? Could she make it so, just by telling him that?

"May I ask you one question?"

"All right."

"Why did you become so furious at the tailor's when you saw the apprentice?"

"He reminded me of someone." The memories were stone upon stone, piled around Matteo's heart. He shoved at one stone, toppling it. "There was a drummer boy. In the infantry. Maybe twelve or thirteen. Hair like corn silk, eyes like two fat, round blueberries. Always laughing and smiling."

The image made him want to put the stone back in place, but he looked at Zdenka and the love in her eyes gave him courage.

"He was so brave and innocent. So willing. His mother was our washerwoman. She begged me to watch out for him. I promised her." He shut his eyes. "I can still see his blue eyes, how the wind lifted his hair like straw flying around his head. It's only when I'm drunk that I can forget."

"You must have been heartbroken." She took his hand and caressed his knuckles.

Heartbroken. He had once had a heart. Now it was buried behind rocks, big as headstones. He wanted to give his heart to her, but he couldn't as long as he had all these secrets, these burdens, all this guilt.

"I found him, lying on his back in a pool of blood, his drum stove in, his blueberry-colored eyes staring at the sky."

She entwined her fingers with his and waited.

Every word was like extracting glass from his mouth, but he was adamant she know the truth. "I couldn't even keep one boy alive. He was barely more than a child. Everyone I'm close to gets hurt"

What he was going to say was going to hurt her more than a fist to the chin. He held took her face in his hands. "You must not get close to me."

"Don't say that. I can help you, if you'll let me. This is only a little of what you experienced."

He shook his head. "Someone died because I failed."

"You can't blame yourself. You may never forget, but you must forgive yourself." She wound her arms around his neck. "See? I still love you."

He pulled her arms from his neck. "I won't risk hurting you again. We can't be together. I can't put you in jeopardy. I could never forgive myself."

He moved her off his lap onto the bed. When he stood, the effort was like lifting a boulder.

"What are you saying?" she scoffed. "I'm not afraid of you. If you're having a nightmare, I won't get too close."

A tremble of fear shook his voice. "Look at what I did to you. Next time, it might be worse. I can't take that chance."

He took her hand and pulled her from the bed. "Even sleeping in my dressing room hasn't kept you safe. I'll move down the hall and install a lock on the door." He led her back to her room. "Only I will have the key. Nothing else will change. We'll still ride together, dine, dance, have breakfast, go to concerts and the opera. Everything else will be the same. I'll lock myself in and carry the key on a string around my neck. That way, if the door is locked from the inside, no one can get in."

"Do you mean we can't be together in bed ever again?"

The wound in her voice nearly made him change his mind. "I would rather cut off my arm than risk harming you. You're not safe from me."

He turned and walked out the bedroom door.

CHAPTER 38

Matteo's refusal to sleep with her strengthened Zdenka's resolve to visit Luther as soon as possible. It wasn't only that he no longer trusted her; he didn't trust himself. Didn't think he could change, or that they could have a marriage like other people. No matter what, she was going to find out what had happened at Königgratz. After Luther, she would ask Edward. If she had to, she would stop every soldier on the streets of Vienna to find out what could be pulling her husband away from her, away from himself.

She waited until Matteo had gone out, then she dressed and hurried to the *Allegemeines Krankenhaus* to speak to Luther.

When Zdenka arrived at Luther's bedside, he was propped up with pillows, staring off into space.

She remembered him as her deranged attacker. Prickles spiked up her arms.

Barrel-chested, Luther's bucket-sized head listed slightly to one side as though he were out of balance. Paw-sized hands spasmed atop his blankets. The clean bandage around his brow contrasted with his sun-browned, leathery skin. He smelled human again; clean, and of lime and chlorinated water.

He stared blankly. "Who you be?"

Luther's voice sounded like two stones rubbed together, and his words were a jumble, but he addressed her with the formal *Sie* form of German. Zdenka's pulse slowed.

It was clear why Matteo had forbidden her to visit Luther in the hospital. Rows and rows of narrow cots with injured soldiers, moaning and groaning in pain, made her stomach clench. The effect on Matteo must have been a hundredfold.

A nurse in starched whites glided to Zdenka's side. "I'll be over there, attending to someone if you need anything."

Zdenka assumed the nurse was worried about the proprieties of a woman sitting alone with a patient in a ward full of ex-soldiers. "Don't worry. We'll be fine." Though she wasn't actually sure. She perched on a chair beside Luther's bed. "I'm Mrs. von Ritter, but you must call me Zdenka." It felt good to use Matteo's last name, to claim her identity as his wife, even if she had gambled away her wedding ring.

Luther squinted. "Where seen you before?"

Of course, the last time, she had worn pants. Today, she wore the last outfit she still owned: a burgundy day dress with black ribbon trim and a silly hat the milliner told her accented her eyes. Zdenka pulled the pins out of her hat and removed it. Her curls sprang free.

Luther's face broke into a grin. "Ah! A swarm of orange butterflies."

She laughed, relieved. "I suppose so. And they're always trying to get away."

"*Ja*. Prater. Lieutenant's wife. Lady in pants."

He grimaced. She wondered if he was in pain and if she should call the nurse.

"Giant black devil horse." His voice rose in volume and his hands began dropping, rising, dropping rising, opening, closing.

Best to direct the conversation away from the park and horses. "Matteo said you were looking better."

Luther looked down the aisle as if expecting someone. "Is Lieutenant here? Nurse says he comes at night, but I'm sleeping."

So, this was where Matteo roamed at night. Why not visit during the day? She turned her hat around and around in her hands.

"Try staying awake, but ..." He touched his bandage. "This makes me sleepy."

"You don't need to mention I paid you a visit. I wouldn't want my husband to worry."

Luther lay his head back and closed his eyes. Was she tiring him? Should she leave?

"The Lieutenant told the nurse I'm to go stay with Kurt."

"Kurt?" She sat so still she didn't even blink.

"Plays the violin. I'm gunner. Pack the powder in the cannon. Kurt rams it in. We were in the Fifth Cavalry. All wounded."

This was more than Matteo had ever told her. She crushed the brim of her new hat. If only Luther wouldn't peter out before she got more information. "Where is Kurt?"

"My head doesn't remember."

"It's alright. Don't worry, I'll ask my husband," she said, giving a bright lilt to her voice.

"Thank the Lieutenant."

"I will." She glanced at her hat. She had crushed it so that it looked trampled. "How long will you stay with Kurt until you return home?"

His eyes bulged, and his cheeks reddened. "Farm was in Schleswig."

In the Treaty, Emperor Franz Josef had ceded the Austrian state of Schleswig to the Prussians. Luther didn't have a state left, let alone a home. Like her, he'd lost the place he loved most in the world. Where would he go after leaving Kurt's? Who would care for him? How would he live?

Fear vibrated inside her as if someone had struck a tuning fork.

She plumped Luther's pillow. He leaned back again.

"I know how you must miss your home. I grew up on my family's farm in Hohenruppersdorf called Friedenheim. We ... It doesn't belong to us anymore." She couldn't help sharing with him the tiny nugget of hope still nestled deep in her heart. "But I intend to own it again one day."

"Friedenheim. Peaceful home. Good name."

"Would you like me to tell you about it?"

He gave a tiny nod and closed his eyes again. She teared up as she gave a lengthy description of the farm, Kessler, the stallion she had once owned, her *Braunes Bergschaf* sheep, the mountainsides covered in black pines, and the larch trees, her dog, Harbin. How she loved to sit by her grandmother's grave where she could see the valley below.

"I like to visit," he said.

"When I move back, you are most welcome, but ... it may be awhile. I know you would find it peaceful and lovely. In fact, you must promise to visit me."

"Yes. I will." He winced.

What experience did the two men share they couldn't forget? Did the experience affect Luther the way it did Matteo? His hands had stilled on his blanket. He seemed calm enough for her to ask the more sensitive questions she had come to ask. Luther might have the key that would allow her to help Matteo.

"Do you ever have nightmares about the war?" She slid the question out smoothly. Off-hand.

His eyes swiveled to her, his gaze sharp as a razor.

"Nightmares?" He raised his gnarl-knuckled hand and swept it in an arc to encompass all the men in the room. "Everybody."

The ward must sound cacophonous at night if all these men had nightmares like Matteo.

Inhaling deeply, she asked, "What can you tell me of the battle of Königgratz? How you and Matteo were wounded?"

Luther's breathing sped up. His chest rose and fell. His nostrils flared, and his eyes widened. His lips moved, but no sound came out. Then, "Want to forget."

Bur for Matteo's sake, she needed Luther to remember. It was selfish, she knew, but she justified it by reassuring herself that if Luther told her enough, she could help him, too. He might give her enough information to allow Matteo to achieve his dream of helping other soldiers.

Luther grabbed her wrist with an iron hand, nearly yanking her out of her chair. He twisted her skin where the thorn had scratched her. Pain radiated up her arm to her shoulder. His fingers dug into her flesh. The air crackled the way embers do when landing in dry grass. Blood hammered in her ears. Her mouth went dry. She had made a mistake. She glanced around for a nurse but saw no one.

"I should go." Her voice wobbled.

His eyes went unfocused. "Too much smoke." He waved his hand and coughed as if breathing smoke. "Horses. Huge. Black. Coming like Lucifer." Sweat beaded his forehead, and he trembled all over. His eyes narrowed. He looked at her with contempt. "Your horse. You rode me down."

She tried pulling her hand away, but his grip tightened. "I really must be—"

"Made us go. Followed him." He twisted the blanket in his hands. "Couldn't get through. Rocks—" he looked at her imploringly.

"Rocks? There were rocks?"

"Wall. Trapped." His free hand pulled at the blanket. His feet kicked back and forth.

Where in God's name was the nurse? A doctor? Anybody? Why had she come? How could this help Matteo?

Summoning her courage and her voice, she asked, "Was Matteo with you?"

Luther blinked rapidly, his eyelids fluttering like the wings of a panicked bird. "Yes. For some time. He went away." He focused his eyes on her. "Where did he go?"

She tugged her hand again, but he had no intention of letting her go. He pinched the slender bones in her wrist so her fingertips were turning blue.

His breath came in shallow gasps. "They came out of the smoke. Trampled us."

"Who trampled you?"

"Prussian horses."

"So ... you were at a rock wall, with no escape, and Prussians on horses attacked you?" She was relieved, but she was certain there was more to the story. Either Luther couldn't articulate it, or he didn't remember. If his reaction was so violent, what kind of inner strength did Matteo require to keep memories at bay? Or was the loss of those memories worse? What kept Matteo from letting her love him? She needed to know, but not at Luther's expense.

His voice reflected his increasing agitation. "The horses. Huge. Black. Riding us down. Straight from hell." His grip on her wrist tightened. Her skin burned under his twisting grasp.

He was sinking in the mud of a bloody battlefield, trying to stay alive.

She had to calm him. Had to find a way to get him to forget what she had made him remember. "It's all right." She took a long, shaky breath. "You don't have to talk about it. I can see it pains you. I'm sorry I upset you."

He let go of her wrist. She jerked back her arm and rubbed the angry red welt he'd left.

"No escape. Where's von Ritter?" Luther's eyes widened, and he stared from side to side, looking for Matteo.

Her stomach sank, as though she'd swallowed a hard, frozen stone with sharp edges. *Where's von Ritter?* Had Matteo abandoned his men? Where had he gone when they were under fire?

She held her breath. Now she could see why they didn't want to remember. It must have been an experience beyond words or description. Only soldiers who had experienced battle could understand.

Going against all propriety, Zdenka reached out and clasped Luther's hands. When they stopped trembling, she said, "You don't have to go back. The war is over now."

The nurse appeared, her skirts rustling. Her voice was sharp. "It's time to change his dressings. I think you should go, Madame.

Zdenka would have felt less insulted if the nurse had grabbed her by the collar and heaved her down the stairs.

She stood, placed her crumpled hat on her head, and passed the rows of cots. Outside the hospital, pewter colored clouds hung from the sky and the air's scent promised rain. Her feet dragged as she walked to the tram stop. She caught a glimpse of herself in a shop window and saw how she'd mangled her hat.

Her questions had disturbed Luther, setting off a spell of madness. The only information she had gleaned was that sometime during the battle, his men couldn't find Matteo.

CHAPTER 39

When Zdenka arrived home from visiting Luther, Edward's *fiaker* waited at the curb. What did he know of Matteo's experiences in the war? Did he have any insight? She couldn't expect Edward to break a confidence, but he might be able to help her figure out the nature of Matteo's nightmares and where he went at night.

Edward's sharp words the night in the alley brought a flush back to her cheeks, and she was momentarily embarrassed to inquire after Matteo. But she was running out of sources to ply for information. After all, Edward knew about her gambling and the loss of her ring and gowns. She had no choice but to trust him.

In the foyer, Zdenka removed her caplet and mashed hat and handed them to Phillipe.

"Herr Edward is waiting in the drawing room." Phillipe stared at her gloves. She avoided his gaze, and he didn't ask to take them. Phillipe indicated a satchel beside the staircase.

The satchel she had left at Madame Bonterre's, filled with her dresses.

Her heart tumbled. Had Edward bought back her dresses?

She raced into the drawing room.

Edward sat in a high-backed, blue brocade armchair, legs stretched out in front of him, hands folded over his flat stomach, newspaper spread over his face. A soft snore came from beneath the newspaper.

She tiptoed across the room, gently lifted the newspaper from his face, and kissed his forehead. "Thank you for retrieving my dresses."

It was only after planting a kiss on Edward's forehead that Zdenka thought it might be improper, that the servants might gossip. But then, nothing at Thea's was proper.

Edward cocked open one eye. "My pleasure." She let the newspaper drop back on his face. He straightened his long frame in the chair and folded the newspaper.

As usual, Edward wore trousers pressed to a knife's edge and a smart waistcoat of blue and silver brocade. His morning coat of soft charcoal grey made him look distinguished and accomplished, but she knew he was probably recovering from having engaged in one of the seven deadly sins.

He squinted at her. "My God! What happened to your lip?"

Gingerly, she licked her lower lip with the tip of her tongue. Even that hurt.

Edward launched from his chair. He grasped her chin in his hand and turned her face from side to side. "Are you forgetting that you promised me no more adventures?" He took her elbow and sat her in the armchair opposite his own.

She tried stalling. "Why did you get my dresses back?"

"I don't want your marital bliss disturbed." He pointed at her lip. "First, confess how you broke your promise."

"I didn't break my promise. But if I tell you, please don't get mad at Matteo."

Edward's face hardened. "Matteo did this to you?"

She answered quickly, "Don't blame him. He was sleeping."

"Sleeping? How's that?"

She swore him to secrecy. Zdenka recounted how Matteo went out at night, sometimes returning drunk. As she spoke, Edward's eyebrows drew down. She described Matteo's nightmare and the incident where he knocked her off the bed.

"He's worse than I thought," Edward said. "He needs you. He's calmer and steadier when he's with you, but you can't put yourself in danger."

He sounded like Matteo, warning her off for her own safety. "I'm not afraid of him. I was too close to him. I know better now."

Edward studied her. "You *do* love him, don't you?"

Loving Matteo was an ache, a flip-flop, a sorrow, a thrill, and she held all those feelings in one place—her heart. "More than anything in the entire world. More than I thought possible."

"I retrieved something else, but after a split lip, perhaps you won't want it." He withdrew something from his pocket and opened his fist.

Her wedding ring rested in his palm.

Zdenka let out a gleeful squeal. "Oh, heavens! You got it back. However, did you do it?" She tore off her bothersome gloves and threw them on the side table. The gold circlet was warm around her finger. A chunk of worry the size of a boulder melted from her mind. "I can't thank you enough." Edward rose from his seat and crossed to the fireplace. He propped his elbow on the mantel, his face serious.

She held her hand out in front of her and admired the way the thin, gold band caught the light.

"If things get too bad, you must leave him," Edward said.

"I'll never leave him. I love him. As you said, he needs me."

"That's what his mother said about his father. Look what happened."

"He's only violent in sleep. He would never hurt me or anyone else."

Deep in thought, Edward stared at the carpet. "I don't know if this was the right thing to do, but—," He withdrew papers from the inside pocket of his coat and handed them to her.

The deed to Friedenheim.

Zdenka gasped.

It seemed too miraculous to be true. She received the folded deed with two hands as if it were a sacred document. The yellowed parchment was tied with the same black ribbon that had always bound it. She turned it over, its distinctive crinkle, the heft of its weight, familiar to her fingertips. Holding it to her nose, she smelled the musty aroma of the Argentinean's cigars. She had nearly been killed for this slim packet of papers.

And if she had the chance to do it again, she would do it. Giggles bubbled up from inside her.

"It's been my dream to take Matteo home. We'll turn it into a place where other soldiers can come to get better, far away from Vienna. We'll have a life together and pass Friedenheim on to our children." She clasped the deed to her bosom.

"It's yours. He can't take it from you."

"How did you get this?" She untied the threadbare black ribbon and unfolded the papers. She spread it open on her lap and gazed at the black ink, declaring she was the owner. The thrill tingling in her heart was something she never expected. The farm was hers.

Edward smoothed his cravat and gave a low chuckle. "It wasn't easy. I lost a packet before I figured out how the Argentinian was cheating. I bided my time then pulled the winning card out of my sleeve. You should have seen his face. A cheater out-cheated at his own game." His hearty laugh filled the room.

How she wanted to hear Matteo laugh like that. "I can't thank you enough."

"I would do anything for Matteo, and he for me." He gave her a reproving look. "Now, Prince Dimitry tells me you had yet another escapade."

She recounted the tale of riding with Matteo in the Prater and being attacked by Luther.

"You could have been killed." He rubbed his temple and muttered, "Gambling with murderers. Falling off horses. You're a menace to yourself. What are we going to do with you?"

"I'm fine. A bump or two. Nothing serious. But the soldier, Luther Klesper, turned out to be from Matteo's regiment. He wasn't in his right mind due to a terrible head wound at König-gratz. His farm was on land that now belongs to the Prussians. He had nowhere to go, so he was living under the Kaiser Josef Bridge."

Somewhere, a door opened and closed.

"Where is this Luther fellow now?" Edward asked.

"Matteo took him to the *Allegemeines Krankenhaus*. I've just come from visiting him." She sat back in her chair, letting the softness surround and support her.

"You visited him?" Edward's eyebrows raised. "Don't tell me you went alone."

She jutted her chin. "Why shouldn't I?"

He muttered something about her being incorrigible and threw up his hands. "You'll let me know how I can help?"

Zdenka stood and went to him. She lightly kissed him on the cheek. "You've already done so much. Thank you for getting back the deed to Friedenheim."

"You did *what*?" Matteo stood in the archway, his face red, eyes bulging.

CHAPTER 40

Hairs on the back of Matteo's neck bristled as he strode into the drawing room. *What the hell*? Zdenka was kissing Edward.

She backed away from Edward and stumbled.

Edward reached out a hand and steadied her.

Had they been discussing him? Was there something between them?

Edward, hands behind his back, projected an air of studied innocence. Matteo knew not to trust that look.

"I ... I didn't hear you come in," she stammered, with a smile too faint to be believed.

"Why were you kissing Edward?" he growled.

Her eyes flicked away, and he followed her gaze. On a side table lay a folded clutch of papers along with her gloves.

Her smile went crooked. "I was thanking Edward for getting back the deed to Friedenheim."

"How is that possible?" Matteo's eye twitched. He stared at Edward.

Edward's 'charming' smile was pasted on his face. Many a

woman fell prey to that smile, but Edward was a fool if he thought Matteo was so gullible.

"I happened across the Argentinean in a card game," Edward said.

Edward's nonchalance chafed Matteo. Everything his cousin did was calculated. Did he have designs on Zdenka? She was probably the only woman in Vienna he hadn't bedded.

"He'd been trying to pass it off as a stake, so I got it for a song."

"You paid for it?" Matteo said. "How much?"

"Inconsequential. It's heavily mortgaged and he was departing, so he was glad to get rid of it." Edward waved his hand self-deprecatingly.

"Isn't it wonderful?" said Zdenka. "It's ours again."

A lump balled up in Matteo's throat. How could Edward have done this? It was insulting to have to depend on Edward to give *his* wife something he planned to give her—when he wasn't spending his every last cent caring for Luther and Kurt. "Ours? It's not ours, it's his. It was his money—or more likely—Thea's."

Edward tilted his chin to the side in a condescending manner that infuriated Matteo. "Don't be stubborn, Matteo. Actually, I paid it out of my allowance from Mama, so it is my money."

Edward's jovial tone did nothing to soften the insult.

"Consider it a wedding present."

"We'll have our own home." Zdenka's eyes shimmered with excitement. "You'll feel so much better away from Vienna. It will be calm and quiet."

Through gritted teeth, Matteo said to Edward, "I can provide for my wife. I intended to buy the farm back for her at the earliest opportunity. You need all your money for whoring."

Edward's face colored from his collar to his hairline. His smile slipped.

Zdenka put her hand over her mouth. "Matteo," she whispered, her face paling.

"You needn't be an ass. I did it for her," Edward growled.

Matteo snatched the deed from the table.

Zdenka gave the tiniest cry. Her gloves slipped to the floor.

He strode across the room to Edward and slapped the deed against his chest with enough force to make Edward stumble back a step. "I'm returning this to you. When I am able, I'll redeem the note."

Ever unflappable, Edward took the deed. He ambled across the room with measured steps, taking his time. "I gave it to your bride." With an elegant half-bow, he folded her two hands around the document. "She has a right to it, even if you're too stubborn and proud to accept it."

With a slow, casual grace, Edward walked to the drawing room door, stopped and turned back. To Matteo, he said, "Be careful. She might go back without you." And he slammed the door.

Matteo and Zdenka stood silently. She blinked back tears. Cords on his neck tightened like a garrote.

"Why did you accept the deed?" he said, his voice hard-edged as a sword.

She took a step back.

He crossed to the opposite side of the room, sat on the sofa, and clasped his hands. "I'm sorry. I didn't mean to frighten you. I will never, ever knowingly strike you."

Color returned to her face. "I accepted it because I want to take you away from Vienna. From the noise and close crowds. You'll feel better in the fresh air."

"I can't leave Vienna right now." He still had to get Luther and Kurt settled. Apologize for abandoning them on the battlefield. He had to be strong for them a little while longer.

"Does your reluctance have anything to do with Luther?"

He raised his eyes and stared hard at her. "Did you visit him after I'd asked you not to do so?"

She jutted her chin at him. "Yes. But before you scold me, I did it for you too."

"How could Luther possibly help me?"

"I wanted to see if he had nightmares like you. If he knew something that could help me help you. You said you don't remember what happened at Königgratz after you were shot. I asked him what happened."

She circled her thumb and forefinger around her left wrist and rubbed. It was an odd gesture. "What did he tell you?"

Her pause was a beat too long. Had Luther told her Matteo had abandoned them? That she married a coward?

With measured steps, as if not to startle him, she crossed the room. Sitting next to him, she laid her hand on his thigh. "When I asked him about Königgratz, he was gripped by a fit of madness and babbled horrible nonsense."

Her sleeve rode up slightly. A dark purple bruise bloomed at her wrist. He turned her hand over and examined her wrist. "Did he do this?"

She withdrew her hand from his and tugged her sleeve down. "He's no more responsible for that than you are for bumping me the other night. I know you visit him at night—"

"Are you following me?"

Her eyebrows shot up, as if she'd realized something. "Luther told me. If you visit him during the day, I could go with you. I could help you. Now that we have the farm back, we can set about arranging for Luther and Kurt—"

Her hand flew to her lips.

Kurt? Luther had told her about him too. What more did she know? The back of his throat burned, and he fought to remain calm. "What did Luther say about Kurt?"

"Only that he's from your regiment and was also wounded.

Luther said you told him to go live with Kurt when he is able to leave the hospital. But they could both come to us, on the farm. It's been your dream to start a veteran's association. This is our chance."

Her naïveté snapped his thin wire of patience. He snatched her wrist again. "Look at what he did to you. He's capable of doing worse. His mind is gone. It will take more than fresh air and being away from Vienna for soldiers like Luther and Kurt to get better."

She met his eyes. Despite his anger at her taking such foolish risks, the band tightening around his chest eased.

"And what about you?" she asked. "What will it take for you to get better? I haven't seen any sign that roaming around at night, visiting Luther and getting drunk, improves your disposition."

"I can't leave Vienna right now."

"All right. But why? And when can you?"

The only thing she'd ever asked of him, he couldn't give her. Clearing his name had to come first, or he could never respect himself.

"Your pride made you reject Edward's gift and his love. It makes you push me away. You only visit Luther at night, as if you're ashamed for anyone to know. You have secrets you won't share." She stood and crossed to the door where she turned. "If you insist on pride above all else, in the end, you will have nothing and no one."

As she left the drawing room, her words left him feeling like he'd just taken a cannonball to the center of his being.

CHAPTER 41

For three nights, after chaste goodnight kisses, Matteo retreated to his bedroom down the hall, making it impossible to hear if he had a nightmare. She was willing to risk another fist to the mouth if her presence comforted him, but he refused. Did he think himself weak if he let her help him? Did he think she couldn't hear the truth of what happened at Königgratz?

Luckily, he still had to pass by her door to depart by the back stairs. Each night she pulled on her pants, blouse, and riding jacket, hung her cap on the back of the chair, and put her boots by the door. This arrangement would allow her to follow him in the blink of an eye, should he leave the house. She kept her hairbrush in her hands, bristles pointed upwards, so if she nodded off and her head slumped forward, the bristles would waken her. Then, she sat on the floor, knees up, back against the bedroom door, listening for the sound of his footsteps.

Doubts about her plans assailed her. Would he discover her following him? Perhaps he was going somewhere she wouldn't want to know. Was he visiting Luther or someone else? Kurt perhaps?

Arabella's words kept coming back to her: '*Only when you know where he's going can you fight whatever draws him away from you.*'

One last time, dressed as a gentleman, she would fight whatever drew him away. She would fight for him with her mind and heart.

Four nights into her plan, her hand tucked into his elbow, Matteo escorted Zdenka to her bedroom. When he stepped over the threshold of her bedroom, her lower abdomen filled with shivery expectation. She slipped her arms around his neck and dug her fingers into the curls at his nape. His body softened to her embrace, and he pressed the tall muscled length of his body against her. He was solid and strong and so very male.

"Wouldn't you like to sleep in my bed tonight?" she asked.

"Not yet, my dear. You must trust me on this. When I know I am safe, I'll return to your bed."

His lips brushed hers, his tongue darting and seeking. Hungrily, she curved her body against his. He hardened.

"Dear god in heaven, I can't wait to ..." he whispered against the soft spot beneath her ear. He trailed kisses down her neck to her collar, and her skin went hot. He disentangled her arms from around his neck. "Good night."

He closed the bedroom door behind him.

She clutched her skirts in her fists and flailed and twisted and yanked at them, then hurled herself on her bed and stared at the ceiling. Could she possibly die of desire before he gave into her? After allowing herself to wallow in her misery, she rose, dressed in pants, and took up sentry at her bedroom door. Her eyelids were heavy with sleep when the *Pummerin* at St. Stephan's struck midnight.

Footsteps sounded. The third step on the back stairs creaked. Matteo was leaving. She jerked on her boots and ran to the window that looked down on the rear garden. The moon was bright and full, but the fence and the trees provided a strip of darkness. A shadowy figure slipped along under the trees toward the back gate. If she didn't hurry, she would lose her chance. She stuffed her hair under her cap and dashed down the back stairs two at a time. The instant she stepped out the back door into the garden, the gate closed with the 'clack' of a metal latch.

Zdenka ducked low and stayed close to the fence. She wanted to exit the garden before he spotted her. She slipped through the gate as quietly as possible and stepped into the alley.

Recalling Edward's words gave her pause. Following her husband at night wasn't exactly a secretive adventure, was it? If she got into trouble, which she highly doubted she would, she could always call out for Matteo. As he had done when Luther attacked, he would come to her rescue.

It was something of a source of pride to her that she hadn't listened to anyone's cautioning before. Why start now?

Matteo turned, but not in the direction of the hospital. His pace was brisk and purposeful. Her heart thundered as she tried to keep up, aware her boots echoed on the street.

He looked back over his shoulder.

She jumped into a doorway and waited as his footsteps receded. Did he suspect he was being followed or was this simply his usual wariness? If he discovered her trailing him, in pants, it would be over between them. But her love for him drove her to foolish, rash, impulsive acts.

Zdenka followed him into the worst part of town, passing the sorts of establishments she hadn't known existed. The streets went from disreputable to dangerous. Drunks staggered out of *bierkellers*. Ladies in face paint lurked in shadowy doorways. Men rolled dice against brick walls. A slap. A woman's scream.

Matteo seemed to be descending into darkness and with

every footstep. Her heart sank lower and lower. What if she didn't want to know his destination? She couldn't imagine him doing anything depraved.

Gas streetlights cast yellow auras, creating circles of light on the pavement. He glided from light to dark, from light to dark, and on again. He disappeared into a narrow alley.

She dashed after him.

He knocked on the wooden door of a small house. A light glowed in the windows. The door opened, and he disappeared inside.

She stood in a pool of moonshine, panting and shaking. It was as if all the air around her disappeared and she couldn't breathe.

Did this place afford him comfort she couldn't provide? Was he compelled to come here, and afterwards, did he feel better or worse?

Would it make *her* feel better or worse?

She jutted her chin. It didn't matter how she felt. Whatever it cost her, she would find out what he was doing and why. Whatever it took to help him, she would find it. She would follow wherever he led.

Even if, ultimately, it meant losing him.

CHAPTER 42

Matteo hadn't had a drink for two days. Now he was so irritable he felt as though he was walking on nails. But best be cold sober when he faced Kurt, so he could feel the full impact of Kurt's questions, as well as any answers Kurt might offer up. Kurt's ramshackle apartment wasn't much further. Still, Matteo had the distinct feeling someone was following him. Perhaps his poor night vision made him wary. He rounded the corner of Heiligen Strasse and peeked behind him. A shadowy figure stepped behind a *fiaker*. A dog trotted crossed the road. Two men staggered out of a *bierkeller*.

A woman in a gaudy, low-cut dress and excessive rouge sashayed up. "Hello, *schatzy,* I can take that frown off your face in ten minutes."

"No thanks. I always look like this." He wasn't the least bit tempted. No one compared to Zdenka.

This would be his first visit to Kurt's to face the man whose musical career he had cut short. Previously, Father Benedict had taken care of the details, all of which Matteo funded. Now it was time to ask Kurt how Matteo had caused his injuries and to apologize. Not that he expected the apology to be accepted.

Matteo strode up a walkway of broken stones to Kurt's doorstep. When Matteo first rented the apartment for Kurt, he chose it for the west-facing window, which would provide the most daylight. Tonight, he noted the overgrown shrubbery obscuring the window.

Something behind Matteo rustled.

His heartbeat spiked. He slewed round to check behind him.

A rat scurried from behind a trash can.

Stupid, to be so alarmed at every little noise. Matteo smoothed his hair back, straightened his jacket, and knocked on Kurt's door.

The door opened. Kurt stood with a blanket draped over his shoulders. Even after the rigors of war, he was a handsome man. His patrician cheekbones, straight nose, and intense blue eyes contrasted with his boyishly tousled blond hair. At twenty-two, he retained the air of the youthfully enthusiastic, perpetually curious musician. Matteo winced at the sight of Kurt's crumpled hand. With that hand, he had made some of the most exquisite music Matteo had ever heard. Music that was now, and forever, silent. At Königgratz, many nights, Kurt had played Johann Strauss's *Czardas* on his violin. It always comforted Matteo, but he didn't think he could ever hear the tune again without regret.

"Lieutenant von Ritter." Kurt smiled as though greeting a long-lost friend. "What are you doing here?"

"I know it's late, but I was passing by and thought I might stop for a moment." A sense of fraudulence hammered at Matteo, but he shoved it away. He carried the pressure of massive guilt, and Kurt was his first confessor.

"I'm always glad to see a fellow soldier." Kurt stepped back and motioned for Matteo to enter.

The room was smaller than Matteo remembered. A bed with

a body-shaped sway and night table were along one side of the room. The threadbare armchair Matteo had rescued from Thea's attic sat before a cold fireplace. Matteo made a mental note to have a load of coal delivered. A side table held a dented pan, an iron skillet, two pottery plates and two mugs. Kurt gathered up his copyist's paper, music manuscripts, inkwell and pen, which lay spread out on the rickety dining table, and set them to the side.

On the side table, lying next to half a loaf of bread, was Kurt's bayonet dagger.

"Please, have a seat." He pulled out a spindle-backed chair and sat. Matteo, still feeling uneasy, moved around to the other side of the table to watch the door for intruders.

When they'd ridden out of Vienna, Kurt's face was as smooth and soft as a girl. Now, lines etched the corners of his eyes, carved parenthesis around his mouth, made a 'V' between his brows. Were they lines of pain? Regret? Bitterness? Anger?

"Are your dwellings suitable?" Matteo asked.

"Father Benedict says all this has come from some mysterious benefactor." He wiped his ink-stained hand on a rag. "Whoever it is, I'm grateful." With his good hand, he rubbed his injured one.

A white flash of pain caused Matteo's hand to spasm involuntarily.

"How is your head?" he pointed to Matteo's scar.

Matteo actually had to stop and think about the words to use. He'd spent so much time trying to ignore it, he wasn't entirely sure how to describe it. "I don't see well at night and occasionally headaches, but I manage."

Matteo nodded toward Kurt's hand. "Does it hurt you much?"

"Some days are worse than others."

"Do you miss playing violin?"

"Yes. When I came home, I saw no way forward. The violin was my life. To play is—was—as if I drew out a magical thread from the universe, and it turned into music with my bow. It was like breathing."

His eyes grew soft and pensive, the way Matteo remembered him.

"In my head, I hear music I used to play. At night, I dream music. Now, I can only copy the music of others." Kurt gestured to the papers on the table. "Father Benedict said someone told Herr Brahms I was a musician and have fine handwriting. Now, I copy his orchestra scores. The music is beautiful. Ethereal. I can hear it in my head."

"Johannes Brahms?" Matteo pretended surprise. It had taken a few weeks, and a good deal of inveigling, trading on Thea's social connections and impassioned importuning to get Brahms to entrust Kurt with copying the great composer's scores.

"The money is all right and, the music is wonderful." He used his good hand to pry the curled-up fingers on his injured hand. "I satisfy my musical desires by composing."

"What have you written?"

"A violin concerto. I send my originals along with copies of Herr Brahms's music, and he sends back with comments and notations. It's an entirely new experience of music."

"I'll be sure to attend the premiere," Matteo said.

Kurt hummed a few bars of the *Czardas* tune. "So, are you my mysterious benefactor?"

Matteo's arms prickled. He ducked his head to hide his embarrassment. "Forgive my subterfuge. I wasn't sure you would be receptive to my assistance. It's the least I could do after what happened."

"What do you mean?"

Matteo lifted his head and met Kurt's gaze. "I led you into the culvert where we were attacked. It was my fault you were hurt. I should have turned back. I ... I want to apologize for your injuries. I know it's insufficient, but I'm sorry."

Kurt's eyebrows raised. "That is war, Lieutenant. We followed orders. After what you did, how could I blame you? I'm alive because of you."

The last statement made little sense. If only he could remember. Despite Kurt's easy acceptance, Matteo's shoulders sagged.

Kurt eyed him closely. "You look worn out. Exhausted, really. Can I help you in any way?"

To think Kurt offered to help *him*. "I don't sleep much these days." In fact, sometimes, he thought he would drop from lack of sleep.

"Nightmares?" Kurt asked.

Matteo straightened his shoulders. "Nothing I can't manage."

"I don't care to talk about it, either."

A flash of shadow in the window caught Matteo's attention.

His pulse raced. His heart catapulted to his throat. He knocked over his chair and snatched Kurt's bayonet dagger. Anyone who tried to hurt one of his men again would find death.

He yanked open the door and charged into the darkness.

♫

Zdenka ducked below the window into which she had been peeping.

Matteo threw open the door, his bulk filling the space. "Who's out here?" he bellowed.

Her stomach plummeted. It was too late to run, so she clambered deeper into the shrubbery.

Matteo dashed off the doorstep into the yard, a knife glinting in his fist. He reached into the shrub again and again, searching, until his iron fist snatched her by the collar and dragged her out. She scrambled backwards, seeking purchase with her boots. Gravel skidded under her heels and cut into her hands. Branches scratched her face and snagged her hair.

She found herself dangling in mid-air. Her throat tightened, leaving her unable to speak.

He dropped her to her feet and grabbed her before she fell to her knees. He flipped her around and held her back to his chest.

Cold steel pressed the vein under her left ear.

"Declare yourself and your business, or prepare to meet your maker," Matteo growled.

Her pulse raced. Sweat dotted her hairline. She didn't dare swallow, the knife squeezed so hard on her flesh. "Don't kill me," she squeaked out.

"Tell me why I shouldn't kill you for sneaking around out here." He loosened the knife so she could answer.

"Because I'm your wife, Zdenka," she said.

Matteo let her go and spun her around. "What ...?"

With trembling hands, she pulled her cap off and her curls sprang free. "See? It's me." She tried a smile, but it melted away in the heat of his blazing gaze.

He staggered back and gasped, "*Gross Gott,* I could have killed you."

The man inside the house peered from the doorway and gawped. "Your wife? In pants?"

Matteo dropped the knife and staggered back a few steps. "Yes. In pants." Matteo sounded as though he was about to collapse in a faint.

Zdenka's entire body trembled. There would be hell to pay now. He would never trust her again.

"Well," said the man, sounding embarrassed. "I, um, suppose I'll leave the two of you to sort this out." He withdrew into the dwelling and shut the door. Then, the door opened again. "Lieutenant?"

"What?" Matteo shouted.

"I don't want to intrude, but may I have my knife back?" The man asked with speech much more refined than his circumstances indicated.

Matteo looked at the knife lying in the dirt at his feet. His eyes widened. His jaw worked but no words came out. Swearing under his breath, he retrieved the knife and returned it to the man.

"Thank you." The man closed the door.

Matteo gripped Zdenka's elbow and marched her from the courtyard.

CHAPTER 43

Matteo's mind throbbed with urgency as he dragged Zdenka by her elbow down the darkened alley toward the main street. Thinking of her in danger made his lungs hurt.

How could she have been so foolish? He should have known her curiosity would outrun her underdeveloped common sense. "I have to get you away from here and to safety as fast as possible."

She stumbled along after him. He stepped over a pile of trash and kept going.

"Can you slow down?" she panted.

"As soon as I find a *fiaker*, I'll slow down." If he didn't explode before he found one.

They came to an unlit corner where an urchin rifled through the pockets of a man lying in the gutter. Matteo reached into his pocket for a *pfennig*, but the boy pocketed his booty and scampered off into the shadows.

"Even dressed like a gentleman, you look like an adolescent, ripe for robbing. You could have been killed." Matteo pointed to the drunk. "That could be you, only with your skull stove in."

She lifted her chin, but her eyes were wide with fear. "I'm a grown woman. I can make my own choices."

He jerked to a stop beneath a gaslight, and she bumped into him. The softness of her body reminded him of her vulnerability. He said, "You think you don't need looking after. You imagine yourself to be wholly independent, without need of help. As much as you despise social conventions and seek to break them, I still want to take care of you because *you are my wife.*"

She ducked her head but looked up at him from beneath her lashes.

"I should have realized you would follow me." He set off down the street, towing her after him. "Where is a *fiaker* when you need one?"

At last, a dilapidated *fiaker*, hitched to a cadaverous horse, clattered around the corner. Matteo shouted, "Ho, there!"

"Which bawdy house for you two genel'men?" the driver asked in a bored tone.

"No bawdy houses," Matteo bit off. "*Himmelpfort Gasse* on the Park Ring."

"You sure?" slurred the driver. "Pretty fancy."

"I'm sure I know where I live." Matteo lifted Zdenka into the *fiaker,* climbed in after her and slammed the door.

He sat on the seat opposite her. He felt like his pants were on fire. Like smoke billowed from his nose and flames shot from his ears. "Why did you follow me?"

"I wanted to see where you're going. Does that man have something to do with Königgratz? With your nightmares?"

"Have you always been so relentless? If so, you must have driven her parents mad." He yanked back the shredded curtain to let in some fresh air. "That's Kurt."

"I followed you because it's the only way I have of understanding you. I'm worried about you, and I want to help."

He wasn't sure anyone could help him, let alone his deceptive wife. "Now you know where I go."

"All I know is that you went to visit a fellow soldier named Kurt. Why?"

With all his will, he pushed back the urge to tell her everything. It wasn't time yet. He couldn't tell her until he'd made his peace with Kurt and Luther. Which he was about to accomplish when she interrupted.

"You don't have to tell me everything." She held up a thumb and forefinger, an inch between the two. "Just a little. Like when you told me about the drummer boy."

Her gentle, inquisitive voice corkscrewed into his tight heart. "If you must know, I help him because his hand was injured at Königgratz."

Her pretty eyebrows bent into a frown. "What is it about those two men that you must be so secretive when all you're doing is helping them?"

Clever girl. Too clever.

Despite everything that had happened, he wanted nothing more than to gather her to his chest and keep her safe. But he didn't excel at keeping people he loved safe, did he? Insisting she marry him had been a mistake. He hadn't expected to fall in love, and he hadn't known her love would become the very breath keeping him alive. Distrusting her made everything so much easier. Safer. For him. But the distance between them was murdering her love.

"I was beginning to trust you, but as before, you deceive me. We'd agreed you would only wear pants to ride in, not to sneak around, spying on me. How do you expect me to trust you when you break promises you made me? You'll never change your stripes. You'll never be trustworthy."

Her head snapped back as if he'd slapped her. In a softly plaintive voice, she said, "I know you want to keep me safe, but I want to keep you safe as well. And for the same reason. Because I love you."

"I can't believe anything you say." Pushing her away was the only method of keeping her safe from him. At least until the nightmares stopped, which he was sure they would, when he finished with Luther and Kurt.

She cowered into the seat corner. "I can't convince you of my love. You continue to accuse me of being deceptive. You will never forgive my past mistakes. You accuse me of being dishonest, but you sneak about, visiting these men at night, for some strange reason you refuse to divulge."

"I've stopped drinking, as you asked. I don't whore around. I don't have a mistress, and I don't patronize opium dens. That should be sufficient to calm any worries you have about me."

"I can't take it anymore. Your accusations, your anger, your coldness. I want to help you, but you refuse to let me. I never expected you would love me in return." Her voice broke and along with it, a piece of his heart. "I held out hope you would let me love you."

The *fiaker* rolled to a stop in front of Thea's. He reached for the door to help her down, but she threw it open and stepped out. In a shaft of moonlight, the tears on her cheeks glistened like tiny diamonds.

"I'm leaving for Friedenheim in the morning."

CHAPTER 44

When a knock on the door woke Matteo, he wasn't certain that the pounding wasn't in his head. He burrowed back under the blankets.

The door opened and curtain rings slid against the rods. Light pried at his swollen eyelids. He squeezed them shut tighter and groaned.

Edward pulled the pillow from Matteo's head. "Get up," he commanded in the voice of an army general.

"Did the Prussian army march through my mouth during the night, because it certainly tastes like it." Matteo groaned. Every part of his body hurt, even his toenails.

"Good God, you look like an exhumed corpse," Edward sneered. "You look worse than you did when I saw you two weeks ago."

If Edward thought he was a disaster, he must really be on the brink of utter dissolution. When he drank as much as he had the night before, the only mercy was that the scar on his temple didn't hurt. Or at least his temple didn't hurt separately from the rest of his head.

"Why are you here again?" Matteo groused.

Edward had been conspicuously absent from the house since the two had fought over Edward giving Zdenka the deed to Friedenheim. Matteo's anger at his cousin had, for the most part, dissipated, but he still resented the assault on his pride and manhood.

"Mama says she hasn't seen you in the two weeks since Zdenka left. She suspects you've only been out of bed to go drinking, and I see she's right. She asked me to get you up."

"Why?" Matteo scrubbed a hand over three days of stubble.

"Tonight, there's a new premiere of *Der Freischutz* by von Weber. She was sure you would want to go, and Prince Dimitry isn't here to escort her. God knows why, but she wants you to take her."

The prospect of navigating the press of crowds filled Matteo with dread. These sorts of occasions made his skin feel too small to wear. Except when Zdenka had been here, his skin tingled as if he had plunged into an invigorating bath.

Edward leaned his shoulder against the door frame, crossed his arms, and fixed Matteo with a withering stare. "I thought you'd stopped drinking."

"I had, but I changed my mind." Matteo eased into a sitting position on the side of his bed. The room swam.

"Do you think you should consider not drinking again? At least for a while? Get more exercise? Get out more?" Edward sniffed. "Bath more frequently?"

Grosse Gott! Not drink? How would he be able to stand himself? "Drinking keeps the nightmares at bay. Or at least I don't remember them in the morning when I wake."

In his cold, wretched bed, alone.

Edward's posture relaxed. "Since you got home from that infernal war, you're irrational, irritable, jumpy, and you drink far too much. At least when Zdenka was here, you were boring like the rest of us."

Matteo gave his cousin a scowl intended to shut him up, except that such scowls only egged Edward on.

Edward didn't disappoint. "I can't imagine why she was willing to not only tolerate you, but she was silly enough to actually love you!"

"What are you doing here, anyway? Don't you have some poor woman to seduce?" Matteo slowly rose to his feet, and the floor tipped from side to side as though he were in a boat in a storm.

Edward poured steaming water from the ewer into the washbasin. Matteo performed his ablutions, and he actually felt less dead.

"Will Zdenka be returning soon?" Edward handed him a towel and Matteo dried off.

A streak of lightning jabbed Matteo's spine, and he could keep silent about the deed no longer. "If you hadn't given her the deed to the damn farm, she wouldn't have left me."

With an insufferable smile, Edward asked, "You think she left you because of the farm? I think she left you because she loved you and you weren't returning her love. Instead, you skulked around at night, doing God knows what—"

"At least I wasn't in some other woman's bed." Matteo swished his shaving brush on the soap cake and soaped up his face to shave. He looked hard at Edward. "Are you sure you didn't give her the deed because you had designs on her?"

Edward threw his head back and snorted a laugh. "Your brain is positively pickled." He opened Matteo's straight razor, stropped it up the leather strap, tested the sharpness with his thumb, and handed it to Matteo. "The only designs I had on her were for her happiness and your happiness. Nothing more. She loves you so much, no man—not even me—could turn her head."

Matteo looked into the mirror, held the blade to his face, and promptly nicked his chin. A thin thread of blood trickled down his neck. The blood smelled like iron, smoke, dead men. He breathed deeply, counting, as Zdenka had taught him. "What makes you such an expert on marriage and love?"

"Let me do this before you slit your own throat." Edward pulled the straight-backed chair over and motioned to Matteo to sit. Edward flipped the towel around Matteo's neck and shaved him. "I claim no expertise on marriage or love, but I am experienced with women. You need to stop pushing her away."

Matteo opened his mouth to say something, but Edward said, "Don't talk, or I'm liable to take off half your Adams's apple."

Matteo had to protect Zdenka from the disappointment of loving a coward. If she knew of the truth about him, she would lose all respect for him. Love without respect wasn't love at all, it was pity.

Edward swished the blade in the water and handed Matteo a wet washcloth. He wiped the remaining soap from his face. "You know, she followed me dressed in pants in order to spy on me? How can I love a woman who's so untrustworthy and duplicitous?"

Edward snorted a laugh. "Resourceful woman. All that talk of your honor and how she had to marry you because she'd tricked you, when truly, she was the best friend—aside from me—you've ever had. Now, you condemn the lengths to which she will go to show her love for you."

"But she's so stubborn and hardheaded. She risks her own safety because she insists on being so damned independent."

And since Luther's attack, her riskiness set guilt, panic, and protectiveness warring inside him when she did something impulsive. An emotional combination he couldn't unweave and couldn't stand.

Edward handed him a comb and pointed at Matteo's

haystack of hair. "You've decried the sorts of women I've consorted with, calling them ninnies, simpering simpletons, amoral. Then, the boldest, smartest, most surprising, most forthright woman in existence marries you, and you drive her off as though she were a Prussian."

Matteo put down the comb. "What would you have me do? You know I hate lying."

Looking over Matteo's shoulder into the mirror, Edward smoothed his pomaded hair back, cocked one eyebrow and feigned his 'seduction' smile. "Then stop lying to yourself. Set your pride aside. If you apologize sufficiently, she might forgive you and give you another chance."

Matteo set his comb next to his shaving implements.

Edward said, "Much as I care for you, you don't deserve her. You need to earn her love again. Her respect. Or you will lose her forever."

♫

Matteo put on his shirt, his black evening suit, cravat, and gold cufflinks. The demons of *Der Freischutz* seemed to be hammering their anvils inside his head. Edward had a way of putting things so they couldn't be ignored.

Once he was finished dressing, Matteo headed downstairs. There was enough time for a cordial before they departed for the opera.

At the moment he passed Zdenka's bedroom, a breeze blew the door open. The maids had been going in daily, opening the windows and airing out the room. Zdenka's vanilla fragrance wafted out of the door, daring him to come inside.

He stopped and stared into her room. Had she returned? Perhaps she was there, stretched out on the bed, waiting for him, her smile welcoming and tender, green eyes beckoning. He reached out his hand, then, and shook his head. His brain sloshed from side to side. What a foolish hope. Once the woman made up her mind to do something, she would do it, no matter what or how dangerous. And that included leaving him.

Determined not to be swayed by Edward's arguments, Matteo marched into the room to close the window, close the door, and close his heart.

When he reached the room's center, he was overcome with a need to see, to touch what she had touched, that which carried her scent, her essence. Even a hint of her fragrance reminded him of Zdenka's curves, the silk of her skin, her mad, springy ginger hair.

For all his anger, his hunger for her was a drive so powerful, he couldn't resist.

He went to her armoire and opened it. She had left most of the gowns Thea had bought her. He rubbed a gown of dark green velvet between his fingers, feeling the soft fabric. When she'd worn this dress and he'd looked in her eyes, he'd been the happiest he could ever remember. What would it take to be that happy again?

But that would require him admitting being wrong, apologizing; letting her love him.

Confessing to her about what he'd done.

He shut the door to the armoire and crossed the room to her dressing table. Her silver hairbrush, hand mirror, a crystal box containing hairpins, and a thin green satin ribbon were arranged on top of the dressing table. The hairbrush and mirror had been wedding gifts from Thea and Prince Dimitry, the crystal box from Edward.

She had left the gifts. Did that mean she would return for them, or did it mean she never wanted to be reminded of anything that had to do with him ever again?

The last time he'd been in her room, he'd seen her music

box. Now, it was gone, the only thing she'd taken. The box played the Mozart tune from *Die Zauberflöte*. He took comfort in the fact that she wanted to remember the music they had both loved. And perhaps remember having been, for a short time, man and wife.

Matteo lifted the lid of the crystal hairpin box, took a single long pin, and replaced the lid. He held the pin up to the light and remembered unpinning her hair the afternoon in the Prater, the way her ginger curls sprang into his hands. Sweet memories stung him like a nest of hornets.

Tucked into the corner of the mirror was a dried pale mauve rose—the flower he'd given her from the meadow on the day she'd given herself to him. He would do anything to get back that moment when they were bound together in love.

He sat on the edge of her bed and let his hands hang between his legs.

Edward was right.

Matteo hadn't thought she would make good on her promise to leave. Rage at her deception, guilt—no, fear she wouldn't love him—had overridden his love for her.

He lifted his head and looked around the room. Whatever it took to get her back, he would do. She deserved better from him; she deserved a real husband. If she required him to slay dragons, swim the length of the Danube in mid-winter, trek the Alps barefoot, he would do it.

He made a mental list.

Stop drinking. Meet his obligations to others, and not just Kurt and Luther. Apologize to Luther and Kurt. Stop accusing her of deception. Ask her to forgive him for hurting her. Pursue his dream of beginning a veteran's association.

The list was daunting. Where was the brandy?

No, where was his wife?

A gust of wind slammed the bedroom door shut.

"All right, all right." He couldn't help laughing.

He opened the door, determined to fight the most difficult battle he'd ever faced: that of transforming himself into the man he knew his wife deserved.

♪

It didn't matter how hard Zdenka worked at Friedenheim or how exhausted she was at the end of a long day, she still dreamt about Matteo. She touched her cheek, longing for the way his fingers grazed her face, for the tickle of his hair brushing against her neck. She buried her nose in the pillow next to her, seeking his masculine scent. In the morning, she often felt more tired than she had when she'd gone to bed. She believed that if she held onto these memories, Matteo might come for her.

Using what little money was on hand, Zdenka had bought the most magnificent horse she could find. It was impulsive, but she was tired of only working and talking to her black and white dog, Harbin. The horse was an enormous black *Shagyar-Araber* stallion, bred as a racehorse in Bábolna, Hungary, the town from whence the famous Viennese Royal Lipizzaner horses hailed.

At the end of every day, she leaned over his neck and let him run at will, his flowing black mane and tail flying out behind her like flags of sorrow. But she could never ride fast enough to leave her heartache behind.

She named him Schwartzkönig.

One afternoon, aching with exhaustion, Zdenka climbed the high hill behind the house where her ancestors were buried. Beneath a towering, hundred-year-old oak, she sat against her grossmutti's headstone. The headstone was flecked with white lichen and weathered a dark grey. Zdenka had planted her grossmutti's favorite rose, *My Beloved*, on top of her grave. Heavy with blush-colored blossoms, the branches bent downward.

This was the same rose Matteo had plucked for her after they made love in the Prater. She had tucked it into her mirror frame at Thea's.

When she and Matteo had departed their secret bower, her heart had been bursting with hopes for a happy future, only to have those hopes dashed by Luther's mad attack. Luther's appearance had changed everything, igniting a firestorm of Matteo's nightmares, increasing his absence at night, making him more fearful of her safety.

She took out pen and paper she had brought along and wrote to her sister.

Dear Arabella,

It has not rained in weeks and the land is dry. If it does not rain soon, we will lose the few crops which were planted. There are so many things to do, I grow weary simply thinking about them. I never thought it would be so hard. I will try to sell a bit of timber so I can hire some workers. For now, I will make do, despite missing both you and Matteo terribly.

Your loving sister,

Zdenka

P.S. Last week, Francine, our best milker, gave birth to a wobbly calf. He has a black spot on his side that looks like Graf Elemer's profile, so I named him Elemer. If we get a bald one, I'll name it Lamoral.

She slipped the letter into her pocket, but it popped out a hole.

She sighed. Another chore.

From this vantage point, she could see to the end of Waldner lane where a pair of hundred-year old stone plinths stood, carved with her grandmother's name, *Friedenstock*. This ancestral land was where she wanted to spend the rest of her life. It was *her* responsibility to ensure all of this remained in the Waldner family for generations to come.

But Matteo was her responsibility too, because he was her husband. It crushed her heart to leave him, but if he came here, he could forget the war and heal. They could have a life together, but as of their final meeting, that seemed highly unlikely.

With her arm slung over Harbin's neck, she squinted and spotted another loose shingle on the barn roof. "Herr Klopstein wasn't much of an estate manager, but at least he took good care of you and the other animals. Thanks to Papa's gambling, there wasn't enough money to keep anything else up."

She turned her gaze to the field furthest from the barns.

"That wheat should be taller, so that means a poorer harvest."

Her horse, old Sophie, limped along the pasture where she grazed alongside the sheep. The sway-backed mare rubbed her nose on a fence rail, which promptly fell from its posts.

"*Ach!* And the rails around the paddock are rotting."

Harbin prodded her hand with his wet nose.

She sighed wearily. "Yes. You're right. If we're to make this place ready for Matteo, there's no time to waste." Standing up, she breathed in the clean, sharp air wafting over her land. She kissed her fingertips and pressed them to the top of the headstone.

"I promise, Grossmutti," she whispered. Then she strode down the hill towards the farm.

CHAPTER 45

Zdenka scratched Harbin behind his ears. "Wait here. I'll be back, hopefully, having sold some of the timber." Harbin lay down with his nose on his paws. She was sure he was smiling at her.

Her stomach knotted as she stepped into the *Milch Halle*, the beer hall in Hohenruppersdorf where landowners, many of whom were dairymen, took a lager in the afternoon. She recalled bitterly how Papa lost her stallion, Kessler, to Herr Blasen, her westerly neighbor, in a card game. She'd learned to ride on Kessler, and it broke her heart when Papa gave him to Blasen to settle the debt. For that reason, approaching Blasen to buy her timber was like swallowing ground glass. But she needed the money to get help on the farm.

The room hadn't changed. Dim light and grimy walls. Pipe tobacco, sweat, and stale beer still hung in the air. Hand-hewn benches and tables cluttered the room. A chess board had been painted on the top of a table, its pieces were scattered as if the last players, too drunk to finish, had abandoned their game.

Through the dim light, she recognized Herr Blasen and Herr

Wilmerstein, and her neighbor, Herr Fredrickson, another local landowner, sitting at a table, drinking lager from metal tankards.

They glanced her direction and laughed.

Heat spread across her face. She stiffened her spine.

Much as she wanted to wear pants, she decided it would make a better impression if she wore one of Arabella's old dresses and a hat. The dress was too short, her boots showed beneath the hem, and the drab brown dress made her look pale and washed out. Or perhaps she was really a washed-out old scrub rag, threadbare from all the work she'd been doing. Every muscle in her body ached, and her hands were scratched and callused from work. Still, there was so much to do, and she had to have the money from selling some of the timber.

With steady steps, shoulders back, Zdenka approached their table.

Blasen glanced sideways at her. "Ah, if it isn't the female farmer."

Tempting as it was to knock him in the head with his tankard, she instead forced a smile. "Yes, here I am."

She looked from one man to the other, waiting for an invitation. Women seldom entered here, and then, only with husbands, but this was the place where townsfolk—men, really —conducted business.

"May I sit, *mein Herren*?" she asked in her sweetest voice. Without waiting for an answer, she pulled up a chair.

Ordinarily, gentlemen, even country farmers, rose when a lady entered and offered a chair, but these men merely traded glances. Blasen smelled like he had rolled in his pig sty, and his beard was full of crumbs.

Zdenka tilted her chin the way she'd seen Arabella do sometimes. "I'm sorry if I've interrupted your discussion, but I have a business proposal for you."

Scrawny Wilmerstein was known by that name precisely

because he looked like a tough old, featherless chicken. He laughed and showed his rotten teeth. "Women have no business doing business."

She bit the inside of her lower lip. "As you know, the farm is mine now, and I'm running it."

"Into the ground, no doubt," Fredrickson muttered into his tankard. His cheeks, threaded with root-like purple veins, sagged like hog jowls.

Determined not to be put off, she ignored his comment. "I have timber to sell. Oak, ash, spruce—all big, old stock. Hardy. Herr Fredrickson, I know you are planning an addition to your house in the next few years."

"Who told you that?" Fredrickson asked.

She batted her eyelashes at him. "Why, your wife has told everyone."

His mouth dropped open slightly, and he frowned.

"I know you'll need to purchase good timber to season." She said it as a statement, not a question, hoping he would understand her certainty as the mark of a seasoned businesswoman.

"No, not I." Fredrickson downed the last of his beer and stood. "I've better things to do with my time than try to be sold a lot of fiddlesticks by a female." He trudged out the door. To go home and berate his wife, no doubt.

Zdenka's cheeks grew hot. "How about you, Herr Wilmerstein? You have a big herd of milkers. If you build a new barn, you can increase milk production."

Wilmerstein leaned his elbows on the table. "My cows have plenty of room. What would a slip of a girl know about dairy cows anyway?"

She clenched her hands together under the table to keep them from shaking. "I know you to be a good dairy farmer, but your barn is old and overcrowded. I read an article in the agricultural section of *Die Zeitung* that said if you allocate more space for your cows, their yield increases." She had read it and intended to build more stalls in her own barn as her herd increased, so as not to crowd them all together.

He glared at her as if he were looking at a two-headed cow. "You don't need to read. It'll do you no good. Book-learning makes a woman restless. Irritable. What you need to do is find a husband." He looked over at Blasen and snickered. "But I can't imagine a man in the whole of the county that would marry a girl walks about in pants."

She bit the end of her tongue until she tasted blood, but she kept a smile on her face.

Wilmerstein shoved his chair back, threw a coin on the table, and left. The door slammed behind him.

That left only Blasen. She hoped she could disguise her hatred of him. "And what about you? I'm sure you could use some timber. I've noticed you've thinned your own timber a great deal, and what remains is not readily accessible because it runs up the hill at the foot of the mountain."

Blasen blinked his protuberant eyes at her. Manure smelled better than his breath.

She tried not to sound desperate. "Even a few trees. You could choose what you want and buy the rest in a few months."

He reached out and patted her head.

She wanted to bite him, kick him, shove his head in a barrel full of pickles.

"Go home, little miss, and do like Fredrickson says. See if you can find some man to take you on." He shuffled out, his fat stomach proceeding him through the door.

Her body burned with humiliation. Perhaps she should have worn pants. Maybe they would have taken her seriously then. She hadn't come begging for help, but they had to have known that was what she needed. She had known it would be perhaps an unpleasant negotiation but didn't expect to be ridiculed.

Never again would she ask these narrow-minded fools for help. Why hadn't she expected such a reaction from a bunch of stupid, uneducated oafs? She would do it all herself. Straightening her spine, she stood and marched out into the sun.

To hell with them. She didn't need anyone's help.

CHAPTER 46

H arbin's barking roused Zdenka. She had been napping, drool pooling on her sleeve. Lifting her head from her folded arms, she blinked and rubbed her eyes. When she had sat at the garden table under the tree, she had promised herself she would only nap for a few minutes. The sun had been high in the sky, but now it was much lower. Her shoulders ached, and her hands were no less blistered than when she had fallen asleep.

She yawned and stood to see Harbin charge down the lane, aimed at two men straggling toward the house. Shielding her eyes from the late afternoon sun, she saw that one man was tall and slender with an elegant walk, the other had a lumbering gait which threw him side to side rather like a barrel on legs. As they drew nearer, she recognized Luther. She had only seen Kurt in the dark, but she assumed the other man was him.

Her heart jumped. Maybe they had word of Matteo.

"Harbin, come!"

Tail wagging, the dog bounded back to her, and stood protectively beside her. "I invited them. It will be nice to have a bit of company." She scratched Harbin's head. "I like you, but you don't have a very big vocabulary."

Carrying rucksacks with bedrolls, Kurt and Luther were covered in dust, bedraggled, and she supposed, hungry. Luther removed his cap and turned it around in his hands.

With his expressionless Schleswig accent, she struggled to understand him. "Frau von Ritter, we come for the Lieutenant."

Her heart plummeted. "No," she choked out. "Isn't he in Vienna?"

"We don't hear from him in weeks. Hope he's not dead," Luther said in a flat tone.

Her legs wobbled.

"Luther, you're frightening her." Kurt pulled out a chair at the table. "Frau von Ritter, you should sit." He pointed to the pump. "Luther, get her some water."

Luther ambled over and pumped a bit of fresh water into a cup hanging on a hook. He brought it, sloshing droplets over the edge. Despite his clumsiness, he placed the cup carefully in her hands.

She drained the contents and set the cup on the table. She felt so vulnerable, asking these two strangers, Matteo's friends, where her husband was. What must they think of her? She was alone, asking virtual strangers for help. Truthfully, she was a little scared being alone with her neighbors so far away. Luther was expressionless and melancholy. What if he became unhinged again? Were either of them unpredictable or dangerous?

"He's not here, coming soon?" Luther asked.

Luther's words were so disjointed and lacking in intonation, she was unsure if he was making a statement or asking a question. His wound had healed, but he had an indentation and jagged scar imprinted on his forehead. He was broader than he had appeared beneath his hospital sheets, and the agitated man she had met in the hospital seemed to no longer exist.

"He's sold his commission. He's no longer an officer," she said.

"I'm Kurt Lescht. We didn't come to upset you, Frau von Ritter," Kurt said.

"Please, you must call me Zdenka." She wiped her dirty palms on her pants and offered her hand. Kurt shook it. His other hand was twisted into a scarred, useless claw.

Pain whip-cracked through her chest.

Matteo had never mentioned that hand.

"We've ... met before. Briefly," she said.

"We have?" Kurt's brow furrowed.

Her cheeks scalded. "Late one night when I, um, arrived at your lodgings during one of Matteo's visits to you."

Kurt pulled out the chair across from her and sat. "I recall, but I didn't see you in the dark."

Peeping through the grimy window, she had only gleaned a bare idea of Kurt's figure, but he seemed hardier, more filled out, than he had that night. Too-long blond hair trailed over his collar. His intense crystal-blue gaze and elegant assurance, were, she supposed, a result of playing violin in public for many years.

"When did you last speak to Matteo?" she asked, her worry spinning out of control. She didn't want to embarrass herself by blubbering. She had thought she could handle whatever fell into her lap. Everything except losing Matteo for good.

"Nurse say he stopped coming, maybe, three week ago," Luther said.

Just when she had left Vienna. Her stomach curled against her spine.

"I know he came only at night to see you both, but it's not like him to abandon something he considers his responsibility." She shook her head.

Kurt's brow furrowed. "About three times a week, Father Benedict from St. Stephan's brought me something and said it was from a mysterious benefactor. When Matteo visited that night, he admitted he was my benefactor. It was the only time I ever saw him."

"We worried," Luther said.

Not as worried as her.

"That night, he apologized. We didn't finish talking because you ..." he cleared his throat. "I haven't seen him since. He helped us so much, we wanted to find him to thank him. When we couldn't find him, and Father Benedict hadn't seen him, we became worried. We told Father Benedict we were coming here to look for him and to tell him we were all right."

"Did you ask at his aunt's house? He had to be there." Her heart raced. Surely Thea and Edward knew where he was.

Luther pushed out his lower lip. "Butler came to the door. Said he didn't know."

Perhaps Phillippe was protecting Matteo. She never should have left him. He needed her. If only he hadn't continuously accused her of deceiving him, she would have stayed. Was he lying drunk in a gutter somewhere?

"I'm sorry we've upset you. Could you write someone and ask after him?" Kurt said.

She swallowed back her tears. "I'll write to Edward, his cousin, first thing in the morning. He has to know where Matteo is. Perhaps I should return to Vienna."

Harbin bumped against her leg as if to remind her of her responsibilities. It was up to her to see to the animals and take care of things. But what of Matteo? She had to have a few minutes to herself to think.

Luther's stomach rumbled and gave her the reason to leave them for a bit.

She jumped up. "You must be hungry. Let me fetch you something to eat."

"There's no need," Kurt said, but she pretended not to hear.

In a few minutes, she had prepared food and returned to the men. Her arms were like noodles as she carried a tray bearing an earthen pitcher, two glasses, and two plates with thick slices of ham and buttered bread. She set the plates on the table before the men then went to the pump and filled the pitcher. When she returned, as she poured a glass of water, her hands trembled, and water splashed on the table.

Kurt leaped up and pulled out a chair for her.

"I ... I'm sorry, I guess I'm a bit out of sorts." She sat.

As the men ate, her mind churned. What happened to Matteo that he stopped doing the things which he had taken so much care to plan and execute? He had been so secretive about helping these men, but now, to disappear without a word? It wasn't like him at all. Why did no one know where Matteo was?

Why didn't she know where he was?

"Thank you." Kurt pushed his plate away. "I was hungrier than I realized."

"*Ja,* thanks. Sorry bring bad news." Luther pushed his chair back. "We go now. Long walk back."

Kurt, his irritation obvious, said, "We wouldn't have to walk, if you were willing to ride a horse."

Luther's smile vanished. "No horse for me, thanks. I like walking."

Zdenka remembered Luther's horrifying description of the battle and Matteo's dream of giant black horses riding down on them. No wonder Luther was afraid to ride horses.

It had been a windless, cloudless, sun-drenched day. Now, the sun dipped behind the mountains, and the day had begun to cool. Zdenka didn't want to be alone. For the first time in her life, terror gripped her. If Matteo went to Father Benedict, he would tell him that Kurt and Luther were here. Maybe he would come too.

It wasn't a likely answer, but the only one her frantic mind came up with.

"It's late. Stay and rest. You can go tomorrow. If you wish, you can sleep in the barn tonight," she offered.

"Are you sure?" Kurt asked. "We don't want to impose."

"It's no imposition. I'm glad to have you. Matteo would want it, and so do I." She rose from her chair. "Come, I'll show you where you can put your things. You can wash up in the stream, beyond that row of spruce trees."

Wearily putting one foot in front of the other, she led them across the lane to the barn. Harbin trotted along at her heels.

Luther said, "Beautiful farm, but barn need shingles."

Kurt nudged him with an elbow.

"I know. It's on my list of things to do, but I always seem to run out of time." Her arms were so tired, they might have fallen out of her shoulder sockets. Worrying about Matteo and the needs of the farm left her feeling utterly overwhelmed.

"You? Are you here alone? Haven't you got a hired man to do it?" Kurt asked.

"No hired men," she said on a long sigh. "Just me and Harbin."

In the barn, she pointed out the hay loft. "You can sleep up there."

In his stall, Schwartzkönig whinnied.

Luther's eyes widened. He backed away from the stall. "I sleep outside." He turned and, almost running, left the barn.

She reminded herself to lock and barricade her bedroom door.

CHAPTER 47

Matteo kept his head down, staring at a scuff mark on the toe of his right boot. Now and then, Thea paused on the stairs of the opera house to bid good evening to one of her friends. Edward was behind him, and Matteo had a sense that Edward knew what a struggle it was for him to go to the opera tonight. Being in public, sober, was equivalent to having forks dragged across his skin. Zdenka's presence, as a gentleman or as his wife, had always calmed him. In such a crowd, her absence made him feel as though he should have brought a sword in case he needed to defend himself. The audience chatter about von Weber's opera rattled in his ears like gravel tumbling in an empty barrel. The brush of every cloak was like the slap of a hand. His eye began to twitch, and the scar on his back burned. But he wasn't about to let Thea down. He was a dependable man. He was responsible.

At least, he would be, if he tried not to drink. Not try. Just not drink.

"Here we are." The livery-clad usher opened the door to Thea's box.

"I have someone to see," Edward said to Matteo. "I'll be

along shortly." He disappeared, off to speak to one of the many women who had smiled and laughed coquettishly as he passed.

Not a one of those women had caught Matteo's attention. Zdenka was more beautiful than all of them when she strutted about in her pants. Finally, he was able to identify the constant ache he couldn't assuage. He wanted his wife. In his arms, in his bed. At his side. Under him.

The solitude of the opera box was a relief from the press of the crowd. Matteo's stomach rumbled. He was a bit light-headed from hunger. They would have supper in the box at the interval.

When they were settled in their seats, Thea placed her hand on his arm. "I haven't had a chance to speak to you until now. I understand how grieved you must be over Zdenka's leaving, but you must stop drinking so much. You have to get out and live." Her eyes were moist in the low light. "If you could let go of your pride, go to her and apologize, I'm sure she would take you back. She loves you."

If only it were pride and not shame. He had to protect Zdenka from disappointment at having married a coward. "I'm not ready yet. I don't think I'm yet the man she deserves."

Thea squeezed his arm. "Oh, my dear, she adores you and wants you to love her in return. Be honest with her. Love isn't so much more complicated than that. If she loves you, she will forgive you, whatever is weighing on your mind."

It couldn't possibly be so easy. Men had been hurt, nearly killed because of him. When they had forgiven him, he would go to her.

Edward entered the box, flustered and out of breath, relieving Matteo of the need for further confession.

"Off seducing some poor woman?" Matteo asked.

Edward crossed his legs and straightened his bow tie. "I'm curtailing my activities," he said with a mysterious smile.

"Has Hell frozen over?" Matteo asked with exaggerated

astonishment.

"Have you finally lost your heart to someone?" Thea asked Edward, with genuine astonishment.

"Ask any one of a dozen Viennese women. He has no heart," Matteo said, ignoring his aunt.

Edward didn't answer but leaned over the railing and smiled the idiot grin of a man who *had* lost his head and his heart.

Was that how Matteo looked when he stared at Zdenka? When he looked at her, he knew something happened inside him. Something like a green blade of grass pushing through rock. A sharp inhalation of disbelief. Zdenka loved him!

Then, the urge to protect her overpowered everything else.

Matteo followed his gaze and recognized Fanny Bösendorfer, the daughter of the piano builder to the Emperor, her eyes blazing with adoration at Edward. Had Edward lost his mind as well? Fanny was rather plain-faced, sharp-tongued, a fantastic pianist and a gossip. "Fanny Bösendorfer?" Matteo said, incredulous.

Edward threw him a sizzling glance. "She's a rather an intelligent young lady. I've given up my ideas of what is of paramount importance in my life." Edward smoothed the front of his pristine starched white shirt. "You might want to consider doing the same thing, *mon cousin.*"

"I've stopped drinking. What else do you suggest I give up?" Matteo asked.

"Honor has served you well, but making that your defining personal characteristic, has, unfortunately, caused the departure of your wife," Edward's sarcasm was friendly, but delivered with his usual pointed panache.

Thea frowned. "Don't be cruel."

The theater lights dimmed, and the conductor entered the orchestra pit. Matteo had looked forward to the solace of the evening's music, but after the first act, he thought the overture tedious, the tenor unbearably flat, and the soprano screechy. He couldn't keep his mind on the music. Edward's admonishment kept coming back—

Vibration shocked Matteo's bones.

There was a brilliant orange flash and the unmistakable crack of a gunshot.

A few members of the audience gasped. Some of the ladies made sharp, high cries.

Matteo's heart jumped in his chest. His forearms and thighs tensed. He launched out of his seat, looking around for the source of attack.

Protect her.

He threw his arms around Thea and pulled her to the floor. Her chair tipped sideways, clattered against his, and fell to the floor with a thud. The floor vibrated with pounding feet. *Or hooves. They were coming.*

Edward sprang from his seat. "What in the devil are you doing, man?"

"We're under attack. Have to protect her." Matteo dragged Thea deeper into the back of the box and lay over her to shield her. He had failed to protect his men, but this time he would not fail his beloved aunt.

In the boxes on either side, alarmed guests arose from their seats and gawked.

"Is everything all right, Vicomtess Prokovsky?"

"Do you need assistance?"

"Shall we summon the police?"

"What on earth?"

The orchestra halted. The curtain rang down and the house lights went up. Titters rippled through the opera house.

"Have you gone completely mad?" Edward yanked him off Thea. "Get up before you hurt her. There is no attack. It was a shot from onstage. It's part of the opera."

Matteo's breath was ragged. His face burned. His heart jammed in his chest. *Is she safe?*

Edward helped Thea off the floor and placed himself protectively between her and Matteo. "Mama, are you all right?"

Matteo blinked. He got to his feet. His shirt was damp with sweat, and his eye twitched madly. The scar on his temple throbbed. "Part of the opera? Are you sure?"

Thea's hair had come undone and tumbled down her shoulders. The sleeve of her dress was torn. "Matteo, what's the matter?"

Thea sounded as worried and unnerved as he had ever heard her. And it was his doing. His throat was too tight to apologize. He looked over the balcony. The entire audience stared up at their box. The rustle of murmurs. Titters. Tsk-ing. Gaping mouths.

He flung open the door to the opera box and staggered blindly down the staircase, through the doors, and out into the black night.

♫

Outside the opera house, Matteo walked as fast as he could, unsure where he was headed. He yanked his cravat free and gulped the brisk night air. He hunched against the early-spring cold and marched, head down into the wind, but he had forgotten his overcoat in the opera box. The chill wind cut through his evening jacket. Blood pounding in his ears slowed as his heartbeat returned to normal.

The only normal thing about him.

Why hadn't he stayed home this evening? He had wanted to Thea to be able to depend on him, to be responsible, to honor his commitment.

His insides curdled, remembering the people staring, their

eyes stabbing at him like pinpricks. Titters scratched in his ears. He had been able to keep his unpredictability private thus far, confined to a few small incidents, but now, all of Vienna knew. No one would hire him. Who would trust him not to go berserk?

If he hadn't driven Zdenka away, this would never have happened. Her resilience made his soldiering look like he had the backbone of a blushing debutante. Her core of steel drew him like a needle to the North Pole.

The wind rose, beating at him, pushing him back, flapping his coat. He put one boot in front of the other, blind to his direction, until, at last, the muddy, damp odor, told him he had reached the bank of the Danube.

He sat on an iron bench, the seat cold as ice, and stared out over the churning waters. How could he get her back? Moreover, could he be the man she deserved? How could he tell her how he had failed?

Wind whistled in his ears. The air smelled of rain. A scrim of clouds obscured most of the stars. He pulled his coat tightly around him. Lights from houses and apartments blinked off. He leaned his elbows on his knees and wondered how cold the water was.

Such an independent, courageous woman could never love ... a *coward*. How had he convinced himself otherwise?

Clouds swept off the stars and the wind died down. A slice of moon, bright as a molten scythe shown on the water. Amber light danced on the water and reminded him of the way sunlight glinted on Zdenka's hair. From somewhere behind him, the sound of a violin floated across the night. It was Mozart's duet, *Bei Männer welche Liebe fühlen* from *Die Zauberflöte*. He had hummed that tune, when he had waltzed Zdenka, dressed as a boy, about in the woods. The tune in the music box he had presented her for their wedding. The music box she had taken with her when she left him. The words came back to him.

In men who feel love, a good heart too, is never lacking.

Then a few lines later,

The high purpose of love proclaims there is nothing higher than wife and man.

A realization hit him with the force of a well-placed punch to the jaw. If he *loved*, and dear God above, did he love her, his heart *was* good. The love of man and wife was the highest love of all. He had lost her because he hadn't trusted in her to love *him*, but it was loving which *made* you good, made you whole, raised you above anything that made you *unlovable*.

Nothing, not honor, not duty, not responsibility, surpassed his love for Zdenka. And her love surpassed his guilt and shame. Her love lifted him beyond the realm of human, to the realm of *beloved*. It was worth his pride to take the chance and tell her his cowardice was responsible for Luther and Kurt's injuries. She would love him, or she would not, but he had to know.

He stood, filled with a kind of propulsive light. It took him a moment to realize that light filling him was hope. It streamed into every crevice of his being. He would tell her everything and trust in her to love him. It was impossible going on without knowing if she wanted him as much as he wanted her.

Throwing his head back, he laughed out loud. Laughed at the river, the moon, at his foolishness, at his pain. Laughed that he had been so pigheaded, that he had scolded her for her faithfulness to her family when she was just as faithful to him.

Elated, he turned toward the Franz Josef Train Station to catch the next train for Hohenruppersdorf. It left at midnight. He checked his pocket watch. Ten minutes. If he ran, he could catch the last train. He ran until he thought his lungs would burst.

On the train, panting, one thought pummeled his mind over and over.

What if she never wanted to see him again?

CHAPTER 48

In the grey, half-light of dawn, huddled in one of her father's old coats, work pants, and a moth-eaten sweater, Zdenka sat at the kitchen table, drinking cold, weak coffee.

She knew when to bring the grain in from the field, but she didn't have the least idea of how to make a cup of coffee.

Her worries about Matteo had kept her awake most of the night. She had penned a letter to Edward asking for word of Matteo, and she planned to ride to town to post it.

The day stretched ahead with a list of endless, backbreaking chores. This farm was her responsibility. She stiffened her spine. She could do this on her own. She didn't need help.

Feed Harbin. Milk the cows. Turn them out to pasture. Feed horses, sheep, chickens. Collect eggs. Mend paddock fence. Repair holes in the hen house, and—

She glanced out the kitchen window and startled. How did the cows get out to the pasture? Was the barn gate broken as well?

The thud of a hammer reached her ears.

Who was that?

Oh ... and see to her guests. She left her coffee on the table and opened the back door. Harbin and his wagging tail greeted her. "What are our guests up to so early?" she asked the dog.

On the barn roof, Luther banged away at shingles. He gave her an unsmiling wave. Kurt came out toward the house, carrying a bucket of milk. They hadn't hurt her last night. Maybe they weren't unpredictable. Perhaps Luther was only afraid of horses, nothing more. Kurt had seemed perfect happy when she had showed them the barn.

Warmth wrapped itself around her. How kind it was of them to help her when she had so little to offer them. She held the kitchen door open for Kurt. "Thank you for doing the milking."

"It's the least we could do." Kurt came into the kitchen and set the bucket on the table. "I got to work because your milk-maid hadn't shown up."

She held her arms out, the old coat billowing. "Behold the milkmaid."

"You do the milking as well?" he asked, skeptically.

She fisted her hands on her hips. "Yes, and everything else." She didn't mean for her tone to be tart, but it irritated her that men doubted her ability to manage the farm. She had done all these things before, just never alone. And now she was alone with two strangers. What if one of the neighbors came asking about the timber, or someone came to inquire about Schwartzkönig's stud services? There was bound to be talk of that mad woman farmer letting roaming soldiers stay here. What if Matteo came? What would he think of her, capering about in pants, with two of his men?

Kurt pulled out a chair and sat. On the tabletop, he folded his good hand over his injured one. "We thought we'd stay a few days. Help out. Maybe Matteo will turn up."

She didn't want them to think she couldn't manage on her own, but the two chores they had seen to this morning made her feel lighter already. Not that there wasn't more to do.

And of course, there was no money, since she had invested every last cent on Schwartzkönig.

"You needn't worry about propriety," Kurt reassured her. "We'll sleep outside. If anyone asks, we'll say we're hired hands."

Was he hinting at being paid? Her cheeks flushed. "It's kind of you to offer, but I can't pay you."

"We aren't asking to be paid. Matteo has done enough for us. We owe him plenty."

She had wanted Luther and Kurt to come and recover from the war, but she had expected Matteo would be here too. If they stayed, perhaps she might find out something that would help Matteo. She sagged against the counter. She had never been so tired in her entire life. Turning her back, she busied herself at the sink so Kurt wouldn't notice tears of relief pooling in her eyes. When she found her voice, she turned around.

"I would be grateful, but you don't owe Matteo. He did what he did for you because he thought you deserved it. Don't stay because you feel indebted."

"We don't. We want to help." Kurt rose from his chair and went to the counter where the bucket of milk sat. He took a wooden ladle from a hook and dipped it into the milk. Without spilling a drop, he poured it into an earthen mug which sat on the counter and handed it to Zdenka. He said, "Every day, I have to learn that I don't have to do everything by myself. Sometimes, it's hard to accept a gift of help, seeing it not as pity, but simple human kindness."

His eyes were warm, and somehow, forgiving. He seemed to understand without her saying, how it rankled her to accept help. But they were more in need of assistance than she. Helping soldiers was Matteo's dream, and here, the opportunity presented itself.

She sipped the still-warm milk and stared out the window, watching Luther descend the ladder. "But what about Luther?

He was mad when he attacked me and rather agitated in the hospital. But now, he speaks without any inflection and last night, he wouldn't sleep in the barn. Is he unpredictable?"

Kurt dipped his chin into his collar and stared at the floor. "He has some skittish moments. Mostly around horses."

She noted Kurt's reticence to say more, but she had to know if Luther was safe. "I know you want to protect your friend, but why is he afraid of horses?"

Kurt hunched into his jacket. His blue eyes turned the color of a winter sky before a harsh snowfall. "We were ambushed at Königgratz by Prussian *Cuirassiers* riding *Mecklenburgers*. A minute more and the horses would have stomped him to death."

Mecklenburgers were practically the size of draft animals. This sounded like Matteo's nightmares. "But Matteo wasn't afraid of horses when he returned, so I don't think he was bothered by the ambush."

Kurt raised his eyes to her. "No, but remember how he reacted so violently the night he came to my lodgings? He thought we were being ambushed. You could have been killed."

Cold slithered up her spine.

What if she couldn't help Matteo, even if he did come to Friedenheim? Maybe something so terrible had happened, he would never get better. Kurt leaned against the counter, waiting, his blue eyes offering help she so desperately needed. She didn't want to disclose Matteo's infirmities, but there was no one else to trust but Kurt.

"He sustained a head wound so he can't remember everything." Her insides quaked and her voice dropped to a shaky whisper. "What did you mean by 'a minute more, and Luther would have been killed'?"

Kurt looked at her strangely. He pulled out a chair and sat at the table. "Matteo saved our lives."

CHAPTER 49

Even though it was only mid-morning, perspiration dotted Zdenka's face as she lifted the upper wooden rail that had fallen out of the paddock fence. With some jiggling, she fitted the rail into the post notch. She smiled and stepped back, hands on hips, to admire her work.

The rail thudded to the ground.

Two sheep stood inside watching the proceedings. "I suppose I'll have to climb into your side."

She lifted a leg over. The crotch of her pants snagged on the lower rail.

"Just fine," she muttered. Straddling the rail, she looked around for Luther or Kurt then remembered they had gone off to the house to repair some loose bricks in the chimney. They would never hear her if she called out, not to mention the humiliation of having one of them free her pants. In the last two days, they had completed more chores around the farm than she had in the two weeks she had been here alone.

Harbin trotted up and sat on the other side of the fence, wagging his tail.

"Are you laughing?" she asked the dog, who thumped his tail faster. "I guess I'll have to get myself out of this mess."

Harbin laid his head on his paws, settling in to watch.

She twisted round to see a neighbor striding down the road, pointed at her lane. "Uhhh! He'll tell the whole village I can't even put up a fence rail without losing my pants."

Harbin woofed, and his mouth parted in a definite dog-smile. She scowled back at him and wiggled her behind to loosen her pants.

She'd had the sense to stake Schwartzkönig in back of the orchard. He might have hoofed over to Blasen's mares, and she would be out a stud fee. The man coming up the road was nearing. He had a familiar, forward tilting gait, massive shoulders and a determined set to his head.

Matteo.

A thousand butterflies took flight in her chest. She tingled all over. Her breath caught at the back of her throat in a suppressed cry.

He waved to her. "Zdenka!" He broke into a run, arms pumping, chestnut hair blowing.

He was probably wondering why she wasn't running toward him. "Matteo!" She hopped from one foot to the other, trying to get loose to no avail.

He pelted down the lane, and she gave one last heave. As he reached her, she pitched over backwards, tore her pants, and landed in the paddock on her backside. Heat flushed her face, but her heart did a twirl.

Laughing, he easily stepped over the fence rail. His muscular arms encircled her and lifted her to her feet. "My sweet, mad wife," he said, crushing her to his chest.

She murmured over and over, "Matteo, you're here at last." He picked her up and swung her in an arc. She couldn't help but laugh.

He set her on her feet and covered her lips, her temple, her cheekbone, her freckled nose, with kisses. Every kiss sang though her right to her fingertips and toes.

"Are you all right?" he asked. He brushed his thumbs over her cheeks and wiped away her tears.

"Aside from landing on my behind, I'm fine." Her pants were muddy at the knees, her fingernails ragged, and her hair was probably a crazy mess. "But I'm a sight. If I had known you were coming, I would have bathed and put on a dress."

His eyes twinkled in a way she had never seen. "I'm glad you didn't. I like seeing you in your element. And you're more beautiful than ever." He pointed to the fence rail lying in the grass. "Can I help you put this back up?"

"I hate to ask. Don't get a splinter."

Together, they easily fitted the unwieldy wooden rail back into the notches of the fencepost. Then, she flung her arms about his neck, let herself collapse against the ridged muscles of his chest. "I haven't stopped thinking of you for a minute. What made you finally come?"

His face clouded. "I had an incident. At the opera."

Her muscles tensed. "What kind of incident?"

"A shot went off on stage. I thought we were being attacked. I threw Thea to the floor and made a spectacle of myself."

"Oh my. You must have been embarrassed. I'm sorry I wasn't with you." Was he running away from Vienna, or was he running toward her? "You're here now. You'll get better here at Friedenheim. I'm sure it won't happen again."

He stiffened, and his eyes lost their twinkle. The air around them went cold. She withdrew her arms. Had she misread his coming to see her? "That incident showed me I'm not safe to be around."

"I'm not afraid of you."

"That's to decide later." His face was solemn when he

stepped back and held her at arm's length. "I've come to apologize and tell you why I had nightmares. To tell you why I left the house, and where I was going so late at night. About," he swallowed, "about Kurt and Luther."

His somber tone frightened her. He was here, and she didn't think she could bear to lose him again. "Come up to the house and rest. We can talk later." She took his hand to lead him, but he pulled back.

"You may not want me to stay after I say what I have to. I must tell you a few things first."

Her stomach balled up. Was he not ready to stay? Would he force her to make the decision for him? She took his hand and led him into the shade of a massive black walnut tree. She sat, leaned against the trunk, and patted the grass beside her. "Come, sit here with me."

He dropped to the grass beside her. His face sagged as he stared out into the distance. "First, I apologize for accusing you of deception. You loved your family, and they were your first duty. I should not have blamed you for doing what circumstances demanded of you."

She reached up and touched the scar at his temple with a single finger. "When we first met, I should have declared myself sooner, but I wasn't assured of your affections." Heat raced from her neck to her hairline. "I'm sorry I lured you to Arabella's room."

A rakish grin lightened his handsome face. "I'm not. Not anymore. It was quite memorable."

He drew her on to his lap, and she rested her head against his shoulder. The memory of his kisses shot through her. Her body ached for his touch, for the mindless want; for him to answer her want with his own. But before that, she had a few apologies of her own to make.

"You were rightfully angry that I spied on you at Kurt's. I was impulsive and failed to consider the consequences. I'm sorry."

He twirled a curl around his finger. "If I had been more honest and forthright about my nightly wanderings, you would not have followed me to Kurt's. It was that you put yourself in danger that made me so angry. Unreasonably so. I'm sorry."

She laid her head on his shoulder. "Why did you keep secret your kindness? From Kurt, Luther, and me."

He tangled his fingers in her unconquered curls, and she felt utterly safe.

His chest rose with a long inhale. "You may despise me for what I am about to tell you. I was a coward not to tell you, but I was afraid if you knew what I had done, I would lose you. After I tell you, if you wish me to leave you in peace, I shall."

What had he done? Murdered someone? Taken advantage of a woman? Did he have another wife or a child somewhere? If it was something heinous, would she ask him to leave? Could she bear it if he did leave?

"I love you," she said.

"Loving me is one thing. Pity is another. I could not stand it if I thought you pitied me." His voice was gravely and edged with anger.

She sat on the grass and drew him to her so his head lay in her lap. He squinted up into the leaves for a bit until he was ready.

Then, he began.

"As you may have guessed, Kurt, Luther, and I were together at Königgratz. Our troops were massed, waiting for orders. General Benedek wanted the cavalry to charge, but the Prussians had taken cover in the forest, making a charge on horseback impossible. We outnumbered the Prussians, but they had a new gun. A breach-loader."

"What's that?"

"The gun loads from the other end of the barrel, so it doesn't require the infantryman to stand to reload. Our infantry had to stand and muzzle-load."

Her skin grew cold. "Our soldiers were standing targets."

"Exactly. They were decimated. Our artillery pounded the Prussian position. But for the trees, we couldn't tell if we hit our target." His voice turned bitter. "General Halasz—fool if there ever was one—ordered Kurt, Luther, and I to find a way behind enemy lines. It was a suicide mission."

His eye twitched.

"Kurt and Luther were inexperienced. Neither knew how to handle a sword and could barely shoot."

She laid her palm on his chest. His heart pounded through the thick fabric of his jacket as he relived the terror of that day.

"We rode as far as we could then dismounted and ran, dodging around trees and crawled through mud, through dead bodies and carcasses of slaughtered horses. So many men ..." He closed his eyes and his Adam's apple bobbed several times before he continued.

"A bullet grazed my temple, and I became dizzy. Disoriented. I thought we still had a chance to win the battle if we could find a way behind enemy lines. Eventually, we wandered into a deep culvert, hemmed on all sides."

This was the culvert he always talked about in his nightmares. But here at Friedenheim, these memories would fade into blurry images. She would love him until they no longer bothered him. Her heart ached for what he had seen, for the torture he carried with him.

His jaw tightened, and the tendons on the side of his neck stood out. "Two Prussian cavalrymen with swords, riding enormous Mecklenburger horses, attacked us."

He sat up and crossed his legs. "That's the worst of it. I don't remember. The next thing I knew, I awoke in a field hospital with a bandage on my head. I don't remember what else happened so ... I must have abandoned Kurt and Luther. I displayed cowardice on the field of battle."

The skin around his mouth was tight, and he seemed like a man who had given his last testament before going to the gallows.

"But if you don't remember, why do you assume you abandoned Kurt and Luther?"

"I led my men into a death trap. I cost Kurt the use of his hand and Luther, possibly his mind. Abandoning them is the only explanation for why I don't remember what happened when the Prussians attacked."

"Perhaps you became unconscious."

"Then why do I have dreams of being attacked by mounted Prussians?"

"You followed orders. I'm sure there's an explanation for why you don't remember."

He shot to his feet and whirled on her. "I am—was—an officer. I deserted my men. It was dishonorable. Irresponsible. I was supposed to take care of them, and I didn't. To make up for my cowardice, I went out at night to help other soldiers, not just Kurt and Luther. I brought food, helped with rent, found them places to live, brought them books, helped them find jobs. In the case of Luther and Kurt, I kept my identity a secret. I thought they would be too angry to accept my help. I didn't want you to know because I would have had to tell you why I was keeping my identity a secret."

That her husband was so kind and compassionate touched Zdenka. Even after the war and the horror he had seen and experienced, he still retained his humanity, his wish to care for others. It was a miracle that his instinct hadn't been extinguished in the war.

His voice dripped self-loathing. "Don't you see? Everyone

who gets close to me gets hurt. I should have been able to save them."

"Like you should have been able to save your mother?"

His eyebrows shot up. He took a few unsteady steps backwards.

"Since you saw your mother die, it seems that you have made it your responsibility to save people."

"What do you mean?"

"You tried to save the drummer boy. Me from Luther. Me from my own impulsiveness. And you thought you were going to save the whole of the Austrian army from terrible generalship?" She rose from the grass and moved to him. "You set yourself impossible tasks. You're not to be condemned, but lauded."

"I wish that were true. Now you know I'm a coward. I abandoned my responsibility. I have to regain my honor by helping Kurt and Luther. Then, I'll be worthy of your love."

"You are worthy now." She had to get Kurt and Luther to tell him everything they had told her. Only that would ease his mind.

"Why didn't you ask Kurt and Luther what happened?"

He jammed his hands in his trouser pockets. "Soldiers don't discuss those sorts of things."

"You could ask them now." She placed her hands on his shoulders and turned him to face her.

"They're in Vienna. Are you sending me packing, then?"

"Even if what you say were true—and it is not—I wouldn't send you packing. Come up to the house and ask Kurt and Luther."

"They're here? Not in Vienna?"

For a moment, she enjoyed the surprise in his eyes. "They became worried when you stopped visiting, so they came here looking for you." She took his hand and tugged him along the lane toward the house. He followed with stuttering steps. "When

I visited Luther in the hospital, I invited him to come for a visit, so he knew where to find me. He brought Kurt along. They've stayed to help me around the farm."

He tugged back on his arm. "You've been here alone with two men, one of whom attacked you? Why do you take such risks?"

"They're helping me because they appreciate how much you did for them, and they haven't attacked me. You needn't doubt their loyalty, which, by the way, extends to me. Now, come along and stop worrying." She couldn't wait to see his reaction when they told him what had happened in the culvert. That he was a hero, not a louse.

He stopped and rubbed the back of his neck. "I want to face them alone. I want them to be brutally honest. If you're there, they may think they have to be circumspect. I want to know what they experienced. To apologize for what I did to them."

CHAPTER 50

Unsure of his reception, Matteo paused at the kitchen doorway. At the table, Luther and Kurt drank coffee. Matteo's eye twitched. They knew what had happened on the battlefield.

Despite Zdenka suggesting a different history, Matteo steeled himself for their condemnation.

When the two men saw him, they went silent as stones. Kurt smiled broadly, and they rose.

"Lieutenant, look good." Luther's speech was strangely expressionless, but he crushed Matteo's hand in a hearty handshake.

Welcome and concern shaped their expressions. It was as if they weren't the same men he had led into the culvert. Then again, none of them were the same men who had gone to war.

"Sit, sit." Kurt offered him a chair. "You look tired. I'll bring you a cup of coffee and something to eat."

Bone-weary, Matteo sat at the table. A fat, round loaf of black bread sat on a cutting board in the center of the table. A knife the size of a dagger lay beside it.

Matteo glanced at Luther whose attention was riveted by

some minuscule nick on the tabletop. After the way Luther had attacked Zdenka in the Prater, Matteo doubted that it was safe to allow him around knives.

At the sideboard, Kurt poured a cup of coffee and placed it in front of Matteo. Luther poured him a glass of water. Kurt balanced a plate on his lame hand and loaded it with a slab of cheese, a dollop of raspberry jam, and a finger's-width slice of ham. He set the plate in front of Matteo then returned to his chair. Back in Vienna, Kurt had mourned the use of his hand, but here at Friedenheim, he seemed to have adjusted easily.

Matteo's throat thickened, remembering the beautiful violin music Kurt had once made with that hand. If Kurt could get over losing a hand, Matteo could get over the loss of a few hours-worth of memories, but not the loss of his honor.

"When you stopped visiting ..." Kurt's eyes flicked to Luther. "We were concerned you had been hurt or worse."

"Wife invited us. We come looking." Luther picked up the knife and plunged it into the bread.

Hairs on the back of Matteo's arms raised.

Luther sawed off three thick slices of bread and handed them around. He tore his slice apart with his fingers, making a mess of crumbs on the table. He had always been roughhewn, with his Schleswig accent and crude manners, but Luther had been a loyal soldier. All fine on the battlefield, but in Zdenka's home, cause for apprehension.

"I'm glad to see you both looking so well. Zdenka tells me you've been a great help." Out of the corner of his eye, Matteo watched Luther for signs of madness. If he showed the least sign of imbalance, Matteo would insist he leave. He couldn't allow Zdenka to be in danger.

Then, Matteo considered that his wife might not be safe from him. The eviscerating thought wrung out his heart.

"We hoped you would come home so we could thank you properly," Kurt said.

Luther rubbed the jagged scar above his right eye. "You took me to hospital. Thanks, Lieutenant."

The military rank struck him as ill-fitting as a wooden shoe. It wasn't as if he deserved the rank any longer. "No need to call me lieutenant. I've sold my commission."

"So, your wife said. Seen enough of the cavalry?" Kurt asked.

Matteo's mouth filled with the bitterness of all he had seen. "Yes. And of war and its consequences."

"I didn't have a chance to thank you properly for all you did for me," Kurt said.

"Oh ... that." Matteo splashed milk in his coffee, trying to be as casual as possible, and began eating. He wanted to convey normalcy, responsibility. He wanted them to believe he could withstand whatever they had to say to him.

Luther's wooly eyebrows lowered. "I left hospital, but I ..." he paused, his eyes darting back and forth as he searched for words. "I didn't know where you lived."

Matteo found it odd that the two men didn't simply haul him outside, stand him up against the barn, and shoot him. How could they not hold a grudge?

"At your aunt's house, the butler he said he didn't know where you were," Kurt said. "Perhaps he didn't want to tell us."

Phillipe hadn't mentioned their inquiry. Most servants weren't as loyal or tightlipped as Phillipe. Matteo would tell Thea to give Phillipe a raise.

"Why did you keep your identity a secret when you were helping us?" Kurt asked.

Matteo's bite of bread stuck in his throat. "I wanted to make sure you weren't so angry at me that you refused my assistance."

Kurt stared at him questioningly. "But we are surely the ones indebted to you for saving our lives."

Matteo's fingers tingled. He stopped chewing. "What do you mean? I nearly got you killed."

"Remember you saved me." Luther made the pronouncement as though he had mentioned it might rain.

If Matteo admitted he couldn't remember, they would think *he* was mad. But he had come here to make a clean breast of things. And he hated lying. He bowed his head and stared at his plate. He pulled the words from deep inside where they were embedded like bullets. "I don't remember what happened."

"Can't remember cause a' that?" Luther pointed to Matteo's temple.

Matteo blinked. "I suppose that's possible."

Kurt leaned his elbows on the table and stared hard at him. "Do you remember the two Prussians on horseback attacking us?"

Matteo's mouth went dry. His palms grew damp. Fog clouded his mind, twisted, coalesced into a solid vision. Inky *Mecklenburgers* frothing at the bit. Slashing silver cuirassiers. Sprays of rock shards. Air vibrating with thundering hooves. Rumbling of the earth.

But nothing more.

He remained fairly certain that he had abandoned them. Bolted. Left them to face the Prussians alone. His eye twitched.

"Yes. Those I remember. Like the hounds of Hell, those horses, but nothing more."

Bit by bit, to Matteo's amazement, Kurt, and occasionally Luther, pieced together what happened that day. He rummaged about in his own mind as one would look for a missing sock in a drawer. Hard as he tried, he could not conjure the events in his own memory.

When Luther drew a finger across his neck and told, in choppy words, of the head rolling into the underbrush, surprise exploded in Matteo's brain. Had he done that?

They described his bleeding wounds as he brought them to safety. How he urged them forward when they thought all was lost.

When they finished, Luther took a long, deep breath. In one rush of words, crammed together, he said, "Prettygoodforahalf-dead lieutenant."

Pretty good for a half-dead lieutenant.

The air grew thin and still. Sun spread across the kitchen floor. A bird sang.

"This ...can't be ..." Matteo said haltingly.

A darkness dissipated, burned away by truth, and left only ashen smudges of guilt. A space inside him filled with something warm and bright and glowing. Hope. He recognized it as hope. Something he'd given up, let go of completely. They were giving him a great gift in return for him saving their lives.

"Of course, it is. You saved our lives." Kurt's blue eyes flickered with the light the way they did when he had played the violin.

Matteo's head emptied of thoughts. Air rushed into his lungs, and he was so light, he thought he might float out of his chair. He *was* good. *He* was responsible. He was *not* a coward.

"I couldn't remember anything that happened after the Prussians rode in, so I assumed I had ... abandoned you."

"Not bloody likely." Kurt laughed.

Luther shook his work-roughened fists. "You fight only having fists."

"You thought you had abandoned us?" Kurt said. "General Benedek would abandon his men before you would."

Had Matteo really done this? Saved their lives? He had led them to their near deaths, but he had saved them, and they were *grateful.* They were concerned enough for *him* to come all the way from Vienna to look for him. All these months, he had thought himself a coward, but it was the opposite. He had followed orders he knew were impossible, and still his men respected and cared for him. If he had it to do again, he would stand up to Halász, turn back, take a different route. He had redeemed his mistake with bravery he didn't know he possessed. It was as if Königgratz had receded into the distant past for them. They didn't blame him. Only he blamed himself for something that had *never* happened.

Perhaps Zdenka was right. Maybe Friedenheim did have some kind of magic that allowed soldiers to heal and put the war behind them. If Kurt and Luther could let go of the war, perhaps, with her at his side, so could he.

And then he could sleep with his impulsive, extraordinary, matchless, wife in his arms every night for the rest of his life. If she would have him.

He turned his hands over, opening and closing them. These hands had killed two men. To save his *own* men. Hands that led his men back from the brink of death.

Hands that would never again cause harm to another living soul. Never.

He was lightheaded. His insides pushed his heart against his ribcage. The scar at his temple no longer throbbed, but pulsed softly, almost like a tiny reminder of his forgetting.

Mozart's *Bei Männer, welche Liebe fühlen* breezed through his mind again. He was imperfect, but he was good. Almost as good as whole.

Almost safe for Zdenka.

CHAPTER 51

When Zdenka looked up from grooming Schwartzkönig, Matteo entered the barn, a stunned look in his eyes. Luther and Kurt had upended his world. Gone was the wariness, the hard-edge suspicious glance. It was as though he had cast off some hard shell to reveal a man who could trust.

He laid his arms on the railing of Schwartzkönig's stall. "You knew everything when I arrived, didn't you?"

She stepped out of the stall, prepared for another accusation. "I wasn't deceiving you."

"Why didn't you tell me?"

His voice had a smile. "I thought it better you heard it from them. Then, there would be no doubt."

"Nothing is as I imagined it. And I remember nothing of my efforts."

"Now, you know the ... truth." She squirmed inside as the pressure mounted to tell him how she had gotten Friedenheim back. "You're a hero, not an irresponsible, dishonorable man."

"It will take me the rest of my life to believe the story they told me."

She stroked the horse's soft, hair-covered nose.

"To whom does this splendid stallion belong?" Matteo asked.

She brought a bit of oat cake from her pocket, palmed it, and fed Schwartzkönig. Trying for a lilt of innocence, she said, "He's mine."

Matteo rolled his eyes and thumped his forehead with his palm. "You didn't," he groaned.

She knew he was worried about her safety, but still, his scold irritated her. "I missed you terribly, so I bought a horse."

"Should I take that as a compliment?"

Schwartzkönig had finished his oat cake. He stomped the floor like an impatient child.

"Yes, you should." She opened the barn gate, and Schwartzkönig whinnied and thundered away into the paddock, his black mane and tail flying behind. Matteo helped her push the heavy wooden gate closed. "I wanted to remember how we rode together. Remember what we did in the Prater. I don't think I could have survived without him. He kept me from being melancholy for the hours I rode him. He means so much to me."

The horse covered half the paddock in great strides with speed and strength that thrilled her.

"I know you think it was an impulsive purchase, but I want to start a breeding program, and the stud fees will pay the debts."

"I might be able to help you with that." His chin dipped into his collar. "That is, if you would let me help."

Her heart flip-flopped. He was staying! "I would like that."

He wrapped her in his arms and covered her mouth with his. Her spine melted. His tongue invaded her, and she surrendered. Cradling her head in his big hands, he nipped her lower lip, sucking and teasing until she thought she couldn't breathe. Their tongues met, tangled, darting and tasting. One hand slipped down and cupped her breast. A thumb played over her nipple. She gasped and dug her fingers into the folds of his jacket, reveling in the touch for which she had longed. He tangled his fingers in her hair, tugged her head back, and burned his kiss onto her neck. She was starved for his skin and wanted her clothes off. Wanted his off. She wanted to caress every inch of him, to give herself to him.

He pulled away and it was as though he'd plunged her into icy water. He stared out across the paddock where Schwartzkönig romped under a big oak tree. "He's a magnificent beast. He must have been expensive." He frowned at her. "Edward?"

She couldn't go on much longer, letting him think Edward bought the farm for her. She had to tell him the truth about gambling at Dommayer's. About Edward rescuing her. But what if he became angry at yet another deception? What if he wouldn't forgive her?

Her voice trembled. "I have a few things to tell you."

One eyebrow rose. "Hmm. This sounds as if I should sit. I don't know how many more surprises I can take today." He glanced about and sat on wooden tack box, rested his elbows on his knees, and dangled his hands between his legs. "I'm listening."

Her face flushed. She couldn't bear to see the disappointment and distrust she expected from him. She turned away. "I'm afraid you'll be so angry with me."

"My dearest, look at me. If you can still love me after the way I behaved toward you, I doubt there's much that will make me angry at you."

She turned to face him, clenching her hands to still the shaking. "I dressed as a man and went to Dommayer's to win the farm back from the Argentinean in a game of *Schwimmen*."

His eyebrows shot skyward. "*Schwimmen*? You abhor gambling."

"I do, but I had learned a lot from standing at Papa's elbow, begging him to leave the tables. It was the only way I could think of to get the farm back."

He made a guttural sound of disgust and stared at the ground. He covered his eyes with a hand. "But Edward gave you the deed. How did he come to have it in his possession?"

"I'd lost everything I had. Edward came in just as I was accusing the Argentinean of cheating. Edward dragged me out, blistered my ears, and sent me packing. Then, he returned to the game and won back the deed for me."

He dropped his head into his hands for a moment, then lifted, and shook it in disbelief. "I'll have to thank him for that. But if you gambled, what did you wager with in the first place?"

She winced.

He tilted his head and smiled. "Go on. I promise not to be angry."

"I pawned my gowns and dresses back to Madame Bonterre." She glanced up at him from below her lashes. "She was quite understanding. I don't think it's the first time she's made such a bargain."

"I'll have to tell Aunt Thea to change dressmakers." He laughed. "Is that everything?"

She brushed some dirt from her sleeve. "Well, not entirely."

He sighed, but he smiled. "Well then, out with it."

Her voice went thready. "When it came down to the final wager, I ... I ..." She twisted the plain gold wedding band around her finger. "I bet my wedding ring."

He waved a hand dismissively. "That's everything? All of it?"

She planted her feet solidly, waiting for the blast, expecting him to break his promise not to be angry.

"I don't mind so much about the ring, but *Heiligen Gott!* Gambling is dangerous business. Don't you know you could have been killed? And what if they'd found out you were a woman?" He rose and took her in his arms and tucked her head beneath his chin. "Why did you risk your life for the farm? It's not worth it."

"I did it for you. I wanted you to come because I knew you'd feel safe here. I wanted to make your dream of a veteran's association come true. To have a place for soldiers to heal after the war." She tried to impart her own zeal and certainty. "And look, we're doing it. We have our first two guests, Luther and Kurt. They're doing so much better in even the few days they've been here."

For a long time, he was silent. With the reverence one would use in church, he said, "You risked everything, your life, for me? For my dream?"

"You were my dream, so ... in a way, I guess I was selfish. I wanted to make you happy. Help you feel safe."

He kissed her temple. "You are a confoundingly, impulsive woman."

She exhaled a breath. "Is that a compliment?"

"Yes." He sat back on the wooden tack box and pulled her onto his lap. "But your gowns are back in your closet. How did Edward manage that?"

"He won enough money to redeem them from Madame Bonterre." She giggled. "And Edward hinted that she was quite grateful when he came to retrieve my gowns."

He snorted. "So, it wasn't all sacrifice and danger on his part."

"I know you were hurt and angry when you thought he bought the farm for me, but does this make you less angry?"

He laughed. "How could I be angry? Edward saved you from nearly being killed, he won the farm, your wedding ring, and bought your gowns back. He's my hero. I'll have to thank him properly."

Zdenka burrowed against his voluminous chest. His body

was like an unbending tree she could take shelter under for the rest of her life. "I'm sorry I masqueraded as a boy again. That I snuck around."

"How could I be angry when you did it for me?"

They kissed, letting their lips brush, then linger, building heat. Schwartzkönig wandered up to the barn door and snorted. They broke their kiss. Both laughed.

"I think he's a bit jealous," Matteo said.

"My heart's secure with you."

"Now, show me around your Eden, before I drag you up into the haymow and have my way with you."

Her knees went weak at the suggestion, and she considered submitting to his threat.

As she showed him the fields, the tool shed, and pointed out the boundaries of the farm, he asked questions and listened patiently as she explained.

When they reached the orchard, she said, "Now you see why this is the perfect place for soldiers to recover from the war. For example, Luther's afraid of horses. I think if he's here for a while and works with Schwartzkönig, he can overcome his fear."

Matteo jerked to a stop. "You can't make everything right with fresh air, hard work, and good food. War and the scars it leaves are ... more complicated than that."

"You have no faith in me. That I can help you." She didn't want to argue, but until she had proof, neither was she willing to concede healing here wasn't possible.

"Don't you think I *want* to get the war and what I saw out of my mind? Don't you think I *want* to forget?"

She heard the frustration in his voice but couldn't bear to think he would suffer forever. She would be the one who helped him feel normal again. "But here, you *will* forget."

He gathered her in his arms. Tenderly, he said, "I'm not sure *any* of the three of us is safe to be around."

Something in her heart tumbled when he emphasized the word 'any.' She withdrew from his embrace. "What are you saying?"

"I should leave until I know I'm safe to be around. I don't want a repeat of what happened in Vienna. I think I should take Luther and Kurt too."

By the set of his mouth, she knew he'd made up his mind. He had pulled the plug on her full heart. All her excitement dribbled away and hurt flooded in. "You can't leave. I just got you back."

She wanted to say *I need you*, but she couldn't allow the words. Giving into that made her feel too vulnerable. She counted on her own strength and ingenuity, sometimes on her impulsivity, to see her through. Admitting she needed him might make him feel as if *he* couldn't rely on *her*.

"Nothing is more important to me than your safety. I can't think of any other way to keep you safe than not to be with you." He turned and started back toward the house.

CHAPTER 52

Matteo lay awake, alone in his bed, as watery sunlight crept over the windowsill. Birds chirped with annoying happiness. A cow bellowed. Curtains fluttered at the open window.

He was going to break her heart. Again. To leave her would be as painful as cutting off his arm.

Swallowing hard, sat up in bed and leaned against the headboard. His eyes burned, and his head ached from sleeplessness. All night, images of Zdenka threaded his mind. Her pillowy breasts, the way her waist narrowed and flared to her hips, the perfect muscular plumpness of her bottom-the real reason he had grown to like her in pants.

A soft knock sounded on his door. Zdenka peeped in. "Are you awake?"

"Yes. Sit here." He patted the bed beside him.

She entered and closed the door. Ginger curls framed her face like the ruff of a baby fox. Her muslin nightgown was sheer enough to show the dark shadow below her belly. A shawl draped her shoulders, and her dainty, feminine feet were bare.

He slept nude, but the coverlet lay across his waist, exposing his naked chest. Her eyes widened, and she stared. Her gaze drank him in. He felt loved by the greedy hunger in her eyes, and he hoped she wanted him as much as he wanted her. But it would be unfair to bed her if he wasn't going to stay.

She padded over and clambered onto the bed. He pulled her close, and she curled under his arm. He rested his cheek on her crown, breathing in her vanilla-scented soap. Through her nightgown, his fingers played along her arm. For a minute, they were content to lay quietly in one another's arms.

With her next to him, he was at peace. How had he not known how much he needed her? Because of her, his world had righted itself. The war was over, as were his days of being a soldier. His wife forgave him his cowardice and suspicion. His honor was intact. His men were safe, and he had their respect.

"I listened at your door last night and didn't hear a nightmare. I think Friedenheim has made them disappear."

To keep her from going along that line of thought, he pulled her atop him so that she straddled low across his abdomen. They lay chest to chest. Her weight against his cock only made him want her more. Not bedding her was getting increasingly difficult. With his hand, he cupped her bottom and squeezed, feeling her flesh yield to the gentle pressure of his hand.

"No nightmares, but then, I wasn't sleeping much anyway." He kissed her nose. It was as much as he dared. If he kissed her lips, his self-control might fail.

She folded her arms and rested her chin atop them. "So then, do you think you're safe enough to sleep with me?"

He rolled her off to the side and put some space between them. The disappointment and confusion in her eyes nearly made him change his mind. But he had to protect her.

"There's no point in delaying telling you. In two hours, Kurt, Luther and I are taking the train to Vienna."

She sat upright, eyes blazing. "Why?"

He tied a sheet around his waist and edged off the bed. "If I'm going to keep you safe, from me and them, we have to leave."

"But I'm not afraid of you, and you haven't even given Friedenheim a chance."

"Your love for me keeps you from seeing I might hurt you. When I'm sure I'm not a threat to you, and if Kurt and Luther are well enough, we'll return. In our absence, I'll find an estate manager to help you. He'll take care of everything."

Her eyes flashed for an instant. "I don't need an estate manager. I'm capable of taking care of things myself."

He'd insulted her. Not the best way to tell her he was leaving for a while. At the washbasin, he poured water from the ewer, splashed his face, and dried with a towel. His evening scheme, the only clothes he had, lay folded on a chair. He sat on the edge of the bed and pulled on his smallclothes, then his pants.

If was as though he was dressing for a funeral.

"You could sleep in another room and lock the door," she blurted, all in a rush to convince him.

He slipped his arms into his shirt and buttoned it. Sleeping in another room for the rest of their lives wasn't a reliable strategy. Every time she was within arms-length, his body raged against the restraints he put on himself. If he stayed, he would give in to the pull she had on him. He wanted her beneath him, to be in her, pleasure every inch of her body; to kiss her sex as he had in the Prater.

Her pleas threatened his resolve. "What if I give a repeat performance like I had at the opera? Then what?" He cinched his belt tight. "In the course of my mad frenzy, I *hurt* Thea. What if I lose myself in such a way again? I can't take a chance I would hurt you."

"Can't we find some way for you to stay?"

"And what of Luther and Kurt? What if one of them hurts

you? You should never have allowed them to stay." He buttoned his shirt cuffs.

She jutted her chin at him, her flag of stubbornness. "Luther is sleeping in the hayloft now. He's hardly afraid of the horses anymore. And if you would stay, I'm sure you would find the memories of the war fading."

"I suppose I could sleep in in another room and lock the door, but that only takes care of the night." He took her by the shoulders and lowered his lips to hers. They were soft and velvety, and made his mind go blank for a minute. Nothing else mattered except kissing her. His hands wandered to her breasts. "I want you." He kissed down her neck all the way to her cleavage.

Her breath was hot and ragged against his temple. "What about sleeping in the barn with Luther and Kurt? You're around during the day so you'll know if one of them tries to hurt me, and you'll know if they get up at night. If you thrash about or punch one of them in your sleep, they'll know."

Sleeping in a hayloft with two men didn't hold much appeal, but it was a far sight better than leaving her.

He cupped a breast in his palm. "All right, but how will I keep my hands off you in the meantime?" He nuzzled her neck which smelled sweetly of sleep.

"Must we?" She arched against him.

He nibbled an earlobe. Between bites, he said, "A week. Then we'll see if I've had any nightmares or thrashed about."

She jerked away and squeaked, "A week?"

Who was he fooling? He doubted his self-control would hold out that long. "Five nights."

Her eyes narrowed. "Three nights."

If she drove as hard a bargain with those buying her crops and stud services as she did with him, the farm would be flush with cash in no time. He couldn't help smiling. "All right. Three nights."

That, he could manage. And if he didn't thrash, kick, or punch Luther or Kurt as they slept, he might finally trust himself with his wife.

CHAPTER 53

It had been three days since Matteo arrived at Friedenheim. Every night, he had retired to the hayloft with Kurt and Luther and listened to Kurt's snoring and Luther's muttering about Prussian soldiers and black horses. Every morning, they were all where they had slept and no one had a black eye or any bruises, so Matteo knew he hadn't been violent during his sleep.

During the days, he worked near Zdenka so he could keep an eye on Luther and Kurt. He had the best intentions of keeping his hands off her, but when he was within arms-length, he was drawn to her like a magnet. Every furtive squeeze, ravening kiss, and tantalizing touch only made him want her more and, she not only welcomed his caresses, but initiated languid kissing and delicious fondling of her own.

Once, he raced out of the barn and dunked his head in the watering trough.

On the fourth morning, he sat at the breakfast table, waiting for her to come down. His jaw hurt from smiling so broadly.

"We'll be gone most of the day," Kurt said to Matteo. "We're mending the fence between Friedenheim and Herr Blasen's farm."

"All right. I'll help Zdenka." Matteo sipped his coffee, glad they would be alone most of the day.

Zdenka entered the kitchen wearing a pair of snug-fitting, dark blue pants. They exchanged greetings, and she sat at her place next to him. He poured her a cup of coffee and put his mouth to her ear. "You look positively delightful in pants, but I must say, I can't wait to take them off of you."

His cock heard him and responded accordingly.

"We have a full day of work ahead of us," she said as two red spots appeared on her cheeks. In the vein below her ear, the pulse jumped.

Later that morning, Matteo worked in the barn on various chores. He mended a hole in a stable, tightened a hinge on a stall gate, and oiled some of the tack. All the while, he kept an eye on her and noted how hard she worked, never asking for help, refusing his help when he offered.

Matteo watched as she mucked out the stalls, weeded a vegetable garden she had planted, fed chickens, and collected eggs. Even with his brawn, he would weary with such incessant labor. She needed and deserved rest. If only she would accept help from him and let the other men take over some of the heavier chores. She was determined to do the lion's share of the work. It was almost as if she considered it a personal failure to accept help.

She reminded him of the way he had refused her help in Vienna.

He had married a stubborn, impulsive, independent woman and had come to love precisely those characteristics about her. He wasn't about to try to change them. Those things made her bold enough to wear pants, to not care what others thought. If wearing pants and being knee-deep in straw and smelling like hay made her happy, then he was happy.

After lunch, while she took a brief rest for an hour, he hiked to her grossmutti's grave. He remembered when they were in the Prater together, she had told him about the roses called *My Beloved*, which she had planted on the grave. He gathered an armload of blossoms, returned to the house and put them in a vase on the kitchen table. The fragrance filled the kitchen and took his mind back to the afternoon in the Prater—how exquisite she had tasted, how her own fragrance had mixed with that of the roses.

Women were confounding, complex, and as necessary as breathing, but he was fairly sure they all loved flowers.

Late in the afternoon, when Zdenka and Matteo were in the barn, he noted the sky had begun to darken. Skeins of slate-gray clouds clumped around the mountain peaks. As the afternoon wore on, dark masses filled the sky. In the higher elevations, lightning stabbed across the sky. A distant trembling of thunder vibrated against his skin. The air pressed heavy as a blanket and the wind gathered strength, as though a hand pushed against his chest when he crossed the farmyard.

As the day wound toward evening, still no rain came.

He pointed out the cloud banks to Zdenka. As she gazed out the door, worry creased her face. "I hope Kurt and Luther make it back before that breaks."

"Is there something we should do to prepare for the storm?" he asked, taking the pitchfork out of her sweet, callused, hard-working, hands.

"I thought it would blow the other direction, but it seems it's headed this way."

"How do you know?" he asked.

She pointed to the animals in the paddock. The sheep raced from one side to the other and the cows bawled without provocation. Schwartzkönig was more unruly than usual, neighing, galloping up and down the meadow, and kicking up his heels.

"They're scared." Matteo's concerns mounted.

"I wanted to spread this straw before we bring them in." She took the pitchfork back and jabbed it into a pile of clean straw.

Matteo took the pitchfork back from her. He reached out and tucked a flyaway lock of hair behind her ear. Anything to touch her.

"I'll do it. Start rounding up the stock," he said.

"It's my responsibility to do all this." She reached for the pitchfork. "I can do it."

He turned his back so she couldn't get the pitchfork and flipped in the last forkful of hay.

She stood with folded arms, looking slightly offended.

"I know you're capable of doing it." He bent and brushed a kiss across her lips. "But you don't have to, and I want to help. I want to be useful to you. I want to lighten your load. It's what husbands and wives do for one another. You deserve to have flowers and perfume, to be treated like a princess now and then. To sleep in fine sheets and dress in the most elegant gowns. To be savored and cherished, not have to slave out here, shoveling manure."

Her shoulders drooped and she smiled. Something in her eyes flickered. "But I like--"

He laid a forefinger on her lips. "If you are happy wearing pants, being dirty, running your farm and smelling like hay, then I am happy." He slid a palm over her hip and down her backside, where he gave it a pat. "Besides, when you wear pants, I find you almost irresistible."

She leaned into him. He lowered his lips to hers and kissed her soundly.

"Let me bring in the livestock, then I promise I'll go," she said, holding up a forefinger.

He propped the pitchfork against the stable wall. "I will help you bring in the livestock, then, after dinner, I'll draw you a bath."

♫

Zdenka peeled off her dirty clothes in the small warm room off the back of the kitchen. Matteo had filled the big copper slipper tub with hot water and laid out vanilla-scented soap. Candles placed around the room created a sheer, pale light.

Her heart filled with warmth. He had sprinkled pink rose petals on top of the water. They were from the rose bush on her grossmutti's grave, her favorites. *Mein Liebling;* My Beloved.

She stepped into the water and, with a sigh, laid her head back against the edge of the tub. The animals were safe in the barn, Kurt and Luther had gone to bed in the hayloft, and Matteo had retired somewhere.

Everyone was taken care of. Most of the day's chores were done. She could rest at last.

Closing her eyes, she settled back and let the water soothe her body. So many things had happened in a short time. Her husband had come home, they were actually starting a military veterans' association here on the farm. Luther was getting better. The farm was getting set to rights. So many dreams had come true. She was fulfilling her destiny.

Fulfilling one's destiny was tiring and worrisome.

As her sore muscles released, she remembered Matteo's firm squeeze on her behind, the way his kiss smoldered deep in her belly. They had waited three days. He was free of his nightmares, free of his shame, free to make her his wife. If she hadn't smelled like manure, she might have thrown herself down on the straw and begged him to take her right then and there.

When you wear pants, I find you almost irresistible.

The rose petals, the candelabra, the bath Matteo had drawn for her, all made her feel so feminine, so taken care of. It was a strange sensation, and a pang of guilt pricked her conscience; she didn't deserve such fine things, such time to herself, not working.

She dunked her head under the water until she ran out of breath. She bobbed out of the cooled water. Matteo had left two fresh towels folded on a chair. She wrapped her hair in one and buffed her skin dry with the other. He had even brought her comb and brush from her room, so she sat on the chair and dragged the comb through her tangly curls.

A stack of fresh clothes sat on a shelf. He had thought of everything. A fresh cotton chemise, lacy pantalets, a white lace-collared blouse with pearl buttons and ... a pair of pants? She frowned. She had expected a nightgown and robe.

If you are happy wearing pants ... then I'm happy, was what he had said.

Tears sprang to her eyes. Matteo understood her. He understood her independence, her need to be treated different from all the frilly girls, how much she loved the farm, and how hard she had to work to make it a success. He had felt betrayed and duped when she masqueraded as a boy, and in Vienna, after their wedding he had asked her only to wear pants for riding, but now, he *gave* her pants to wear. No one had ever made her feel so understood, so cared for, so totally, utterly, completely loved. Never again would her wearing pants come between them.

She put on the lacy undergarments and blouse and pants. Where were the socks? She glanced around, but she had on everything he'd brought her. When she walked into the kitchen, something tickled her bare feet.

Pink rose petals, like those in the bath, were strewn on the floor and trailed through the kitchen and up the stairs. Her heart jumped in her chest like a grasshopper as she followed the trail and ended at her closed bedroom door.

♫

While Zdenka bathed in the private room off the kitchen, Matteo washed at the kitchen sink. As he prepared to finally make Zdenka his fully wedded wife, he recalled the precise pink of her rounded, perfect breasts, the quaking of her legs when she climaxed, the almost musical sound of her sighs. His need made him feel like he was burning up from the inside out.

As he dried off, he spotted their boots next to the back door on a mat. Hers lay on top of one another where she'd left them. He went over and set them upright, side by side, next to his. He stood for a moment, staring down at his tall ones listing to the side against her shorter boots. The sight made him feel like he was home. It was ordinary and simple but held such permanence. He wanted to belong to someone, to a place, the way she belonged at Friedenheim. He wanted them to set their boots and shoes, their bathrobes, their coats, their rocking chairs, side by side forever.

He went upstairs to his bedroom, took the vase of roses he hid in his room, and placed them on the dresser in her bedroom. Because it was the largest in the house, Zdenka had taken her parent's bedroom, but remade it for herself. The decor surprised him. A coverlet with pink roses and green twisting vines draped the dark walnut bed. Lace curtains adorned the windows. Only the fireplace mantel was plain and unadorned with two candles in simple white candleholders. He lit the candles, and the room was awash in a golden glow. The room reminded him of the young, girlish side of Zdenka which he knew she possessed, but with her parents demands, had had little occasion to show itself.

On her vanity was the music box he'd given her. He wound it tight and set it back in place.

He promised himself he would give her every opportunity for ribbons and lace, if she desired. And if not, he loved that plush bottom in pants.

Her footsteps padded down the hall. He lifted the lid on her music box and *Bei Männer, welche Liebe fühlen,* from *Die Zauberflöte,* played. His heart swelled in his chest.

She knocked on the door.

He opened it. She stood before him, her soft, lavender pants hugging her curves, her skin glowing, her eyes sparkling, and her lavish mouth, waiting to be kissed.

Without a word, he bowed and offered his hand. She laid her slender fingers in his grasp. As if they were at the most brilliant Viennese ball, he placed his other palm in the arch of her lower back and drew her to him. Then, gazing into those green eyes that dazzled and bewitched him, he waltzed her around the room, certain there was no man happier than him.

"You are a much more accomplished dancer than you let on in the woods when you were a boy," he said.

She blushed, and he was sorry he made her feel as if he were accusing her. Again.

"Pretending to let you teach me was the one way I could get you to put your arms around me," she said, laughing.

Lights from the candles caught the coppery glints in her hair. He twirled her around the room as though she were a queen. He marveled that the girl in his arms was his. That once she'd been a boy, who'd been a girl, and now, was everything he could have hoped for.

They danced until the music box wound down. She wrapped her arms around his neck and laid her cheek against his chest. She smelled fresh, like roses, and vanilla.

He was filled with light, music, and need.

Gently, he unwound her arms from his neck and guided her slowly back to the edge of the bed. She sat. Her thick-lashed eyes were half closed, her cheeks flushed. She worked the buttons on his shirt, and he noticed her hands shook slightly. With anticipation, he hoped. When she had unbuttoned his shirt, she ran her hands up his stomach, over his chest muscles to his shoulders, and pushed his shirt onto the floor.

He worried that the scar on his back would remind her that he wasn't a man entirely in control of his own reactions. That he wasn't a man who could be trusted.

She kissed his chest and raked her fingers through the patch of hair on his chest.

Goosebumps raised on his arms.

Her fingers played over his flat abdomen and he inhaled as the sensation ran directly to his penis. She laid her cheek against his chest, and he dug his fingers into her ginger locks, desire racing in his veins.

Lightning flashed through the curtains and thunder smashed overhead, rattling windows. Matteo's mind was so fixed on her, he ignored the weather, which could have easily been the sights and sounds of battle.

He sat beside her on the bed, and she glided her hand over the scar on his shoulder blade. He had never looked at it because he regarded it as a mark of shame, but he assumed it was an ugly, twisted mess.

Her finger tenderly traced the ragged eight-inch scar.

He drew a sharp breath. Hairs at the nape of his neck prickled.

Her lips, damp and soft, kissed the length of his scar with unimaginable tenderness. He froze until she drew back. His body, all sinews and muscles, knots of strength made for killing, vibrated with a kind of life he had not known for so long.

The tightness, the rigidity of the scar loosened as if it had untied itself from a dark place in his soul. The scar was no longer a mark of failure. At her touch, his scar became a stripe of hard-earned pride, a kind of military ribbon worn on his skin, marking him forever as a hero.

He eased her down on the bed and kissed her deeply, possessively. She yielded to his enormously aroused body. He took his time, teasing her mouth with his tongue, until she answered his gentle probing with her own. The sensation charged his groin, building to an almost uncontrollable physical heat. With agonizing self-control, button by button, he slowly removed her shirt and chemise and let them drop to the floor.

Her pale skin was luminous and delicate as a rose petal, flushed pink with desire. Her breasts with their tight, dark nipples made something in his body, like a long-crouched animal, spring loose. He took one nipple in his mouth and suckled her while he cupped the other, turning the nipple between thumb and forefinger and tugging gently.

She purred moans of pleasure, wordless encouragement.

Zdenka was his. Her femaleness, the reactions of her body, her lithe limbs wrapping around him, floated him off somewhere outside himself. It was a place of forgetting yet focus, satisfaction yet greediness. A place he had given up on finding ever again, but he found it in her body.

Thunder crashed.

Zdenka jumped, but he held her in his arms and murmured endearments, of his love, her beauty, their future, and she settled back into his arms.

When she reached for her waistband, he stopped her. "Allow me."

She lifted her abundantly curved hips to help as he inched her pants down. He paused and, through her fine linen pantalets, he rubbed his stubbled cheek against her mound, inhaling her lusty musk. He licked her crevice through her pantalettes and she gasped and thrust her pelvis up. He drew off her pants, he slowly dragging his hands down over her hips, her thighs, her shapely calves, her small ankles, each curve stoking his passion. He tugged the ribbon of her pantalets and repeated the slow caress down her body as he removed them. With soft mewls, she shivered and tipped her head back.

Reddish curls adorned the mound between her shapely legs, which he longed to explore with his tongue, but first, he had to see the beautiful bottom he'd been dreaming of.

He grasped one hip, rolled her over on her stomach, and admired the firm domes, shaped like the two halves of a sweet peach. He bent and squeezed, kissed, nibbled, each delectable cheek, until, giggling, she wriggled face up onto her back.

Matteo kissed the length of her taut belly, working his way lower. She clamped her legs together when he feathered his tongue along her inner thighs, but he gently pushed them apart with his hand. He fought his desire, stunned by his need to possess her.

With a single finger, he parted the curls, until he found the lips protecting the secret center of her body. Wordless whispers came out of her mouth. He stroked the hidden cleft gently with his middle finger until the lips swelled and her curls glistened with her inner honey. Then he slid his finger into her wetness.

Her eyes flew open, and she gasped. "Oh! What ...?"

He murmured soothing words into her ear, and her inner muscles relaxed. His erection begged satisfaction, but he couldn't—wouldn't—hurt her. He wouldn't try until he knew she was ready for him. With slow movements, he drew his finger in and out, preparing her body for the coming union.

Finding the nub of her sex, he rubbed lightly with his thumb making her gasp. Her legs tightened and she pressed into his hand as he teased the sensitive spot.

"Tell me if you don't like anything, and I'll stop," he whispered.

"Don't stop," she sighed on an exhale.

He slid off the bed, kneeled on the floor, and parted her legs. With his tongue, he probed the curls. His body pulsed with expectation. She moaned low as he licked and dove in and out of her wetness, returning always to the most sensitive part of her body. She tasted salty, sweeter than any wine, more intoxicating than laudanum. He took what he wanted, savoring, loving her with his mouth, relentlessly flicking her sex with his tongue. Her groans drove him on. All thoughts except to please her evaporated from his mind. Her knees bent and her thighs quivered, and he lost his mind in her body, in her female flesh, as his entire world contracted to the smallest spot between her legs. He watched with pleasure as she seemed to levitate off the bed, and her head vaulted against the pillow, her mouth in a soundless cry. He kept at her, never pausing, until she shuddered twice more, her body limp with satisfaction.

She lay back on the bed, panting, an amazed look about her eyes.

He stood at the side of the bed and peeled off his pants and smallclothes, letting them fall to the floor. His swollen cock sprang loose, and she stared, transfixed. She blinked. With two fingers, she caressed his length, driving a shudder of pleasure through his body. Droplets of liquid glistened on the tip, and she took her thumb and swiped then circled his hot silken head. He groaned and moved his hips forward as she gripped him and stroked his erection, testing the limits of his self-control.

"I want you," she said thickly.

Her words fired his blood.

She lay back on the bed and opened for him. He eased between her legs and prodded gently between her legs. Her breasts rubbed against his chest as he braced his hands on either side of her. Her arms slid around his neck and she pulled him to her.

Lightning flashed and thunder drummed overhead. He knew, after making her his wife, there was no going back to who he was, who they were separately. Their lives would be forever entwined. And he wouldn't have it any other way. He was safer, yet needier, with her than he had since he'd been a little boy.

He moved slowly again, and her body tilted eagerly to meet him. Her luscious dampness slicked him in, and he experienced the most exquisite sense of completeness he had ever felt in his life.

Her fingernails dug into the muscles of his back as he drove deeper. She was so lush, her body cushioning his, rising to meet his motions. Lust swamped his senses, and he allowed all restraint and self-control to drift away on the waves of erotic sensation. He focused every nerve in his body on the delight of thrusting into her as she met his every motion with her own, seeking her own pleasure.

He held himself back until the tendons in her neck were rigid and she bucked her hips.

Then he gave himself over to need. He drove deeper and faster into her recess until the well within him brimmed and overflowed into her. His body shuddered. He groaned against the side of her neck, his hips pumping, blood thundering in his ears, feeling the release more deeply than ever before.

As he quieted, she made little circles on his back with her fingers. When he rolled off her, she tried to hold him in place. "Stay," she mumbled.

"I'm just going here," he said as he tucked her under his arm.

He marveled at what had happened. It was like two stars had come together and exploded in a massive conflagration of lust and desire. He was changed, transformed, really, into a man whose heart had shed a bony carapace. He was alive, for the first time ever.

She moved. "I'm ... sticky."

"Wait." He went to the wash basin and poured fresh water on a clean flannel for her. Gently parting her legs, he said, "This will be soothing. You might be a little sore tomorrow."

She gave him a sleepy, sweet smile. "It was worth it."

When he finished tending her, he climbed back in bed. He put his arm across the swell of her ribs and pulled her to him. The warmth of her skin against his was velvet against silk.

"I'm exhausted," she murmured.

"Then go to sleep," he whispered against her neck.

"Not very romantic."

"You want more romance?" He nibbled the top of her ear and she groaned.

"Not tonight, please."

"Then sleep."

Despite his own exhaustion, he couldn't sleep. He lay back and watched the flashes of lightning through the window, feeling her steady breathing against his chest. He had never been so satisfied in his life. The ice around his heart had melted. He wanted for nothing more. The woman at his side wanted all of him—scars, nightmares, irritability, and whatever else the war had bequeathed him. His honor was intact, he was home, his men were safe, and the war was over. What else could he wish for?

Friedenheim wasn't magic; she was.

The mirror reflected the light of the candle. He reached over his shoulder and touched the ribbon of scar on his back. He waited until her breathing was deep and steady and her body was slack with sleep before he slipped out of bed. Standing with his back to the mirror, he held up her hand mirror, and, for the first time, looked at the scar on his back.

It didn't bother him anymore. It was him. And she loved him.

He climbed back into bed and turned on his side. Easing his arm around her, he pressed his happily worn-out cock to her soft bottom and smiled to himself.

Before drifting off to sleep, his last thought was of how peaceful it was to be here next to her.

CHAPTER 54

Outside, a crack sounded, as though something had struck and split the earth open.

Zdenka sat bolt upright in bed. "What was that?" She glanced around in the dim light, trying to orient herself. A strange glimmering orange light filtered through the curtains.

"I didn't hear anything," Matteo mumbled sleepily. "Lie back down, my love."

She threw back the covers, raced to the window, and pulled aside the curtains.

Her heart pushed into her throat.

"Fire!" she shrieked. "The barn's on fire. Kurt and Luther are in there."

Matteo vaulted out of bed. He yanked on his pants, jammed his feet in his boots, and grabbed a jacket. He bounded down the stairs while she was still groping for her pants. She prayed that Kurt and Luther were still alive. After all they had been through, to die on her farm would be a tragedy.

Her blood froze.

Schwartzkönig was in his stable, as were the rest of the livestock. If she didn't get him out, he would die. Without the stud fees she was counting on, she would lose the farm.

She threw a shirt on, wriggled into pants, jammed her feet into her boots, and dashed down the stairs after Matteo.

The farmyard was chaos. Harbin raced back and forth, barking. Smoke choked her. Lashing wind whipped grit into her eyes. Matteo had opened the front door of the barn. A barn cat carried out her kittens. Horses screamed. Sheep bleated. Cows bellowed. Fire roared, loud as an oncoming train.

The doors to the paddock flew open and Kurt burst out, with Schwartzkönig running before him. The horse, wild with fear, screamed and kicked and pawed the air.

Luther staggered out of the smoke, coughing so hard, he doubled over and knelt on the paddock grass.

The horse bucked and pawed the air. Luther was nearly below him. He screamed, rolled away, and got to his feet. Waving his arms over his head, Luther shouted something Zdenka couldn't make out. Luther picked up a rock and hurled it at the horse.

The horse raced across the paddock, and with a single mighty leap, he cleared the fence, except for one rear hoof which caught on the top rail and knocked it down. The top rail collapsed onto the lower rotted rails and they gave way, leaving a gap from which all the other livestock could escape.

"Schwartzkönig!" Zdenka shouted, her arms outstretched towards the horse as if she could catch him.

A sickening feeling swelled in Zdenka's stomach as she watched her investment gallop into the distant forest. Luther stood dumbly watching the horse disappear into the night.

"Luther, please! Do something," she pleaded.

He hesitated a moment, his eyes growing wide. The others weren't around. If he didn't go, she might never see her horse again.

Luther stared at her for a moment, then, he grabbed a piece of burning wood for a torch and a loop of rope from a fence post and charged after the horse.

Where was Matteo?

Wind gusts whipped the fire into a raging blaze. Orange flames raced across the great center ridge beam of the roof, eating through the old barn like a monster chomping through twigs. Last winter's hay in the hayloft made for perfect fire fuel. So did the expensive feed she had planned to give Schwartzkönig. A timber crashed to the ground. Smoke billowed out the doors and windows. Orange embers floated up against the night sky like escaped stars.

She looked around wildly. Matteo stood before the front door of the barn. The flashing flames lit his face, twisted in terror. His fists clenched and unclenched, his chest heaved, but he was frozen in place.

His face was contorted the way it did when she had watched him having a nightmare in Vienna. He was reliving some dreadful scene from the war. He was supposed to be safe here at Friedenheim, but he was anything but safe.

She dashed to him and threw her arms around his neck. "Schwartzkönig is out."

His eyes focused on her face as though he had awakened from whatever nightmare replayed in his mind. He gripped her shoulders so tightly it hurt. "I'll get the other animals."

"I'll go!" she shouted above the din.

"It's too dangerous," he shouted. "You stay here."

She was about to protest, but he was already racing into the barn. Her heart battered against her chest when he plunged inside the burning structure.

Animals poured out of the barn through the paddock door. Smoke burned her lungs as she sprinted around to the opposite end of the barn in time to see her two frightened milk cows, bawling loudly, run out of the blazing structure.

Matteo didn't emerge.

Kurt led the cows to the far side of the paddock and tied them to a tree so they wouldn't escape through the broken fence.

Why hadn't Matteo come out?

Smoke made her eyes tear, and the fire threw off heat like a burning sun.

She was about to go into the barn when, bleating madly, her half-dozen sheep trotted out into the paddock as fast as their legs could carry them. Harbin took over and herded the sheep to a far corner of the paddock. He was in charge of them now.

It was her farm, her livestock, her responsibility. She should have gone in.

Part of the ceiling crashed to the floor.

Her pulse raced. Had anything dropped on Matteo?

She poised to go into the barn, when, like a Greek god walking out of a cloud, Matteo dashed through a wall of smoke, carrying the brown-spotted calf, Elemer. He put the calf down and he wobbled off to his mother.

Her stomach clutched. The back of Matteo's jacket was smoking.

He was on fire.

She hurtled across the meadow to him and, with her bare hands, beat out the smoldering embers.

Her hands stung from the embers.

"That's everyone," she said.

Matteo looked around the paddock. "I didn't see Schwartzkönig in the barn. Did he get out?"

"Kurt brought him out, but he jumped the fence. He ran through the orchard toward the forest. Luther went after him." She pointed out Luther's torch moving through the orchard.

Panic lumped in her belly. "If Schwartzkönig is hurt or lost, I'll lose the farm."

"I'll go. Pump as much water into the troughs as you can." His long legs ate up the ground as he bolted after Luther.

White lightning ripped across the canopy of night sky. Thunder, loud as an exploding bomb, rattled her bones. She had only ever seen a dry storm like this once before. When she was twelve, on a hot summer's day, black clouds carrying thunder and lightning blew down from the mountains. Lightning hit a tree in a neighbor's field and some crops had burned, but nothing like this.

Kurt struggled to put the fence back in place. She careened up to him, panting and coughing, and helped finish the task.

"Where's the alarm bell?" he asked. "We have to alert the neighbors."

She paused, trying to remember. Every second wasted was more of a chance for the house to catch fire from a spark, for the chicken coop to go up in flames, for the shed to burn to the ground. "Somewhere in the kitchen. I'll go look for it."

"I'll pump."

She dashed up the slope. The smoke was so thick, she couldn't get enough breath. Wind tore at her hair and flung dirt in her face. Thunder crashed furiously, as if her head was caught between two cymbals.

Once she reached the kitchen, she leaned against the wall and gulped air. She was covered in black soot and ash.

Every farm kept a brass bell as an alarm to summon neighbors in an emergency. She grabbed her bell from the shelf by the stove, sprinted out of the kitchen, and pelted back down the hill.

In front of the blazing barn, Kurt pumped water into the animal's drinking troughs. He threw several buckets of water on the barn, but it was only delaying the inevitable. The fire was too far gone.

Her heart sank.

The barn, which her great-great-grandfather had built, was lost.

Kurt took the bell from her. "I'll go and wake the neighbors." He shot off across the wheat field. She watched him go until he was beyond the perimeter of firelight and the darkness swallowed him. The sound of the clanging bell receded.

She was alone.

Tears streaked down her face. Never had she been so helpless, so ineffective. She couldn't do this. She was impulsive and inadequate, and this fire exposed all her weaknesses. How could she ever have thought she could run the farm herself? The neighbors would laugh at her, as they had when she tried to sell them her lumber.

The howling wind twisted and sawed the treetops. Somewhere, a branch cracked and broke and landed with a thud. The brass bell clanged and clanged. Thunder pounded. Jagged flashes of lightning flared overhead, adding a ghostly light to the fire-tinged night sky.

If only it would rain!

Gleeful flames licked up board after board of the ancient wooden barn. Clouds of black smoke billowed skyward. With a sound like an avalanche of boulders, the walls of the barn crashed down, sending sparks into the air like fiery moths. All that was left was the fieldstone foundation.

Her stomach was hollow as a wooden bucket. That was the end of the barn. Her shaky knees gave way, and she sank to the ground. At least the fire was over.

Then the wind shifted.

Lifted by the wind like wicked snow, smoke, embers and white ash, blew up the hill in the direction of the house.

The house might catch fire. She had to wet down the roof. For that, she needed the ladder.

She staggered to her feet and charged across the farmyard to the shed. The long, heavy wood ladder was around the back, lying on the ground. Splinters dug into her palms as she lifted it. It was too big to carry so she dragged it up the hill to the house. One step in front of the other, over and over, she told herself.

Three times she tried to lift the ladder to the house roof, but it was too heavy for her to do by herself and it fell. Her arms felt as if they were going to fall out of their sockets. Her legs shook, her lungs burned, and her heart was in shreds.

How had she ever thought she could do this? Run the farm, pay her father's gambling debts, make the farm productive, start a horse breeding business, sell lumber, everything that this farm needed to remain in the Waldner family. She had been in charge of the farm only a short while and had already failed miserably. Kurt should have stayed and helped douse the fire. The neighbors wouldn't come to help her.

Why would any of the other neighbors come to save her farm now? If she failed, they could buy the land cheaply. The farm would leave Waldner hands forever, and it would be her doing.

"What else can I do, Grossmutti?" she cried to the stars. She dragged the back of her sleeve across her face and wiped her tears and runny nose.

'My destiny was here, and so is yours,' her grossmutti had said.

Zdenka couldn't give up. Not yet.

Where was Matteo? Why weren't they back yet? Was he all right?

In the forest, she spotted Luther's torch moving through the trees like a fiery ghost. They were still pursuing Schwartzkönig. She should have gone after him. He wouldn't allow himself to be caught by anyone but her. She would have to go help them.

She remembered a coil of rope hung on a hook in the shed.

Racing down the hill, she stumbled and went head over heels for a few yards. She found the rope, grabbed it, and took off towards the orchard. Her feet ached and her legs trembled as she crashed up the path through the orchard, keeping her eyes on the orange glow of Luther's torch. Hopefully, Matteo could help Luther if he became disoriented.

This path was as familiar to her as the hallway to her bedroom, so she didn't need a light. In the distance, Luther's torch shimmered deep in the forest. It was less smoky in the orchard and she was able to stop coughing. When she reached the other side of the orchard, she paused and looked back at the barn, a heap of sputtering, smoking wood. Sparks lifted into the air and disappeared as they extinguished. Entrails of smoke curled upwards.

Somewhere ahead, deep in the forest, Schwartzkönig screamed. She scanned the woods for Luther's torch.

The torch wasn't a flickering dot any longer, but a flame the size of a tree.

Blood beat in her eardrums. Her knees went weak. Panic carved an icy hole in her chest.

The forest—her forest—was burning.

CHAPTER 55

"Luther! Luther!" Matteo shouted. But the black night, the forest and wind, swallowed his voice. He ran through the forest, dodging trees, tripping over roiling tree roots, leaping over fallen logs. He followed the orange flicker of Luther's torch as he zig-zagged deeper and deeper into the woods, pursuing Schwartzkönig.

Branches whipped his face. Thunder pummeled his ears. His heart pounded in his chest as he raced after Luther. Sweat and ash clung to his face. Smoke choked him and burned his eyes.

At last, Matteo caught up with Luther. Somehow, he had gotten a rope around Schwartzkönig's neck.

Blood pounded in Matteo's ears.

Luther thrust a flaming torch at the horse.

"Prussian bastard, kill you, I will!" Luther screamed.

The horse bucked and reared and knocked Luther to the ground. He rolled about, holding his head. The torch fell onto a pile of dry pine needles. Fire flared up in an instant. Matteo tried to kick dirt on the flames, but the fire was too fast and ran across the woodland floor, spreading in all directions. Low branches caught fire. Flames rushed up the trunk and jumped to the next tree. Smoke billowed. Sparks flew. Sap sputtered. Branches cracked.

The horse reared wildly but the rope had caught on a fallen tree and he was unable to escape.

Luther staggered to his feet.

Smoke blinded Matteo.

"Luther! We have to get out of here! Leave the horse. Let's go."

"No, we're going to kill them!" Luther snatched a burning branch from the ground.

He shouted as if all the emotion he had not expressed, boiled out of him. His eyes were as mad as the day he had attacked Zdenka in the Prater.

"It's a Prussian horse," he screamed. "Means they're in the woods. The fire will smoke them out!"

Matteo went cold inside. Flames surrounded them. The horse reared this way and that, snorting, squealing, and stomping, trying to get loose.

With all the calm he could muster, Matteo said, "Come, Luther. It's me, Matteo."

Shadows from the fire made Luther's face, twisted in hatred, seem demonic. "That's a Prussian jacket." Luther pointed at Matteo.

Matteo looked down at the jacket he had hurriedly snatched. It was Graf Waldner's old coat, which for some reason, had been hanging in the armoire. The same color as the Prussian uniform.

"I saved you once, and I'll save you again if you let me. Put the branch down. We have to get out before we're surrounded by the fire. Let me help you."

Luther answered by swinging the torch at him.

Matteo jumped out of the way, rolled on the grass, and came

up on his feet. He grabbed a stick and swung it back and forth to keep Luther at bay.

Luther bent low and circled around, his mouth open and gasping for air. His face was sooty and sweaty, and his eyes filled with insane hatred.

Matteo stumbled, fell, scrambled to recover.

Luther ran at him, the wooden torch held over his head.

Matteo clutched a rock.

He rolled and bolted into a standing position. He froze.

Zdenka's words rang in his mind: *The war is done for you, Luther, and Kurt. You never have to kill anyone again.*

He could not kill Luther. He was done. The war was over. Even if it meant he had to die, he would not kill again. Ever.

There was honor in dying for another human being, or for one's country, but he simply could not live with himself if he took another life. And he didn't think Zdenka could live with him if he did, either. War had turned him into a killer, but he didn't have to remain a killer.

Matteo dropped the rock. "I won't kill you, Luther. If you think I'm a Prussian and you want to kill me, go ahead."

With a roar, Luther leapt at him. Matteo spun sideways, caught his arm, and threw him on to his back.

Matteo straddled Luther and pounded his arm on the ground until he dropped the flaming torch.

Luther picked up the rock Matteo had dropped and struck him aside the head.

Lights flashed. His temple throbbed in agony.

Matteo swung his fist. Connected with something. He slumped off Luther.

Gasping, Matteo struggled to stay conscious. If he couldn't subdue Luther, he would not kill him. He struggled to his hands and knees, staggered to his feet, and leaned against a tree.

Schwartzkönig roared and snorted. Fire danced up in the

trees, skipping along the canopy. Smoke choked and blinded him. Blood and sweat dripped into his eyes. He blinked.

A face appeared out of the darkness.

"Zdenka?"

What was she doing here? Get her out; Luther be damned. Nothing—not fire, not Luther, not hell, not a horse, nothing, was going to separate him from his love.

Luther lurched to his feet but fell again. Matteo glanced at the man's feet. Zdenka had looped a rope around Luther's ankles.

"Are you all right?" she shouted over the roar of the fire.

He nodded. "We have to get out of here." He removed the rope from Luther's ankles and tied his wrists in front.

Zdenka untied Schwartzkönig. Matteo gave her his jacket, and she draped it over the horse's head so he couldn't see the fire. Matteo hoisted Luther across the horse's back.

"Go!" Matteo shouted.

Heads down, they ran through the smoke, heat driving at their backs. They splashed through a stream, zig-zagged past burning trees, and dodged falling limbs until they reached safety at the edge of the forest.

When they were out in the clear, they paused to rest.

Zdenka turned back to the forest and watched as the last stand of timber belonging to the Waldner's was consumed by fire.

CHAPTER 56

The storm passed without a drop of rain. Zdenka and Matteo, coughing and rubbing their smoke-stung eyes, led Schwartzkönig with Luther atop, out of the forest. When they reached safety, they slowed to a stagger until they passed out of the orchard. The acrid stench of burned wood stung their nostrils and tendrils of smoke ghosted into the air.

Zdenka stopped at the end of the path and stared in disbelief.

A line of people snaked from the water trough up the hill to the house. Pumping with his good hand, Kurt filled buckets. Dozens of neighbors, people she didn't recognize, passed buckets, dishpans, and cooking pots, filled with water, from hand to hand. Even Blasen, who had laughed at her because she was a woman trying to sell her lumber, was there on the bucket line. Someone was on the ladder, wetting down the roof so sparks from the forest fire wouldn't catch. Other people dashed water onto the spots on the barn that still glowed orange. As they sluiced the water, embers hissed and sent up steam.

Zdenka sat on the ground and stared.

"Stay here and rest a minute." Matteo led the horse to the paddock and tied him to a post. He helped Luther down from the stallion's back. Luther alternately babbled and shouted, so Matteo tied Luther's wrists to another post some distance from the horse.

Someone Zdenka didn't know pulled her to her feet and handed her a clean handkerchief to wipe her face. The person led her to the table beneath the tree and sat her on a chair.

A fist of tears knotted her throat.

They had come. The neighbors, their farmhands, their sons and daughters, their tenants, had all come to help fight the fire. She had expected them to wave Kurt off when he came ringing the bell for help. She had been so sure of their scorn. Her pride and independence had made her believe she didn't need help, that she could do anything the farm required, by herself.

The fire showed her how wrong she had been.

With buckets and shovels, on foot, on horseback and carts, on the run, all the neighbors—people she knew and some she didn't—had come to help.

The sight renewed her courage. She rose, took a place on the bucket line, and passed a bucket on to someone she didn't know.

Kurt pumped water at the trough, filling all manner of containers. Water sloshed out of buckets as people passed them along the fire line and up the hill. She dared to hope that the house might yet be saved. Even without the noise of the wind or fire, there was no less a wall of sound as everyone worked feverishly to save the house.

She looked toward the forest and saw the line of blazing trees. Her hopes turned to ash. The forest had been a cash crop. Now there was nothing.

Another ember fell on the lilac bushes below her bedroom window. There had been so little rain this year, everything was tinder dry.

A tiny flame flashed on the lilac and jumped to the next bush. It, too, caught.

Fear punched her stomach. Where was Matteo?

He was at the top of the bucket line, dumping bucket after bucket on the fire cindering the bushes.

She was surrounded by shouting voices, running feet, banging buckets, gushing water, shoveling dirt, sloshing water.

So many people.

She wasn't alone. They were working as hard as if it were their own houses. They were saving her.

Saving her from herself, her idea of independence, from her wild folly that she could run the farm on her own.

What if Kurt and Luther had died in the blaze? What would have happened if she hadn't found Matteo and Luther in the forest? If they hadn't made it back? If Kurt hadn't gone for the neighbors? She shuddered.

They were safe.

Luther gave a bellow. How could she have been so stupid as to think all he needed was a little time working with the horses to get used to them again? It had been naïve to think fresh air and good food would make him right again, even when Matteo had warned her repeatedly that Luther might still be dangerous. Healing took more than a few weeks or months. It might take a lifetime. Next time, she wouldn't be so stubborn about helping someone if it put her or Matteo, or anyone she loved, in danger.

Her stubbornness, her independence, had nearly cost her everything she loved so dearly, including Matteo. He had risked his life to save her horse. The least she could do was not risk her own life, as he had so often asked her.

He needed her. But she needed him more. Tears streaked down her face as the realization sunk in. Her mistake could have cost Matteo his life, the man she loved more than her life.

Light peeped over the eastern ridge of mountains. Someone

took her elbow and sat her down against a tree. She had no strength to resist.

At dawn, Zdenka woke, shivering, under the tree where she had fallen asleep. The forest smoldered, having burnt out. The barn was an ash-covered pile of charred wood, but the house stood proudly atop the hill where it had for so many years.

The fire-fighting neighbors finished dousing the last smoldering lilac bushes.

She clambered to her feet and thanked them one by one, even Herr Blasen.

"I can't thank you enough for coming." She was almost too tired to stand, but, unwaveringly, she looked him in the eye.

Blasen made a grumbling noise. "Always willing to help a neighbor. Have to stick together. Can't do it alone."

"Thank you. Thank you very much." Zdenka thought she detected the slightest curl on his upper lip, as if he had to eat something distasteful.

Blasen nodded and patted his fat stomach. "Then we need to discuss my purchase of what timber is left." He pointed at the forest. "And I have a good mare I'd like to put to that stallion of yours."

She smiled and put her hand out, and they shook on it.

The neighbors trudged off, mounted their horses, climbed back in their wagons, and waved goodbye as they departed.

She was touched by the deep sense of friendship and kindness in those tired waves. When she helped Kurt and Luther heal, she had benefitted more than they. Matteo had shown her that she needn't give up her independence to accept his love.

Now, the aid of her neighbors made her realize, though she was a woman of her own will and mind, she could not—need not—do everything on her own. Asking for help didn't need to cost her pride, freedom, or the respect of others.

Matteo put his arm around her waist as they waved farewell to the last of the neighbors.

He didn't say a word but took her dirty face in his two hands and kissed her.

Even if she had been able to, she no longer wanted to do anything without him.

"Doesn't Vienna look beautiful?" Zdenka gazed out of the carriage window at the new-fallen snow. Light streamed from the windows of the grand *palais* making the snow glitter like a million diamonds. On the other side of the Park Ring, people skated on the pond in the park. Horses trotted along at snappy clip, snorting steam into the cold night air. A stiff wind blew through the cracks in Thea's carriage, and Zdenka snuggled closer to Matteo. He tucked the heavy woolen blanket tighter around her and kissed her gloved hand.

"Looking forward to the opera?" Matteo asked her.

"I am. It's worth a return to Vienna. I've never seen *Die Zauberflöte* before." She laid her head against his solid shoulder. "It's funny to come to this year's *Fasching* and not be forced by my parents into looking a husband."

"And I'm glad I don't have to beat a path to your door." Matteo clasped her hand.

Almost a year had passed since she came to Vienna with Arabella. Since then, Zdenka had unveiled herself as a woman, she and her sister had both married, Arabella had given birth to her first child, a boy she named Zdenko in honor of all the Viennese machinations by which she and Mandryka finally married. Most exciting, Zdenka awaited the birth of their first child.

Matteo hummed 'their' tune from the *Die Zauberflöte*. She patted his hand and peeked at him from the corner of her eye. His mouth was drawn tight, and a muscle along his jawline jumped.

As they had been getting ready for the opera, Zdenka was fully aware of Matteo's increasing tension. He'd become relaxed and comfortable at Friedenheim, but the chaos of Vienna—crowds, unexpected noises, the sights of wounded soldiers he had yet to help—made his eye twitch.

"Don't worry about the people and noise. Squeeze my hand if you're feeling uncomfortable, and we'll go for some fresh air." One thing she had finally learned over the last six months was that she couldn't heal him, but she could help him.

Matteo flexed his gloved hands. "Edward seems to be keeping up his schedule of seductions, because I haven't yet had time to thank him for winning back the deed to Friedenheim."

"Thea writes that he will be here tonight." She said, "Hopefully."

Matteo shifted in the carriage, trying to stretch his long legs. His posture remained tense. "It's been half a year. Do you think everyone will remember what happened last time?" Matteo asked, his face pinched.

"It doesn't matter," she said, matter of factly. "You and your fellow soldiers sacrificed so they could keep their lives. Thea said your reaction to the sound of the gunshot spurred more concern about the soldiers returning and helped with her campaign to build a new wing at the military hospital. Think of it as a deed that changed people's minds."

"It was humiliating," he grumbled.

"It brought you to me." She caressed his cheek.

"And that made it worthwhile," he said.

They followed *Schülerstrasse* and turned onto the Stephansplatz. The massive cathedral's spire pointed into a cloudless sky filled with stars. The mighty *Pummerin* began to ring, its huge note tolling the hour across Vienna. The note vibrated in Zdenka's chest, and the thrill brought tears to her eyes.

She was so much more emotional now that she was with child. She sniffled. Without comment, Matteo handed her his handkerchief. It was dizzying, how different she felt about so many things. She still wore pants at the farm, but they didn't mean what they had before. Now, they were just work attire, not a shield and sign to the world of her independence. She no longer needed her pants to prove anything to anyone, certainly not to her husband. Her heart was melded with Matteo's in a way which sometimes surprised her and caused her to marvel at how their love for one another had remade them into vastly different people than they were before.

"Do you suppose anyone will recognize me as Arabella's non-existent brother?"

"Who cares?" he said, flicking his hand, as though brushing off a pesky fly. "You're her beautiful sister now, if anyone asks."

She realized how, with worrying about him, she had stuffed her own worries down, so she hadn't noticed them until now. As long as Matteo loved her and was by her side, she could endure anything. The loss of the barn and admitting she was wrong about Luther and so many other things had shown her that strength wasn't the act of merely holding on to what you *thought* to be true, but *letting go* of what wasn't.

The carriage springs creaked as they jounced over a hole. Zdenka gave a little squeak. His hand flew to her swelling belly.

"Are you all right?" he asked, anxiously.

She chuckled. How he worried. Another thing she had to get used to—allowing him to fuss and take care of her.

"Don't be afraid. Women can endure a great deal while pregnant and still have a lovely, healthy baby."

"I marvel at the things women know that men haven't a clue about." His voice filled with admiration. "How do you know?"

"I read about it," she said simply. "A little bump is nothing."

He cleared his throat, and his voice took on a concerned tone. "I've been meaning to talk to you about how much farm work you're doing. Might you take it a bit more slowly, now that you're so far along?"

"There's too much to do." She ticked off on her gloved fingers. "I know it's only February, but there's still—"

He clasped her hands and stilled them. His voice was resolute and determined. "Let me and the other men help you. It doesn't make you weak or helpless. We must protect you and the baby."

"Yes, you're right. I should stop working so hard. I am getting tired these days." Then she admitted another worry. "But I'm afraid to ask the others to do more."

"I like taking care of you, and I know the other men are quite prepared to help out more." He kissed her temple. The warm damp of his breath on her skin made her want to return home and do the very thing that had put her in this condition in the first place.

Their driver pulled into a line of carriages and passengers, many of them soldiers, clambered out into the fallen snow. Women in gowns and men in evening schemes and top hats climbed the marble staircase to the double doors of the opera house. When their carriage reached the front of the line, Matteo alighted and turned to help Zdenka.

"Don't worry. I'm not yet so pregnant I can't descend stairs."

"I enjoy playing the gallant, my lady," he said and bowed.

She had to remember she deserved to be cared for and that

it was one of the ways he showed he loved her. She gave him her hand and let him help her down.

"You look magnificent," he said, his eyes burning in the dark.

A flush of pride swelled in her chest. The very same Madame Bonterre, who had bought her dresses so she could gamble for her farm, had created this gown. It was made of peach satin with a low neck. Her breasts, preparing for a child, nearly burgeoned over the top. The front was loose across the abdomen to allow her belly plenty of room. A pelisse lined with a sheepskin from one of the sheep in her flock wrapped her shoulders. Instead of arranging her coiffure in the complicated manner of most Viennese women, she displayed a bit of social rebellion and allowed her ginger curls to tumble down her shoulders.

"I never tire of hearing you compliment me," she said.

Matteo tucked her hand in the crook of his arm, and they started up the marble staircase. He still had his military bearing: back as straight as a saber, chin level to the ground, drawn up to his tallest.

His eye twitched. A weak scowl traced around his eyes.

She patted his arm. "We won't spend much time in the foyer, chit-chatting. Let's go right to the box so you don't have to talk to many people."

His shoulders relaxed a bit, and he smiled down at her. She couldn't get enough of those smiles. He enchanted her with so much as a raised eyebrow, but when he smiled, her heart did pirouettes.

They swept through the double doors into the brilliantly lit foyer where satin rustled, laughter boomed, people milled about, and soldiers chatted.

She expected Matteo to hesitate. He didn't; instead, he plunged into the crowd toward Thea and Prince Dimitry who waited at the foot of the stairs.

Thea embraced Zdenka and then Matteo. "I'm glad you felt well enough to come, Zdenka. Edward will join us later."

Prince Dimitry stared pointedly at Zdenka's round tummy. "You look marvelous in a gown."

Zdenka gazed up at Matteo. "I like it now and then, as long as I know I can wear pants again when necessary."

"Nice not to be defined by your attire, isn't it?" Thea said, with a touch of acid in her voice.

"How is the farm coming, Zdenka?" Prince Dimitry asked.

"Very well. I have two more requests for stud services for Schwartzkönig, and my little calf is going to be quite a bull someday."

"And what of the new barn you wrote about?" Thea asked.

"Finished two weeks ago. We built right on top of the old foundation but expanded somewhat, as our livestock is multiplying faster than expected."

Matteo lifted her hand to his lips and kissed it, sending a sparkle of heat up her arm.

"And you? How is the veteran's association coming?" Prince Dimitry asked Matteo.

"Quite well. We have four men on the farm now. They're building a sort of barracks behind the house so we can house more soldiers. They've increased farm productivity to the point that we can afford to house two more men in the spring."

"How marvelous." The Prince tucked his hands behind his back and rocked back on his heels. "And who tells these fellows what to do? Who runs the farm, now that Zdenka is in ...?" He gave his mustache a swipe. "...a delicate condition?"

Zdenka smoothed her skirt with her hands. She felt so feminine and lovely, but the Prince's question scratched at her temper. She jutted her chin, but kept her teeth clamped shut behind a smile.

Matteo's arm wound around her waist, and he gently tickled

her ribs. Probably because he knew the question would put a frown on her face. "She runs the day-to-day operation of the farm. I know nothing about crops or raising animals. I hire out the studs, but Zdenka does everything else."

Even Thea raised her eyebrows and smiled broadly. The Prince nodded approvingly.

"Do you tire easily?" Thea asked.

"I lie down for a nap sometimes," Zdenka said.

Truthfully, many afternoons, she and Matteo 'napped' together in their bedroom.

♫

Matteo thought he recognized the Major General who was approaching him, but the name and place of acquaintance didn't come to him. The man was outfitted in his white dress uniform with medals and ribbons jingling from his chest.

Matteo's back stiffened, and his eye twitched.

Zdenka squeezed his arm and whispered, "Shall I have a bit of a swoon?"

"Not yet," he whispered out of the side of his mouth. Just having her near him steadied his nerves.

The Major General's posture was rigid, but his eyes glowed warmly. He was missing two fingers on his right hand. He extended his left hand. "Matteo von Ritter, I'm Major General Doctor Vaslosch, First Medical Division."

Even his voice sounded familiar. Matteo introduced Zdenka, Thea, and the Prince. The officer bowed.

To Matteo, he said, "I was assigned to your cavalry unit, and I was in the field hospital when you brought two soldiers in off the field. I want you to know I've never seen such bravery under fire in my life. Congratulations. I've put in for a medal for you."

Matteo's eyes widened. He wasn't sure he wanted recognition for saving only two lives when he wished he could have saved more.

"Thank you, but it's what anyone would have done," Matteo said. He didn't like to be noticed. Many others, unrecognized and nameless, had died, but he'd had the great, yet unmerited, fortune to return.

Vaslosch continued. "I also understand you've established a military veteran's association on a farm somewhere."

Matteo turned to Zdenka. "Yes, on Friedenheim, my wife's farm in Hohenruppersdorf."

"Excellent idea." He clapped Matteo on the shoulder. "I'm going to take it up with the medical staff of the Army and try to replicate what you're doing. I hear you're doing good work, rehabilitating the men back into society."

Zdenka, Thea, and Prince Dimitry beamed.

Matteo's heart swelled as though it would burst out of his chest.

He smiled and glanced down at his wife. "We do it together, sir. She deserves most of the credit. Initially, she established the veteran's association without my help."

"But it was entirely his idea," she interjected quickly.

The Major General looked up. Upstairs, ringed around the balcony, soldiers, officers, and enlisted men looked down. The Major General clapped. Thunderous applause, foot stomping, and 'hurrahs' echoed off the walls of the foyer.

Stunned beyond words, Matteo gazed up at the faces of the men.

The Major General shook Matteo's hand and disappeared into the throng of patrons.

Turning back to his wife, Matteo watched her eyes fill with tears. Thea dabbed a handkerchief to her eyes. Even Prince Dimitry seemed choked up.

As strangers shook Matteo's hand, he was too surprised to say much except, "Thank you."

Zdenka whispered, "Even they think you're a hero. Now will you believe it?"

Matteo was almost relieved when the gong rang out, calling the patrons to their seats.

"Shall we?" The Prince motioned to the stairs.

The applause continued to sound until Matteo entered Thea's opera box. Once inside, he plopped into his chair, overcome with disbelief. When they were seated, the door at the rear of the box opened and shut quietly. Edward appeared at Matteo's side.

First, Edward kissed his mother's upturned cheek then Zdenka's. "I've never seen a lady with child who looks more divine than you, Zdenka," he said. "Is my cuz taking care of you?"

"Of course," she said with a laugh. "When are you going to find someone to take care of you?"

"Such an angel doesn't exist," Edward quipped in return.

Matteo rose from his seat and thumped Edward on the back as a substitute for an embrace.

Edward flipped his coattails and sat. He leaned over the rail and gazed at none other than Fanny Bösendorfer, who was flirting with a male companion.

With a growl, Edward plopped back into his chair, crossed his arms, and glared down at Fanny.

Matteo poked Zdenka in the ribs and nodded at his cousin. He had never seen Edward behave like this. He was clearly besotted with a woman, who, for the first time in Edward's existence, didn't seem to notice he was alive.

Matteo leaned over and whispered to Zdenka, "Shall we compose a letter and send it to Fanny?"

She giggled. "Don't you dare."

The lights went off, and the curtain rose. Accompanied by audience applause, the conductor entered the orchestra pit. He bowed and the house went silent. Turning, to the orchestra, he gave the downbeat to the overture to Mozart's *Magic Flute*. Matteo slipped his arm around Zdenka, and she lay her head on his shoulder. In the second scene of the first act, Papageno, the bird man, and Pamina, the heroine, sang the duet *Bei Männer, welche Liebe fühlen* about the joys of married bliss.

Matteo kissed his dear wife's temple and whispered, "No one knows this better than us."

THE END

Dear Reader,

If you enjoyed this book, please head over to your favorite retailer or other social media sites and leave a review. Reviews help others to discover books and I would greatly appreciate your taking the time to do so.

Future books

I hope you'll join me for my next books a series of six books called The Marriage Survivor's Club. It's about six diverse, single, Episcopalian 50-something women, living in a suburban New England town, drinking, dancing, cursing and praying their way through menopause. All while unsuccessfully trying not to fall in love.

Sign up for my newsletter at www.annettenauraine.com to find out when these fun, crazy women will dance into your life.

Be sure to check here for more books:
https://www.annettenauraine.com/home/purchase-books/

ACKNOWLEDGMENTS

No book is born alone. It takes many hands, hearts, and minds to bring a book to life. I have many people to thank.

My husband, Peter, has believed in me through every hairbrained scheme I've ever undertaken, including writing this book. When I had doubts, he would say, "Just keep writing," which was the best advice I ever got.

Raising my two boys, Lincoln and Ulysses, is still the best thing I've accomplished. They were instrumental in my writing because they kept me sane when I thought I'd lose my mind.

A shout out to my plotting partners, Isabel Morin, Libby Waterford, and Kate Kettler, who have taught, supported, and guided me through this, and forthcoming, books. Guys, I couldn't have done it without you. I value your friendship and thoughts and look forward to our journeys together.

L.A. Mitchell, my editor and coach, (la-mitchellwrites.com) has made me the writer I am, and she continues to encourage me to write better and deeper prose, to plot (I still hate it!), and to delete every exclamation point. I can't thank her enough.

Thank you, dear reader, for granting me the gift of your time to read my book. Without you, there would be only a dream.

ABOUT THE AUTHOR

Annette Nauraine is a former opera singer. She has loved singing, reading and writing for as long as she can remember. She writes because stories are the deepest, most profound ways to understand ourselves and others. Her stories are about the grace of love and how love saves us from ourselves, if only we let it. She's inspired by Proust, Shakespeare, opera, the writing of Grace Burrowes, Lisa Kleypas, Julie Ann Long, Mozart and his librettist, Lorenzo Da Ponte.

Made in the USA
Middletown, DE
09 March 2021

35058977R00241